THE HASH KNIFE OUTFIT

Center Point
Large Print

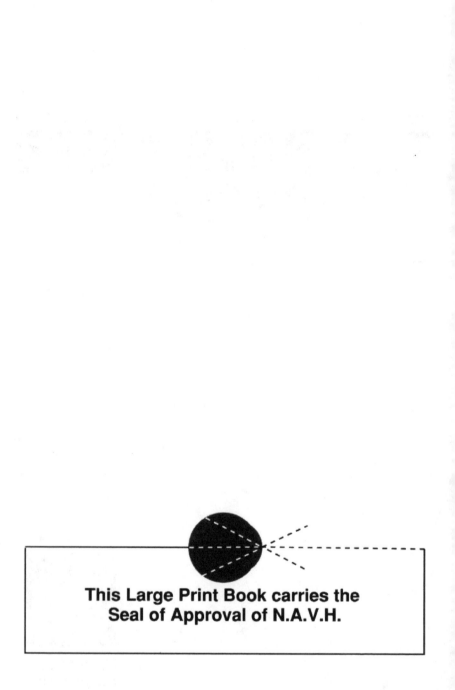

**This Large Print Book carries the
Seal of Approval of N.A.V.H.**

THE HASH KNIFE OUTFIT

Zane Grey

CENTER POINT PUBLISHING
THORNDIKE, MAINE

This Center Point Large Print edition
is published in the year 2010 by arrangement with
Golden West Literary Agency.

The text of this Large Print edition is unabridged.
In other aspects, this book may vary
from the original edition.
Printed in the United States of America
on permanent paper.
Set in 16-point Times New Roman type.

ISBN: 978-1-60285-650-9

Library of Congress Cataloging-in-Publication Data

Grey, Zane, 1872-1939.
  The Hash Knife outfit / Zane Grey.
    p. cm.
  ISBN 978-1-60285-650-9 (library binding : alk. paper)
  1. Large type books. I. Title.

PS3513.R6545H37 2009
813'.52--dc22

2009033915

Chapter One

IT WAS a rainy November night down on the Cottonwood. The wind complained in the pines outside the cabin and whispered under the eaves. A fine cold mist blew in the open chinks between the logs. But the ruddy cedar fire in the huge stone fireplace gave the interior of the cabin a comfortable aspect and shone brightly upon the inmates scattered around. A coffee-pot steamed on some coals; browned biscuits showed in an open iron oven; and thick slices of beef mingled a savory odor with the smoke. The men, however, were busy on pipes and cigarettes, evidently having finished supper.

"Reckon this storm looks like an early winter," remarked Jed Stone, leader of the outfit. He stood to one side of the fire, a fine, lithe figure of a man, still a cowboy, despite his forty years and more of hard Arizona life. His profile, sharp in the fire glow, was strong and clean, in no way hinting of the evil repute that had long recorded him an outlaw. When he turned to pick up a burning ember for his pipe the bright blaze shone on light, rather scant hair, on light eyes, and a striking face devoid of beard.

"Wal, early or late, I never seen no bad weather down hyar," replied a man back in the shadow.

"Huh! Much you know about the Mogollans.

I've seen a hell of a winter right here," spoke up another, in a deep chesty voice. "An' I'll be trackin' somethin' beside hoofs in a couple of days." This from the hunter Anderson, known to his comrades as Tracks, who had lived longer than any of the others in this wild section, seemed to strengthen Stone's intimation. Anderson was a serious man, long matured, as showed in the white in his black beard. He had big deep eyes which reflected the firelight.

"I'll bet we don't get holed up yet awhile," interposed Carr, the gambler of the outfit. He was a gray-faced, gray-haired man of fifty. They called him Stoneface.

"What do you say, Pecos?" inquired the leader of a long-limbed sandy-mustached Texan who sat propped against the wall, directly opposite the fire.

"Me? . . . Shore I don't think nothin' aboot it," drawled Pecos.

"We might winter down in the Sierra Ancas," said Stone, reflectively.

"Boss, somethin's been eatin' you ever since we had thet fight over Traft's drift fence," spoke up Croak Malloy, from his seat against some packs. His voice had a peculiar croaking quality, but that was certainly not wholly the reason for his significant nickname. He was the deadliest of this notorious outfit, so long a thorn in the flesh of the cattlemen whose stock ranged the Mogollans.

6

"I ain't denyin' it," replied Stone.

"An' why for?" complained the croaker, his crooked evil face shining in the red light. "We got off without a couple of scratches, an' we crippled them two Diamond riders. Didn't we lay low the last nine miles of thet fence?"

"Croak, I happen to know old Jim Traft. I rode for him twenty years ago," answered Stone, seriously.

"Jed, as I see it this drift fence of Traft's has split the range. An' there'll be hell to pay," snapped the other.

"Do you reckon it means another Pleasant Valley War? That was only seven years ago— thereabouts. An' the bad blood still rankles."

Croak Malloy's reply was rendered indistinguishable by hot arguments of Carr and Anderson. But the little rider's appearance seemed silently convincing. He was a small misshapen man of uncertain age, with pale eyes of fire set unevenly in a crooked face, and he looked the deadliness by which he had long been known to the range.

Just then the sodden beat of hoofs sounded outside.

"Ha! that will be Madden an' Sonora," said Stone, with satisfaction, and he strode to the door to call out. The answer was reassuring. He returned to the fire and held his palms to the heat. Then he turned and put his hands behind his back.

Meanwhile the horses thumped on the other side

of the log wall. Then the sliddery sound of wet leather and heavy packs, and the low voice of men, attested to what was going on out there. Stone went again to the door, but evidently could not see in the stormy gloom. His men smoked in silence. The rain beat on the roof, in some places leaking through. The wind mourned hollowly down the stone chimney.

Presently a man entered the cabin, carrying a heavy pack, which he deposited against the wall, then approached the fire, to remove dripping sombrero and coat. This action disclosed the swarthy face and beady bright eyes of the Mexican whom Stone had called Sonora.

"Glad you're back, Sonora," said the leader, heartily. "How about things?"

"No good," replied Sonora, and when he shook his head drops of rain water sputtered in the fire.

"Ahuh," ejaculated Stone, and he leaned against the stone chimney, back in the shadow.

The other rider came in, breathing heavily under another pack, which he let fall with a thud, and approached the fire, smelling of rain and horses and the woods. He appeared to be a nondescript sort of man. Water ran off him in little streams. He hung his coat on a peg in the chimney, but did not remove his battered black sombrero from which the rain drops dripped.

"Wal, boss, me an' Sonora got here," he said, cheerfully.

"So I see," returned Stone quietly.

"Bad up on top. Snowin' hard, but reckon it won't last long. Too wet."

"What you want to bet it won't last?" queried Carr.

Madden laughed, and knelt before the fire, his huge spurs prodding his hips.

"Lemme eat," he said. "It'll be the first bite since yestiddy mornin'."

Whereupon he drew the coffee-pot away from the fire at the same moment that Sonora removed the biscuits and meat. Stone, though nervously burning to ply questions, respected their hunger, which appeared to be of a ravenous nature. He paced the cabin floor, out of the shadow into the light, and back again, ponderingly, as one who had weighty thoughts. The firelight struck glints from the bone-handled gun which swung in a belt-sheath below his hip. The other men of the gang smoked in silence.

The youngest of the group, a cowboy in garb and gait, rose to put more wood on the fire. It blazed up brightly. He had a weak, handsome face, with viciousness written all over it, yet strangely out of place among these hardened visages. No one need have been told why he was there.

The returned members of the outfit did not desist from appeasing their appetites until all the drink, bread, and beef were gone.

"Cleaned the platter," ejaculated Madden. "Gosh! there's nothin' like a hunk of juicy salty meat when you're starved. . . . An' here's a real cigar for everybody. Nice an' dry, too." He tossed them to eager hands, and taking up a blazing stick he lighted one for himself, his dark face and steaming sombrero bent over the fire. Then he sat back, puffed a huge cloud of white smoke, and exclaimed: "Aghh! . . . Now, boss, shoot."

Stone kicked a box nearer the fire and sat down upon it. Then from a shadowed corner limped a stalwart man scarred of face and evil of eye, with a sheriff's badge glittering like a star on the front of his vest. Some of the others edged closer. All except Croak Malloy evinced keen eagerness. Nothing mattered to this little outlaw.

"Maddy, did you fetch all the supplies?" asked Stone.

"Yep. An' kept them dry, too. There's four more packs out in the shed. The tobacco, whisky, shells—all that particular stuff is in the pack Sonora fetched in. An' I'm here to state I don't want to pack down Cottonwood any more in the snow an' rain. We couldn't see a hand before our eyes. An' just follered the horses."

"Any trouble at Flag?" went on Stone.

"Nary trouble," answered Madden, brightly. "All our worryin' was for nothin'."

"Ahuh. Then neither of those drift-fence cowboys we shot up died?"

"Nope. Frost was around with a crutch. An' Hump Stevens will live, so they told me."

"How did Jim Traft take the layin' down of nine miles of his drift fence?"

"Which Jim Traft do you mean?"

"The old man, you fool. Who'd ever count that tenderfoot of a nephew?"

"Wal, boss, I reckon you'll have to count him. For he's shore countin' in Flag. . . . Of course I could only get roundabout gossip in the saloons an' stores, you know. But we can gamble on it. That nine-mile drop of Traft's drift fence didn't make him bat an eye, though they told me it riled young Jim somethin' fierce. Jed, the old cattle king is goin' through with that drift fence, an' with more'n that, which I'll tell you presently. As I got it the drift fence is comin' more to favor with cattlemen as time goes on. Bambridge is the only big rancher against it, an' shore you know why he is. But the fence ain't the only thing talked about. . . . Boss, the Cibeque outfit is busted."

"No!—You don't say!" ejaculated Stone.

"Shore is. Most owin' to that cowpuncher Hack Jocelyn who left the Diamond outfit an' throwed in with the Cibeque. That split the Cibeque. It seems Jocelyn lost his head over that little Dunn girl, Molly, sister to Slinger Dunn. You've seen her Jed, at West Fork."

"Yes. Prettiest kid in the country."

"Wal, Jocelyn was after her hard, an' he double-crossed the Haverlys an' Slinger Dunn by tryin' to play both ends against the middle. He hatched a

11

low-down deal, if I ever knowed one. But it fell through. He got away with the girl Molly, however, an' thet precipitated hell. Slinger quit the Cibeque, trailed them to a cabin in the woods. Back of Tobe's Well somewhere. Must have been the very cabin Anderson put up there years ago. Wal, Jocelyn an' the rest of the Cibeque had kidnapped young Jim Traft for ransom. But Jocelyn meant to collect the ransom an' then murder the boy. The Haverlys wasn't in on this, so the story goes. Anyway, things worked to a hot pitch at this cabin. Jocelyn had a drink too many, they say, an' wanted to drag the little girl Molly off 'n the woods. An' she, like what you'd expect of Slinger Dunn's sister, raised hell. Jocelyn tried to shoot young Jim. An' she fought him—bit him like a wildcat. Wal, Slinger bobbed up, Injun as he is, an' killed Jocelyn. Then he had it out with the Haverlys, killin' both of them. He was terrible shot up himself. They fetched him to Flag. But he'll live."

"I'm dod-blasted glad, though there ain't any love lost between me an' Slinger," said Stone, forcibly. "No wonder Flag wasn't excited over our little brush with Stevens an' Frost."

"Wal, thet's all of thet news," went on Madden, importantly. "Some more will interest you-all. Bambridge lost his case against Traft. He had no case at all, accordin' to the court. It seems Traft got this Yellow Jacket Ranch an' range from Blodgett, years ago. Bambridge didn't even know the deeds were on record in Flag. He was hoppin' mad, they said, an' he an' Traft had it hot an' heavy after the court proceedin's. Traft jest about accused Bambridge of shady cattle deals down here. Bambridge drew a gun, but somebody knocked it out of his hand. Wal, thet riled the old cattle king. What do you think he said, boss? I got it from a fellar I know, who was in the court-room."

"Maddy, I'll bet it was a heap," replied Stone, wagging his head.

"Heap! Reckon you hit it. Traft swore he'd run Bambridge off the Arizona ranges. What's more, he made a present of this Yellow Jacket Ranch, which Bambridge an' you reckoned you *owned* yourselves, to his nephew, young Jim, an'—but guess who?"

"I'm not guessin'. Out with it," rejoined Stone, hardily.

"No one less than Slinger Dunn," announced Madden, with the triumphant tone of the sensation-lover.

"What?" bellowed Stone.

"I told you, boss. Old Traft gave this ranch an' range to young Jim an' Slinger—half an' half. Providin' thet Slinger throwed in with the Diamond outfit an' helped them clean up Yellow Jacket."

"Haw! Haw!" croaked Malloy, with vicious humor.

"Slinger Dunn an' the Diamond!" exclaimed Stone, incredulously. Evidently it was a most astounding circumstance, and one fraught with bewildering possibilities.

"Thet's it, boss, an' they're ridin' down here after Thanksgivin'," ended Madden, and took a long pull on his cigar.

Stone once more leaned in the shadow, his dim profile bent toward the fire. Madden stretched himself, boots to the heat, and gave himself over to the enjoyment of his cigar. All except the leader puffed white clouds of smoke which rose to catch the draught and waft through the chinks between the logs.

"What do you make of it, boss?" finally queried Anderson.

Jed Stone vouchsafed no reply.

"Humph!" grunted the hunter. "Wal, Frank, you're the green hand in this outfit. What you make of Maddy's news?"

The cowboy stirred and sat up. "I reckon it can't be done," he replied.

"What can't?"

"Cleanin' up Yellow Jacket."

The hunter took a long draw at this cigar and expelled a volume of smoke, while he thoughtfully stroked his black beard.

"Whar you from, Frank?"

"Born in Arizonie."

"An' you say thet? Wal. . . . Reckon it ain't no

wonder you ended up with the Hash Knife outfit," said Anderson, reflectively. Then he turned his attention to the Mexican, who sat nearest. "Sonora, you been herdin' sheep for years on this range?"

"Si, señor."

"You've seen a heap of men shot?"

"Many men, señor."

"Did you talk to sheep-herders in Flag?"

"Si. All say *mucho malo*. Old Traft bad medicine. If he start job he do job."

Whereupon Tracks Anderson, warming as to a trail, set upon the long-limbed, sandy-mustached Texan. "Pecos, what was you when you rode thet river you're named fer?"

"Me? Much the same as I am now," drawled the rustler, with an easy laugh. "Only I wasn't ridin' in such good safe company."

"Safe, huh? Wal, thet's a compliment to Jed an' the Hash Knife. But is it sense? . . . To my way of thinkin' this —— drift fence has spelled a change fer Arizona ranges. There's a mind behind that idee. It's big. It throws the sunlight on trails thet have been dim."

Croak Malloy did not wait to be interrogated. He spat as he emitted a cloud of smoke, which hid his strange visage.

"If you ask me I'll tell you Maddy's talk is jest town talk," he croaked. "I've heard the same fer ten years. An' Yellow Jacket is wilder today than it ever was. There's more cattle runnin' than then. More rustlers in the woods. More crooked ranchers. An' one like Bambridge wasn't ever heard when I first rode into the Tonto. . . . An' what's a bunch of slick-ridin' cowboys to us? I'll kill this young Traft, an' Sonora can do fer Slinger Dunn. Thet'll be the last of the Diamond."

"Very pretty, Croak. It might be done, easy enough, if we take the first step. I ain't aimin' to class thet wild Diamond outfit with the Hash Knife. It ain't no fair fight. Boys ag'in' men. An' this is shore allowin' fer Slinger Dunn an' thet Prentiss fellar."

"Tracks," spoke up Pecos, dryly, "you're plumb fergettin' there's a Texan in the Diamond. Lonestar Holliday. An' you can bet the Texas I come from wouldn't be ashamed of him."

"Humph!—Lang, you swear you come honest by thet sheriff badge," went on the hunter, in a grim humor. "Let's hear from you."

"There ain't no law but might in the Mogollans an' never will be in our day," replied the ex-sheriff.

"Kirreck," snapped Anderson. "Thet's what I'm driving at. *Our* day may be damn good an' short."

"Aw, hell! Tracks, you need some licker," croaked Malloy. "Let's open the pack an' have some."

"No," came from Stone with sharp suddenness, showing how intent he was on the colloquy.

16

"Wal, it narrows down to Stoneface," continued Anderson, imperturbably. "But seein' he's a gambler, you can't ever get the straight from him."

"Tracks, I'll bet you them gold wheels you'll be hibernatin' fer keeps when spring comes," said Carr, clinking gold coins in his palms.

"*Quién sabe?* But I won't bet you, Stoneface. You get hunches from the air, an' Gawd only knows—you might be communicatin' with the dead."

A silence ensued, during which the hunter gazed with questioning eyes at the shadowed leader, but he did not voice his thought. He returned diligently to the cigar that appeared to be hard to smoke. The rain pattered on the roof; the wind moaned under the eaves; beyond the log wall horses munched their feed; the fire sputtered. And presently Jed Stone broke the silence.

"Men, I rode on the first Hash Knife outfit, twenty years ago," he began. "An' Arizona never had a finer bunch of riders. Since then I've rode in all the outfits. Some had good men an' bad men at the same time. Thet Texas outfit in the early 'eighties gave the Hash Knife its bad name. Daggs, Colter, an' the rest didn't live long, but their fame did. Yet they wasn't any worse then the cattlemen and sheepmen who fought thet war. I've never had a real honest job since."

Stone paused to take a long pull on his cigar and to blow smoke. He kicked a stick into the fire and watched it crackle and flame.

17

"An' thet fetches me down to this day an' the Hash Knife outfit here," he went on. "There's a heap of difference between fact and rumor. Old Jim Traft knows we're rustlin' his stock, but he can't prove it—yet. Bambridge knows we are stealin' cattle, but he can't prove it because he's crooked himself. An' same with lesser cattlemen hereabouts. If I do say it myself, I've run this outfit pretty slick. We've got a few thousand head of cattle wearin' our brand. Most of which we jest roped out on the range an' branded. We knowed the mothers of these calves had Traft's brand or some other than ours. But no posse or court can ever prove thet onless they ketch us in the act. We're shore too old hands now to be ketched, at least at the brandin' game. But . . . an', men, here's the hell of it, we can't go on in the old comfortable way if Traft sends thet Diamond outfit down here. Yellow Jacket belongs to him. An' don't you overlook this Diamond bunch if Slinger Dunn is on it. Reckon thet will have to be proved to me. Slinger is even more of an Indian than a backwoodsman. I know him well. We used to hunt together. He's run a lot in the woods with Apaches. An' no outfit would be safe while he prowled around with a rifle. I'm tellin' you—if Slinger would ambush us—shoot us from cover like an Indian, he'd kill every damn one of us. But I'll gamble Slinger wouldn't never do thet kind of fightin'. An' we want to bear thet in mind if it comes to a clash between the Diamond an' the Hash Knife."

"If," exploded Anderson, as the leader paused. "There ain't no ifs. Any kind of reasonin' would show you thet Traft has long had in mind workin' up this Yellow Jacket. It'll run ten thousand head, easy, an' shore will be a fine ranch."

"Wal then, we got to figger close. Let me make a few more points an' then I'll put it to a vote. I wish I hadn't always done thet. For I reckon I see clear here. . . . We've had more'n one string to our bow these five years. An' if we wasn't a wasteful outfit we'd all be heeled right now. Bambridge has been playin' a high hand lately. How many thousand unbranded calves an' yearlin's we've drove over to him I can't guess. But shore a lot. Anyway, he's figgerin' to leave Arizona. Thet's my hunch. An' he'll likely try to drive some big deals before he goes. If he does you can bet he'll leave the Hash Knife to bear the brunt. Traft has come out in the open. He's on to Bambridge. There's no slicker cowman on the range than Traft's man, Ring Locke. They'll put the Diamond down here, not only to watch us, but Bambridge too. An' while we're at it let's give this young Jim Traft the benefit of a doubt. They say he's a chip of the old block. Wal, it'd jest be a hell of a mistake for Croak to kill thet younger fellar. Old Traft would rake Arizona from the Little Colorado to the Superstitions. It jest won't do. Slinger Dunn, yes, an' any of the rest of the outfit. But not young

Jim. . . . Wal, I reckon it'd be wise fer us to make one more drive, sell to Bambridge, an' clear out pronto."

"My Gawd!" croaked Malloy, in utter amaze.

"Boss, do I understand you to hint you'd leave the range your Hash Knife has run fer twenty years?" demanded Stoneface Carr.

And the Texan rustler Pecos asked a like question, drawling and sarcastic.

"Men, I read the signs of the times," replied the leader, briefly and not without heat. "I'll put it up to you one by one. . . . Anderson, shall we pull up stakes fer a new range?"

"I reckon so. It ain't the way of a Hash Knife outfit. But I advise it fer thet very reason."

Sonora, the sheep-herder, leaned significantly and briefly to Stone's side. But the gambler was stone cold to the plan. Malloy only croaked a profane and scornful refusal. The others came out flat with derisive or affronted objections.

"Wal, you needn't blow my head off," declared Stone, in like tone. "If you do there shore won't be a hell of a lot of brains left in this outfit. . . . It's settled. The Hash Knife stays until we are run out or wiped out."

That ultimatum seemed to be final. The force of Stone's grim voice had a thought-provoking effect, except upon the cold Malloy, and perhaps the silent Texan. One by one they unrolled their beds, talking desultorily and sleepily. Madden had already fallen asleep with his head on a sack. His sombrero had slipped back, exposing a heavy tired face, dark with shadows.

Jed Stone still stood in the darkening shadow by the chimney. Presently, when the members of his gang had quieted down he stepped out to seat himself on a box by the fire, and took to throwing chips on the red embers, watching them burn.

Outside, the storm appeared to be letting up. The wind moaned faintly and intermittently; the rain pattered softer; the trees ceased to lash their branches against the roof.

Stone must have been thinking of the past. He had the look of a man who saw pictures in the glowing embers. Twenty years ago he had been a cowboy riding the ranges, free, honest, liked, with all the future before him. The dark sad eyes told that then there had been a girl. Only twenty years! But the latter number of them were black and must be expiated. He had seen cattlemen begin honestly and end by being hanged. Sighing, he evidently dispelled something familiar yet rare and troublesome, and rising he began to pace the floor before the fire.

The replenished embers glowed fitfully, augmenting the shadows on the walls, playing on the sinister faces of the sleeping men. Malloy's had a ghastly sardonic mockery. Even in sleep he showed his deadliness. What were life and death to him? Young Reed, the cowboy lately come to

21

the outfit, lay flat, his weak handsome face clear in the ruddy light. Stone pitied him. Did he have a mother living—a sister? He was an outlaw now at twenty-two. That should have meant nothing to Jed Stone, considering how many cowboys he had seen go to the bad. But somehow for the moment it meant a good deal. Stone saw with eyes grown old in the wild ways of the West. Sonora there—he had a dark sleek face, inscrutable like an Indian's, that did not betray he was thief and murderer. The gambler Carr, too, wore a mask. Pecos was the only other member of the gang who lay with face exposed to the firelight. Silent, mysterious Texan, he had always fascinated Stone. Pecos was a deadly foe, and to a friend true as steel. He cared little for money or drink, not at all for cards, and he shunned women. Could that be his secret?

Stone went to the door and looked out. It had cleared somewhat. Stars shone in the open spaces between the black clouds. A misty rain from the pines wet his face. A mountain to the East stood up wild and black. Out there a wolf bayed a deer. A chill in the air—or was it the haunting voice of the wolf? struck down Stone's spine. He had an honest love for this lonely range, which sooner or later, and one way or another, he must leave.

He went back to unroll his bed near the fire, and he for one pulled off his boots. Throwing more chips and bits of bark on the coals, he stretched his long length, feet to the warmth, and his head high, and watched the blaze rise and fall, the red glow pale, the ruddy embers darken, and the shadows dim and die.

Chapter Two

THAT same stormy night in early November, when the members of the Hash Knife gang had their fateful colloquy in the old log cabin on the Yellow Jacket range, Jim Traft sat with his nephew in the spacious living-room of the big ranch-house on the edge of Flagerstown.

It was a bright warm room, doubly cosy owing to the whine of wind outside and the patter of sleet on the windowpanes. Old Traft had a fondness for lamps with rosy globes, and the roaring fire in the great stone fireplace attested to his years on the open range. A sleek wolf-hound lay on the rug. Traft occupied an armchair that looked as ancient as the hills, and he sat back with a contented smile on his fine weather-beaten face, occasionally to puff his pipe.

"Dog-gone-it, Jim, this is somethin' like home," he said. "You look so good to me these days. An' you've come through a Westerner. . . . An' the old house isn't lonesome any more."

He nodded his gray head toward the far end of the room, where Molly Dunn curled in a big chair,

23

her pretty gold-brown head bent over a book. Opposite Molly on the other side of the table sat Mrs. Dunn, with eager expectant look of enchantment, as one who wanted to keep on dreaming.

Young Jim laughed. It looked more than something like home to him, and seldom was there a moment his eyes did not return to that brown head of Molly Dunn.

"Shore is, Uncle," he drawled, in the lazy voice he affected on occasions. "You wouldn't think we're only a few weeks past that bloody fight. . . . Gosh! when I think! . . . Uncle, I've told you a hundred times how Molly saved my life. It seems like a dream. . . . Well, I'm back home—for this *is* home, Uncle. No work for weeks! No bossing that terrible bunch of cowboys! You so pleased with me—though for the life of me I can't see why. Molly here for the winter to go to school—and—and then to be my wife next spring. . . . And Slinger Dunn getting well from those awful bullet wounds so fast. . . . It's just too good to be true."

"Ahuh. I savvy how you feel, son," replied the old rancher. "It does seem that out here in the West the hard knocks and trials make the softer side of life—home an' folks—an' the girl of your heart— so much dearer an' sweeter. It ought to make you keen as a whip to beat the West—to stack cunnin' an' nerve against the wild life of the range, an' come through alive. I did. An', Jim, if I'd been a drinkin', roarin' cowpuncher I'd never have

24

lasted, an' you wouldn't be here tonight, stealin' looks at your little Western girl."

"Oh, Uncle, that's the—the hell of it!" exclaimed Jim. "I'm crucified when I realize. Those weeks building the drift fence were great. Such fun—such misery! Then that fight at the cabin! O Lord! I could have torn Hack Jocelyn to pieces with my hands. Then when Molly was fighting him for possession of his gun—hanging to him like grim death—with her *teeth,* mind you—when he lifted and swung her and beat her—I was an abject groveling wretch, paralyzed with horror. . . . Then when Slinger leaped past me round the cabin, as I sat there tied and helpless, and he yelled like an Indian at Jocelyn. . . . I thrill and shiver now, and my heart stops. . . . Only since I've been home do I realize what you mean about the West. It's wonderful, it's glorious, but terrible, too."

"You've had your eye teeth cut, son," said Traft, grimly. "Now you must face the thing—you must fight. I've fought for forty years. An' it will still be years more before the range is free of the outlaw, the rustler, the crooked cattleman, the thieving cowboy."

"Uncle Jim," called Molly, plaintively, "please hush up aboot the bad West. I want to study, an' I cain't help heahin'."

"Wal, wal, Molly," laughed Traft, in mild surprise. "Reckon I thought you was wrapped up in that school book."

25

"An', Jim—shore the West's not as wicked as Uncle makes out," went on Molly. "He wants you to be another Curly Prentiss—or even like Slinger."

"Ha! Ha!" roared the rancher, rubbing his hands. "That's funny from Molly Dunn. My dear, if *you* hadn't had all the Western qualities I'm tryin' to inspire in Jim, where would he be now?"

Even across the room Jim saw her sweet face blanch and her big dark eyes dilate; and these evidences shot an exquisite pleasure and happiness through him.

"Uncle, I'll answer that," he said. "I'd be in the Garden of Eden, eating peaches."

"Maybe you would, Jim Traft," retorted Molly. "A little more bossin' the Diamond outfit an' your chances for the Garden of Eden are shore slim."

Mrs. Dunn spoke up, exclaiming how strange and delightful it was to hear the sleet on the pane.

"Wal, this is high country, Mrs. Dunn," replied Traft. "Down on the Cibeque where you live it's five thousand feet lower. There's seldom any winter in the Tonto. But she's shore settin' in here at Flag."

"Will there be snow on the ground, tomorrow?" asked Molly, wonderingly.

"I reckon, a little. Couple of feet."

"How lovely! I can go to school in the snow."

"I'm sorry, Molly," interposed Jim. "Tomorrow is Saturday. No school. It will be very tame for you, I'm afraid. Only wading out to the corrals with me. A snowball fight or two. Then a sleigh ride into town."

"*Jim!*" she exclaimed, ecstatically. "I never had a sleigh ride in all my life."

Her rapture was reflected in the old cattleman's face. Jim imagined it must be pure joy for his uncle to see and hear Molly. What a lonely hard life the old fellow had lived! And now he wanted young folk around, and the children that had been denied him. Jim's heart swelled with longing to make up to his uncle for all that he had missed.

Mrs. Dunn rose to come forward and take a chair nearer the fire. "It's getting chilly. Such a big room!"

"Molly, come over an' be sociable," called Traft.

"But my study, Uncle. I—I've missed so much," replied the girl, wistfully.

"Molly, I'll not allow you to wear your pretty eyes out," decared Jim, authoritatively. "Learning is very good for a girl, but beauty should not be sacrificed."

"You won't allow me?" she asked, demurely, and resumed her study.

Whereupon Jim walked over, picked her up bodily, and carried her back to set her, blushing and confused, in his own chair.

"You're such a slip of a girl, Molly," he said, wonderingly. "In size I mean. You're heavy as lead and strong as the dickens. But you're so little.

There's quite room enough in that chair for me, too."

And Jim slipped into it beside her, not quite sure how she would take this. But his fear was unfounded.

"Now, Uncle, tell us the story about the time you came West as a boy. How you rode in a caravan across the plains and were attacked by Indians at Pawnee Rock. I was six years old when you told me that story. I've never forgotten. It'll make Molly think the Cibeque a quiet, peaceful country."

Later, when the ladies had retired, Ring Locke came in with his quiet step and his intent eye. Since Jim's return from the disastrous failure of the drift fence (so he considered it, in contrast to his uncle's opinion) and the fight at the cabin below Cottonwood, he had seemed to be in the good graces of this Westerner, Ring Locke, a fact he hugged with great satisfaction. Locke was a keen, strong, and efficient superintendent of the old cattleman's vast interests.

"Some mail an' some news," he announced, handing a packet of letters to Traft.

"How's the weather, Ring?" asked the rancher.

"Clearin' I reckon, but we won't see any green round Flag till spring."

"Early winter, eh? Wal, we got here first. . . . Son, letter for you from home—two. An' in a lady's fancy hand. You better look out Molly

28

doesn't see them. . . . Ring, help yourself to a cigar an' set down."

Jim stared at the first letter. "By gosh! Gloriana has written me at last. It's coming Christmas, the little devil. . . . And the other from Mother. Fine."

"Glory must be growed into quite a girl by now," remarked his uncle.

"Quite? Uncle, she's altogether," declared Jim with force.

"Wal, I hardly remember her, 'cept as a pretty little kid with curls an' big eyes. Favored your mother. She shore wasn't a Traft."

Locke lit a cigar. "Some of the Hash Knife outfit been in town," he announced, calmly.

Jim forgot to open his lettters. Old Traft bit at his cigar. "Nerve of 'em! Who was it, Ring?"

"Madden and a greaser whose name I've forgot, if I ever knowed it. Reckon there was another of the gang in town, but I couldn't find out who. They bought a lot of supplies an' left Thursday. I went around to all the stores an' saloons. Dug up what I could. It wasn't a lot, but then again it 'pears interestin'. One thing in particular. Curly Prentiss swears he saw Madden comin' out of Bambridge's, after dark Wednesday, he says. But Curly has had a ruction with his gurl, an' he's been drinkin', I'm sorry to say. That cowboy would be the grandest fellar, if he didn't drink. Still drunk or no, Curly has an eye, an' I reckon he did see Madden."

"Funny, his comin' out of Bambridge's," growled Traft, and the bright blue eyes narrowed.

"Awful funny," agreed Locke, in a dry tone, which acquainted the listening Jim with the fact that the circumstance was most decidedly not funny. "Anyway, it started me off. An' the upshot of my nosin' around was to find out that the Hash Knife crowd are at Yellow Jacket an' all of a sudden oncommon interested in you an' young Jim, an' the Diamond, an' Slinger Dunn."

"Ahuh. Wal, they'll be a heap more so by spring," replied Traft. "Funny about Bambridge."

"The Hash Knife have friends in Flag, you bet, an' more'n we'd ever guess. Shore, nobody knows our business, onless the cowboys have talked. I'm afraid Bud an' Curly have bragged. They do when they get to town an' guzzle a bit. Madden did darn little drinkin' an' none 'cept when he was treated. Another funny thing. He bought all the forty-five caliber shells Babbitt's had in stock. An' a heap of the same kind, along with some forty-fours for rifles, at Davis's. He bought hardware, too. Some new guns. An' enough grub to feed an outfit for a year."

"Winter supplies, I reckon. An' mebbe the Hash Knife are in for another war, like the one it started in 'eighty-two. Ha! Ha! . . . But it ain't so funny, after all."

"It shore doesn't look like peaceful ranchin'," drawled Locke.

"Damn these low-down outfits, anyway," growled the rancher. "I fought them when I rode the range years ago, an' now I'm fightin' them still. Locke, we'll be runnin' eighty thousand head of stock in a year or two."

"Eighty thousand!—Then you can afford to lose some," replied Locke.

"Humph. *I* couldn't lose a calf's ear to those thievin' outfits without gettin' sore. They've kept me poor."

"Uncle, we appear to have the necessities of life around the ranch. Nice warm fires, and some luxury," remarked Jim, humorously.

"Just you wait," retorted his uncle. "Just you wait! You'll be a darn sight worse than me, pronto."

"Locke, who is this Madden?" asked Jim, quietly, with change of tone.

"One of Jed Stone's gang. Hard-ridin', hard-drinkin' an' shootin' hombre. Come up from the border a few years ago. The murder of Wilson, a rancher out of Holbrook, was laid to Madden. But that was only suspicion. In this country you have to catch a man at anythin' to prove it. Personally, though, I'd take a shot at Madden an' ask questions afterward."

"Tough outfit, Uncle tells me," went on Jim, reflectively.

"Boy, the Cibeque was a summer zephyr to thet Hash Knife outfit. Stone used to be a square-shootin' cowboy. Rode fer your uncle once. That was before my day here. He's outlawed now, with crimes on his head. An intelligent, dangerous man. He's got a Texas gun-fighter in his outfit. Pecos something or other, an' I reckon he's 'most as bad as any of the killers out of Texas. Croak Malloy, though, is Stone's worst an' meanest hand. Then, there's Lang an' Anderson, who've been with him for years."

"Is Slinger Dunn the equal of any of these men?" queried Jim.

"Equal? I reckon. Yes, he's ahaid of them in some ways," replied Locke, thoughtfully. "Slinger could beat any one of them to a gun, unless mebbe this Pecos feller. But Slinger is young an' he has no crimes on his haid. That makes a difference. None of his Hash Knife outfit could be arrested. They hang together, an' you bet they'll die with their boots on."

"Then we're in for another fight?" mused Jim, and though he sustained a wonderful thrill—cold as a chill—he did not like the prospect.

"Traft," said Locke, turning to the rancher, "strikes me queer that Stone hangs on in this part of Arizona. He's no fool. He shore knows he can't last forever. If the Diamond doesn't drive him out it'll break up his outfit. An' other riders will keep on his track."

"Wal, you know, Stone will never be run out of anywhere. But he's an Arizonian, an' this range is home, even if it has outlawed him. He's bitter an' hard, which is natural enough. Stone ought to be a rich cattleman now. I—I feel sorry for him, an' that's why I've let Yellow Jacket alone."

Jim thought his uncle spoke rather feelingly.

"Wouldn't it be better to drive off what stock's left there an' let the land go?" went on Locke.

"Better? Humph! It can't be done. We've got to organize against these rustlin' outlaws or they'll grow bolder an' ruin us. Take that case over in New Mexico when a big cattleman—crooked, of course—hired Billy the Kid an' his outfit to steal cattle, an' he sold them to the government. That deal lasted for years. Everybody knew it, except the government officials. Wal, I'm inclined to think there's *some* ranchin' man backin' Stone."

"Ahuh. I know how you incline, Traft," returned Locke, dryly. "An' it's likely to get us into trouble."

"Wal, if Bambridge is buyin' in our stock we ought to find it out," said Traft, testily.

"Suppose your suspicions reach Bambridge's ear? He *might* be honest. In any case he's liable to shoot you. An' I say this Yellow Jacket isn't worth the risk."

"Ring, I don't like the man. I suspect him. We've clashed from the first. He was hoppin' mad when he found out I owned Yellow Jacket an' had the range rights there. It'll be interestin' to see what move he makes."

"Like watchin' a game of checkers," rejoined Locke, with a laugh. "All right, Boss. I'm bound to admit you've made some sharp guesses in my days with you. Reckon I'll go to bed. Good night."

In the silence that succeeded after he had gone, Jim slowly opened the letters he had been idly holding.

"Uncle, I'm afraid Locke is against this Yellow Jacket deal, especially the Bambridge angle."

"Locke is cautious. He hates this sort of thing as much as I do. But what can we do? I take it as my duty to rid Arizona of this particular outfit, an' I'm goin' to do it."

"Then it isn't a personal grudge against Bambridge?"

"Not at all. I shore hope we find out my suspicions arc wrong. An' I'm relyin' on your Slinger Dunn to find out. He's the man we need, Jim. I shore appreciate your gettin' hold of him."

Jim spread out one of the letters on his knee and read it.

"Good heavens!" he ejaculated, blankly.

"Son, I hope you've no bad news. Who's the letter from?"

"Mother," replied Jim, still blankly.

"Wal?"

"Uncle, what do you think? Mother is sending my sister, Gloriana, out here to stay with us a while. . . . Doctor's orders. Says Gloriana has a weak lung and must live a year or more in a high dry climate. . . . By gosh! Glory is on her way right now!"

"Wal, wal! I'm shore sorry, Jim. But Arizona will cure her."

"Cure! . . . Cure nothing!" snorted Jim. "Gloriana has no more trouble than I have. She's the healthiest girl alive. It's just a trick to get her out here."

"Wal, I reckon there ain't no need of tricks. We'll be darn glad to have her, won't we?"

"Uncle, you don't understand," replied Jim, in despair.

"Tell me, then."

"Gloriana will upset the ranch, and break the Diamond and drive me crazy."

"Haw! Haw! Haw!"

"It's no laughing matter."

"But, Jim, you've been away from home 'most a year. Your sister could have failed in health in much less time."

"That's so. . . . Oh, I hope not. . . . Of course, Uncle, I'll be glad to have her, if she's really sick. But . . ."

"Son, don't you care for this little sister?"

"Gosh, Uncle, I love her! That's the worst of it. I can't help but love her. Everybody loves her, in spite of the fact she's a perfect devil."

"Humph! How old is Gloriana?"

"She's eighteen. No, nearly nineteen."

"Wal, the Trafts were all good-lookin'. How does she stack up?"

"Glory is the prettiest girl you ever saw in all your life."

"Shore then it'll be fine to have her," replied the rancher. "An' I'll tell you what, Jim. When we once get her out heah we'll keep her."

"What?" queried Jim, weakly.

"We'll never let her go back again. We'll marry her to some fine Westerner."

Jim felt it his turn to laugh. "Ha! Ha! Ha! . . . Uncle, there're not enough men in Arizona to marry Glory. And I'm afraid not one she'd wipe her feet on."

"Sort of stuck up, eh? Thet ain't a Traft trait."

"I wouldn't say she was stuck up. But she's certainly no plain everyday Traft, like you and I, or Dad or Mother. She's not conceited, either. Glory is a puzzle. She changes each moon. I wonder what she's like now. . . . Jerusalem! Suppose she doesn't take to Molly!"

"See heah, young man," spoke up Traft, gruffly. "Mebbe it'll be the other way round. Molly mightn't take to her."

"Molly? Why, Uncle, that adorable child would love anybody, if she had half a chance."

"Ahuh. Wal, that accounts fer her lovin' you. . . . Jim, it'll work out all right. Remember your first tenderfoot days. Would you go back East now to live?"

"Gosh, no!"

"Wal, the West will do the same for Gloriana, if she has any red blood. It'll go tough, until she's broke in. An' if she's a high-steppin' Easterner,

36

it'll be all the tougher. But she must have real stuff in her. She's a Traft, for all you say."

"Gloriana May takes after Mother's side of the family, and some of them are awful."

"She's got to have some Traft in her. An' we'll gamble on that. For my part, I'm glad she's comin'. I hope she burns up the ranch. I've been so long without fun and excitement and deviltry around heah that I could stand a heap."

"Uncle Jim, you're going to get your desire," exploded Jim, dramatically. "You'll see these cowboys walk Spanish and perform like tame bears with rings in their noses. You'll see the work on the ranch go to smash. The roundups will be a circus. As for dances—holy smoke! every one of them will be a war!"

"Wal, I'll be gol-darned if I wouldn't like the girl all the more," declared Traft, stoutly. "These cow-punchers make me awful sick with their love affairs. Any girl will upset them. An' if Glory is all you say—my Gawd, but I'll enjoy it! . . . Good night, son."

Jim slid down in his chair and eyed the fire. "Gosh! It's a good bet Uncle Jim will be apple pie for Glory. But if she really loves him, why, I reckon, I'll be clad. And I might get aong with her, in a pinch.—But there's Molly. . . . Heigho! I'd better dig into Glory's letter."

He held it to the dying glow of the fire and read:

DEAR BROTHER JIM:

Don't let Mother's letter worry you. I'm not very sick. I've planned to start west the day after I mail this letter, so you won't have time to wire me not to come. I'm just crazy about the West. Your letters have done it, Jim. I've devoured them. Dad is so proud of you he almost busts. But Mother thinks it's terrible. I'm sorry to spring this on you so sudden. I hope you will be glad to see me. It seems ages since you left. You'll never know your Gloriana May.

Expect me on the Western Special, November 7th, and meet me with a bunch of cowboys, a string of horses, and one of those tally-ho things you call a chuck-wagon. I'm starved to death.

LOVE.

GLORIANA.

Jim read the letter twice and then stared into the fire. "Sounds like Glory, yet somehow it doesn't. . . . I wonder if she *is* really ill. . . . Or in any kind of trouble. . . . It was Glory's affairs with boys that stuck in my craw. . . . Well. November the seventh. By jinks! it's Monday! What shall I say to Molly?"

The difficulty, it seemed to Jim, would be serious. Glory was bright and clever. She had graduated from high school at seventeen. She could do 'most anything well, and had a genius for designing and making modish dresses and bonnets. Molly, on the other hand, was a shy little wood-mouse. She had never had any advantages. Two years at a backwoods school had been all the opportunity for education that had ever come to her. She was exceedingly sensitive about her lack of knowledge and her crudeness. The situation would be a delicate one, for Molly, in her way, was quite as proud as Gloriana was in hers.

"I'll trust to Molly's generous heart and the western bigness of her," soliloquized Jim. "In the end Glory will love her. That I'll gamble on."

Chapter Three

JIM lay in bed longer than usual next morning, and when he finally rolled out, convinced that his problem was not so terribly serious after all, a white glistening world of snow greeted him from his window. The storm had gone and a clear blue sky and bright sun smiled coldly down upon the white fringed pines and peaks. He did not take more than a glance, however, because his room seemed full of zero weather. He had to break the ice in his bucket to get water to wash, and he was far from lethargic about it. "I don't know about this high dry altitude," he soliloquized. "It'd freeze the nose off a polar bear."

The halls of the big ranch-house were like a barn. Jim rushed to the living-room. A fine fire blazed in the wide fireplace. How good it felt to his numb fingers! Jim thought the West brought out so much more of a man's appreciation. It was harsh, violent, crude, but it brought home to a man a full value of things.

"Mawnin', Jim," came in Molly's drawling voice from somewhere.

"Hello! . . . Oh, there you are!" exclaimed Jim, gladly, as he espied her at the corner window, gazing out upon the wintry scene. "I was sure you'd be snug in bed. Come here, darling."

Molly had not yet grown used to the impelling power of that word and she seemed irresistibly drawn. She wore a red coat over her blouse, the color of which matched her cheeks. In the few weeks since her arrival at the ranch she had lost some of the brown tan of the backwoods, which only added to her attractiveness. The gold glints in her dark curly hair caught the sunshine as it streamed through the window. Her eyes had that dark, shy, glad light that always thrilled Jim. And her lips, like red ripe cherries, were infinitely provocative.

"Oh—Jim—" she gasped, "some one might come in."

"Kiss me, Molly Dunn," he replied, giving her a little shake. "I'll have to get like Curly or Bud in my lovemaking."

"If you do, Mister Missouri, you'll never get nowhere with me," she returned.

40

"Not 'nowhere,' Molly. Say, anywhere."

"Very well. Anywhere," she obeyed.

"I'll take that back about Curly and Bud."

"You don't need to learn from them. You're somethin' of a bear yourself."

"Don't you love me this morning?"

"Why, Jim—of course!"

"Then?"

Molly's kisses were rather few and far between, which made them so much more precious. Jim both deplored and respected her restraint. She had been raised in a hard school, and often she had regretted to Jim that her lips had not been kept wholly for him. She was strong and sweet, this little girl of the Cibeque, and she had earned Jim's worship.

"There!" she whispered, shyly, and slipped out of his arms. "Gee, your hands are cold. An' your nose like ice."

"Molly, I've news for you," he said, thinking it wise to broach the subject in mind.

"Yes?"

"My sister is coming out here." He tried not to be sober, but failed. It seemed lost upon Molly, however, who smiled her surprise and gladness.

"Oh, how lovely!—Gloriana May! You told me aboot her—how pretty she is an' what a little devil. . . . Jim, thet'll be nice for you to have her heah. I'm glad."

Jim hugged her quite out of all reason. "Lord!

but you're a sweet, fine, square kid! I just love you to death."

"J-Jim—let me go. . . . I see no call for rastlin' me."

"No, I dare say you don't. Please excuse my violence. . . . Molly, my sister is in poor health, so Mother writes. And she's sending Glory out to get well."

"I'm sorry. What ails her, Jim?"

"Weak lung, Mother said. It's hard to believe. But Glory said in her letter for me not to let Mother's letter upset me. Uncle Jim was tickled. Began figuring right away on marrying Glory to some Westerner. Isn't he the old match-maker?"

"He's the dearest, goodest man in Arizona," returned Molly, warmly.

"Sure he is. But all the same he's a son-of-a-gun for some things."

"When is Gloriana to be heah?" asked Molly, becoming thoughtful.

"Monday, on the Western Special."

"So soon? Oh! . . . I—I wish I'd had time to study more. . . . Jim, suppose she doesn't like me?"

"Molly! She can't help but adore you."

"Jim, I never noticed that any of these Flag girls went ravin' crazy over your Molly Dunn of the Cibeque," replied Molly, a little satirically.

That was perfectly true, thought Jim, and she might have mentioned how green with envy some of them were. But Molly Dunn was generous.

"Gloriana isn't like these Flag girls. She has more breeding. She couldn't be jealous or catty."

"She's a queer girl, then," mused Molly. "After all, Jim, you're only a big overgrown boy who knows nothin' aboot females. . . . Reckon it's thet breedin' you speak of thet scares me."

Jim reflected that, as usual, he had made a tactless remark.

"Molly, don't distress yourself. I'm sure you will love Glory and—and she'll adore you. Naturally, since you're going to marry me, you'll have to meet all my family sooner or later."

"Yes, Jim, but I—I wanted a little time to study—to improve myself—so they wouldn't be ashamed of me," replied Molly, plaintively.

Jim could ony assure her by tender word and argument that she was making a mountain out of a molehill, with the result that Molly's heart seemed satisfied, if her mind was not. They went out to breakfast, and Jim hugged her disgracefully in the dark corridor. When Molly escaped into the dining-room a less keen eye than that of the old rancher, who stood back to the blazing fire, could have made amusing deductions.

"Mawnin', Uncle Jim. I—I been chased by a bear," laughed Molly.

"Good mornin', lass. Shore I seen thet. . . . Howdy, son! What do you think of Arizona weather?"

"Terrible. And you're sending me to camp out

after Thanksgiving!" protested Jim. It seemed to him there was going to be good reason for him to stay in Flagerstown.

"Wal, Yellow Jacket is five or six thousand feet lower, an' if it snows it melts right off. Molly can vouch for thet. An' the valley of the Cibeque is higher than Yellow Jacket."

"I've seen snow every winter I can remember, most up on the Diamond. Down at my home it never lasted a day," replied Molly.

"That's some consolation."

"Jim, I think it's grand. I shore hope you won't go back on your promise," said Molly.

"What promise?"

"Aboot takin' mc to town in a sleigh, with bells ringin'. An' snowballin' me. Oh, I'm shore I'll love this winter.

"Yes, I'll keep my promise, and I bet you beg for mercy."

"Me!"

Uncle Jim laughed heartily. His interest in their talk and plans, in all that concerned them, hinted of the loneliness of his life and what he felt he had missed.

"I like a little winter, too. Shore makes this here beef steak taste good. . . . Son, have you told the little lady your news?"

"Yes. And there's further proof she's an angel."

"Oh, Jim, such nonsense!" she protested. "Being glad with you don't—doesn't make me no angel.

I keep tellin' you thet I'm shore not related to no angel yet."

"Haw! Haw! I'll bet he finds thet out, Molly," put in the rancher, heartily. "Reckon if I'd ever been keen on girls I'd have wanted one thet would scratch an' bite."

Molly blushed. "Uncle, I hope I've not got thet much cat in me," she said, anxiously.

Jim made good his promise, and when he had Molly bundled in the sleigh beside him, her cheeks like roses and her dark curls flying, he was as proud as she was delighted. Much to his satisfaction, all the young people of Flagerstown appeared to be out sleigh-riding also; and many a girl who had made Jim uncomfortable when he was a tenderfoot saw him now with Molly.

They had lunch at the hotel and drove home in the brilliant sunshine, with the white world so glaring that they could hardly face it. All too soon they arrived at the ranch.

"That was glorious," said Molly, breathing deeply. "Jim, I'm shore a lucky girl. I'm so—so happy it hurts. I'm afraid it won't last."

"Sure it'll last," replied Jim, laughing. "Unless you're a fickle little jade."

"Jim Traft, I'm as—as true as steel," she retorted, vehemently. "It's only you may tire of me—or—or your family won't accept me."

"Say, you're not marrying my family."

The word marriage or any allusion to it always silenced Molly. She betrayed that she saw the days fleeting by toward the inevitable, and her joy submerged any doubts.

Jim drove around to the barn, having in mind the latter half of his promise to Molly, which surely she had forgotten. As they went by the big bunkhouse Bud Chalfack poked his ruddy cherub face out of the door and yelled, "Hey, Boss, thet ain't fair."

Jim yelled back, "Get yourself a girl, you cowboy."

At the barn he handed the reins to a Mexican stable boy, and helped Molly out. Then he led her into the lane toward the ranch-house. She was paddling along beside him through the deep snow and babbling merrily. When fully out of sight of the hawk-eyed cowboys Jim snatched up a big handful of snow, and seizing Molly he washed her rosy face with it.

"Jim Traft—you—you—" she sputtered, as he let her go. Then before she could recover her sight and breath he snatched up a double handful of snow and pitched that at her. His aim was true. It burst all over her in a white shower. She screamed, and bending quickly she squeezed a tight little snowball and threw it at Jim. He managed to save his eye, but it struck him on the head. Molly, it appeared, was no mean antagonist. Then fast and furious came the little snowballs. Never a one missed!

"Hey, you said—you'd never had a snowball fight," he panted.

"Shore never had. But I can lick you, Missouri," she replied, her high gay laugh pealing out.

Jim realized that she would make good her word unless he carried the battle to close range. Wherefore he rushed her, getting a snowball square on the nose for his pains. She dodged.

"Aw, Jim—stand up—an' fight square," she squealed.

But he caught her, tumbled her into the snow, rolled over and over, and finally swept a great armful upon her. Then he ran for dear life, tinglingly aware of the snowy cyclone at his heels.

Later Jim emerged from concealment and walked down to the bunk-house. He had not seen the boys for several days. He stamped on the porch.

"Hey, don't pack no snow in hyar," yelled a voice. "I gotta do the sweepin' fer this outfit."

Jim opened the door and went in. The big room was cheerful with its crackling fire, and amazingly clean, considering it harbored the hardest cowboy outfit in Arizona.

"Howdy, boys!" he sang out.

"You needn't come an' crow over us," answered Bud. "Sleighridin' with Molly Dunn!"

Jackson Way looked askance at Jim's snowy boots, his lean young face puckered and resentful. "Boss, I reckon you had this snow come on purpose."

Hump Stevens spoke from his bunk, where he lay propped up, cheerful and smiling.

"How are you, Hump?"

"Rarin' to go, Boss. I been walkin' around this mornin'. An' I won all the money the boys had."

"Good work," said Jim, turning to Uphill Frost, who sat before the fire in a rocking-chair, with a crutch significantly at hand. "And you, Up?"

"Boss, I ain't so damn good, as far as disposition goes. But I could fork a horse if I had to."

"Great! Where're Cherry and Lonestar?" went on Jim.

"They hoofed it in town to see Slinger," replied Frost.

"I haven't been to the hospital for three days," said Jim. "How's Slinger coming around?"

"He was up walkin' around, cussin' Doc fer not lettin' him smoke all he wants. Reckon time hangs heavy on Slinger. He can't read much, an' he says he wants to get back in the woods. Asked why you didn't come to see him. Didn't he, Bud?"

"Sure. Slinger complained like hell of your neglect, Boss. I seen him yestiddy. An' I told him thet no one never seen you no more. Then he cussed Molly fer not fetchin' you."

"I'm sorry. I'll see him tomorrow," replied Jim, contritely.

Curly Prentiss, the handsome blond young giant

48

of the Diamond outfit, sat at a table, writing with absorbed violence. He alone had not appeared to note Jim's entrance.

"Curly, I've got news for you."

But Curly gave no sign that he heard, whereupon Jim addressed Bud. "What ails Curly?"

"Same old sickness, Boss. I've seen Curly doubled up with that fer five years, about every few months. Mebbe it's a little wuss than usual, fer his girl chucked him an' married Wess Stebbins."

"No!"

"Sure's a fack. They run off to Winslow. You see, Curly come the high an' mighty once too often. Caroline bucked. An' they had it hot an' heavy. Curly told her to go where it was hot—so she says—an' he marched off with his haid up. . . . Wal, Carrie took him at his word. Thet is—he'd unhooked her bridle. Wess always was loony over her, an' she married him, which we all reckon was a darned good thing. Now Curly is writin' his funeral letter, after which he aims to get turrible drunk."

"Curly," spoke up Jim, kindly.

"Cain't you leave me alone heah?" appealed the cowboy.

"Yes, in a minute. Sorry to to disturb you, old man. But I've news about Yellow Jacket, Jed Stone and his Hash Knife outfit."

"To hell with them! I'm a ruined cowboy. Soon as I get this document written I'm goin' to town an' look at red licker."

"Nope," said Jim, laconically.

"Wall, I jest am. Who says I cain't?"

"I do, Curly."

"But you're not my boss. I've quit the Diamond. I'll never fork a hoss again."

"Curly, you wouldn't let us tackle that Hash Knife gang without you?"

"Jim, I cain't care aboot nothin'. My heart's broke. I could see you all shot. I could see Bud Chalfack hung on a tree an' laugh."

"Curly, didn't you and I get to be good friends?"

"Shore. And I was durn proud of it. But friendship's nuthin' to love. Aw, Boss, I'm ashamed to face you with it. . . . Caroline has turned out to be false. Chucked me fer thet bowlegged Stebbins puncher! Who'd ever thought I'd come to sech disgrace?"

"Curly, it's no disgrace. Wess is a good chap. He'll make Caroline happy. You didn't really love her."

"Wha-at?" roared Curly. And when his hearers all greeted this with a laugh he sank back crestfallen.

"Curly, there're some good reasons why you can't throw down the Diamond at this stage," said Jim, seriously, and placed a kindly hand on the cowboy's shoulder.

"Jest you give me one, Jim Traft," blustered Curly, and he lay down his pencil.

Jim knew perfectly well that this wonderful young Westerner could not be untrue to anyone.

50

"First, then, Curly. You've already got a few head of stock on the range. In a few years you'll be a rancher on your own account."

"No reason atall. I don't want thet stock. I'd have given it to Bud if he hadn't been so nasty aboot Caroline. Swore she'd finally come to her senses. Then I gave the cattle to Hump, heah."

"Well, Hump can give them back. . . . Another reason is Uncle Jim is throwing us plumb against the Hash Knife outfit. Now what would the Diamond amount to without Curly Prentiss?"

"I don't give a—a damn," rejoined Curly. But it was a weak assertion.

"See there, Boss," yelled Bud, red in the face. "He hates us all jest because thet red-headed Carrie Bambridge chucked him."

"Curly, it's just as well," went on Jim. "Listen, and all of you. This is a secret and not to be spoken of except among ourselves. Uncle Jim is sure Bambridge is crooked. Making deals with the Hash Knife."

All the cowboys except Curly expressed themselves in different degrees of exclamation.

At length Curly spoke. "Even if Bambridge was crooked—that'd make no difference to me."

"Did you ask Caroline to marry you?" queried Jim, kindly.

"Dog-gone-it, no," replied Curly, and here his fine, frank face flamed. "Boss, I never was sure I cared that much, till I lost her."

"Curly, it wasn't the real thing—your case on Caroline."

"Ahuh.—Jim, you haven't given me any argument why I shouldn't go out an' drown my grief in the bottle—an' shoot up the town—an' kill somebody or get put in jail."

"No? All right. Here's another reason," replied Jim, and he drew a photograph out of his pocket and laid it on the table in front of Curly.

The cowboy started, bent over, and became absorbed in the picture.

Bud Chalfack started, too, but Jim waved him back.

"My Gawd! Boss, who is this?" asked Curly.

"My sister, Gloriana May Traft."

"Your sister?—Jim, I shore ought to have seen the resemblance, though she's ten million times better-lookin' than you. . . . But how is she a reason for my not goin' to the bad?"

"Curly, it's as simple as pie," said Jim. "Gloriana is a sick girl. She's coming West for her health. She'll arrive on Monday, on the Western Special. Now, I ask you, have you the heart to bust up the Diamond—to get drunk and worry me to death—when I've this new trouble on my hands?"

Curly took another look at the photograph, and then he turned to Jim with all the clouds vanished from eyes and face. To see Curly thus was to love him.

"Boss, I haven't got the heart to throw you

52

down," he replied. "It's my great weakness—this heah heart of mine. . . . I reckon I wasn't goin' to—anyhow. . . . An' I'll go down to meet the Western Special with you."

Jim, if he had dared, could have yelled his mirth. How well he had known Curly.

"Lemme see thet pictoore!" demanded Bud, advancing.

Curly handed the photograph back to Jim, and said, blandly, "Bud, gurls of high degree shouldn't interest you."

"Boys, I want you all to see Glory's picture," said Jim calmly, though he reveled in the moment. "Come, take a look."

Bud and Jackson Way leaped forward; Uphill Frost forgot his crutch; Hump Stevens hopped out of his bunk; and they all, with Curly irresistibly drawn, crowded around Jim.

The long silence that ensued attested to the beauty of Gloriana Traft.

Finally Bud exploded: "Lord! ain't she a looker?"

"Prettier even than Molly Dunn," added Way, as if that was the consummation of all beauty.

"I never seen no angel till this minnit," was Uphill Frost's encomium.

"Ef I jest wasn't a crippled cowpuncher an' had a million dollars!" exclaimed Hump Stevens, with a sigh. "Boss, her name fits her."

Curly Prentiss reacted peculiarly to all this. It

seems he resented the looks and sighs and fervid comments of his comrades, as if they had profaned a sacred face already enshrined in his impressionable heart.

"Wal, I'm informin' you gentlemen of the range thet I saw her first," he said, loftily.

Bud took that as an insult. Frost swore his surprise. Hump Stevens stared in silence. Jackson Way laughed at the superb and conceited cowboy. Then Curly addressed Jim. "Boss, it's shore plain the Diamond will be busted now."

Chapter Four

JIM did not see much of Molly on Sunday. She kept to her room except at meal hours. He found opportunity, however, to ask her to go into town with him on Monday to meet his sister.

"I'd rather not, Jim," she replied, as if her mind had long been made up. "She'd rather you didn't fetch any girl, especially *your* girl, to meet her, thet's shore."

"But why, Molly?" he queried.

"It'll be a surprise to her—the way things are with you an' me. An' it oughtn't come the minute she gets heah."

"We don't need to tell her—right away."

"She'd see it. . . . Jim, you should have written home weeks ago—to tell your folks aboot me."

"I suppose I ought. Really I meant to. Only I just didn't write."

"Wal, I reckon it'd be better not to let her know right away. I could hide it. But I'm shore afraid you couldn't. Uncle Jim will blurt it out."

"Molly! The idea—not telling Gloriana we're engaged," he protested, mystified by her gravity.

"Jim, it'll be all right if only she takes to me, but if she's like you when you first struck Flag—she won't."

"I was pretty much of a snob," he admitted. "Molly, I'm the better for all I've gone through. . . . You realize, don't you, how much I—"

The entrance of Molly's mother prohibited the rest of that tender speech. And Jim presently left the living-room perturbed in mind. He could not rid himself of a premonition that Gloriana's coming heralded disaster. No further opportunity to speak privately to Molly presented itself that day; and early Monday morning Molly trudged off to school like any country girl, wading through the snow. How serious she was about her studies!

In the afternoon Jim sent Curly Prentiss, who appeared as if by magic, most gorgeously arrayed in the gayest and finest of cowboy habiliments.

"For goodness sake! Why this togging up?" exclaimed Jim.

Curly appeared to be laboring under stress.

"Had hell with the outfit," he said. "Come near punchin' Bud. He swore I ought to wear a plain suit—which is somethin' I don't own—but I'm no business man, or even a rancher yet. An' I want to look what I am."

"Oh, you mean you want my sister Gloriana to see you're a real cowboy?"

"Shore do."

"Big hat, gun, spurs and all?"

"I reckon."

"Well, Curly, she'll see you, all right. She could see you a mile away."

"Jim, don't you give me any of your chin aboot how I look. I had enough from Bud an' Jack an' Uphill. An' my feelin's are hurt. . . . They're goin' to meet thet train, all of them except Hump. He wanted us to carry him on a stretcher. Up is goin' on a crutch—the damn fool!"

"Fine. The sooner you all see Gloriana May the sooner you'll be miserable. . . . I've ordered the buckboard to meet the train. Let's walk in, Curly, and stop to see Slinger."

"It's a good idea. A little movin' around might steady me. I'd shore hate to meet Jed Stone or thet Pecos gun-thrower."

So they strode out into the snow. The weather had moderated somewhat and the day was superb, with crisp tangy air. Curly manifestly was on the eve of a great adventure. Jim had to laugh when he thought again of how Glory would affect these simple, sentimental cowboys. It would be murder. He reflected that she would very likely be more

Gloriana May at nineteen then she had been at eighteen. Worry over them he had no room for; all that seemed centered upon Molly. Curly stalked like a centaur, his spurs clinking, and talked like a boy engaged upon some lofty venture.

Meanwhile their long steps soon brought them to the edge of town and eventually the modest hospital, which, unpretentious as it was, had become the boast of cowboys.

They found Slinger Dunn the only inmate, besides an attendant or two, and he was limping up and down a warm and comfortable room. His dark face, bronze and smooth like an Indian's, wreathed into a smile at sight of his visitors. He had gained since Jim had last seen him. His long hair, black as the wing of a crow, hung down over the collar of the loose woolen dressing-gown he wore, in which obviously he felt ill at ease. Jim aways thrilled at sight of Slinger, and had reason to do so, beyond appreciation of his striking figure and piercing eyes. Anyone who had ever seen Molly Dunn would at once connect Slinger with her.

"Howdy, boys! It's aboot time you was comin'," he drawled. "Molly came in on her way to school, or I'd shore be daid now."

"Patience, Slinger. Why, you've made a marvelous recovery!" said Jim, cheerily.

"Slinger, you backwoods son-of-a-gun, only five weeks ago you was a sieve of bullet holes,"

57

declared Curly. "An' heah you can walk aboot."

"Wal, it's easy fer you fellars to talk, but I'd like to see you stand stayin' heah. Day after day—night after night. Thet damn Doc won't give me any more cigarettes an' only a nip of whisky. Set down, boys, an' tell me some news."

"Slinger, just as soon as you can ride we're off for Yellow Jacket," announced Jim.

"Wal, pack up fer tomorrow mawnin'."

"Not till after Thanksgiving. Three weeks yet. And now listen." Whereupon Jim related all the late news and rumors about the Hash Knife outfit.

"Shore, I'd expect thet of Jed Stone," said Dunn. "An', Boss, if you want to know, I've long had a hunch Bambridge is back of the Hash Knife."

"No!" ejaculated Jim, aghast at so definite a statement from this backwoodsman.

"Slinger, we reckon you mean Bambridge ain't above buyin' a few haid of stock from Stone now an' then?" queried Curly, slow and cool, but his blue eyes flashed fire.

"Hellno! Buyin' a few steers nuthin'," drawled Dunn, forcibly. "Bambridge's outlayin' ranch is across the divide from Yellow Jacket. Thirty miles around by road. But by the canyon—Doubtful, we call it—there's less'n ten miles. An' Bambridge is gettin' stock through Doubtful an' drivin' it to Maricopa."

Curly whistled his amazement. Jim simply stared. This was getting down to hard pan. It did not occur to either of them to question Slinger Dunn.

"Shore, I cain't prove it, Jim," he continued. "But it's what I reckon. An' my hunch is fer us to keep our traps shet—an' go down to Yellow Jacket to make shore."

"Right, you bet," agreed Curly. "But if it's true, the Hash Knife will stop operations until either they or the Diamond are settled."

"We've got to find out," interposed Jim, emphatically. "Ring Locke advised against Uncle sending the Diamond on that job. Said we could do easier and more important work. He's afraid Bambridge might shoot Uncle."

"Wall, there's shore risk of thet," rejoined Dunn. "But Traft could keep out of the way. When we get the trick on these fellars we can do a little shootin' ourselves. . . . You know, Boss, there ain't no other way oot of it."

"So Uncle says," assented Jim, gloomily. "Slinger, you don't think it'll be another Pleasant Valley War?"

"Lord, no," declared Dunn, showing his white teeth. "Thet war hed hundreds of sheepmen an' cattlemen behind it, with rustlers on the side of the sheep fellars. This heah deal is a matter of a little gun-play."

"Slinger, you've got a lot of time to think it over," said Jim. "Do so, and I'll come in after a few days. I'm a little upset just now. My sister is coming today. She's ill. They say the climate will agree with her."

"Thet's too bad, Boss. But mebbe it'll all turn oot right. . . . Molly never told me you hed a sister. I reckon I know how you feel."

"Here's her picture, Slinger," said Jim, producing the photograph and handing it over.

Dunn bent his piercing eyes upon the likeness of Gloriana May. He was not a volatile cowboy. His expression did not change. Only he gazed a long time.

"Wal, I never before seen any gurl or a pictoor of one thet could beat Molly. But this heah shore does."

"Molly is totally unlike Gloriana. Just as pretty in her way, I think," he said, stoutly.

"Boss, you're loco. Molly is a slick, soft, pretty little woodmouse. But this sister of yourn is like the sun in the mawnin'."

Jim felt a surprise he did not betray. The compliment to Gloriana at Molly's expense did not find great favor with him. Receiving the picture back he took a look at it, somehow seeing Glory differently, and then he returned it to his pocket.

"It was taken a year ago," he explained. "And if Gloriana has improved in looks since I've been gone as much as she did the year before—whew! but she'll be something to look at. I hardly expect improvement, though, since she has been ill."

"Huh! Thet gurl couldn't be ailin'," returned Dunn, positively.

Conversation reverted to other channels then—the Diamond, the incompleted drift fence, winter, horses, until finally Jim rose to go, with Curly following suit.

"Slinger, I'm awful glad you're doing so well," said Jim.

"Wal, you fellars have cheered me right pert. Come again soon. . . . An', Jim, would you mind lettin' me borrow that pictoor fer a spell? I get hellsrattlin' lonesome—an' it'd be good to look at."

"Why, certainly, Slinger," declared Jim, hastily producing it. "I'm sure Glory will be flattered."

"Thanks, Boss," drawled Slinger. "Your havin' a sister, too, kinda makes us closer, huh? Wal, adios."

All the way out Jim heard Curly growling under his breath. This ebullition came out in force once they reached the street.

"Jim what'n hell did you want to let Slinger Dunn borrow Gloriana May's picture fer?" demanded Curly.

"Why, cowboy, I never thought not to. What could I say? It was a perfectly innocent request of Slinger's."

"Shore. It was innocent enough. But cain't you see straight? The dam' backwoodsman was shot plumb through the heart."

61

"What! By Glory's picture?"

"Shore. It did the same fer me. An' I've no call to kick. But, my Gawd! Boss, I couldn't stand for a rival like Slinger Dunn. Now aboot Bud an' the rest of the Diamond, I'm not carin'. But Dunn is darned handsome, an' shore fascinatin'. Any girl would lose her heart to him—if he let himself go. . . . I'd hate to have to shoot it out with Slinger."

"Ha! Ha! Ha! I should think you would," replied Jim, after a hearty laugh. "But, Curly, don't be a jackass. Let me give you a hunch. Glory will be sweet to you cowboys—let you saddle her horse or carry something for her. And she *might* dance with you. But she could never see one of you seriously, even through a microscope."

Curly looked crestfallen, yet sustained a little dignity.

"Jim, you're her brother an' you fell in love with Molly Dunn."

The remark was thought-provoking, but Jim could not keep it before his consciousness.

"True, Curly, old boy. But I'm not Glory. Wait till you see her!"

"I'm a-waitin' best I can," averred Curly, "An' I'll bet a handful of gold eagles against two bits, thet Bud an' Up an' Jack are waitin', too, right now at the station. Let's rustle."

For a cowboy who had been born on a horse and who had spent most of his life in a saddle, Curly Prentiss could certainly walk. He might have had on seven-league boots. In quick time they arrived at the station, to find Zeb there with the buckboard; Bud, Jackson, Lonestar Holliday, Cherry Winters, and Uphill in a state of vast excitement, that seemed strange in their plain business suits, at least three of which were brand new; and lastly that the Western Special was two hours late.

Curly groaned. Jim did not know whether this expression of pain was due to the lateness of the train or the presence of the cowboys. Probably it was for both.

"Zeb, drive over to the stable and keep the horses there till you hear the train whistle," directed Jim. "And, boys, what do you say to a game of pool at Raider's?"

"I ain't dressed fer thet," objected Bud, eyeing his nice clean cuffs. "You-all go an' I'll hang around here. Mebbe the train will make up some time."

"Wal, you're a rotten pool-shot," remarked Curly, "an' you cain't be missed."

"Say, rooster, I beat you last time we played," retorted Bud.

"Cowboy, you couldn't beat a carpet," put in Jim, knowing full well how to work Bud.

"Got any money with you, Boss?" asked Bud, sarcastically.

It was noticeable that when the company reached Raider's, Bud was following along. This Raider place, a saloon, gambling-den, as well as pool-hall, did not bear a very respectable name.

But as the other places were uptown, Jim thought he could take a chance on it.

"No drinks, boys," said Jim.

"What?" demanded Curly, who was edging toward the bar.

"Not a drop of anything. You're meeting my sister," replied Jim, sharply.

"You big hunk of cheese," added Bud, scornfully. "All dressed up as for a rodeo, an' now you want to soak in a gallon of licker."

"Curly, jest because you're a good-lookin' cuss you cain't meet the boss's sister with a whisky breath. Why, you plumb ought to be ashamed!" said Uphill Frost.

"Where's your manners, Curly?" asked Cherry Winters. "You get wusser every day."

Jim was inclined to revel in the situation. Never would he recover from the innumerable and infinitely various tricks these boys had perpetrated upon him when he had come to them a tenderfoot. They were still capable of the same, if he was not sharp enough to detect them. Molly had helped him circumvent them—had given him something of revenge. And Gloriana May would surely fill his cup to the brim. They were such a devilishly lovable lot.

"Nope. There'll be no more drinking for the Diamond," said Jim, simulating cheerful satisfaction. "Glory hates drink. And I want her to be happy out here. She's a sick girl, you know."

"Aw!" breathed out Bud Chalfack, enigmatically. He might have been profoundly impressed or only regretting the ban on liquor.

"Haw! Haw! Haw!" roared Curly Prentiss, in derision of something or somebody.

"Laff, you dressed-up kangaroo," shouted Bud. "Fine chance *you'll* have!"

"Shut your faces, you cowboys," ordered Jim, genially. "Now let's see. There are seven of us. . . . Reckon Uphill can't play, with his game leg. We'll—"

"The hell I can't. I can beat any of you with only one leg," remarked Frost, speaking for himself.

"Ex-cuse me, Up. . . . We'll each put in a dollar. Play rotation pool. Every time one of us misses his shot he puts in two bits. And whoever gets the most shots takes the pot."

"Great stuff!" agreed Curly, who imagined he divided honors with Jim in pool.

"Turrible stiff game," said Bud.

"You might jest as well stick your hands in my pockets," added Uphill, derisively.

"I'm game, but it's highway robbery," put in Cherry Winters.

"Suits me. I can jest aboot pay fer these heah new clothes," said Lonestar Holliday.

So the game began. Probably it never could have been started but for the state of mental aberration the boys were in. Not often had Jim prevailed upon them to play, after they had a sample of his game. They were atrocious shots. With fifteen balls on the table, all numbered, it was no easy task sometimes to hit the number called for, and Bud never did it once during that whole game. He had to produce nine two-bits, two dollars and a quarter in all, and he was perfectly furious. Jim won the game and pocketed the cash. Then they began another. Curly appeared to be next to Bud in poor playing. In fact, he was away off in his game, a fact the other boys soon made much of. Jim won this time also.

"Might as well steal our wages and be done with it," said Bud.

But in the third game, when Bud started off by pocketing three balls in succession and Curly began to miss, he changed his tune. This time Jim deliberately made poor shots, which, playing along with other retarding chances of the game, prolonged it. Bud played beyond his actual ability and altogether got nine balls, which won him the money and recovered his good humor.

"Curly, I told you I could beat you all holler," he said. "Same in poker. An' likewise in affairs of the heart."

"Bah, you little bow-legged runt," scoffed Curly.

"I can lick you, too," concluded Bud, belligerently.

Jim consulted his watch. "Whoopee! she's due in two minutes. Don't forget to pay the bill, you losers." He ducked out of the hall and ran across to the station, thrilling at the whistle of the train. And he found the boys at his heels, except poor Uphill, who had to labor behind on his crutch. Jim knew perfectly well that his partners in the pool game had not tarried to pay their score.

The Special roared into the station, all ice and snow, with the steam hissing and the smoke obscuring the platform lights. It was almost dark. When the engine and mail and baggage car passed the air cleared, and the bright lights shone again. In his excitement Jim quite forgot his comrades. The second coach stopped opposite his position and he was all eyes. A porter began sliding bags and suitcases off the step. Then a slim form emerged from the car upon the vestibule. The furs proclaimed it feminine. But there was too much shadow. Then she stepped down and paused in the bright light. It was Gloriana, Jim said to himself, conscious of inward tumult. The tall slim shape, with its air of distinction, the cut of the long fur coat, the set of the stylish little hat, would have been enough. But Jim stared a moment longer. Gloriana's face shone like a white flower out of the black furs, and her great eyes, dark in that light, strained eagerly to and fro, and then fixed on him.

"Jim!" she cried in a rapture. When had she ever called to him with a voice like that? He ran to the steps and lifted her down in a bearish hug. She

did not appear as substantial and heavy as he remembered his sister.

"Glory!—Dog-gone, I'm glad to see you!" he said, and certainly returned the warm kiss she gave him, which struck him even more unusual then the poignant tone of her voice. Something had changed Jim Traft's value in the eyes of his sister.

"Jim, you can't be—half as glad—as I am to see—you," she panted, gayly, clinging to him. "Is this the—North Pole? Who are these young men? . . . Jim, I thought Arizona was desert—sunny, hot—all golden ranges and pine trees."

"Hey, boys, grab the bags," ordered Jim, with a laugh. "Fetch them into the waiting-room." Then he led Gloriana into the station, where it was light and warm. "The rig will be here in a minute. . . . Gosh! . . . I just don't know you, Glory. Your eyes, maybe."

No one, not even a brother, would ever have been likely to forget Gloriana May's eyes. At this moment they were traveling over Jim, brilliant with amaze.

"I know you and I don't. You great big handsome man. Oh, Jim, you're so wonderfully different. Arizona has improved you. . . . I'll bet you've fallen in love with some Western cowgirl."

Jim should have said she had guessed right the very first time, and he would have done so but for the something familiar and disconcerting that was merely Gloriana. Then the cowboys came bustling in with bags and suitcases. Even Uphill carried one with an air of importance. Curly disengaged himself from the excited group and strode forward. Sight of him filled Jim with glee, and a quick glance at Glory took in her eyes, fixed and beautiful. Now it was a natural function of Glory's eyes, even in her most casual glance, to shine and glow and give illusion of a thousand thoughts that were not in her head at all. They were so alive, so speaking, so eloquent, so treacherously lovely, that Jim sustained a second thrill at sight of them.

"A cowboy!" she whispered. "Jim, I believe you now."

It probably was a magnificent moment for Curly, but he did not betray that in the least.

"Boss, Zeb is heah with the buckboard," he announced, in his cool lazy way.

"Gloriana, this is Curly Prentiss, one of my cowboys—and quite a cattleman in his own right," introduced Jim. "Curly—my sister."

Curly doffed his sombrero and made a gallant bow that, though easy and slow like his voice, was as singularly pleasing.

"Miss Traft, I shore am glad to meet you-all," he said.

"How do you do, Mr. Prentiss. I'm pleased to meet you," she replied, with a dazzling smile. "You are my very first cowboy."

Gloriana May probably did not mean she had

taken possession of Curly at first sight, but Jim saw that this identical circumstance had come to pass.

"Wal," drawled Curly, not in the least knocked off his balance, "I'm shore happy to be the first an' I'll see to it I'm the last."

"Oh," laughed Glory, merrily, and turned to Jim with her first appreciation of a cowboy.

The other boys lined up, with Uphill Frost hanging a little behind to hide his crutch. They presented a bright-eyed, shiny-faced coterie, at the moment devoid of any trace of devilment or horns and hoofs.

"Boys, this is my sister Gloriana," announced Jim. "Glory, meet the rest of the Diamond, except two that are laid up for repairs. . . . Bud Chalfack."

Bud took a step out and his smile was cherubic. "Miss Gloriana I reckon there ain't no one any gladder to welcome you to Arizonie."

"Thank you, Mr. Chalfack. I'm happy to meet you," replied Gloriana.

"And this is Lonestar Holliday," went on Jim. Lonestar in his eager confusion stepped on Bud's foot and could not find words to answer Glory's bright acknowledgment.

"And Jackson Way . . . and Cherry Winters . . . and Uphill Frost. . . . There, Glory, you've made the acquaintance of most of the Diamond, which, according to Uncle Jim, is the most terrible cowboy outfit in Arizona."

70

"Oh, I'm sure Uncle Jim is wrong," said Gloriana, sweetly. "They look very nice and mild to me—except Mr. Prentiss—who *is* quite terrifying with his gun and those awful spurs."

Somehow Jim got the impression from Glory's speaking eyes that she meant Curly's handsome presence was something calculated to stop the heart of a girl fresh from the East.

Bud looked disgustedly at Curly, as if to say he had gone and done it again. If there was anything a cowboy hated it was to be thought nice and mild.

"Miss Glory," he spoke up, most winningly, and Jim made certain that the next time Bud addressed her it would be Glory minus the prefix, "there's some cowpunchers who pack hardware all the time an' sleep in their spurs. But they ain't the dangerous kind."

Thus Jim saw with delight a new species of men and life dawn upon his bewildered sister. Likewise he perceived with fiendish glee that he was going to get even with the Diamond.

"Carry the baggage out, boys," he said. "We'll go home to the ranch. . . . Curly, you can ride with us, so in case we meet any desperadoes or Indians they won't get Glory."

Chapter Five

ON THE way out Jim did not say anything to Glory about the room he had fixed up for her. In fact, he did not have much chance to talk, for Glory addressed her curiosity to Curly. Jim drove fast, so the wind would pierce through his sister, furs and all. It did.

"F-f-fine f-for a g-girl with o-one lung," chattered Gloriana as Jim lifted her out of the buckboard. "G-good n-night—Mr. Curly. If I don't—f-f-freeze to death I'll see you—to-tomorrow."

"I shore pray for a moderation of temperature," replied Curly, gallantly. "Good night, Miss Traft."

"Set the bags on the porch," said Jim, "and hurry those horses into the barn. . . . Glory, I reckon you'll want to get warm before you see Uncle Jim."

Gloriana stood in the cold starlight, looking out at the spectral pine forest and the pure white peaks that notched the sky. "W-w-wonderful!"

Jim almost carried her to her room, which was in the west end of the rambling ranch-house. When he opened the door a blaze of light and warmth and color greeted Gloriana's eyes. Jim had spent a whole day on making this room different from any Glory had ever seen, and one that would be livable, even for a sick girl in zero weather. It had an open fireplace where logs were snapping and blazing; Navajo rugs covered the floor; Indian ornaments of bead, basket and silver work hung on the walls; a fine elk head, with massive horns, stood out over the mantel; the bed had a coverlet of deep, woolly, soft red, most inviting to the eye. Even the lamp had a shade painted with Indian designs.

Gloriana gasped with delight, threw off her furs and hat, and rushed to the fire, where she stretched her gloved hands.

"Pretty nifty, huh?" asked Jim.

"Just lovely. But wait a minute until I can see."

Jim went out to fetch in the luggage. He had to make three trips to the porch and back. "Glory, from the looks of this you've come to stay awhile."

"I've three trunks, too," rejoined Gloriana.

"Is that all? Gee! I didn't figure on trunks when I worked over this room. But there's a big closet. . . . Turn round, Glory, so I can look at you."

She did so, and he saw his sister strangely changed, but how he could not tell at once. She appeared taller, which might have accounted for her slimness. But Jim looked in vain for a frail, flat-chested girl bordering on consumption. Her face, however, was exceedingly white, and herein lay the change that struck him. She looked more than her age. She wore her dark chestnut hair in a fashion new to him, and very becoming. But

Glory's great purple eyes were as he had them pictured in a loving memory.

"Well, how do I look?" she asked, soberly.

"Prettier than ever, Glory, only different. I can't figure it yet," said Jim.

"Thanks. I didn't hope for compliment. . . . Jim, you've been away almost a year."

"So long? Gee! time flies. Well, sister, it has been a terrible and a wonderful year for me. I've sure got a story to tell you. But that can wait. Sit down. You look fagged. And tell me about yourself. Mother's letter scared me."

She did not take the chair he indicated, but sat down on the arm of his, and rather timidly took his hand. Jim remembered how seldom Gloriana had ever touched him voluntarily. They had never gotten along well together. Gloriana could not bear criticism of her actions or any antagonism to her freedom. And Jim had always been the bossy older brother, until she reached eighteen, when he had been flatly rebuffed. After that there had been a slowly widening breach. It all returned to him now, a little sadly, and he wondered at her. Perhaps she really had cared something for him. Gloriana had never been shallow; quite the reverse. Jim began to feel a deeper significance in her coming West, in her presence now, than at first had occurred to him.

"Jim, you're my last bet," she said, frankly.

"Glory! . . . I don't understand," exclaimed Jim,

74

blankly. "You were a belle when I left home. You had so many friends that *I* never saw you. Then all that money Aunt Mary left you. . . . And now I'm your last bet!"

"Funny, isn't it, Jim? . . . Retribution, I guess."

"For what?"

"I was never—a—a real sister."

Jim caressed the soft thin little hand while he gazed into the fire and pondered. A chill of fear of he knew not what crept over him. Glory had always worried him. Her childish pranks—then her girlish escapades—but now she seemed a woman!

"Perhaps that was my fault," he replied, regretfully.

"Jim—you've changed," said his sister, quickly.

"Sure. I'd not been much good if this Arizona hadn't changed me."

"I hope it does as well by me," she continued, wistfully.

"Glory . . . what're you driving at?" burst out Jim, no longer able to repress a mounting anxiety.

"Please—ask me questions."

That from Gloriana May was indeed a strange request. Jim felt an uncomfortable constriction of his throat.

"Glory, have you really got lung trouble?" he queried, sharply.

"No. Mother and Dad think so because I got so white and thin. I coaxed Dr. Williamson to hint of that. I wanted to come West."

"Thank goodness!—But, you deceitful girl!—Why such an extreme? And are you really ill?"

"Only run down, Jim."

"From what?"

"Worry—unhappiness."

Jim imagined his ears were deceiving him. Yet there his sister sat, slipping closer to him. She was now half off the arm of his chair and her head rested on his shoulder. A faint fragrance came from her hair. He let a long silence ensue. He could not ask just then what was forming in his mind.

"Love affair?" he finally asked, lightly.

"Affair—but not love," she replied, scornfully.

"So that's it?"

"No, that's not it. Still, it had a lot to do with it."

"Gloriana!" That was how he had used to address her when he was on his dignity or wished to reprove. She laughed a little, remembering it.

"Jim, I—I have disgraced the family," she admitted, with a catch in her breath, and suddenly she sat up.

"My God! . . . Oh, Glory—you can't be serious!" he exclaimed, distressed, yet uncertain.

"I wish to heaven I wasn't serious."

Jim tried to prepare himself for a blow. Contact with the rough and wholesome West had knocked pride and prejudice out of his head. Nevertheless, something of the former reared its hydra head. In his gathering apprehension and horror he sensed that he was on trial. He must react differently to this revelation. Glory had come to him in her trouble. If he repulsed or scorned her! If he showed any of the old outraged brotherly disfavor! Suddenly he happened to think of Curly Prentiss—that cool, easy, careless firebrand of a Texas cowboy. How would he take such a confession from a once loved sister? Beloved still, he discovered, poignantly! But that thought of Curly was sustaining. Its content typified the West.

"Well, so little sister has kicked over the traces?" he queried, as coolly as ever Curly could have said it.

"Jim, don't misunderstand," she said, quickly. "I've been wild, crazy, out of my head. But I can still look you in the eyes."

And she sat up to give him a straight full glance that was as searching as it was revealing. Jim hid his relief. And he realized the moment gave birth to his existence as a brother. The purple blaze of Gloriana's eyes failed to hide her sadness, her hunger.

"Shore, I never had any notion you couldn't," he replied, essaying Curly's drawl. Then he put his arm around her, which action brought Glory slipping into his lap. Her head went down with a suspicious haste. Her nervous hand tightened on his. "Tell me all about it."

"Jim, you remember when I was sixteen the Andersons took me up," began Glory, presently.

"That began my gadding about, my desire for fine clothes—excitement, dancing—and so forth. Then Aunt Mary left me that money. And you remember the summer I graduated—how gay I was—what a wonderful time I had! . . . Even before you left I was traveling with a pretty fast set. But we younger girls hadn't really gotten into it yet. After you left home I was about ready for it, I guess. But something happened. I met a man named Darnell—from St. Louis. He was handsome—and all the girls were crazy over him. That tickled me. I—I thought I was in love with him. It *might* have been just as well—the way things turned out. I could have done worse. Mother wanted me to marry Mr. Hanford—you know him—the dry goods merchant."

"Not Henry Hanford?" broke out Jim, incredulously.

"Yes, Henry Hanford. He was more than old enough to be my father. But Mother nagged me nearly to death. I dare say she wanted me to be— safe. Dad hated my running around—and he didn't like Ed Darnell. So we had a bad time for some months. . . . I thought I was engaged to Ed. So did everybody else. All the same, I wasn't. He said he was mad about me, but he didn't ask me to marry him. . . . He borrowed a lot of money from me. He was a gambler. Then he embezzled money from Dad. Oh, how wretched it was! He left town, without a word to me. The truth came out—and—

and the Andersons, the Loyals, the Millers—all my old friends dropped me. Cut me dead! . . . That broke Mother's heart. And it went hard with Dad. . . . Well, I had reached the end of my rope. You know what gossip is in a little town. And gossip made it a great deal worse than it actually was. I had been a fool over Ed Darnell. I had snubbed some of the boys because of him. I had been wild as a partridge—so far as parties, dancing, running around were concerned. But I wasn't as bad as I looked. Still that queered me at home, when the crash came. . . . And, Jim, it knocked me out. I began to go downhill. I realized I was done for there. I worried myself sick. Many and many a night I cried myself to sleep. I went downhill. . . . And then I got to thinking about the West—your West. I read all your letters to Mother. You never wrote *me.* And I thought, if I could get out West, far away, it'd be my salvation . . . and here I am."

"Well, is *that* all?" drawled Jim, true to his imitation of Curly. "You shore had me plumb scared."

"Jim!" she cried, and then she kissed his cheek in much gratitude. By that Jim felt how hard it had been for Gloriana to confess to him—how little of a brother he had been in times past. Then before he could say more she burst into tears, which was another amazing thing, and Jim could do no more than hold her. There must have been much dammed-up misery in Gloriana, for when she suc-

cumbed to weeping it gradually grew uncon-
trollable. Jim thought, to judge her emotion, that
the situation at home had been insupportable for
the proud, vain young lady. She had come to him
as a last resource, doubtful of her reception, and
he had overwhelmed her by making light of her
trouble. As a matter of fact Jim felt exceedingly
relieved, and even happy that what he had sus-
pected had been wrong. Glory had been on the
verge of disaster. That seemed enough for him to
know. There might have been details which
would have hurt him to hear. Pity and tenderness
welled up in his heart for his sister. Indeed, there
had been cause for her to come West and throw
herself upon his protection. The very idea was
incredible, yet here she was, sobbing softly
now, and gaining control of herself.

"Thank God I—I had the—courage to come,"
she said, speaking a thought aloud. "I—I never
knew how—good Jim was!"

That established a character Jim regretted he
hardly deserved, and one to which he felt he
must live up.

"Glory, I've got a little confession to make,
myself," he said, with a happy laugh. "Not that
I've actually fallen by the wayside. But I've
gone back on the East. And I'm—"

"Wait," she interrupted, sitting up to dry her
eyes. "I haven't told all—and what seems the
worst to me."

"Gosh!" ejaculated Jim, with a sinking sensation in his chest. "Perhaps you'd better not tell me more."

"Jim, I met Ed Darnell in the station at St. Louis," went on Glory, hastily, as if eager to impart what seemed important. "Quite by accident. I had to change trains there and wait five hours. And it was my bad luck to run into him first thing. . . . Well, he raved. He made a thousand excuses. . . . The liar! The thief! . . . I absolutely refused to have any more to do with him, yet I was scared stiff at him. He had some queer power over me. But I had sense enough to realize I despised him. Then he threatened me —swore he'd follow me. And Jim—that's exactly what he'll do. He knew, of course, about Uncle Jim, the rich ranchman. Mother gabbed a lot. At first she was fascinated by Ed. I didn't tell him where I was going, but he could find out easily. And he'll come. I saw it in his eyes. . . . And that'd be dreadful."

"Let him come," replied Jim, grimly. "I hope he does. It would be a bad move for Mr. Darnell."

"What would you do?" queried Gloriana, with all a woman's curiosity.

"Glory, you're out West now. It'll take you some time to realize it. . . . I'd impress that fact upon Mr. Darnell pretty pronto. And if it wasn't enough, I'd tell Curly Prentiss."

"That wonderful-looking cowboy!" exclaimed

Gloriana. "He seemed so kind and nice. He wouldn't hurt anyone."

Jim laughed outright. Gloriana would be the tenderfoot of all tenderfeet who ever struck Arizona.

"Glory, I'm engaged," he blurted out suddenly, with a gulp.

"Jim Traft!—You've kept up with that catty Sue Henderson," exclaimed Glory, aghast.

At first Jim could not connect any of his Missouri attachments of bygone days with that particular name. When he did he laughed, not only at Glory's absurd guess but at the actual realization. Ten times ten months might have elapsed since he left home.

"No, Glory. My girl is a real Westerner," he replied.

"Real Westerner? What do you mean by that? Uncle Jim was born in the East. He couldn't be Western."

"He's pretty much so, as you will discover. Molly was born in Arizona. She's about eighteen. Twice in her life she has been to Flagerstown, and that is the extent of her travels. She lives down in the Cibeque, one of the wildest valleys in Arizona."

"Molly.—Molly what?" queried Glory, her white smooth brow wrinkling and her fine eyes dilating and changing, as she bent them upon Jim.

"Molly Dunn. Isn't it pretty?" rejoined Jim, warming to his subject. He had need to.

82

"Rather. But sort of common, like Jones or Brown. Is *she* pretty?"

"Glory, I reckon there's only one prettier girl in the world, and that's you."

It was a subtle and beautiful compliment, but somehow lost upon Gloriana May.

"You were always getting a case on some girl—back home. It never lasted long," said his sister, reflectively.

"This will last."

"How about her family?" came the inevitable interrogation.

"Arizona backwoods. And that's as blue-blooded as the skies out here," replied Jim, rising to the issue. "Her father was ruined by a range feud between cattlemen and sheepmen. Her mother has been a hard-working pioneer. You will learn what that means. Molly has one brother. Slinger Dunn. I don't know his first name. But the Slinger comes from his quickness and use with a gun. He has killed several men—and shot up I don't know how many."

"Desperado?" gasped Gloriana.

"Of course an Easterner would call him that. I did at first. But now he's just Slinger to me—and the very salt of the earth."

Dismay, consternation, and sincere regret succeeded one another on Gloriana's expressive face.

"Dad called me the black sheep of our family," she said. "But I'm afraid there are two. . . . It'll kill

Mother . . . Jim, they have no idea whatever of all this. Dad brags to his friends about you. How you are in charge of his brother's big cattle ranch. Nothing of this—this you tell me ever crept into your letters. I know them by heart."

"That's true, Glory. I left out the real stuff which was making me over. And besides, it all sort of bunched just lately. . . . Look here." Jim unbuttoned his flannel shirt at the neck, and pulled his collar back to expose a big angry scar on his breast.

"My heavens! what's that?" she queried, fearfully.

"My dear sister, that's a bullet hole," he replied, not without pride.

"You were shot?"

"I should smile."

"My God!—Jim this is awful! You might have been killed."

"Shore I might. I darn near was. I lay in the woods two days with that wound. Alone!"

"And you can smile about it!" she ejaculated, her eyes dark with awe and fading terror.

"It helped make a man of me."

"Some desperado shot you?"

"Yes, one of the real bad ones."

"Oh, Jim," she cried. "I hope—I pray you—you didn't kill him."

"It turned out I didn't, Glory—which was darn lucky. But at the time I'd have shot him to bits with great pleasure."

"This terrible West has ruined you." Mother always said it would. And Dad would only laugh."

"Nope, Glory. You've got it wrong. I'm not ruined by a long shot. And I hope you've sense and intelligence enough left to see it."

"Jim, I've nothing left," she replied. "You're wild, strange to me—sort of cool and indifferent like that Prentiss fellow. I'm just terribly sorry this West has made you rough—crude. I know I'll hate it."

"Glory, you just misunderstand," rejoined Jim, patiently. "It'll jar you at first—more than it did me. You were always a sensitive, high-strung thing. And your trouble has only made you worse. But please give the West—and me—the benefit of a doubt, before you condemn. Wait. Glory. I swear you will gain by that. Not have any regrets! Not hurt any of these Westerners."

But he saw that he made no impression on her. He had shocked her, and it nettled him. She had quite forgotten already how kindly he had taken her dereliction.

"Where is this Molly Dunn?" asked Gloriana, curiosity strong.

"She's here."

"In this house?"

"Yes. She and her mother. I fetched them up from the Cibeque. Molly is going to school. It's great—and a little pathetic—the way she goes at study. Poor kid—she had so little chance to learn. I expect to marry her in the spring, if I can persuade her."

"Persuade her!" echoed Gloriana, with a wonderful flash of eyes. "I dare say that will be extremely difficult."

"It probably will be," replied Jim, coolly. "Especially after she meets you. But Uncle Jim adores her and he's keen to see me married."

"Well, I deserve it," mused Gloriana.

"What?"

"A dose of my own medicine."

"Glory, I don't want to lose patience with you," said Jim, slowly, trying to keep his temper. "I can understand you, for I felt a little like you do when I landed out here. . . . Now listen. I'm glad you've come to me. I'm sorry you've made mistakes and suffered through them. But they are really nothing. I predict the West will cure them in less than a year. You won't know yourself. You could not be dragged back to Missouri."

Gloriana shook her beautiful head in doubt and sorrow.

"If you only hadn't engaged yourself to this backwoods girl!" she said, mournfully.

"But she saved my life," declared Jim, hotly. "She fought a fellow—one of those desperadoes you mentioned—fought him like a wild cat—*bit* him—hung on him with her teeth to keep him from murdering me as I sat tied hand and foot. . . .

Saved my life until her brother Slinger got there to kill Jocelyn."

"The wretch!" exclaimed Gloriana, in passion and horror. Her face was white as alabaster and her eyes great dark gulfs of changing brilliance. "Did this Slinger Dunn really kill him?"

"You bet he did. And two other desperadoes. They shot Slinger all up. He's in the hospital at Flag. I'll take you in to see him."

"Wonderful!" breathed Gloriana, for the moment thrilled out of her disgust and horror. "But, Jim, why all this bloody murdering? I thought you worked on a cattle range."

"I do. That's the trouble," said Jim, and forthwith launched into a brief narrative of the drift fence and subsequent events which led up to his capture by the Cibeque gang, to Hack Jocelyn's arrival with Molly, who had consented to sacrifice herself to save Jim, of Jocelyn's treachery and how Molly fought to keep him from killing Jim until Slinger got there.

When Jim concluded there was ample evidence that Gloriana did not lack heart and soul, though they were glossed over by restraint and sophistication. This reassured Jim in his stubborn hope that Gloriana was undeveloped and needed only the hard and wholesome contacts she was sure to get in Arizona.

"But, Jim, you can't *marry* a girl who bites like a little beast, no more than I could the brother who kills men," was Gloriana's grave reply.

"I can't—can't I?" retorted Jim goaded at the regurgitation of a forgotten phase of the Traft boy he had once been. "Well I am going to marry her, and I'll think myself the luckiest fellow on earth."

Plainly she thought he was out of his head or that Arizona had broken down his sense of values. But she did not voice either conviction.

"Gloriana, I think I'd better take you in to meet Uncle Jim—and the Dunns," concluded Jim.

"Yes, since it has to be," she replied soberly. "Give me time to make myself presentable. Come back for me in fifteen minutes."

"Sure. I'm curious to see what *you* call presentable," said Jim, and went out whistling. Nevertheless, his heart was heavy as he proceeded down the hall toward the living-room.

Chapter Six

JIM found his uncle alone in the living-room. "Hey!" he said, "when are you going to trot my neice in?"

"Pfetty soon. She was tired and wants to clean up after the long ride."

"How is she, Jim?" he asked, anxiously.

"White and thin. Looks wonderful, though. You could have knocked me over with a feather, Uncle."

"Wal, I reckon I'm plumb ready for mine."

At this juncture Molly and her mother came in,

and it was certain Jim had never seen Molly so pretty, so simply and becomingly attired. He did not see how Gloriana could help admiring her.

"Oh, Jim, did your sister come?" she asked, eagerly.

"You bet. Curly and the boys were there with me. It was a circus."

"I shore reckon," agreed Molly, her eyes round and bright. She was excited, trembling a little.

"I'll fetch Glory in pronto."

"Does she look sick, Jim?"

"Well, you won't be able to see it," laughed Jim. "She'll dazzle you. But when I remember Glory a year ago—how tanned and strong—I confess she looks ill to me. She's white as the snow out there. She has dark circles under her eyes and that makes them bigger. She's very slender."

"Oh, I—I'm crazy to see her," exclaimed Molly. "What did the boys say an' do? Was Curly knocked silly?"

"They were funny, Bud especially. Curly wore his best cowboy outfit, gun and all. The other boys had new suits and they looked most uncomfortable. Curly had the best of them. . . . Well, I'll go fetch Glory in."

Jim went out and thoughtfully wended his way to the west wing of the huge ranch-house. In a certain sense this event was a thrilling and happy one, but in the main it was shadowed by misgivings. He tapped at Gloriana's door, and at her call he entered.

He stared. Was this lovely white creature Gloriana Traft? She wore a pale blue dress, without sleeves, and cut somewhat low. She was slender, but there was not an ungraceful line about her. And she had a little color in her cheeks, whether from excitement or from artificial means Jim could not tell.

"Glory, if you let the boys see you in that rig— we can't go on ranching," he said, with grave admiration.

"Why not?" she asked, not knowing how to take him.

"Because this place would beat the Pleasant Valley War all hollow. You just look like—like some beautiful sweet flower."

His genuine praise brought more color to her cheeks. "Thank you, Jim. It's nice to hear I look well. But this dress is nothing. I've some new ones and I'll have to wear them, even if your ranching can't go on. . . . Guess I'd better put my coat around me. That hall was like Greenland's icy mountains—"

"This house is a big old barn. But the living-room is comfortable," said Jim as he replaced the screen before the fire.

"Jim, if I catch cold again it'll be the end of little Glory."

"Don't talk nonsense. This is a beginning for you, Glory," he replied, warmly, and he kissed her. Gloriana caught his hand and clung to it. Her action and the sudden flash of her face toward him gave Jim a clue to something he had not before guessed. Glory might resemble a proud, cold, aloof young princess, but she really was unconsciously hungering for love, kindness, sympathy. By that Jim judged how she had been hurt, and through it he divined he could win her. Right there Jim decided on the attitude he would adopt with his sister.

"Jim, my failure and disgrace do not alter the fact that I represent your family out here," she said, as they went out.

The remark rather flustered Jim. He was not used to complexity, and he could find no words in which to reply. He hurried her down the hall to the living-room, and opened the door for her to enter. When he followed and closed it Gloriana had let her coat fall to the floor and was advancing quickly to meet the rancher.

"Oh, Uncle Jim, I know you," she said, happily, as if she had expected not to.

"Wal—wal! So you're my niece, Gloriana?" he replied, heartily, yet with incredulity. "I remember a big-eyed little girl back there in Missouri. But you can't be her."

"Yes, I am, Uncle. I've merely grown up. . . . I'm so glad to see you again." She gave him her hands and kissed him.

"Wal, it can't be, but if you say so I'll have to believe," he said, quaintly. "I reckon I'm powerful pleased to have you come West. . . . Gloriana, meet some friends of ours—Arizona folks from down country. . . . Mrs. Dunn and her daughter Molly."

The mother appeared embarrassed at the introduction; Gloriana graciousness itself. Then Jim experienced a sort of fright as this lovely sister and the little girl so precious to him faced each other. Probably Jim was unaware of his intense scrutiny of both. But as a matter of fact he held them both on trial.

"Gloriana, I'm shore happy to welcome you heah," said Molly, with simple sweet warmth. She was tremendously impressed—Jim had never seen her so pale—but there was no confusion for her in this meeting. Her eyes had a shining, earnest light. Jim could not have asked more. She was true to Molly Dunn. She was Western. She had stuff in her. Never in her life had she been subject to such an intense and penetrating look as Gloriana gave her. Jim's heart leaped to his throat. Was Glory going to turn out a terrible snob?

"Molly Dunn! I'm glad to meet you," replied Gloriana, cordially, and she was quick to accept the shy advance of the Western girl. She met Molly's kiss halfway. Jim almost emitted audibly a repressed breath of relief. But he was not sanguine. Gloriana appeared the epitome of perfect breeding, and she was too fine to let the Western girl outdo her in being thoroughbred. Yet heart and soul were wanting. And Jim thought that if he felt it Molly must have, too.

Uncle Jim beamed upon Gloriana and then upon Molly, and lastly upon his constrained nephew.

"Jim, shore there's such a thing as luck," he said. "I reckon I didn't believe so once. But look there. An' think of your havin' a sister an' a sweetheart like them."

It was a simple warm tribute from a lonely old bachelor who had given his heart to Molly and now shared it with Gloriana. But the compliment brought a blush to Gloriana's pale cheek and broke Molly's composure.

"Wal, I don't know aboot it, as Curly would say," drawled Jim, far from feeling like Curly. "A man can have enough luck to kill him."

This unexpected sally from him made the girls laugh and eased the situation. All took seats except Molly, who stood beside Gloriana's chair, plainly fascinated. It gave Jim a pang to see that Molly had already fallen in love with his sister. If Gloriana would only give the Western girl the smallest kind of a chance!

"You shore don't look sick to me," said Molly, her dusky eyes on Gloriana.

"Perhaps Jim exaggerated," returned Gloriana, with a smile. "I'm not on my last legs, but neither am I so very well."

"You look like you didn't eat an' sleep enough, an' run aboot in the sun."

"I don't. That's just what ails me." It would have been hard for anyone human to resist Molly's sweet simplicity.

"You're lovely right now," murmured Molly. "But in six months out heah. . . ." She could not find words to express her conviction, and they were not needed.

"It's fine pneumonia weather just now. I had that last winter. The doctor said once more and it would be flowers for Gloriana May."

Molly did not quite assimilate this speech, and turned to Jim.

"You mustn't roll her in the snow, like you did me."

"Glory will love even winter in Arizona," said Jim. "It's so dry you never feel the cold. But if Glory freezes too much at first we might send her to Tucson for a while."

"Take her down to Yellow Jacket," interposed the rancher.

Molly clapped her hands. "Thet would be fine. We never have any winter down in the Tonto. It snows a little, then melts right off. Sunny days to ride. The air full of cedar an' pine an' sage. Camp fires at night. . . . Gloriana, you would get well quick down at Yellow Jacket."

Jim spoke up seriously: "Next summer we will have both you girls down. But it'd never do now, even down in that low country. We'll have the Hash Knife outfit to entertain."

Gloriana was all interest. "Pray what is Yellow Jacket? And what is the Hash Knife outfit?"

Uncle Jim hawhawed. "Glory, don't let them tease you. Yellow Jacket is a cattle range, wildest left in Arizona. An' the Hash Knife outfit is a gang of cattle thieves."

"Now you've made me want to go," exclaimed Gloriana. "More than anything I want to see a desperado. I—I want to be scared. And I want to go to some lonely place. And when I'm strong again I want to ride. . . . Jim, have you a horse you will let me have?"

"*A* horse? Glory, you've grown amazingly modest. I have a hundred horses you can ride— that is, as soon as you can stick in a saddle."

"You will take me on trips into the desert?" queried Gloriana, breathlessly, her great eyes shining like stars.

Jim concealed his thrill of satisfaction. Added to Gloriana's need of love there seemed a thirst for something she had never had. Perhaps this was merely for excitement. But if she showed an innate leaning toward the beauty and wildness of nature then Arizona would claim her, and change her body and soul.

"Glory, I reckon I'll have to take you, if we want any work done," replied Jim.

Gloriana was as delighted as nonplussed. "But I don't quite understand your reference to work. I can't do very much."

"Could you bake sour-dough biscuits?"

"Gracious no!"

Molly laughed merrily. "Could you call wild turkeys?"

"I could eat a whole one anyhow. . . . Oh, I'll be the greenest tenderfoot who ever came West."

"Glory, I'll teach you to make biscuits an' call wild turkeys," volunteered Molly.

"You're very good. I'm afraid you'll find me stupid."

"Glory, I didn't mean work for you, though I dare say a little would be good for you. I meant that the cowboys said there wouldn't 'never be no more ranchin' now.' "

"And why not?" queried Gloriana, vastly puzzled.

"I showed them a photograph of you."

Gloriana joined in the laugh at her expense.

"That horried picture of me! I have some really good ones."

"For Heaven's sake, don't let anybody see them!" exclaimed Jim, plaintively.

Thereupon followed a half-hour of pleasant conversation, mostly for Gloriana's edification, and received by her with undisguised enthusiasm. Then she said she was very tired and begged to be excused.

"Jim, take me back to my Indian wigwam. I'd never find it," she begged, and bade the others good night.

When back in Gloriana's room Jim stirred the fire and put on a few fresh sticks of wood.

"Well?" he queried, presently, rising to face his sister, and he was quite conscious of the anxious gruffness of his voice.

To Jim's surprise she placed a hand on each of his shoulders.

"Jim, your Western girl is distractingly pretty, sweet as a wild flower, honest and good as gold— and far braver than I could have been. I saw what you couldn't see. Probably it was harder for her to meet me than that Hack fellow she—she bit to save your life. I'm your family, so to speak."

"Thanks Glory," replied Jim, somewhat huskily. "I—I was afraid—"

"I'd not like her? Jim, I don't blame you for loving her. I *did* like her. . . . But—and here's the rub—she is illiterate. She comes from an illiterate family. She's only a very common little person— and certainly not fit to be the wife of James Traft."

"That's your Eastern point of view," returned Jim. "It might—though I don't admit it—be right if we were back home. But we're out West. I love the West. It has made me a man. It is now my home. I worship this 'common little person,' as you call her. *I* think she is farthest removed from that. She's strong and true and big, and crude like this great raw West. And as I've thrown in my fortunes here I consider myself most lucky to win such a girl. . . . All of which, Glory, dear, is aside from the fact that but for her I'd be dead. . . . But for Molly *you* wouldn't have had any brother to come to!"

"Don't think me ungrateful," she rejoined, in hurried, shuddering earnestness. "I am . . . and indeed you talk like a man. I admire and respect you. But I had to tell you the ethics of it. I wouldn't be a Traft if I failed to tell you."

"Then—you're not against us?" queried Jim, hopefully.

"Jim, I disapprove. But it would be absurd for me to oppose. I have come to you for help—for a home—to find *my* chance in life, if there be one. Besides, I like Molly. . . . The trouble will come not from me, but from *her*. Can't you see it? I don't think I ever was subjected to such study. Yet no trace of jealousy or bitterness! She was just being a woman seeing *you,* your family, your position through me. I saw fear in her eyes as she bade me good night. That fear was not of me, or that I might come between you. It was a fear of realization, of love. She ought not marry you because she is Molly Dunn of the Cibeque! And, Jim, if she's really as strong and fine as it seems she is, she will not marry you."

"I've had the very same fear myself," admitted Jim. "But I always laugh myself out of it. Now you—"

"Make it worse," she interposed. "I'm sorry. I

ought not have come. . . . I could go away some-where, I suppose, and work. . . . But, Jim, the damage is done."

"I wouldn't let you go. I think we're making a mountain out of a molehill. It'll sure come out all right, if you'll help."

"Jim, I promise. I'll do my utmost for you. I'll be nicer to that little girl than I ever was to anyone in my life. I *can* make people like me. But the worst of me is I'm cold. I've been frozen inside since Ed Darnell deceived me. I can't promise to love Molly, though it'd appear easy enough."

She seemed so eloquent, so moving, so beautiful that Jim could have decried aloud her intimation of her indifference.

"Glory, I couldn't ask any more," he concluded. "It's more than I had hoped for. You have made me feel—oh, sort of warm deep down—glad you've come West. We'll win out in the end. We've got the stuff. . . . And now good night. You're worn out. Be sure to put the screen in front of the fire."

"Good night, brother Jim," she said, and kissed him. "I'm glad I came."

Jim left her with her kiss lingering on his lips. Gloriana had never been the kissing kind, and it was easy to tell now that she had not changed. She was older, deeper, more complex, with a hint of sadness about her which he wanted to eradicate. The cowboys would do that. They would change even the spots of a leopard. He went toward his room, and on the way tapped on Molly's door.

"Are you in bed?" he called.

"No, Jim—not quite," she replied, and presently opened the door a few inches to disclose a sweet agitated face.

"I just wanted to ask. . . . Do you like her?"

"Like!—I shore fell in love powerful deep. She's—she's—" But Molly could find no adequate word to express herself.

Jim darted his head downward to give her a quick kiss.

"Darling, I'd gamble my soul on you," he whispered, gratefully. Then louder, "Did your mother like Glory?"

"Shore. But she was aboot scared stiff. . . . An', Jim, me too—a little."

"Well now, you mustn't be. Glory said some mighty sweet things about you."

"Oh, Jim—tell me," she begged, breathlessly.

"Not much. I'll keep them until I want something special out of you. Ha! Ha!—But they're awfully nice. . . . Good night, Molly."

Jim found his uncle dozing before the living-room fire. "Wake up and tell me what I'm to do?"

"Huh?" grunted Uncle Jim.

"Wake up and talk to me," replied Jim. "Did you like Glory? What on earth am I to do with two such girls on my hands? How can I keep the cowboys from murdering each other? Tell me what—"

"One at a time, you Missouri rooster. . . . Wal, Glory is the most amazing girl I ever saw. Bright an' smart as beautiful! She's got a haid on her, Jim. An' only nineteen. I reckon she'll be a bitter pill for Molly. But Molly is true blue. She'll be Western. In the end she an' Glory will be sisters. Not soon, but you can bet on it. An' your part is goin' to be harder'n buildin' the drift fence. Shore, Glory will upset the cowboys. Because she's sweet, she's nice, she'll be intrested in them—an' the poor dumbhaids will reckon they can win her. At that she could do worse than be won by Curly or Bud or Jackson Way."

"I've come somewhere near that conclusion myself," rejoined Jim, thoughtfully. "Confidentially, Uncle, I want to tell you Gloriana has come West for good."

"Fine!" ejaculated the rancher: "Is she thet sick? Or what—"

"She's not so sick as it appeared. Only run down. She got involved in an unfortunate affair back home. Took up with some flashy fellow— thought she loved him when she didn't—and he turned out bad. Borrowed money from her and cheated money out of Dad. It hurt Glory with her crowd, which she was pretty sick of, anyhow, I guess. She's the proudest of the whole raft of Trafts. . . . So she has turned to me, poor kid."

"Ahuh!—Wal, dog-gone! . . . Jim, you ain't implyin' some scoundrel ruined your sister?"

"No, thank God," returned Jim, fervently. "But he ruined her reputation, at least. Fellow named Ed Darnell. And Glory is sure he'll show up out here."

"Wal, if he does I reckon it'll be aboot the last place he ever shows up," replied the cattleman, grimly.

"I said as much. . . . So, Uncle, we've got the happiness and future of two wonderful girls to make. I swear I'm stumped. I'm scared. I'm struck pretty deep."

"Wal, it's a problem, shore. But you're young an' you want results too quick."

"I can be patient. I'll do everything under the sun. But suppose Molly gets upset by Glory? Scared of my family, so to speak."

"Wal, in thet case I'd put Glory up against the real stuff out *heah*. An' have Molly with her. Thet'll square the balance. Then they'll learn from each other."

"It's a good idea," agreed Jim, almost with enthusiasm. "You mean put Glory up against rough outdoor life—horses, cowboys, camp, cold, heat, rain, dust and hail? Hard beds, poor feed, privation—danger—and so on?"

"Shore, an' so on. Put her up against everythin' thet Molly knows."

"It's risky, Uncle. Glory is not strong. It might kill her."

"Wal, you'd have to go slow an' easy till she could just aboot stand it, an' thet's all."

"But, if it *didn't* kill her—" mused Jim, fascinated by the memory of how terrible and wonderful the raw West had been to him. It was that which had won him for Molly Dunn; and now he regarded the stronger and primitive in him more desirable than any development he might have had in the East. The thing had to be gone through to be understood. Gloriana would succumb to it sooner than he had done, despite or probably because of her sensitive, feminine nature. And during this transition of his sister he was going to have trouble holding on to his sweetheart. Jim regretted that he had not persuaded Molly to marry him before Gloriana had come out. Could he do it yet? His mind whirled and his blood leaped at the suggestion. But it would not do, because Molly might suspect the reason. All of a sudden he realized that his uncle was talking.

"Beg pardon, Unce, I was lost."

"Wal, I was changing the subject," replied the rancher. "Locke was in awhile ago an' he's got wind of Bambridge shippin' steers tomorrow from Winslow. We was figurin' thet it might be a good idea for you to run down there an' look 'em over."

"Gee! In this weather?"

"Wal, you forget we're up high heah on the mountain slope. Winslow is down in the desert. Reckon there won't be any snow. Anyway, weather never fazes this Bambridge cattleman, thet's shore."

"What's the idea, Uncle?" asked Jim, soberly.

"Bambridge doesn't know you, nor none of his outfit, so Locke reckons. An' you've never been in Winslow. You could look those steers over without bein' recognized. An' fer thet matter it wouldn't make a whole lot of difference if you were. . . . Whatever is comin' of this Bambridge deal is shore comin'."

"Uncle Jim, you expect trouble with him?"

"Son, I've seen a hundred Bambridges come an' go. I know the brand. I've been forty years raisin' steers. . . . Ten years ago a fine-spoken most damn likeable fellow named Stokes drifted into Flag. Had money. Began to buy stock an' sell. Soon was operatin' big. Everybody his friend. But there was somethin' aboot Stokes thet stuck in my craw. An', Jim, I seen him hangin' to a cottonwood tree—by the neck."

"Queer business, this cattle-raising," mused Jim, darkly.

"Wal, so long's there are big open ranges they'll be rustlers. An' I reckon when the ranges are fenced the cattleman of my type and Bambridge, an' Jed Stone, too, all will have passed. It's a phase of the West."

"You regard Jed Stone as a cattleman?" queried Jim, in surprise.

"Shore do. He's a factor you've got to regard. Yellow Jacket belongs to you, legally, because I bought it, an' *gave* it to you. But Stone shore thinks it belongs to him," replied Traft, with a dry laugh.

"Humph! And for what reason?"

"He's been ridin' it for years, thinkin' it free range, same as the rest. But it's a ranch, an' two sections of land, twelve hundred acres, have been surveyed. The best water—an' by the way, Jim, Yellow Jacket Spring is the wonderfulest in Arizona—an' level ground are in thet surveyed plot. The corners were hid pretty well by the man who first owned the ranch. I haven't been down there for years. But Locke has an' he's seen them. So we can prove our claim."

"Good heavens, Uncle!" exclaimed Jim. "Do you mean we may have to prove to an outlaw that we have a right to a piece of land you bought?"

"Not Stone. You'll have to prove it to him with guns. Haw! Haw! . . . But Bambridge, an' mebbe thet catteman who's in with him—I forget the name—may want to see our proofs. Of course, son, nothin' but a little fight may ever come of this. But I've a hunch Yellow Jacket will catch your eye. It did mine. It's the wildest an' most beautiful place to live I ever seen in Arizona. Yellow Jacket isn't a valley, exactly. Really it's a great wide canyon, with yellow walls. Protected from storms. Best place to hunt in Arizona. Bear, deer, turkey just thick. An' very few hunters ever get in there, because it's a long way an' there's plenty of good huntin' ranges closer. Lots of beaver left in Yellow Jacket an' where there's beaver you bet it's wild."

"Well, I've set my heart on Yellow Jacket, Uncle Jim Traft," declared Jim, forcefully. "And Slinger Dunn has a half interest in the stock running there. That was the deal I made with him, you know, to get him into the Diamond."

"Shore, an' you don't know how good a deal it was. Wish Dunn could go to Winslow with you. . . . An' come to think of it, Jim, you take Curly along."

"Fine. We'll hop the early train."

In the nipping frosty dawn, Jim, clad in jeans and boots, and heavy leather jacket, stamped into the bunkhouse, and yelled, "Curly Prentiss!"

Not a sound. The bunks might have been empty, only they were not. Jeff, the cook, stirred out in the kitchen, and asked through the door, "Boss, is the ranch-house on fire?"

"No. I've got to go to Winslow. Fix some break-fast for two, Jeff. And rustle . . . Curly."

"I'm daid."

"Get up and into your jeans."

"Aw, Jim, I was oot late last night."

"Hurry, or I'll ask Bud," returned Jim, tersely.

That fetched a lithe clean-limbed young giant thudding to the floor, and in the twinkling of an eye, almost, Curly was in his clothes. He stalked into the kitchen. "Water, Jeff, you sleepin' cook, an' if it's not hot I'll shoot at your toes."

Bud poked his cherub face above the blankets and blinked at Jim.

"Funny how this reminds me of camp," he said. "What's wrong, Boss?"

"I'm going to Winslow. Bambridge is shipping cattle, and I want to look over the bunch."

"Dog-gone-it, Jim, don't go," rejoined Bud, seriously.

"I'm not stuck on going, but Uncle says go, and that settles it. . . . What do you know, you mum little geezer?"

"Me? Aw, hell, I don't know nuthin' this early in the mawnin'. . . . Let me go along?"

"I reckon I can't, Bud. Uncle said take Curly."

"An' why thet hombre especial? Looks ain't everythin' in a cowpuncher."

"Well, Bud, I think Uncle is worried about you and the other boys. You need sleep and rest, he says."

"Like hell he does! . . . Jim, I don't like this hyar deal atall," complained Bud.

"I asked you what you knew."

"Sure, I heerd you," replied Bud, innocently. "Jim, are my eyes pore or is thet a gun you're packin'?"

"Yep. I've got in the habit, you know, since I bossed the Diamond."

"But some of these days you'll be throwin' it, sure. Jim, you've got a rotten temper. An' you oughtn't be trusted with a gun, onless the outfit was around."

Curly came in, his tawny hair damp and tousled, his cheeks rosy as a girl's.

"Shet up, you little monkey," he admonished, glaring at his bosom friend.

"All right," said Bud, sinking back into his blankets. "It shore won't be on my haid. But I'm tellin' you, Boss, Curly has been plumb crazy since—"

Bud narrowly escaped a well-aimed bootjack, which thumped hard on the wall, and he succumbed. But the noise awoke other of the cowboys.

"Injuns! We're attacked," ejaculated Uphill Frost, still half asleep.

"I smell ham," said Lonestar Holliday. "What'n'll's goin' on around heah?"

Jim and Curly went into the kitchen, shutting the door, and they warmed their palms over Jeff's fire until breakfast was ready. Curly was not his usual bright self, which might have been owing to the night before, of which he had hinted, but also it might have been the portent of Jim's early call. They had breakfast and hurried out into the snow. The morning was still, with frost crackling, and the fence posts glittering with sunshine on the snow. Curly had little to say until they reached the station.

"Ring Locke was in last night," announced Curly, "an' he shore had bad news."

"Thought you were out late?" queried Jim, gruffly.

"Wal, I wasn't. Ring got wind of this heah Bambridge shippin'. Dog-gone-it, Ring's always gettin' tipped off aboot things we don't want to heah. He has too many friends."

"Wait till we're on the train," replied Jim, tersely. The station-room and platform were not the places just then for indiscriminate speech. Cowboys, cattlemen, Mexican laborers, and other passengers for this early train, were noisily in evidence.

When they got into the train, to find a seat somewhat isolated from those occupied, Jim whispered, "What did Locke hear?"

"Some darn fool sent him word there were Diamond steers in thet bunch of stock Bambridge is shippin'."

"So that's it? Uncle didn't tell me Locke said that. . . . The nerve of this Bambridge! . . . Curly, what're you growling about?"

"Locke ought to have kept his big mouth shet. . . . We shore cussed him last night."

"And why?"

" 'Cause we all knew what'd come off pronto. Old Traft would send you down there, an' if you saw any steers with our brand you'd go right to Bambridge an' tell him—"

"I should smile I would."

Curly threw up his hands, an expressive gesture of his when he was helpless, which in truth was not often.

"Why shouldn't I tell him, cowboy?" queried Jim, somewhat nettled. How long it took to understand these queer cattlemen!

"Wal, we reckon Bambridge oughtn't know we're suspicious, till we've had a spell at Yellow Jacket."

"But, Curly, surely Locke and Uncle Jim know more what is best than you cowboys."

"Hellyes. But they don't have to do the fightin'."

The way Curly spat out those words, as well as their content, gave Jim a breath-arresting moment. Indeed it was true—Locke was an aggressive superintendent, and the old rancher a stern and ruthless dealer with crooked cattlemen. No more was said then, and Jim gazed out at the speeding white and black landscape. The pines had given place to cedars and piñons, and these soon made way for sagebrush. The snow thinned out, and when the train got down on the open desert the white began to give way to the yellow of grass and occasional green tuft of sage or greasewood.

Chapter Seven

THE Hash Knife were back from a drive, the nature of which showed in their begrimed, weary faces, their baggy eyes, and the ragged condition of their garb.

"Home!" croaked Malloy, flinging his crooked

length down before the fire Stone was building.

"My Gawd!" ejaculated Stone, staring at the little gunman. And his men simulated his look if not his speech. The idea of Croak Malloy giving expression to such a word as home was so striking as to be incongruous, not to say funny.

"Did you ever have a home?" added the outlaw leader, more curious than scornful.

"Aw, you can't gibe me," replied Malloy, imperturbably. "What I mean is hyar's rest an' comfort—after a hell of a job."

"It shore was," agreed Pecos.

"An' ain't it good to be down out of the snow an' thet damn Tonto wind," said Madden. "Like spring down hyar at Yellow Jacket. It smells different."

"Wal, we'll sit tight till spring, you can gamble on thet," spoke up the gambler, Carr.

"Mebbe we will," interposed Jed Stone, sarcastically, yet not without pathos.

"Aw hell!" bit out Malloy. "Jed, don't begin your belly-achin', now we're home. We've got supplies till spring, plenty of drink and money to gamble with. Let's forget it an' be happy."

Sonora came in, dragging a pack, and young Frank Lang, the ex-sheriff, also appeared heavily laden. It was about midday, and outside the sun shone brightly warm. The air was cool and sweet with sage and cedar, and had a hint of spring, though the time was early December.

"Reckon Jed built thet fire 'cause he's so absent-minded," remarked some one.

"No, I want a cup of coffee. I'm soured on whisky. . . . At that it ain't bad to be back in the old cabin. . . . —— Bambridge anyhow!"

"He shore pulled a rummy deal," said Pecos, his tone harmonizing with Stone's.

"Wal, no one much ain't a-goin' to connect the Hash Knife with thet winter shippin' of stock. So what the hell?" replied Malloy. "But it wasn't a slick trick to turn."

For Malloy to show disapproval of a cattle-steal seemed to prove it was the last word in bold and careless rustling.

"Bambridge will skip Arizona pronto," put in Anderson, wagging his shaggy head. "I'd have give my pipe to see thet young Traft call him."

"So would I—an' some more," said Stone, thoughtfully. "Nervy youngster. . . . Frank, tell me about it again."

"Boss, I told you twice," complained Reed.

"Sure. But we was on the trail an' it was cold an' windy. You made it short an' sweet, too. . . . Here's a cigar."

Thus importuned the young cowboy rustler lighted the cigar, smiling his satisfaction, and settled himself comfortably.

"I was in Chance's saloon after the shippin', an' I heard a man say, 'damn funny about thet Bambridge cattle-drive. I went by the railroad stockyards late last night, 'cause I live out thet way. There wasn't no cattle there. An' next mornin' at daylight the pen was full of bawlin' steers.'"

"Haw! Haw!" croaked Malloy, gleefully, rubbing his thin brown hands.

"Laugh, you frog!" exclaimed Stone, darkly. "Thet drive was another blunder. We ought to have left the cattle at Bambridge's ranch, which I wanted to do. But he got sore. . . . An' well— Frank—"

"We drove the stock in at midnight, as you-all ain't forgettin'," resumed Reed, puffing his cigar. "It was a slick job fer any cowpunchin' outfit. An' next mornin' at ten o'clock them steers was all on a stock train, ready to move. Thet was another slick job. . . . I stayed at Chance's, sleepin' in a chair, an' went out to the yards after breakfast. Already the railroad men was movin' the cars to the pen. There wasn't no cowboy in sight 'till thet mornin' train from Flag come in. Then I seen Curly Prentiss. Used to ride under him when he had charge of the U Bar. He had a young fellar with him thet turned out to be Jim Traft. They watched the cattle fer about two minutes. No more! An' young Traft jumped right up an' down. You could see Prentiss talkin' turkey to him. I made it my business to foller them back to the station. An' you bet your life Curly Prentiss seen me. There ain't much thet hombre doesn't see. But it was safe, I reckon, 'cause nobody knows I'm with the Hash Knife. Prentiss an' Traft went in the freight office, an' I ducked in the station. As luck would have it, Bambridge came in with a dark-complected fellar, sporty dressed, an' good-lookin'. I edged over an' heard Bambridge ask: 'Where you from?' The fellar said St. Louis. 'What do you know about cattle?' He said nuthin', but he happened to know a stock-buyer in Kansas City who told him to hunt up George Bambridge, if he was goin' to Arizona. 'An' who's this stockman?' asked Bambridge, quick like. He said, 'Darnell'—I got thet name straight. 'Come to my office up town later in the day. I'm busy now with this cattle shipment.' . . . He was shore goin' to be damn busy in a minnit, only he didn't guess it. Just then Prentiss an' Traft come in. They was both packin' guns, which was funny only for Traft, I reckon. Prentiss sleeps in a gun. They looked kinda fire-eyed, an' Traft stopped Bambridge right in the middle of the station, an' he was in a hurry, too."

Reed leisurely drew on his cigar, and puffing out a white cloud of smoke he looked at Stone and Malloy and Lang and Pecos and the others, as if to note if his story was having any effect. Malloy had a sardonic grin. Lang was pale for a weather-beaten outdoor man. Anderson wore an intent anxious expression.

"Talk, an' come to the point," ordered Stone, in a cold, testy voice.

114

"Not much more," replied Reed, casually. "Traft asked, 'Are you George Bambridge?'—an' he got a short answer.

" 'You're shippin' some of my steers,' snapped Traft.

"Bambridge turned red as a turkey gobbler's comb. 'The hell you say, my young cowpuncher! An' who may you be?'

" 'My name is Traft,' said thet young cowpuncher, an' he said it loud.

"Bambridge went white now. 'Jim Traft's nephew?'

" 'Yes, an' you're shippin' steers with my brand.'

" 'What brand is thet?' jerked out Bambridge, sort of husky. He was madder'n hellsfire.

" 'Diamond brand.'

" 'Ahuhm, I see.' . . . Bambridge sort of pulled himself together. 'Sorry, Mr. Traft. Mistakes happen. This is a rush order. An' them Yellow Jacket steers of yours overrun my range. An' I'm runnin' some new cowhands. Send me a bill.'

" 'No, Mr. Bambridge, I'll not send you a bill now, but I'll send a telegram East to have a count made of the Diamond steers in this shipment,' said Traft, an' he shore looked a lot.

" 'You call me a liar—an' a cattle thief?' busted out Bambridge, movin' a hand back.

" 'No. An' don't pull a gun. This gentleman with me is Curly Prentiss. . . . I didn't *say* you was a liar an' a thief. But this shipment has a queer look an' I'll not be satisfied till it's been counted over.'

" 'I tell you if there's Diamond steers on that train it's only a mistake. Any rancher makes mistakes when he's rushed,' yelled Bambridge.

" 'No, any rancher doesn't make *such* mistakes!'

" 'Every cattleman drives stock sometimes thet ain't his.'

" 'But not branded stock.'

" 'Your Uncle does it. An' fer thet matter he's as much of a cattle thief as Blodgett, or Babbit, or me—or any—'

" 'Don't you call my uncle a thief,' broke in young Jim. An' he cracked Bambridge square on his ugly mug. You ought to have heard thet fist. Sounded like hittin' a beef with an ax. Bambridge fell all over himself—damn near knockin' down the stove, an' he didn't get up. It was a good thing he was knocked out, fellars, for when I looked at Traft again there he was waitin' with a gun, an' Prentiss was standin' far over to one side."

"Pretty," croaked Malloy, with relish.

"Is thet all?" asked Stone, tersely.

"Jest about. Some men got around Bambridge an' helped him up. I seen Prentiss eyein' me sort of sharp, so I ducked back to Chance's an' hid there till early next mornin'."

"Bambridge is a damn fool," burst out Stone. "An' I was the same for dealing with him."

"Looks like young Traft has done us a good turn," said Anderson, with satisfaction.

"It shore does, Boss," added Pecos, quietly. "He throwed the light on Bambridge."

Others of the group attested to the same conviction.

"Well, yes, I reckon—mebbe," agreed the leader. "But it'll only make old Jim Traft sorer."

"Jed, the fact that you once rode fer Traft an' stood well with him sticks by you like a fish-bone in the throat," observed Anderson. "We've all seen better days. We was all different once—onless mebbe Croak there, who hasn't changed a damn iota since he was born."

"What's a iota?" inquired the subject of this remark. "Sound somethin' like I-O-U, which you'll all be doin' pronto."

"Men," said Stone, "I'll split this money I got fer this last job, an' let myself out."

"Thet ain't fair," objected Malloy, who was strict in regard to shares of spoil. He had been a bandit at an earlier stage of his career. "You did thet last time."

"An' spoiled my settin' in for you an' Carr to fleece? It's jest as well. I'd be broke soon, anyhow."

"Reckon thet four-flush rancher owes you quite a wad?"

"Ten thousand."

"— — —!" cursed Malloy, in consternation. "Jed, he's goin' to do you. Sure as shootin'!"

"He'd better not, or there'll *be* a little shootin'," declared the chief, grimly. "But I don't mind admittin' thet the Hash Knife has struck a snag in this same hightalkin' crooked cattleman."

Stone left his men to their profanity and humor, both of which expended some force over the debt Bambridge owed him, and he went outside to walk around the familiar grounds.

December was on the way, but it was like spring down here in this protected spot. The air was crisp and full of tang. Blue jays were squalling and black squirrels chattering. A faint sound of wind from the pines above came down, and was almost drowned by the mellow roar of the brook that ran through the boulder-strewn, sycamore-lined glen just below the cabin. There were gold and green leaves still on the sycamores, which was another proof of the peculiar climate of Yellow Jacket.

Stone strolled under the great checker-barked junipers. Bear signs not yet old showed on the brown matted earth, and gave him peculiar satisfaction with its suggestion of the loneliness of this canyon. That feeling did not survive long. He had a premonition that the race of the long notorious Hash Knife was about run. None of his men shared that with him, and not improbably the big ranchers of the Mogollans and the Little Colorado Range would have scouted the idea. But Stone knew better than any of them; and this homecoming, as he bitterly called it, back to Yellow Jacket, had made him pretty sick. He was weary with the toil, the devious crooked ways, the sweat and blood, and, yes, the ignominy of the Hash Knife. He confessed it to himself for the first time and realized it as a factor that would lead to something drastic.

He walked under the pines and spruces, across the log bridge over the brook, where many a time he had angled for trout in the amber water, and under the vine-covered, fern-fringed walls. In places he waded through leaves up to his knees, brown, dry, rustling oak leaves that gave up an acrid dust. And he went back and along the high bank to the beautiful glen where Yellow Jacket Spring poured its amber flood from under huge mossy rocks. From that high point he surveyed the gray-green valley, with its rock walls, its open range of bleached grass, silver in the sunlight, its many groves of cedar and pine, its numberless slopes of shaggy oaks, which the bear and deer and turkey haunted in the early fall, its black timber belt along the rims. All these features presented the isolated confines of the canyon itself. Below, the gray-walled gateway opened into the wildest and most rugged range in Arizona, a wilderness of rock and brush and forest, grassy ridges, brawling streams, thickets of manzanita and mescal, towering cliffs and canyons where no sunlight entered—altogether a big country which only the Apaches had ever thoroughly explored.

Toward the lower end of this country, perhaps forty miles as a crow flies, it was barred from the open range by Clear Creek Canyon. Beyond lay the Little Colorado Range, where the rich cattlemen operated.

Yellow Jacket possessed a very singular feature. High and isolated and inclosed as it was, it yet looked down, at least through that narrow gateway, upon the desert which sloped away into purple infinitude. For that country had the right altitude, neither too high nor too low, and its walls held back the winds and reflected the sunlight.

Some years back Stone had indulged in the illusion that he was going to own Yellow Jacket. Bambridge had promised to give it to him. But Bambridge had failed to get possession, and Stone's dream of quitting the outlaw game and settling down to honest ranching had been dispelled. He hated Bambridge for that, though he blamed himself for indulging in dreams. Hunted man as he was, the plan could have been carried out. Arizona was quick to recognize a cattleman whose shady dealings were in the past.

From that hour Jed Stone was more than ever a preoccupied man, wandering around the canyon during sunny hours, sitting in favorite places, or smoking by the camp fire. His gambling comrades, intent on their daily gains or losses, saw nothing of the almost imperceptible change in their leader. Anderson hunted every day, supplying the camp with fresh meat, while he stuck to his trade of trapping fur, even though he had been an outlaw for years. Sonora was the trusted scout of the band, always watching the trails. Pecos, the Texan, dreamed away his life. The rest of them staked their ill-gotten gold on the turn of a card.

Stone had something on his mind, and it was not only the slow disintegration of the once virile Hash Knife outfit, and therefore the decline of his leadership, but a realization that for the first time in his life he leaned towards betrayal of those who trusted him. And loyalty was the predominating trait of his personality. It was loyalty to a friend that had lost him his place among honest cattlemen.

One afternoon, Jed, returning from a walk up the brook, heard a shot. Rifle-shots were not rare around camp, but this came from a small gun of heavy caliber. It had a dull, ominous sound that echoed from the walls. Upon reaching the cabin he saw some of his men standing in a group—the kind of group he had seen so often and which suggested so much.

"Croak jest shot Carr," said Pecos, coolly and slowly; but there was a glint in his eyes.

"What for?" demanded Stone.

"Ask him."

Stone hesitated at the threshold of the cabin door. He did not trust Malloy, or was it that he did not trust himself? Then he entered. The little outlaw sat at the rude table, smoking a cigarette and shuffling a deck of cards. Carr lay humped over a bench, his head resting on the floor.

"Is he dead?" queried Stone, asking a super-fluous question."

"Thet's funny," replied Malloy, with his little croaking laugh.

"Not so damn funny!" retorted the leader. "What'd you shoot him for?"

"Boss, he cheated at cairds," returned Malloy, almost plaintively.

It was Stone's turn to laugh. Malloy's statement was preposterous, if not in fact then certainly in significance.

"Sure he cheated. But you all turn a trick when you can. Carr was the slickest. You had no call to kill him for what you do yourself."

"Wal, he won all the money. Thet's the difference."

"Ahuh. I see. It's shore a big difference. An' where's all this money Carr won?"

"He was stuffin' his pockets an laughin' at us," said Malloy, with heat. "Thet made me sore. An I cussed him fer bein' a caird sharp. Then, Boss, he got mean an' personal. He swore I stacked the cairds, which you all know is a lie, 'cause I can't do it. The best trick I know is to slip an ace from the pack or hold out a hand. An' the damn gambler threw thet in my face."

Stone called the men in from outside. "Search Carr an' put what he has on the table. Then take him out an' bury him—an' make it a good long way from this cabin."

"Boss, what're you goin' to do with it?" asked Malloy, as the heaps of gold coil and rolls of greenbacks were thumped upon the table.

"Divide it, accordin' to what each of you lost."

Then arose an argument among the gamesters over what amounts Carr had won from them. Lang and Madden, and especially young Reed, lied about it. Malloy frankly admitted he did not know how much he had lost, but certainly all that he had. Stone finally adjusted the difficulty by giving each the exact sum he had portioned out to them as their share of the recent cattle-drive. This caused some grumbling. And it turned out that Stone himself, with the aid of Pecos, had to carry Carr out into the woods and bury him.

"Much good his stone face done him," said the outlaw leader, wiping the sweat from his face.

"Shore not much," agreed the Texan. "Boss, I reckon Carr got his desserts. He was aimin' to slope with all thet money."

"You don't say? Who told you?" asked Stone, in surprise.

"Carr told me aboot it. Made no bones of braggin' he'd quit the outfit soon as he'd won our pile."

"Did he ever say thet before Croak?"

"Shore. We all heahed him."

"Then thet was why Croak shot him."

"I reckoned so myself."

"Pecos, do you hold this job as good or bad for the Hash Knife?"

123

"Wal, both, I reckon. Carr riled the fellars, most of the time. He was a disorganizer. Bad hombre for a business like ours. On the other hand, the fact that he meant to double-cross us an' thet Croak killed him in cold blood shore is serious. . . . Boss, the Hash Knife is ailin' from dry rot."

"Ahuh. . . . Money too easy—no hard work like we used to have—this two-faced Bambridge—"

Pecos nodded his lean hawklike head, acquiescing silently to the leader's unfinished speech.

Two mornings later, rather early, for Madden and Lang were cleaning up after breakfast, Stone was surprised by Sonora darting in the cabin doors with his noiseless swift step.

"Boss, somebody comin'," he whispered.

"Who?"

"Cowboy—on foot."

"Sit tight, all of you," ordered Stone, and faced the door. Then Sonora told him that there was a camp somewhere down outside the gateway of the canyon. He had smelled smoke and had started to hunt for it when he had espied this lone cowboy approaching up the trail.

After a long wait a leisurely footfall was heard outside. A shadow fell across the sunny threshold. Then came a knock.

"Hello! Anybody home?" called a clear voice.

"Come in," replied Stone.

A tall, lithe-limbed, broad-shouldered young

man stepped into sight. He was bareheaded, and the sun shone on a tanned open countenance.

"I'm looking for Jed Stone," he announced, frankly.

"Wal, you're lookin' at him," replied the outlaw tersely. "An' who may you be, stranger?"

"Boss, it's young Jim Traft," spoke up Reed, excitedly.

"Yes. But I can talk for myself," returned the young visitor, with a flash of sharp hazel eyes at Reed.

"Jim Traft! . . . What you want?" exclaimed Stone, in slow amaze.

"I want a straight talk with you."

"Wal, young fellar, thet ain't hard to get, though most ranchin' folks reckon they'd get straight shootin' instead."

"I'd like to talk to you alone," said Traft, eagerly.

"No. What you have to say to me you'll say in front of my outfit."

"Very well, then," rejoined Traft, slowly, and he sat down on a box in the broad sunlight that flared through the wide door. He did not appear to be hurried or nervous; indeed for an Easterner not long in the West he was exceedingly cool. Stone liked his face, the keen curious light of hazel eyes, and his manner. And the thought stung Stone that twenty years ago he was very like this young man. Traft glanced casually over the Hash Knife outfit, his gaze lingering longest on Croak Malloy, who

125

sat on the floor, leaning against a pack, and for once his expression was one of interest. Though the little gunman did not realize it, he had respect for courage.

"First off, my Uncle Jim didn't advise me to call on you. I've done that on my own hook," said Traft.

"Wal, you needn't of told me thet," observed Stone.

"I've made my mind up ever since I got out of that fight at Tobe's Well—to try common sense."

"It ain't a bad idea, if the other party has any."

"Stone, would it surprise you to learn my uncle speaks well of you?" queried the young rancher.

"Reckon it would," replied Stone, slowly. And a pang rent his heart.

"He has done so. To me, and I've heard the same to others. He said twenty years ago he knew you and you rode for him—and there wasn't a finer or squarer cowboy in Arizona. He said you must have been driven to outlawry. Anyway, you never had been and you never would be a cattle thief at heart. . . . And it was a damn pity."

Stone felt a rush of hot blood to his face, and a cold tightness of skin as the wave receded. His breast seemed to cave with a sickening pain. So old Jim Traft spoke openly that way about him? Somehow it had a terrible significance, almost a fatality, coming at this hour. Malloy's hollow croaking laugh jarred on him.

"Wal—thet was—good of Jim—but I reckon—wasted sympathy," he replied, rather hoarsely.

"I'm not concerned with the truth of it—though I believe my uncle," went on Traft. "It's just encouraged me to call on you and have a talk."

"No harm done, young fellar, but shore a little risky."

"I didn't see it. Curly Prentiss called me a crazy tenderfoot. And Slinger Dunn swore it was ten to one I'd not come back. But I couldn't see it that way. I'm not packing a gun or looking for trouble."

"Wal, Traft, I reckon if you'd happened to miss me here—you'd run into trouble all right."

"I took the chance. . . . But, Stone, before I make you the—the proposition I have, I want to talk some more. Making the best of my opportunity." He had to laugh at that, and once more glanced over Stone's men, particularly at Malloy, who appeared to fascinate him. "I went down to Winslow to look over a cattle shipment. Prentiss and I. We saw a big herd of stock being loaded on a freight train. Wildest bunch of steers Prentiss ever saw. . . . Well, we only watched the loading for about two minutes. A good many unbranded cattle—and some wearing the Diamond brand. . . . That's my mark, Stone. They were my cattle, and that was all I wanted to know. . . . I met Bambridge at the station and told him he was shipping some of my steers. He laughed it off as a mistake. I needed only one look at him to see he was as crooked as a rail fence. And that *any* man who dealt with him would get the worst of it. So you can bet my talk was pretty sharp. He got nasty and said old Jim Traft had made many such mistakes—or words to that effect, and—but, Stone, what do you think of him accusing my uncle of stealing cattle?"

"Kinda funny," replied Stone. "But the fact of ranchin' is, every cattleman appropriates cattle thet ain't his. It can't be helped. The dishonest cattleman takes advantage of this. All owin' to the custom of the range. No rancher has ever thought of anythin' better than the individual brand. An' thet shore has its defects."

"Bambridge didn't mean in that way," resumed Traft. "Anyway, I got mad and swung on him—but, Stone, maybe you're a friend of Bambridge's?"

The sly quick query was that of a boy and fetched a hollow croak from Malloy, and a smile to the hard face of the outlaw leader.

"Nope. He's shore no friend of mine, an' I'd have liked to see you slug him."

"I was sorry for it afterward. My outfit regretted it. Said it'd lead to worse. But I got hot under the collar, and saw red—"

"Traft, if I don't miss my guess some one will make you *spill* red before you're much older," returned the outlaw, significantly.

"Lord! I hope not," said Traft. "But I don't know what's come over me. Prentiss told me that after I hit Bambridge I pulled my gun and waited. . . . Well, the other thing I wanted particularly to tell you is that we can't find any of my three thousand head of stock. We're camped down among the rocks, and of course we haven't ridden over Yellow Jacket. But Ring Locke told me we'd find my cattle down there in the brakes. But he was wrong. There are a few bulls and steers, wilder than the deer or bear. . . . I'd like to ask—not insinuating anything—if you know where that three thousand head have gone?"

"Wal, Traft, I shore don't," replied Stone, and he was telling the truth.

"Bambridge could tell me, I'll bet a hundred. He hired some one to rustle my stock. I don't accuse you, Stone. I know there is more than one gang in the Tonto Basin. Take the Cibeque outfit, for instance. So if you tell me straight out that the Hash Knife didn't rustle my Diamond cattle—why, I'll believe you."

Then ensued a queer little silence. Stone's men seemed as much concerned with him as the audacity of this young visitor.

"Wal, thet would be kind of you, Traft, an' I reckon foolish. But I'm not tellin' my business, one way or another," replied the Hash Knife leader.

"Which is answer enough for me," returned

Traft, with a shrewd, almost merry twinkle in his clear eyes. "Well—my job here is to clean up Yellow Jacket."

"Uhuh.—Clean it up of what?"

"Wild cattle, rattlesnakes, cow-eating grizzlies and cougars, brush and cactus—and anything else not good for the making of a fine ranch."

"Your Uncle Jim hasn't give you no job atall," said Stone, with a grin. "Where's the common sense comin' in?"

"This visit to you is my first move, except ride around below to look for stock," rejoined the young man, seriously. "I've made up my mind—that if I live through this job I'll build me a fine big roomy log house here and make this place my home."

"Home! . . . Marry some Western gal, I reckon?" went on the outlaw, with interest.

"I've already found her, Stone. . . . No one else than Molly Dunn."

"Molly Dunn!—You don't say? Thet little brown beauty of the Cibeque!—Wal, Traft, I'll say you're a good picker an' a fast mover. I happen to know Molly. Used to run into her at Enoch Summer's store in West Fork. Last time scarce a year ago. . . . Me an' Slinger, her brother, was friends once. She's the prettiest lass an' the best little woman south of Flag."

"Or north, either," said Traft, happily. "Thanks for your compliment. I'll tell her. . . . And see here,

Stone, don't you agree with me that it'd be pretty tough for me to get killed now or shot up bad—with marriage with Molly coming next spring?"

"Shore would be for Molly. She never had nothin' but tough luck. . . . If you feel thet way about her, why go lookin' up chances?"

"I'm not. I'm trying to avoid them. But this Yellow Jacket is a fine ranch. It belongs to me. It's my job.—What can I do?"

Stone shook his head as if the problem was a knotty one.

"Now here's another reason I want to—well, keep my health. Ha! Ha! . . . My sister, nineteen years old, arrived in Flag a few weeks ago. Came to make her home in the West. With me. She's not so well. The doctors think Arizona will make her strong again. So do I. Already she has begun to improve. . . . She wasn't very happy when she first got here. But that's passing. Stone, she's a lovely girl. Full of the devil—and, I'm afraid, stuck up a little—Eastern, you know, but the West will cure her of that, you bet. . . . Now, she's in my charge, not to say more, and even if there wasn't a Molly Dunn to make life so sweet, I'd hate like sixty to fail my sister. . . . So there you are, Jed Stone."

"Thanks. You're shore kind spoken, confidin' in me. . . . It's a hell of a situation for a young man."

"I wanted you to know exactly how I stand," went on Traft, earnestly. "I'm not afraid of a fight, I'm afraid when I get into one I almost like it. But common sense is best. I'm down here to tell you and your outfit to get out of Yellow Jacket. I want to tell you in a decent way, and that I appreciate this range has been like your own. But business is business. You'd do the same. . . . If you don't move off I'll have to try to put you off. And that's no fair deal. The Diamond, even with Slinger Dunn, is no match for the Hash Knife. I may still be a tenderfoot, but I'm no damn fool. A clash will mean a lot of blood spilled. I'd like to avoid it. Not only for my own sake, but for my men, and for that matter for you, too. . . . So I'm putting it up square to you. I can raise ten thousand dollars. That's my limit. Uncle Jim won't help me buy anybody out. I'll give you that to move off, fair and square, like the good fellow I believe you are."

"Traft, I couldn't accept your offer, nohow," returned Stone, pacing the floor with grave face and intent eyes. He made his last move look casual, but he did not like the gleam in Croak Malloy's pale eyes, and wanted to be within reach of the little rattlesnake. Croak did not have to be stepped upon to show his fangs. "Much obliged to you, but shore I couldn't take the money. I'll say, though, thet Jed Stone ain't the man to stand in the way of a young fellar like you. . . . I'll get out of Yellow Jacket for nothin'."

"You will!" cried Traft, in amaze and gladness. "Well, that's darn fine of you, Stone. . . . Uncle Jim *was* right. I—I just can't thank you enough."

"Shore you needn't thank me atall."

"Gosh!—" The young man arose in relief and with shining face stepped forward to offer a hand to Stone. "Shake. I'll always remember you as one of the big lessons the West has taught me, and already they've been more than a few."

Stone gripped hands with him, with no other reply. Then Traft moved back into the sunlight, and halting at the door proceeded to roll a cigarette, in Western fashion and with deft fingers.

"It'll be great to tell the boys. Good day and good luck to you, Stone. . . . And same to your men."

If he had glanced at these men he might not have expressed such good will. As he struck the match and held it to the cigarette there came a ringing crack of a gun. The match vanished. A bullet thudded into the dark logs. Traft suddenly changed into a statue, his empty fingers stiff, his face blanched in a fixed consternation. Then followed another shot. The cigarette whipped out of his mouth and another bullet thudded into the wood.

"Them's my compliments, Mister Jim Traft, junior," croaked Malloy, in a stinging, sarcastic speech full of menace.

Slowly Traft lost his rigidity and turned his head, as if on a pivot, to fix staring eyes upon the little gunman.

"Good God!—Did you shoot that match—and cigarette—" he exclaimed, hoarsely.

"Yep. I didn't want to see you leave without somethin' from the rest of the Hash Knife," replied Croak, significantly.

"But you—you might have shot me—at least, my hand off!" expostulated Traft, the white beginning to leave his face for red.

"Me? Haw! Haw! Haw! . . . I hit what I shoot at, an' you can go back an' tell your Slinger Dunn an' Curly Prentiss thet."

"You —— crooked-faced little runt!" burst out Traft, furiously.

At this juncture Stone took a noiseless and unobtrusive step closer to the sitting Malloy.

It had chanced that of all opprobrium, of all epithets which could have been directed at Croak Malloy, the young rancher had chosen to utter the worst to inflame the gunman. His lean body vibrated as if a sudden powerful current had contracted every muscle, and his face flashed with a hideous deadly light.

As he raised his gun Stone kicked his arm up. The gun went off as it flew into the air. Malloy let out a bellow of rage and pain, and leaped erect, hoding his numbed arm.

"Croak, I reckoned you'd done shootin' enough fer one day," said Stone, coolly.

The little outlaw had no time to reply. Traft sprang at him and in three bounds reached him. He was like a whirlwind. One swift hand fastened in Malloy's shirt and swung him off his feet. The other, doubled into a big fist, swung viciously the other way round. But it missed Malloy's head by an inch. He flung the outlaw, who went staggering over the floor to crash into the door. Traft, light and quick as a cat, was again upon him, even before he could fall, which he surely was going to do. Traft gave him a terrific slap alongside the face, which banged his head against the door. Then he held him there.

"You dirty—little snake!" panted Traft. "You may be a good shot—but you're a damned yellow—coward."

A hard blow from Traft's right sent Malloy's head with sodden thump against the door post. The outlaw swayed forward, only to meet Traft's left swing, which hurtled him through the doorway, out on the ground, where he rolled clear over and lay still.

Traft stood on the threshold, glaring out. Then he stepped back, produced another cigarette and match. His fingers shook so he could hardly light the cigarette. His ruffled hair stood up like a mane. Presently he turned, to give Stone another thrill. It was something for the outlaw to look again into furious blazing honest eyes.

"Reckon I was a little previous," he said, in a voice that rang. "All the same, Stone, I'm wishing *you* good luck."

As he swept out the door Malloy appeared to be attempting to get up, emitting a strange kind of grunt. He was on his hands and knees, back to the cabin. Traft stuck out a heavy boot and gave him a tremendous shove. The little outlaw plunged face forward and slid into the brush.

Stone stood in the doorway and watched Traft's lithe, erect, forceful figure disappear in the trees. Then he laid a humorous and most satisfying gaze upon Malloy. And he muttered, "Somebody will croak for this, an' I hope it's Malloy."

Chapter Eight

JIM TRAFT did not pause in his rapid stride until he had passed through the walled gateway which permitted egress from Yellow Jacket to the rough brakes of the basin below. Then he slowed up along the brawling brook, waiting to compose himself before he arrived at camp. The fire and tumult within him did not soon die down. "Gosh!" he ejaculated. "I get worse all the time. . . . I'm going to kill somebody, some day—sure as the Lord made little apples." And thoughtful review of the experience he had just passed through in the old Yellow Jacket cabin made him correct his exclamation by adding, "if I don't get killed myself."

The trail followed the brook. No one could have guessed from the environment that the season approached midwinter. White cottonwood trees, with gold and russet leaves, and even some tinged with green, lined the amber stream, sending out gnarled and smooth-barked branches across from one bank to the other. Wild turkeys and deer scarcely made an effort to move into the green brush. Jays were squalling, woodpeckers hammering on dead trees, black squirrels barking shrilly. And there was a dreamy hum of murmuring water mingled with a low sough of wind in the great silver spruces and pines. The wildness and ruggedness of this country increased the farther Traft got down the stream. Grass grew luxuriantly in every open patch of ground, mostly bleached, yet some of it still green.

Jim soon left trail and stream to plunge into the forest toward a mighty wall of red and gray rock which towered above the highest pines. A wild steer, ugly as a buffalo bull, crashed into the brush ahead of him. It afforded Jim amusement to have proof that the remnant of his cattle were wilder than the bears and lions. He had met several bears, one a cinnamon and another a grizzly, without making any attempt to run. But sight of a wild Diamond steer always engendered in him a desire to climb a tree.

He reached the wall and flung himself down in a sunny spot surrounded by green on three sides and dominated by the cracked and caverned cliff. If he was compelled to leave Arizona he would always remember it and cherish it by pictures in mind of this marvelous Yellow Jacket country. If the Tonto

Basin, the Cibeque Valley, and especially the Diamond Mesa, across which he had built the now famous drift fence, had fascinated him, what had this wilderness of canyon and forest done? It brought into expression some deep, long-latent force of joy. Hours he had spent alone like this, not worrying over some problem, nor dreaming of Molly—which happened often enough—but not thinking of anything at all. It was a condition of mind Jim had not inquired into, because he realized it was pure happiness, and he feared an analysis would dispel it. And the enchantment fastened down strong upon him, so that it alternated with a serious consideration of what he had just passed through at the outlaw camp.

"I've made another blunder," he soliloquized, regretfully. "Stone proved to be a decent fellow, as Uncle Jim vowed he was. . . . But Stone is not all of the Hash Knife. Whew! . . . That little hatchet-faced ruffian!—Sure he scared me, and I reckon I wasn't in any danger from his playful bullets. But, my God! when I cursed him—if Stone hadn't kicked his arm up—I'd be dead now! . . . That was Croak Malloy, sure as hops. Reckon I'll remember his face. And any of them. Sure a hard crowd! . . . They'll probably buck against Stone about leaving Yellow Jacket. But he struck me as a man who'd be dangerous to cross. . . . Anyway, I made a good impression on him. . . . I'll put the matter up to the boys and see what they say."

If Jed Stone did really keep his word and abandon Yellow Jacket, how that would simplify the big task there! Jim would put the boys to cutting, peeling, and dragging pine logs down to the site where he wanted to erect a wonderful house. He had meant to clean up that ragged brushy end of Yellow Jacket, but after seeing it he had changed his mind. He would not even tear down the old log cabin where the Hash Knife outfit had held forth so long. In time this cabin would become a relic of Arizona's range days. It would take all winter to cut the logs, rip-saw the boards, split the shingles, and pack in the accessories for the ranch-house Jim had planned.

If Stone moved off peacefully and took his men—about whom Jim was most dubious—then it would be possible for Jim to go back to Flag for Christmas. What a thrilling idea! It warmed him into a genial glow. But another thought followed swiftly—the cowboys of his outfit would go back to Flag also. And that would be terrible. He groaned when he recalled the Thanksgiving dinner and dance which his Uncle Jim had given in honor of Gloriana May Traft. It had been a marvelous occasion, attended by everybody in or around Flagerstown, and something about which the cowboys raved more and more as time passed. Or it was Gloriana about whom they raved! What havoc that purple-eyed, white-faced girl had wrought. She had looked like a princess—and had flirted like a—a—Jim did not know what. She had even enticed Slinger Dunn to dance—a feat Molly avowed was without parallel. And she had showed open preference for handsome Curly Prentiss, which fact had gone to the head of this erstwhile gay and simple cowboy. He had made life for Bud and Cherry, not to mention the others, almost insupportable. Yet it all—the whole situation following that unforgettable dance—was so deliciously funny. All except the stunned look of Molly's eyes—as Jim recalled it! Molly had not been jealous. She, too, had been carried away by Gloriana's lovely face and charming personality. But there was something wrong with Molly. And Jim had been compelled to leave Flag almost before he realized that the advent of his sister had brought about some strange change in Molly's happiness.

It required submission to the dream of love and of the future to dispel Jim's dread, and his regret. His faith in Molly's tenderness was infinitely stronger than all doubt. He knew he had won her and that always he could prevail. This imperious sister, Gloriana, with her charm, and the distinction of family and class which seemed to hang upon her words and every action, might cause the sincere and simple Arizona lass the mortification and realization of what she considered her own humble station, but they were really chimeras, and would pass in time.

Jim had only to recall the last moments he had spent with Molly, her betrayal of self, her utter devotion, and her passionate love, to which she was gradually surrendering. These sufficed here, as they had before in moments of gloom, to lift him buoyantly to the skies again.

At last he got up and wended a devious way toward camp, preoccupied and tranquil. He was so absentminded that when Slinger Dunn appeared as if by magic, right out of the green wall of foliage, he sustained a violent shock that was not all thrill.

"You darned Injun!" he ejaculated, in relief, "always scaring me stiff."

"Howdy, Boss. I reckon you spend a heap of time heah-aboots—sittin' in the sun," replied Dunn.

There was no help for it—Jim could not leave camp or approach it, or hide, or in any way escape the vigilance of this backwoodsman. It rather pleased Jim, who recognized in it a protective watchfulness. His cowboys were always concerned, sometimes unduly, when he was absent. And the acquisition of Slinger Dunn to the outfit had been hailed with loud acclaim.

Slinger leaned on his rifle and regarded Jim with eyes like Molly's, only darker and piercing as the points of daggers. He was bareheaded, as he went usually, and his long hair almost lay upon his shoulders. He wore buckskin, which apparel singularly distinguished him from the cowboys. In his backwoods way Slinger was fastidious, or so it seemed. His simple woodsman's costume partook of the protective hue of foliage and rock, according to which furnished a background.

"Jim, you look sorta worried," he observed.

"Huh! Small wonder, Slinger."

"How'd Jed treat you?"

"Fine. He's a good fellow, even if he is an outlaw."

"Shore I reckoned you'd like Jed. But I was skeered of Croak Malloy, an' thet slippery greaser sheep-herder."

"I didn't get a line on the Mexican you called Sonora. But, Slinger, I formed the acquaintance of Mister Malloy, croak and gun and all. I did! . . . Wait till we reach camp. I don't want to have to tell it twice. . . . How are the boys? I swear I'm afraid to leave them alone these days."

"Hell to pay," grinned Slinger, showing his white teeth, and his black eyes had a gleam of fun.

"Now what?" demanded Jim, perturbed.

"Curly busted Bud one on the nose."

"Oh! . . . Is that all?"

"Wal, it shore was enough, leastways for Bud."

"Aw, they're pards, the best of friends. They worship each other, even if they do scrap all the time. What was it about this time?"

"Somethin' about Gloriana's laigs," drawled Slinger.

"Wh-hat!" exclaimed Jim, astounded and furious.

142

"I didn't heah Bud. But you could have heahed Curly a mile. He roared like a mad bull. An' I near died laffin'. I'll shore have fun tellin' Gloriana aboot it."

"Oh, the —— you will?" queried Jim, constrainedly.

Slinger was an entirely new element in the Diamond outfit and assuredly an unknown quantity. He was naïve to the point of doubt, and absolutely outspoken. "Better tell me first."

It appeared, presently, that Bud Chalfack, as frank and innocent in his cowboy way as Slinger was in his backwoods fashion, had been talking about Gloriana's pretty feet, ankles, and so on, much to Curly's disgust. And when Bud nonchalantly added that Gloriana was not wholly blind to the grace and beauty of her nether extremities Curly had taken offense. He could allow no insult to his young lady friend from the East, and despite Bud's protest he punched him on the nose.

Jim held himself in until he reached camp. He did not know whether to explode with wrath or glee. But the incident might prove to have advantages. Gloriana had upset the outfit; and Jim had found himself at a loss to combat the situation. He grasped at straws.

The camp site, assuredly the most beautiful Jim had seen, was in a break of the wall, where a little brown brook ran crystal clear over stones and between grassy banks. A few lofty silver spruces lorded it over an open glade, which the sun touched with gold. Huge blocks of cliff had fallen and rolled out. Boulders as large as houses stood half hidden by pines. Ferns and amber trailing vines colored the rock wall behind. Camp paraphernalia lay around in picturesque confusion that suited the lounging cowboys.

Jim stalked toward the boys. He must maintain tremendous dignity and make all possible use of this opportunity. Curly got up, his fine face flushing, and made a halfhearted advance, which he checked. Jim divined that this young man was not sure of his stand. Bud sat apart, disconsolate, and nursing a bloody nose.

"What's this Slinger tells me?" Jim demanded, in a loud voice. "You insulted my sister?"

"Aw no, Boss. Honest t'Gawd I never did," burst out Bud, in distress.

"Is Slinger a liar, then?"

"Yes he is, dog-gone-it, if he says so," retorted Bud.

"And Curly slugged you for nothing?"

"Not egzactly nuthin', Boss," replied Bud. "I—I did say somethin', but I meant nuthin'."

"Bud Chalfack, did you dare to speak of my sister's legs—here in this camp of low-down cowboys?" demanded Jim, as he leaned over to jerk Bud to his feet.

"Aw, Jim. Fer Heaven's sake—listen," begged Bud. "Shore I—I said somethin', but it was compliment an' no insult."

Jim placed a boot behind Bud and tripped him, spread him on the grass, and straddling him, lifted a big menacing fist.

"Aw, Jim, don't hit me. I got enough from Curly. An' he cain't hit as hard as you."

"I'll smash your wagging jaw!"

"I'm sorry, Boss. I—I was jest excited, an' talkin' aboot how pretty Miss Gloriana is. An' I reckon I was jest seein' if I could rile Curly. It shore did. . . . I swear I didn't mean nuthin'. An' I apologize."

"What'd you say?" demanded Jim, his fist still uplifted.

"Aw, I forget. It wasn't nuthin' atall."

"Curly, come here," called Jim, sharply, and as the red-faced cowboy advanced reluctantly Jim went on: "Since you had the gall to constitute yourself my sister's champion you can tell me just what this blackguard did say. Don't you dare lie!"

Curly seemed to be in a worse predicament than Bud, though for no apparent cause, unless it was Jim's great displeasure. He did not look like the chivalrous defender of a young girl. But presently he got it out, thereby acquainting Jim with the exact words and nature of Bud's offense. Jim could have shrieked with glee, though he acted the part of an avenging Nemesis. Curly was the deceitful one who had taken advantage of Bud's ravings; and Bud was the innocent victim, scared terribly by Jim's wrath and a dereliction he could not quite understand.

"Ahuh. So this is the kind of a cowboy you are," shouted Jim, raising his fist higher. "I'll beat you good, Bud Chalfack. . . . Do you crawfish? Do you take it back?"

"No—damn' if I do!" cried Bud, righteous anger rising out of his grief. "You can beat all you want. What I said I *said,* an' I'll stick to it. . . . 'Cause it's true, Jim Traft."

Jim solemnly regarded the prostrate cowboy, while poising aloft the clenched mace of retribution. Bud's true spirit had flashed out. In his code of honor he had not transgressed. But Jim did not like the familiarity with which the boys bandied about Gloriana's charms. It was absolutely inevitable, it was Western, and there was not any harm in it; nevertheless, he was inconsistent enough to see the humor of it and still resent.

Suddenly an idea occurred to Jim and in an instant he accepted it as a way of escape out of the dilemma. He certainly had not intended to strike Bud, unless there was real offense. He released the cowboy and got up.

"Bud, you are hopeless," he said, with pretense of sorrow and resignation. "No use to beat you! That'd be no adequate punishment. I'll make you an example. . . . I'll *tell* Glory what you said about her!"

"Aw—Boss!" gasped Bud.

"I shall, Bud Chalfack. Then we'll see where you get off."

"But, Jim, for Gawd's sake, think! You'd have to tell her Curly punched me for it. Then I'd be wuss'n a coyote an' he'd be a hero. Thet'd be orful, Jim, an' you jest cain't be so mean."

"Curly never talked exactly that same way about Gloriana, did he?"

"No, I never heered him, but I reckon he thinks it an' more'n thet, too, you bet."

"Bud, if you admire a girl and *must* gab about her, why not confine yourself to her eyes, her hair, or mouth? Couldn't you be satisfied to say her eyes were like wells of midnight, her hair spun gold, and her lips sweet as red cherries?"

"Hellyes, I could. But I never swallered no dictionary. An' dog-gone-it, any bootiful girl has more'n eyes an' hair an' lips, hasn't she?"

"Nevertheless, I shall tell Gloriana," returned Jim, inexorably.

"Boss, I'll take the beatin'," implored Bud.

"No, you won't, Bud. You'll take your medicine. And pretty soon, too. We're all going back to Flag for Christmas. Jed Stone agreed to get off Yellow Jacket and that leaves us free, for the present, anyway."

"*Whoop-ee!*" yelled the outfit, in a united chorus.

Only Bud was not radiant. "I'll get drunk an' disgrace the outfit," he avowed.

"Listen, men, and tell me what you make of this deal," said Jim, and seating himself on a pack while the cowboys gathered around, he began a detailed account of his visit to the Hash Knife outfit. He took longer than usual in the telling of an incident, because he wanted to be specific and not omit a single impression. When he had finished there was a blank silence, rather perturbing. At length Slinger Dunn broke it:

"My Gawd! Boss, you're as good as daid!" he ejaculated, with the only expression of concern Jim had ever seen on his dark impassive face.

Curly Prentiss broke out: "Jim! You've slugged the dangerousest gunman in Arizona!"

One by one the others vented similar opinions, until only Bud was left to express himself.

"Boss, you're a tenderfoot, same as when you come West," declared that worthy. "You cain't be trusted with a job like thet. Didn't I ast to go? Didn't I *tell* you to take Curly? You dod-blasted jackass! Now you've played hell!"

"So it appears," returned Jim, sober-faced.

"If you'd only shot Malloy when you had the chanct," said Slinger, moodily.

"But I didn't pack a gun," expostulated Jim. "I went unarmed so that I couldn't shoot anybody."

"Wal, Boss, you shore made another mistake," spoke up Curly. "Jed Stone is square. He'll keep his word. But he's only the brains of the Hash Knife. Croak Malloy haids the gun end of thet outfit. An' if he doesn't shoot up Arizona now, I'll miss my guess."

"Well, it's too late. I'm sorry. I sure was mad. And I'd have slammed that dirty little rat around if it was the last thing on earth. . . . But let's get our heads together. What'll we do? Slinger, you talk first."

"Better lay low an' wait while I watch the trails. Jed will go, but he might go alone. An' I'm shore tellin' you *if* he goes alone the Hash Knife will be ten times wuss'n ever."

"I reckon he'll get off Yellow Jacket an' persuade the outfit to follow," said Curly. "Stone is a persuasive cuss, I've heahed men say. An' Yellow Jacket is cleaned out of cattle. They've made way with your Diamond stock, Jim, an' once more you're a poor cowboy. Haw! Haw!"

"They're welcome to my stock, if they only vamoose," returned Jim, fervently.

"Boss, they shore ain't welcome to the half of thet stock you gave me," declared Dunn, darkly. "I was pore, an' all of a sudden I felt rich. An' now—"

"Slinger, you still have your half interest in what cattle are left and what I'll drive in," replied Jim. "My uncle won't see us left stripped."

"Wal, thet's different," said Slinger, brightening.

"You stay off the war-path, you darned redskin," interposed Curly. "We're shore goin' to need you. . . . Now, Boss, heah's the deal in a nutshell, as I see it. An' I know these rustlin' outfits. Jed Stone will change his base. But he won't get out of the brakes. There's rich pickin' on the range below. The Hash Knife will hide down heah, an' then go to operatin' big an' bold. Stone will throw thet outfit down or I don't read the signs correct. An' as Slinger says, then the Hash Knife will be worse. Somebody will have to kill Malloy or we cain't do any ranchin' in these parts. Shore everythin' will be quiet till spring."

Jim maintained a long, thoughtful silence. He respected Curly Prentiss' judgment, and could not recall an instance when it had been wrong. Curly was young, but old in range wisdom. Then his intelligence and education were far above that of the average cowboy.

"Very well," finally said Jim. "We'll stick close to camp, with two guards out day and night. Slinger will watch the Hash Knife gang and report. So until then—I guess we'll have to play mumbly-peg."

"Say, Boss, I ain't a-goin' to stop fishin' fer all the doggone rustlers in Arizonie," declared Bud, rebelliously.

"Fishing? You're crazy, Bud. Something has affected your mind. I declare I don't wonder at Curly's effort to make you think. Fishing in December!"

"Boss, I ain't the only one whose gray matter is off," replied Bud, and from the way he got up and hitched his overalls Jim knew something was coming. Bud's glance had distinctly charged Jim with an affection of the brain. Bud stalked to a spruce tree, reached in the foliage, and drew forth a string of trout that made Jim's eyes bulge and the cowboys yell.

"Jim, you know a heap aboot the West—aboot wild turkeys an' deer an' trout—an' cowboys an' cowthieves—an' Western gurls—now, don't you?"

"Bud, I—I don't know much," admitted Jim, weakly. "Trout in December! . . . Gosh! that's one on me. I thought it was winter. Boy, I'll give you a new gun if you'll show me where you caught them."

"I should smile not," returned Bud. "An' there ain't another fellar in this locoed outfit who could show you, either."

"Shore is a fact, Boss," said Curly. "Bud's a rotten hunter, but as a fisherman he's got us trimmed to a frazzle. Fish just walk out on the bank an' die at his feet."

Jim was studying the disfigured face of the disgruntled Bud. He could read that worthy's mind. Bud would move heaven and earth to keep him from telling Gloriana about the disrespectful gossip.

"Stay in camp. You hear me?" said Jim, sternly.

"I heah you, Boss. I ain't deaf."

Two lazy idle yet watchful days passed. Slinger did not return until long after dark of the second day, so long that it took persuasion by Curly to

allay Jim's anxiety. Slinger came in with Uphill
Frost, who had been on guard down the trail and
who had missed the supper hour.

"The Hash Knife gang is gone," announced
Frost loudly. "I seen the whole caboodle ride by,
an' I damn near took a peg at thet Croak Malloy."

"What!—You sure, Up?" shouted Jim, leaping
excitedly to his feet.

"Yep. I wisht I was as sure of heaven. It was
aboot two o'clock this afternoon. I'd come back
sooner, but Slinger slipped up on me an' told me
to wait till he got back. There was eight of 'em an'
they had a string of pack-horses."

"Slinger, where'd they go?" asked Jim, breathlessly.

"I followed them ten miles, an' when I turned
back they was travelin'," returned Dunn.
"Tomorrer I'll take a hoss. I reckon they're makin'
fer the Black Brakes."

"How far is that?"

"Aboot twenty miles as the crow flies."

"Too close for comfort."

"Boss, I sneaked up almost within earshot of the
cabin," went on Dunn. "Fust off this mawnin' I
seen the greaser Sonora wranglin' their hosses.
An' as he's the only one of thet outfit I'm skeered
of I went up the crick an' crawled up in the brush.
I got close enough to heah voices, but not what
they said. Shore was a hell of a argyment, though.
They'd pack awhile, then fight awhile. Reckon I

didn't need to heah. All as plain as tracks to me. Malloy kicked on quittin' Yellow Jacket an' most of the outfit was with him. But Stone was too strong. An' along aboot noon they rode off."

"Yippy-yip!" yelled Jim, in wild elation. "Gone without a scrap. Gosh! but I'm glad."

"Boss, you shore air previous," spoke up Bud, with sarcasm. "Thet Hash Knife gang hev only rid off aways to hide till you throw up a fine big cabin. Then they'll come back an' take it away from you."

"They will like—h-hob," stammered Jim.

"Thet'll be like Malloy," admitted Slinger. "I'm afeered they went off too willin'."

"Shore is aboot the deal to expect," chimed in Curly, cheerfully. "But life is short in Arizona an' who knows?—Malloy may croak before spring."

"Curly Prentiss, you've somethin' on your mind," declared Jim, darkly.

"Humph! It's only curly hair an' sometimes a sombrero," said Bud.

"Shore. I'm a thoughtful cuss. Always reckonin' fer my friends an' my boss."

"An' your next sweetheart."

"Bud, old pard, for me there'll never be no next one."

"Boys, we'll build the house," interposed Jim with decision that presupposed heretofore he had been only dreaming. "Jeff, we'll break camp at daylight. Better pack some tonight. We'll hit the trail for Yellow Jacket. Gosh! I'm glad! . . . We'll keep Slinger on watch, and the rest of us will cut, peel, an' make pine poles out of the woods."

"Swell job fer genuine cowpunchers," observed Bud, satirically.

"I've ridden all over Yellow Jacket, Jim," spoke up Curly. "Some years ago. But shore there's timber to build a town. Grandest place for a ranch! It'd be tough to spend a lot of coin on it, an' work a good outfit to death, an' haul in stuff to make a nice home, an' fetch your little Western bride down fer your honeymoon—an' then stop one of Croak Malloy's bullets. . . . Shore would be tough!"

"Curly, you're a blamed pessimist," burst out Jim. "Don't you ever have any dreams?"

"Me?—Never once in my life," drawled Curly.

"Boss, he's dreamin' now—an' if you knowed what it's aboot you'd punch *him* on his handsome nose," said Bud revengefully.

"Bud, you surprise me," rejoined Jim, mildly. Then he advised the outfit to turn in and be up at daylight.

Jim rode through the colorful rock-wall gateway of Yellow Jacket, imagining himself Vercingetorix riding his black stallion at the head of his army into one of the captured cities.

On his hurried visit to Jed Stone he had scarcely noted details of this wild and beautiful retreat. But now he had eyes for everything.

"Wal, we'll shore have hell cuttin' a road in heah," Curly was observing. "Reckon it'll have to be at the up end of the canyon."

The trail wound among big sycamores and spruces, a remarkable combination for contrast, of green and white and silver, and of gold. The brook brawled between mossy banks of amber moss, and at the ford it was deep enough and swift enough to make the horses labor.

"Cain't cross heah in a spring an' fall freshet, that's shore," went on Curly. "By golly! this place gets under my skin."

Blocks of red and yellow rock lay scattered beyond the gateway, with tall pines and spruces shading them, except in occasional grassy open sunlit nooks. The gray walls converged from the gate, sculptured by nature into irregular and creviced ramparts, festooned with bright-red vines and bronze lichens, and with ledges supporting little spruces, and with crags of every shape lifting weathered tops to the fringe of pines on the rim.

There was a long slow ascent thinning from forest to parklike ground up to the old cabin. Indeed, Jim meant to preserve this relic of rustler and outlaw days.

"What's thet white thing stuck on the door? Looks like paper to me," said the sharp-eyed Bud.

Curiously they rode up to the cabin, dismounting one by one. Jim saw a dirty page of a lined notebook pegged into the rotten woodwork of the door. Upon it was scrawled in a crude but legible handwriting the word "Mañana." And under it had been drawn the rude sketch of a hash knife, somehow compelling and suggestive.

"Dog-gone! What'd they mean?" exclaimed Jim, in perplexity.

"Clear as print," replied Curly, tersely.

"Wal, heah's four bits thet Croak Malloy left thet," added Slinger.

"Well?" demanded Jim, impatiently.

"Boss, yore mind's so full of ranch an' house an'—wal, an' so forth, thet it ain't workin'," explained Bud. "Mañana means tomorrer. An' the knife says they'll come back pronto to make hash out of us."

"Oh, is that all?" returned Jim, with a laugh. "Bud, life does not seem very bright and hopeful for you just now."

"Hellno! I got brains an' six-sense eyesight," replied the gloomy cowboy.

"We'll throw the packs under the pine trees there. No sleeping in that buggy cabin for me," said Jim. "Jeff, I'd rather you didn't cook here unless it storms. You can build a fireplace under the extension roof there. . . . Say, there's an open-roofed extension at the back, too. Used for horses. Well, here we are. Let's rustle. Slinger, your job is to use your eyes."

"Boss, there's two holes to this burrow," spoke up Bud.

"Where's the other?"

"Reckon its aboot three miles west, where the canyon boxes," replied Curly, pointing. "Higher an' not so rough. If I recollect, the trail grades down easy. We'll cut the road through there. It'll take some blastin'."

"We'll take a chance on that end," said Jim. "Bud, I tell you what you can do. While we pitch camp you ride up and find the best place to cut our poles. But remember, it must be back in the woods, out of sight. No defacing the beauty of this property!"

"Funny how some fellars are," observed Bud, philosophizing. "Beooty first an' last, an' always in wimmen."

Then he rode away. Jim gazed after him in perplexity. "What's wrong with Bud?" he asked.

"His nose an' his feelin's are hurt," replied Cherry Winters.

"You forget, Boss. You swore you'd give him away," drawled Curly. "An' the poor kid is in love. I've seen him like this sixty-nine times."

"Rustle, you gazabos," ordered Jim, rather sharply, as he dismounted. It scarcely pleased him—the implication that Bud was in love with his sister. How true it might be and probably was! Everybody fell in love with Gloriana, who certainly was not worth such wholesale homage. Right there Jim eradicated the last remnant of foolish pride or vanity of family or whatever it was, and acknowledged to himself that Gloriana could do far worse then marry a fine, clean, fire-spirited cowboy like Curly Prentiss. Suppose Curly had looked at a good deal of red liquor—had shot a number of men, some fatally—and had been generally a wild harum-scarum cowboy? That was the way of the West—the making of a pioneer rancher. Jim was beginning to appreciate the place cowboys held in the settling of the rangeland. It could not be overestimated by an intelligent man. Thus he leaned a little, perhaps almost unconsciously, toward Curly in the vague and grave problem of his sister's future.

Jim set the outfit to work, and had no small hand in the cutting and trimming of pine poles. Bud had located a fine stand of long straight trees, growing so close together that there was scarcely any foliage except at the top. This particular grove would benefit by a good thinning out. The peeling of the green bark was no slight task. Some of the boys proved adept at that. And Bud and Lonestar were good at snaking the logs down to the cabin site. Jim had tried this "snaking" job more than once, and he simply could not do it. All it consisted of appeared to be a lasso around the pommel of the saddle, with the other end tied to the small end of a pole, and then a dragging through the woods. The trick was, of course, to keep the small sharp end of the pole off the ground, and from catching under roots and rocks.

By sunset that first day there were a dozen or more skinned pines, yellow and sticky and odorous, lying in a row in the grass where Jim intended to build his wonderful house. It was an actual start. He thrilled, and thought of the dusky-eyed girl for whom he was going to make a home there.

Ten days of uninterrupted labor followed. Slinger Dunn had trailed the Hash Knife outfit to Black Brakes, the very retreat to which he had surmised they would go; and according to him they had stayed there, or at least had not ridden north on the trail toward Yellow Jacket. When Jim allowed himself to think of it he was vastly concerned. The prospect of a ranch and a home within twenty miles of the hardest and most notorious gang in Arizona was almost unthinkable. They would have to be dealt with. Nevertheless, Jim nursed a conviction that Jed Stone would turn out to be the kind of man Uncle Jim had vowed he was. To be sure, all Jim had to substantiate such faith was the fact of Stone's leaving Yellow Jacket, and an undefinable something Jim felt.

One night Jim overheard Curly and Bud talking. It was late, the fire had died down so that it cast only ruddy flickering shadows, and no doubt the boys thought Jim was sound asleep. Bud had seemed more like his true self lately, and had forgiven the blow on his nose and the affront to his vanity. He worshiped Curly like a brother.

"It's a fool job, I tell you, Curly," Bud was saying, almost in a whisper. "Like as not Malloy will burn this pile of logs while we're in Flag."

"Shore he will, or more like wait till the house is half up," agreed Curly. "But, dog-gone-it, Bud, I cain't go against the boss. He has a way of makin' me soft. Shore as hell he'll stop my drinkin'. I'm jest a-rarin' fer a bust. It's due in Flag this heah trip, an' honest to God, Bud, I'll be afraid to take a drink."

"I feel the same, but I'm gonna get orful drunk onct more or die tryin'. . . . Curly, if you don't watch out Jim will argue you or coax you to stop gun-throwin'. An' then you'll be slated for a quiet rest under a pine tree!"

"Uh-ugh. I practice just the same as ever, Bud, only on the sly."

"Wal, I'm glad. If I don't miss my bet we're gonna need some gun-throwin'. Slinger don't like this 'possum-playin' of the Hash Knife. He knows. Curly, what do you think? Slinger was tellin' me he reckoned he oughta dog them rustlers, an' pick them off one at a time, with a rifle."

"Slinger cain't do thet, no more than I could. Shore I'm not Injun enough. But you know what I mean.—What'd you say, Bud?"

"I ast him why he oughta. An' he said for Molly's sake."

"Shore. Thet same thing worries me a lot. I

160

never seen a girl love a fellar like she loves Jim. Dog-gone! It'd shore be . . . Wal, Croak Malloy will shoot Jim the first time he lays eyes on him, no matter where."

"Curly, I agree with you. Croak would. But I bet you Slinger gets to him first. Because, Curly, old pard, our backwoods cowboy is turribly in love with Gloriana May. Did you get thet?"

Curly swore surprisingly for him, and not under his breath by any means.

"Not so loud. You'll wake up somebody," admonished Bud, in a fierce whisper.

"Shore he is, Bud," admitted Curly. "But thet's nothin'. I've lost my haid. So've you, an' all the boys. The hell of it is Glory is in love with Slinger."

"Wow! You *are* out of your haid. He amuses Glory—fascinates her, mebbe, 'cause she's crazy aboot desperadoes, but thet's all, pard," returned Bud, with all the heartwarming loyalty of his nature.

"Shore sounds queer—for me to say that aboot Glory," went on Curly. "Lord knows I mean no disrespect. She's a thoroughbred. But, Bud, jest consider. She's an Easterner. She's young. She's full of sentiment an' romance. An' she's had some kind of trouble. Deep. An' it's hurt her. Wal, this damn Slinger Dunn is far better-lookin' than any of us—than any cow-puncher I ever seen. He's a wonderful chap, Bud. If I wasn't so jealous of him

161

that I want to shoot him in the back—I—I'd love him myself. It wouldn't be so strange for a gurl like Glory to fall haid over heels in love with him. An', honest, I'm scared so I'm afraid to go to Flag."

"Nonsense! Any damn fool could hev' seen you had the inside track with Glory. Sure, if you back out an' show yellow, Slinger, or somebody else, will beat you. Don't you think I'm backin' out. I reckon Glory couldn't see me with a spy-glass, but I'm in the race an' I got a flyin' start. When I raved aboot Slinger havin' her picture she gave me one, an' a darn sight newer an' prettier than his."

Curly swore again. "Wal, can you beat thet? Shore she wouldn't give one to me. . . . Women are no good, Bud."

"I wouldn't say it's thet bad, Curly," replied Bud. "They're damn hard to figger. I reckon Glory just likes me. Why, she laughs an' cuts up with me. She's sorta shy with you."

"Shy nothin'. Shore I haven't seen her a lot of times—that is, to talk to. Twice at the corral—three times in the livin'-room, when I went in to see Jim—once at Babbitt's store—an' at the dance. That was the best. My Gawd! I cain't get back my breath. . . . Bud, she was only curious aboot my gun-play. It makes me sick as a dog to remember the fights I've been in, let alone talk aboot them. But she kept at me till I got mad. Then she froze an' said she guessed I wasn't much of a desperado, after all."

"Haw! Haw!" laughed Bud, low and mellow. "Curly, what thet little lady needs is a dose of Croak Malloy."

Chapter Nine

JIM blazed a road out of Yellow Jacket. His authority was not questioned by any one of the cowboys, but his ability as an engineer certainly was.

"You gotta drive wagons up this grade," asserted Bud, repeatedly. "You wasn't so pore runnin' a straight-line drift fence, but this hyar's a different matter. You don't savvy grades."

"All right, Bud. Maybe I'm not so darn smart as I think I am," replied Jim, laying a trap for Bud. "Suppose we go back and run it all over. You can be the engineer. That'll cut two days off our Christmas vacation in Flag. Too bad, but that road must be right."

The howl that went up from the Diamond was vociferous and derisive, and it effectually disposed of Bud.

"Aw, Bost, mebbe it ain't. I reckon it'll work out—an' any little grade can be eased up after," he rejoined, meekly.

Twenty miles on through the slowly ascending forest they struck a cattle trail which afforded good travel, and in due course led them to the Payson road, and eventually the ranch where they had left the chuck-wagon. They stayed there all night, and the following night camped at the edge of the snow, only one more day's ride to Flag.

Next afternoon late a tired, cold, dirty, unshaven, but happy group of cowboys rode into town, and there they separated. Jim had reasons to shake Curly and Bud, and they manifested no great desire to continue on with him.

Flagerstown was windy and bleak. The snow had been shoveled or had blown off the streets, down which piercing dusty gusts whipped in Jim's face. But it would have taken an unfaceable blizzard or an impassable prairie fire to have daunted Jim's soaring spirits. He had two important errands before rushing out to the ranch, and he did not want them to take long, for his horse was pretty warm. Dismounting in front of the jeweler's, Jim hurried in. The proprietor, with whom Jim had left an order, was not in, but his son was, a young Westerner whom Jim did not like.

"Mr. Miller in?" he asked.

"No. Father's out of town. But I can wait on you. . . . The diamond ring is here—if you still want it," returned the young man.

Jim stared. What in the devil did this nincompoop mean?

"Certainly I want it. I paid in advance. Let me have it, quick, please," retorted Jim.

The jeweler produced a little white box, from which glistened a beautiful diamond. Jim took it, trying to be cool, but he was burning and thrilling all over. Molly's engagement ring! It was a beauty—pretty big and valuable, he thought, now he actually saw what he had ordered. Molly would be surprised. She did not even know Jim had ordered it. And sight of her eyes, when they fell upon it, would be worth ten times the price.

"Thanks. I reckon it's all right. I was careful about size," said Jim, and pocketing the ring he strode out to his horse, which he led down the street. "Funny look that gazabo gave me," he soliloquized, thoughtfully, and he dismissed the incident by admitting to himself he must have been rather amusing to the clerk. Then he went into Babbitt's, where he had left another order, for a Christmas present for his uncle, and one for Molly. Securing the packages, which were rather large and heavy, and which he did not trouble to open, he hurried out through the store. In the men's-furnishing department a bright red silk scarf caught his eye, and he swerved to the counter.

"I'd like that red scarf," he said to the girl clerk, "and a pair of buckskin gloves."

The girl neither spoke nor moved. Then Jim looked at her—and there stood Molly Dunn, with white and agitated face. Jim was perfectly thunderstruck. Could he be dreaming? But Molly's gasp, "Oh—Jim!" proved this was reality.

"What—what does this mean?" he stammered.

"I'm workin' heah, Jim," she whispered. "Mawnin's I go to school an' afternoons I'm heah."

"For Heaven's sake!—A clerk in Babbitt's?" he exclaimed.

"Di-didn't you—get my letter?" she faltered, her eyes unnaturally large and frightened.

"Letter? No, I didn't. How could I get a letter when I've been three weeks in the woods?"

"I—I left it—with your uncle."

"Molly, I just rode in. Haven't been home. What's wrong? Why are you here?" Jim leaned against the counter, fighting to check the whirl of his thoughts. Molly's eyes suddenly expressed a poignant dismay.

"Oh, Jim—I'm so sorry—you had to come in heah—not knowin'," she cried, piteously. "I wouldn't have hurt you. . . . But I—I've left your home. . . . I've broke our engagement."

"Molly!" he ejaculated, in hoarse incredulity.

"It's true, Jim. . . . But you mustn't stand there—"

"Why, for God's sake?" he burst out.

"Please go, Jim. I—I'll see you later—an' tell you—"

"No. You can tell me here why you jilted me," he interrupted, harshly.

"Missouri—I—I didn't," she said, huskily, tears streaming down her cheeks.

"Was Gloriana mean to you?" Jim suddenly demanded.

"She was lovely to me. Kind an' sweet. An' she—she tried to meet me on my own level—so I wouldn't see the difference be—between us . . . but I did. I—I wasn't fit to be her sister. I shore wasn't goin' to disgrace you. So I—I left an' come heah to work. Mother went back home to the Cibeque."

"You swear Glory didn't hurt you?"

"No, Jim, I cain't swear thet. But she never hurt me on purpose. There's nothin' mean aboot your sister. . . . I just loved her—an' thet made it worse."

"Molly Dunn, you're a damn little fool," exploded Jim, overcome by a frenzy of pain and fury. "You were good enough for *any* man, let alone me. . . . But if you're as fickle—as that—"

Jim choked, and gathering up his packages he gave Molly a terrible look and rushed out of the store.

In an ordinary moment he could not have mounted his horse, burdened as he was, but he leaped astride, scarcely feeling the weight of the packages. And he spurred Baldy into a run, right down the main street of Flagerstown. The violence of action suited the violent tumult in his breast. But by the time he reached the ranch-house the furious anger had given away somewhat to consternation and a stunned surprise. That simple, honest, innocent child! But even so she might be protecting Gloriana. Jim left his horse at the barn, and taking his bundles he ran into the house and into the living-room, bursting in upon the old cattleman like a hurricane.

"Jim! Good Lord! I thought it was Injuns," exclaimed Traft. "Wal, I expected you along soon. How are you, son?"

"Howdy, Uncle," replied Jim, throwing aside his bundles and meeting the glad hand extended. "I *was* fine till I struck town. . . . Glad to report the Hash Knife got off Yellow Jacket without a fight."

"Jim Traft!—You're not foolin' the old man?"

"No, I'm happy to say. It's a fact, Uncle."

"Wal!—You long-headed, big-fisted tenderfoot son-of-a-gun from Mizzouri! . . . Jim, I'm clear locoed. I'm dead beat. I'm—wal, I don't know what. How'n hell did you do it?"

"I went straight to see Jed Stone."

"You braved thet outfit?" yelled Traft.

"Sure. Jed Stone was sure decent. He agreed to get out. But Croak Malloy shot a match out of my fingers, then the cigarette out of my mouth. I sure was mad. I cussed him—called him a crooked-faced little runt. He'd shot at *me* then, but Stone kicked his gun. It went off in the air. Then I piled into Croak. I banged him around— then knocked him about a mile out of the door. He was trying to get up when I went out, and I gave him a good stiff kick, and left."

"My Gawd!—Son, don't tell me you punched thet gunman, same as these cowboys?" ejaculated Traft.

"I reckon I did, Uncle. It was foolish, of course. But I was mad. And I didn't know then that the little runt was Malloy. It mightn't have made any difference."

"Croak Malloy! Beat and kicked around by a Mizzouri tenderfoot! . . . Jim, my boy, you're as good as dead," wailed the old rancher.

"Don't you believe it," retorted Jim. "And how long do I have to serve as a tenderfoot. . . . Well, no more about Hash Knife now. We moved up to Yellow Jacket and went to cutting poles. And on our way out we blazed a line out to the road. After the holidays we'll go back, and by spring be ready—"

Suddenly it dawned upon him that something had happened which made the home-building at Yellow Jacket a useless and superfluous task. His heart contracted and sank like cold lead.

"Wal, you're an amazin' youngster," said Traft, with his keen blue eyes full of admiration and pride. "You scare me, though. I reckon it's more a Christian thing to slug a man than to shoot him You 'pear to have a hankerin' to use your fists. I heard aboot your hittin' Bambridge in the station at Winslow. You never told me that, you sly young dog. Didn't want to worry your old uncle, huh? . . . Wal, I can see you've more on

169

your mind. An' I'll wait to hear aboot Bambridge, the Hash Knife deal, an' Yellow Jacket."

"Uncle, I ran into Babbitt's, and there, behind a counter, was Molly," burst out Jim, and the mere telling of it aloud caused a regurgitation of fierce emotions. "She's broken our engagement. . . . She's gone to work. . . . I'm stunned."

"Jim, don't take it too hard," replied the old rancher, soothingly. "Don't imagine it a permanent break. Why, she done it because she loves you so much. She came to me an' told me, Jim. How she wasn't good enough for you—she hadn't the courage to marry you—your family would stick their noses up at her, an' all that sort of thing. I tried to argue her out of goin'. But she's a stubborn little minx. Independent, an' proud, too, in her way. So I jest told her thet you'd understand, but you'd never take her at her word. She cried at thet. Jim, she couldn't hold out against you for five minutes. So don't let it break you all up."

"My word, Uncle, but you're a life-saver," replied Jim, with intense relief. "It's bad enough, Lord knows, but if there's any hope I can stand it. Do you think Glory made it hard for Molly?"

"Wal, I reckon she did," said Traft, seriously. "An' all the time she was tryin' to put poor Molly at her ease. But she couldn't. An' that'll never come until Molly gets Glory on her own ground. Then there'll be a balance struck. Glory an' I have got on fine, Jim. She's a comfort to me, an' has been confidin' a little of her troubles at home. I reckon we'll never let her go back."

"No, we'll keep her out West. Uncle, how is she? Has her health improved?"

"Wal, Glory's got that bad cough yet, an' she gains but slow. I reckon she has improved. It'll take summer an' outdoors among the pines an' cedars to make her strong again. Suppose you hunt her up. Then after supper you can get the rest off your chest."

"All right, Uncle, but just one word more," returned Jim, eagerly. "You tell me not to fear a permanent break with Molly. When she's made it, already! I'm sick. I'm dumbfounded. I was so furious I called her a damn little fool."

"So she is. An' thet won't hurt your cause none. Now, Jim, don't fall into this broken-heart cowboy style an' go to drinkin'. I tell you Molly worships the ground you walk on. An' if I was you I'd jest go an' pack her back home here to the ranch."

"Pack her?" echoed Jim, aghast.

"Shore. She won't come willin', not very soon. So I'd jest fetch her back by force. A good spankin' wouldn't do no harm. But I reckon you haven't nerve enough for thet. Molly has given the town people lots to gossip about. Glory will tell you. An' you in turn can give them somethin' to gossip about."

"Ahuh. . . . Thanks, Uncle," rejoined Jim,

171

soberly. "I'll consider your advice. It appeals to me, especially the spanking part."

Jim left the living-room, absent-mindedly fingering the ring box in his pocket. He did not take all his uncle had said as absolute gospel, but it had surely checked the riot of his feelings. Then he knocked at Gloriana's door.

"Who' there?" she called, in a rather startled voice.

Some devil beset Jim, perhaps the besetting sin of his joke-loving cowboys, and without reflection he announced in a gruff voice:

"Darnell."

He heard an exclamation, followed by quick footsteps, and a sudden locking of the door.

"You nagging scoundrel!" called Gloriana, her voice ringing. "The nerve of you! I'm sick of your chasing after me. Get out of this house or I'll scream for my uncle. You'll reckon with Jim and his cowboys for the way you've treated me."

Jim was thunderstruck again, though in a vastly different way.

"Oh, Glory," he cried, "it's only Jim. I thought I was being funny."

"*Jim!*"

"Sure. Don't you know my voice? I just rode in. Had a word with Uncle and here I am."

"Are you—alone?" she asked, fumbling at the lock.

Wherewith she opened the door to disclose a lovely though most agitated countenance. Jim went in, stricken at the scare he had evidently given her.

"Glory, I'm darn sorry. I don't know what possessed me—to think of that fellow Darnell. Please forgive me."

"Have you heard—anything?" she asked, searching his face with darkly troubled eyes.

"About Darnell? I think I did hear that name. Before I left for Yellow Jacket. But I only just got back. Saw Molly! . . . Imagine my luck! I ran in Babbitt's—and almost fell over her. We had a few words, sister. . . . Then I came home. Saw Uncle for a minute. . . . Aren't you glad to see me?"

"Glad!" she echoed, with a rich deep note. A flash of light, like a golden warmth, seemed to erase the havoc from her face. She closed the door and enveloped Jim. Her embrace, her kisses, were inexpressibly sweet to him that moment. And he hugged her in a way which left no doubt about his own gladness.

"You great big handsome hairy—bear!" she cried, breathlessly. "You look like a tramp. You smell like horses and smoke. . . . Oh, Jim, I'm so glad to see you!"

"We're square on that, then," he said. "Come to the fire. Gee! I'm nearly frozen. I've been so knocked out I hardly knew it was cold. Let me look at you." Turning his back to the cheerful blazing logs, he placed a hand on each of her shoulders and ran searching eyes over her face

173

and form, and back again to her face. It was love-
lier than ever—with a subtle change not wholly of
more rounded contour and a hint of color, but of
less strain. She had rested. She had gained, as he
ascertained mostly by the feel of her shoulders.

"Well, what's your verdict?" she asked, meeting
his gaze with a wistful smile. Gloriana's eyes had
the inscrutable quality of beauty that was a
blending of purple hue and a light which anyone
might well mistake. But Jim saw deeper, and he
was satisified.

"I couldn't ask more. You're on the mend."

"Jim, I was fine until that damned Darnell
turned up here in Flag," she replied. "I told you he
would. It was a couple of weeks ago. But I found
out before I saw him. He came here—coaxed and
threatened. I told him I would have absolutely
nothing more to do with him. He has bobbed up
every time I went downtown, to stores, postoffice,
everywhere. Finally I stayed home. And you bet I
was angry when I took you for him."

"What's he doing out here, Glory?" asked Jim.

"He followed me. But he'll have more than one
string to his bow. Said he had gone to work for a
rancher named Bambridge—"

"Oh, I remember now," interrupted Jim. "I saw
him that day at the station. So your erstwhile beau
has thrown in with Bambridge? Interesting—and
funny."

"Jim, it's not funny to me," she spoke up, hurriedly. "I'm afraid of Darnell. He's a two-faced slicker. But he has become acquainted in town. He's already popular with the girls. I'm deathly afraid."

"Of what?" laughed Jim. He was in fact a little amused at the way he found his Western development disposed of Mr. Darnell.

"He'll talk about me—disgrace you, hurt you in Flag."

"Talk about you, will he? Glory, what do you suppose Curly Prentiss or Slinger Dunn would do—if he so much as spoke one slighting word of you?"

"I—I can't imagine, Jim," she replied, her great eyes dilating.

"Well, it will be funny—unless I get to him first. . . . Glory dear, this Darnell has no claim on you?"

"No, Jim, on my honor," she replied.

"Then dismiss him from your mind. He has struck the wrong place to hound a girl."

"I'm afraid he'll wheedle Uncle out of money," went on Gloriana, slowly yielding to relief.

"Ha! Ha! That's funny. He can't do it, Glory. He's not slick enough. Besides, he has gotten in with the wrong rancher. Bambridge is a cattle thief. We know it, and we can prove it presently. Darnell will have to step mighty slow and careful."

"Oh-h!" sighed Gloriana, and leaned her head against him. Jim could feel the quick beat of her pulse. How sensitive, how highly organized she was!

"Have you had any other trouble, sister? Come out with it."

"Yes, with Molly. Jim, she's the sweetest kid. Honestly, I just fell in love with her. But I made a tactless start. I wanted only to help her. She misunderstood. She thought I was stuck up, and she got the idea she wasn't good enough for you. When she told me she was leaving here I begged and I scolded. I talked sense to her. I argued myself hoarse. I was sincere, too. Only she imagined me afraid of you and lying to her. Then I lost my temper—I have one, if you remember, Jim— and I—well, I made it worse by telling her how lucky she was—that you meant to marry her. . . . But she has a will of her own. She left. And I haven't been able to get her back. I've been to that store I don't know how many times. Then I heard Molly had met Darnell—one of the Flag girls, Elsie Roberts, told me. And she went to a dance with him. I—"

"Molly went to a dance with this Darnell?"

"Yes, she did. But, Jim, you mustn't hold it against her," entreated Gloriana. "She's only a child. I went right downtown and told Molly who and what Darnell was. She didn't believe me. Darnell is attractive and smooth. She doesn't care a rap for him, because she worships you, Jim. But in her present state of mind she'd do anything.

And Darnell is dangerous and unscrupulous. If I had not been pretty wise—despite my infatuation—he'd have ruined me. You mustn't lose any time getting Molly out of his clutches."

"My God! . . . Do I want her?" groaned Jim, dropping his head.

"Yes, you want her. So do I. And so does Uncle Jim. Molly is a treasure. No matter *what* she does, you must stand it, bear with her, and get her back."

Jim raised his head to kiss Gloriana gratefully. "Thanks, Glory. You couldn't have said anything that would mean so much to me. I love that kid. It'd *kill* me to lose her. . . . But Uncle Jim bucked me up, and now so have you. . . . Here's her engagement ring. Isn't it a beauty?"

Gloriana looked at the jewel with eyes that sparkled like it.

"She wouldn't be human if that didn't fetch her. . . . But, Jim, Molly is Western. Diamonds might mean nothing at all to her. Still, I know she loves pretty clothes. She told me she went in debt for a new dress to wear at the Christmas dance."

"Molly certainly must be human and wholly feminine," said Jim, with a tinge of bitterness. "In love with me last month—engaged to me. Now she's going to a dance with another fellow. I call it pretty raw."

"She wrote you—begged Uncle Jim to send it by a rider. But Uncle Jim wouldn't do it. . . . And

177

Molly is just wild with regret and pain and wounded love. Any girl is in peril under a mood of that kind. She wants the town people to *believe* she's no good, so that they can't think she jilted you. It's a sad little story, Jim. But now you're here it will be all right. I *know* it, Jim, unless you're an utter jealous fool. Trust me. I know girls. Molly only needs to learn that you do love her for herself and that neither you, nor I, nor anyone could be ashamed of her—to be the sweetest and happiest girl in the world. That's your job, brother mine. And it beats building the drift fence."

"Glory, I can prove it—with you and Uncle to help. Gosh! I feel as if a mountain had been lifted off my heart. . . . Now what festivities are in order for the holidays?"

"Oh, Flag is quite a social place," laughed Gloriana. "But the dance Christmas Eve, and the party here on the following Wednesday night, are the outstanding events. Uncle is giving that for Molly. She, of course, thinks it's off because she left. But Uncle says no. Wait till Jim comes."

"It's not off, Glory," declared Jim, grimly. "Molly will be here if I have to pack her."

"Romantic, to say the least," replied Gloriana, with a trill of laughter. "I approve. . . . And now, Jim, tell me about Slinger and Curly. And don't forget Bud. He's a dear."

"Your Three Guardsmen, eh?" rejoined Jim,

dryly. "They've managed to live together without actual murder. Slinger looks at his rivals and listens in silent contempt, as down upon lesser men who did not share his secret of power."

Because of the whiteness of Gloriana's face even a little wave of color appeared a startling blush.

"Do they talk about me, among themselves?" she asked, a little confused.

"For three weeks you have shared conversation honors with the Hash Knife."

"How flattering! And what do they say?"

"I've forgotten most of it. At first I got kind of sore. They talked right out before me, with the utmost candor. They were all going to marry you, I gathered. To be sure, murder must be committed. It was funny. You should have been around to listen."

"They are the most amusing fellows—just fascinating to me."

"So I've gathered. Well, dearest, out West you reap as you sow. . . . One day I came back to camp and found Bud with a bloody nose. Curly, his pard, his almost brother, had punched him for talking about your legs."

"Wha-at!" gasped Gloriana.

"Sure. I ascertained that Bud said you had pretty legs and you knew it. Curly took that as an insult and bloodied Bud's nose. When I got there Bud was nursing his nose and his wounded vanity. I thought it a good opportunity for an object lesson, so I pretended tremendous anger, when I really wanted to split with laughter. I threw Bud down on the grass, straddled him, and threatened to smash his face unless he recognized his offense, apologized, and took it back. Do you know, Glory, he couldn't see any offense although he apologized. But he swore it was true and he wouldn't take it back. Then I conceived the idea of greater punishment for Bud by giving him away to you. He almost wept at this, begged me to beat him, said he could stand anything except you thinking Curly a hero and him a low-down skunk, or something."

"I—I don't know what to say," replied Gloriana, but it was plain to Jim that she wanted to laugh.

"Glory, I told you—gave you fair warning. If you flirt with these cowboys you must pay dearly for it. And of course you have flirted, if not intentionally, then some other way. It won't do out here. These boys have hearts of gold. Every last one of them would die for you. They seem like some kind of inflammable tinder. So easy, cool, droll, yet underneath all fire. Curly Prentiss is the highest type of cowboy I know. He is a prince. All the same he's a strutting, conceited jackass who needs a lesson. Bud is the best-hearted of the lot, honest as the day. He speaks right out what he thinks. A raw, crude, common sort of person to any superficial observer from the East, but to me, or Uncle Jim, to anyone who sees clearly, he's a boy to love. The rest of the outfit trail along somewhat similarly, except Slinger Dunn. He's not a cowboy. He's a strange mixture of woodsman and Indian, of country boy and chivalrous gentleman. All the same, if I were you I'd be careful of what I said or did before him."

"I'm afraid it's too late," replied Gloriana, with gravity. "You took us to the hospital to see him. He had my picture under his pillow. Told me right out he'd gazed at it until he was terribly in love with *me*. That you had taken Molly from him and he was going to take me from you."

"Well, I'm a son-of-a-gun!" ejaculated Jim.

"I should have squelched him at once," admitted Gloriana. "But I didn't. I didn't take him seriously. Thought that was just Western. And at a dance here I'm afraid I made it worse. He—"

"Glory, darling," interrupted Jim, plaintively, "I don't want to know any more. I've trouble of my own. I need your help—not to be staggered with your love affairs."

"Silly! My love affairs? The idea!" she retorted, but her cheeks were red.

"But you can't dodge them. I *told* you how to handle these cowboys. Did you listen? I should smile not."

"Misery loves company. We are in a mess, Jim. Only yours is serious. Molly is as stubborn as a mule. I forgot to tell you that some of the Flag girls became very friendly to me, but they snubbed poor Molly. That hurt her—and somehow she associates it with her relation to you and me."

"Ahuh. I see. Glory, those same girls snubbed me, too, at first. Then when they found out I was old Jim Traft's nephew they changed their tune. But nix—I wasn't interested. They were jealous of Molly—the cats. . . . Well, I shall move mountains to make them worse."

Gloriana laid her cheek against Jim's rough and grimy face, oblivious of that or indifferent to it, and she gave vent to a long sigh.

"I'm glad you're back," she said. "I've been lonely, only I didn't guess it. You're a comfort. . . . Jim, when spring comes you must take me to your camp. I'll get well there—and be safer, if you want to know."

Chapter Ten

NEXT morning Jim awakened very early, and lay in bed pondering his problem and mapping out a deliberate course of what he intended to do. He fortified himself against mortification, embarrassment, against all possible contingencies liable to inflame him, and set the limit short of heartbreak. He simply would not and could not face the thought of losing Molly.

It was the 23rd of December, less than two days

before the Christmas Eve dance. His leave of absence from work on Yellow Jacket would expire on New Year's day, following which he and the Diamond outfit must ride back to the range for a long and surely trying stay. Wherefore he had no time to lose. But first he must consult his uncle and Locke, report every detail pertaining to what had happened down at Yellow Jacket, and, consistent with their advice, plan future work.

After breakfast, at which Gloriana was not present, Jim asked for a conference with his uncle and Locke. They repaired at once to the living-room. Jim began with his discovery of Diamond-branded cattle going aboard the train with Bambridge's shipment from Winslow, and slighted nothing in his narrative of what had followed, nor any of his conjectures and convictions, and lastly, the opinions of his men. After he had concluded, his superiors smoked furiously, which appeared their only indication of mental disturbance. Locke was the first to break silence: "I advise givin' up Yellow Jacket."

"Naw," replied Traft, laconically.

"I don't want to," added Jim. "It's a wild, lonely, wonderful wilderness. I want to own it—improve it—and live there part of the year, at least."

"Wal, aside from Jim's leanin' to Yellow Jacket, I wouldn't let it go now," went on Traft. "It'd be givin' in to Bambridge, an' I'll see him in hell first."

"Short an' sweet," said Locke, with a dry cackle. He knew his employer of old. "Then I suggest we arrange some plan of transportin' Mr. Bambridge to the place you name."

"Aw, Ring, don't get funny. This is business. . . . How many head of unbranded stock can you round up this spring?"

"Matter of ten thousand, more or less, countin' new calves."

"Wal, slap the Diamond brand on half of them, this comin' round-up," ordered the rancher, brusquely.

Locke wrote in his notebook, then said: "I'd advise no cattle drive to Yellow Jacket till spring. Let the rustlers have a chance at the lower range."

"Reckon thet's a good idea. Put it down. Now, Jim, tell Locke what you want for the house. He'll order it. Meanwhile the sleddin' will be good an' we'll haul all supplies such as hardware, cement, tools, powder, down to Cottonwood Ranch, an' store it there. Lumber, framework, bricks, and all such to follow fast as it gets here. When the ground dries in the spring you can haul in over your new road. . . . As for the present, wal, stick to our original plan. Take the Diamond back to Yellow Jacket an' clean it up—of varmints, rubbish, an' such includin' any rustlers who might come burnin' your good firewood. . . . Savvy?"

"Yes, sir," replied Jim, quickly.

"Got thet down, Locke?" queried the old rancher, as he rose and knocked the ash off his cigar.

"I'll put it down," replied the superintendent.

"Wal, don't pester me with this two-bit stuff any more," replied Traft, testily. "Help Jim all you can. It's up to him." And he stalked out sturdily, his shaggy head erect, leaving Jim alone with the superintendent.

"Shorter an' sweeter," said Locke, tapping his book with his pencil.

"Gosh!—I never heard Uncle talk like that. What ails him?"

"He's sore at Bambridge. Small wonder. He's had forty years buckin' the crooked side of cattle-raisin', an' he hates it. . . . Jim, he's given you a man-size job. But you've got a hard crew in the Diamond. They're good fer it. Jed Stone's movin' off your range strikes me deep. It means a lot, besides his bein' decent. I've a hunch he's about through, some way or another. But Malloy will have to be reckoned with. If you ever meet him, anyhow, under *any* circumstances, shoot quick an' think afterwards. Don't ever fail to pack a gun, an' keep Slinger or Curly close to you."

"Ring—you mean here—at home—in town?" queried Jim, aghast.

"I should smile."

"Whew!—When will I ever learn?"

"You've been shot once, an' shot at a number of

times. Don't you savvy what it means? Come down on the hard ground, Jim."

After that conference, which left Jim with a keen poignant sense of responsibility, he stayed in his room until after dinner and then started for town on foot. Any sharp observer, at least a Westerner, could have detected the bulge of a gun back of his hip, and the tip of a leather sheath projecting an inch or two below his coat. How he longed for the cool imperturbability of Curly Prentiss or the aloof unapproachableness of Slinger Dunn! But these he could never attain, for he had not been born to the West. Jim had to make determination do for confidence. And when, in accordance with his plan, he walked into Babbitt's store, no one would have guessed the sinking sensation he had in his vitals. He was terribly afraid of Molly Dunn, not to mention the gunman Croak Malloy. Jim knew he was something of a lion when under the sway of righteous anger, but most assuredly he could not muster that at will.

Molly stood behind the counter, and from her wide startled eyes he gathered that she had seen him first. It was early and he appeared to be the only customer present, and at once the object of much interest, both of which facts did not confuse him one whit.

"Good day, Molly," he said, doffing his sombrero. "Yesterday I forgot what I wanted to buy."

"Howdy—Jim," she faltered, huskily, the scarlet coming up from neck to face. How the sight made Jim's blood leap! She could not be indifferent to his presence.

"I want that red scarf and a pair of buckskin gloves," he said.

Molly produced the scarf, and then, with the other clerks snickering openly, she had to try glove after glove on Jim's hand, until he was satisfied with the fit. Her little brown fingers trembled so that she was scarcely able to perform the task; and Jim gloated over this manifestation of weakness, instead of feeling sorry for her.

"Thanks. I reckon these will do," he said, at length. "Please charge to the Traft account. . . . I shall tell Mr. Babbitt you are a very beautiful clerk, but a poor saleswoman."

Molly was staring at the gun-sheath under his coat. Her eye had been quick to see it.

"Jim!—You're packin' a gun!" she exclaimed, breathlessly and low.

"I should snigger I am, as Bud would say," he replied, facetiously.

"Who for?" she whispered, and it was significant that she did not say what for.

"Well, if you care to know, that Hash Knife gunman, Croak Malloy, is looking for me—and I am looking for a fellow named Ed Darnell," concluded Jim, and heartless though he knew himself, it was impossible to look into her eyes then. He took his parcels and went out, most acutely conscious of bursting veins and thrilling nerves.

Jim walked down the street, dropping in at all the business places where his uncle had dealings. Then he visited the saloons, which were more numerous and to him vastly more interesting. He acted, too, like a man who was looking for some one. Next he called at the post-office and the hotel, after which he returned to Babbitt's store.

Molly did not see him enter. She was busy with a customer, which occupation permitted Jim a moment to devour her sweet face with hungry eyes. She looked paler and thinner than he had ever seen her; and these evidences of trouble were dear to Jim's heart. She had not done this cruel thing without suffering. Presently she finished with her customer and espied Jim.

"You again?" she queried, blushing furiously.

"I forgot something, Molly," he drawled.

"Somethin' you wanted to buy?" she went on, a little sarcastically.

"Yes, but I forget. Whenever I see your sweet face I forget everything. . . . Oh yes, buckskin gauntlets for the cowboys—the fringed ones with a horseshoe design on the back. Christmas gifts, you know. My size will do."

"How many pairs?" she asked.

"Have you forgotten how many cowboys in my outfit?"

She did not reply and presently sorted out the

gloves, wrapped them into a parcel and handed it to him. This time he fixed upon her reproachful piercing eyes.

"Molly, you are to understand that I do not accept my dismissal," he said, deliberately. "I'm sorry you feel so. I—I forgive you, I guess. . . . And I'll not give you up."

"But, Jim, everybody heah knows," she said, shrinkingly.

"What?"

"Thet I gave—you up—'cause I wasn't good enough—for you."

Jim could scarcely refrain from leaning over the counter and snatching her to his breast.

"I know Molly. But you're terribly mistaken. Uncle Jim knows you're good enough for me. I know you're too good for me or anyone else. And Glory, she's heart and soul for you."

"Jim, I reckon you're somethin' of a liar," she returned, a red spot forming on each cheek.

"Ordinarily, yes, but not in this," he said, cheerfully. "Anyway, it doesn't make the slightest difference who and what you are. You're going to be Mrs. James Traft."

"I—I am—not."

"You bet you are. . . . Oh yes, that reminds me. I forgot something else. Look here." He slipped the little ring-box out of his pocket, and bending over the counter opened the lid. The big blue-white diamond seemed to leap up. Jim glanced

189

quickly at Molly's face. And that was enough, almost even for him.

"I thought you'd like it," he said, remorsefully, but not now meeting her tragic eyes. "We'll try it on first chance. . . . So long, till tomorrow."

Taking up his purchases, Jim hurried out, his pulse tingling, his heart singing. Molly loved him still. And all the way out the bleak cold road he could have danced. Upon arriving home he went in to see Gloriana, who was gorgeously arrayed in a dressing-gown and demonstratively glad to see him. Jim recounted his adventure to Glory.

"Men are brutes, devils, fiends," responded his sister. "But since the female of the species is what she is and self-preservation the first law of life, I don't see what else you can do. Hurry and get Molly back here."

"Give me a little time, Glory," declared Jim, somewhat daunted.

"Get her here before she goes to the dance with that darn Darnell," advised Gloriana, with a wonderful purple flash of eyes.

"Reckon I don't want to, till afterwards. I sure am curious to see how she acts—and, Darnell too—and what the cowboys do."

"Will you tell them?"

"I will, you bet, and between you and me, Glory, I wouldn't be in Darnell's boots for a million."

"You are beginning to make me feel the same way. . . . Jim, you showed the ring to Molly?"

190

"Yes—and you should have seen her eyes. Oh!—I felt like a coyote, but, gosh! I was happy."

"It's a lovely ring, Jim. Let me have it a little—just to look at. I won't put it on."

"Sure. But wait till I come back from the bunk-house. I want to show it to the boys."

"Jim, if you're going to tell them about Darnell, put it strong."

"Huh! Trust me. I've already told them something. . . . Glory, I don't feel so sick this afternoon."

"You loving goose!—Heigho! I wish somebody loved *me* that way."

"That's funny. As if you hadn't had and didn't have more love than any girl ever had."

"But, Jim, only to be loved because you're pretty!" she exclaimed. "Would even these sentimental cowboys love me—if they knew I couldn't cook, sew, bake, darn a sock—that I'm a useless ornament—that the thought of babies scares me stiff?"

"Sure they would. Men *are* loving geese, Glory. Don't worry. Only begin to deserve it."

He made his way to the bunk-house, finding all the boys in, as he had expected, and recovered from any indulgence they might have treated themselves to the night before.

"Fellars, hyar's the boss, lookin' like a thundercloud," announced Bud.

"Packin' a gun, too, the Mizzouri hayseed," added Curly.

Their separate greetings were all in the nature of comment upon his appearance. The moment seemed propitious and Jim chose to act upon it.

"Boys, friends, pards," he began, dramatically, "if it weren't for my sister and you I'd blow my brains out."

Silence! Staring eyes and awed lean faces attested to the felicity of his acting.

"Why, Jim, what the hell?" uttered Curly, without his drawl.

"Listen. Let me tell it quick," he announced hurriedly. "We go back to Yellow Jacket after New Year's. No more town till spring, if then. The old man is sore at Bambridge—at this two-bit rustling. We've got the job of clearing the range of varmints, rubbish, rustlers, and so forth. He'll throw five thousand head of cattle on to Yellow Jacket in less than a year. That's that, and it isn't a marker to what I'm going to tell you."

As he paused, Curly interposed, coolly: "Wal, Boss, maybe it isn't a marker, whatever thet is, but it's sure rattlesnake poison, gunpowder, and bad whisky, all mixed up."

"Let me get it off my chest," went on Jim. "Maybe you remember I hinted of a fellow named Darnell, who made trouble for my sister back in Missouri. Anyway, he's here in Flag. Has taken a job with Bambridge. He has been hounding poor Glory until she has stopped going to town. She is deathly afraid of him. Afraid he will disgrace me

192

by talking about her. Mind you—Glory is straight and fine and good. So don't get the wrong hunch. She was only a crazy girl and this Darnell is a man, handsome, slick as the devil, a gambler and cheat at cards, and crooked otherwise. He beat Glory out of money, and my father, too. She thinks he'll beat Uncle Jim the same way. But you all know Darnell can't fool the old man. . . . Now does that sink in?"

"Wal, it shore doesn't sink very deep in me, Boss," drawled Curly. "Mister Darnell has shore picked an awful unhealthy climate."

"You saw Darnell with Bambridge that day at the station."

"Shore. An' thet was enough fer me an' Bud an' all of the outfit."

"All right . . . here's the worst—Lord! how am I to get—it out?" continued Jim, and now he did not need to simulate trouble. He was genuine. He felt clammy and nauseated. He paced a step here and there, flung himself upon the chair before the fire, and all but tore his hair in his distress and shame.

"Molly Dunn has—jilted me. Broken her engagement—left my uncle's house. . . . Says she's not good enough to marry me. And it's just the other way around. Poor kid! Just let that sink in, will you? . . . She's a clerk in Babbitt's store in the afternoons. Mornings, she goes to school. All that's tough, boys. But listen to this. She's going around with that — — — Darnell! . . . I can't realize it, let alone understand it. But Glory says Molly is only distracted—out of her head—that it's really because she loves me she's done it. Wants everybody in Flag to *see* she's not good enough for us! That's why she's carrying on with this Darnell! I'm so sorry for her I—I could cry. And so mad I could bite nails. And so scared I can't think."

Jim paused for breath. What relief to get this confession made! When he looked up he gathered a singular conception of the regard in which he was held by the Diamond. It was rather a big moment for him.

Slinger Dunn, without a word, put on his cap and glided noiselessly toward the door.

"Hold on, Slinger. Where you going?"

Dunn turned. At any moment his sloe-black eyes were remarkable; just now they made Jim shiver.

"I was shore wonderin' why my sister hadn't sent fer me to come up to the house," he said. "An' I reckon it's aboot time I hunted her up. Then I'll take a look round fer this Darnell fellar."

"Slinger, by all means go see Molly, but let Darnell alone for the present," rejoined Jim, earnestly.

"Jim, air you electin' to boss me aboot Molly?" asked Slinger.

"No indeed, Slinger. Only asking you to wait."

"What fer?"

There did not appear to be much to wait for, Jim

admitted to himself, and he felt he had been hasty in stating the case to these firebrands.

"Listen, Slinger, and all of you," said Jim. "Tomorrow night is this Christmas Eve dance. We'll all go. We'll look this Darnell over. I won't do anything and I ask you not to—until after that. But understand me. I—I couldn't stick it out here in the West without Molly. You all know how I care for her. It's far more serious for me than the Hash Knife deal. . . . I've confided my intimate feelings because I believe you all my pards. I reckon I'll be laughed at and ridiculed by the Flagerstown young people, as I was at first. But I don't care. All I care for is to get Molly back, to make a home for Glory, and to have the Diamond stick to me."

Curly might have been spokesman for the outfit. Usually in critical cases he assumed that position. Now he laid a lean brown pressing hand upon Jim's shoulder.

"Jim, all this heah Diamond cares for is thet you grow a little more Western overnight," he drawled, in his careless cool, inflexible tone, that seemed to carry such moment. Curly's ultimatum intimated so much. It embodied all of Jim's longings. He divined in that cowboy's droll words an unutterable and unquenchable loyalty, and more, the limitless spirit and the strength of all that the wild range engendered.

"By Heaven—I will!" cried Jim, ringingly, as he leaped to his feet.

Chapter Eleven

JIM had resisted an impulse to bribe the cowboys to call in a body and singly at Babbitt's store to make purchases of Molly and incidentally remind her of him.

In his own case he went downtown late, and everywhere except Babbitt's, trying to screw up his courage. It was not that overnight he had not become transposed to a thorough Arizonian, but that his genuine tenderness for Molly had asserted itself. This he knew he should not yield to. Still he did. On several occasions he espied some of his cowboys, laden with bundles, mysteriously gay and full of the devil. They had not required prompting to do the very thing he had so sneakingly desired. He could just imagine the drawling, persuasive Curly telling Molly she was out of her "haid." And Bud—what that cherubic volcanic friend would say was beyond conjecture. And Slinger! Jim had forgotten that Slinger was Molly's brother, her guardian, in his own estimation, at any rate. It rather frightened Jim to guess what Slinger would do, considering he was not given to much speech. And the rest of the cowboys—they would drive Molly frantic in their Western fashion.

Ruminating thus, Jim lounged in the lobby of the hotel. All of a sudden he saw Molly go into

Davis' store, on the far corner. He jumped. It was only four o'clock, and she should have at least another hour of work. What a chance! It quite took his breath. He went out, crossed the street, and stood back in a hallway, close to the door of the store, where he could see and scarcely be seen. Once he had to dodge back to escape detection when Lonestar and Cherry passed, each with a load of packages. "Gosh!" ejaculated Jim. "They've been in Babbitt's. I can tell by the wrapping-paper on those parcels."

He had to wait what seemed an endless while before Molly appeared. Then he stepped out as if by magic, and Molly bumped into him. It startled her so that she uttered a cry and dropped some of her bundles. Jim picked them up, and rising he coolly faced the scarlet Molly and appropriated the rest of her parcels.

"I reckon I'll carry these. Where you going?" he said, naturally, with a smile.

Molly looked both furious and helpless. Evidently this was the last straw. "You—you—"

"Careful, honey, this is the main thoroughfare of Flag. People all about. If you want to swear, wait till we get somewhere."

"Jim Traft—I could swear—a blue streak," she replied, and her appearance certainly verified her words.

"Shore, but it ain't ladylike, as Bud would say," he drawled. "Molly, I'm going to talk to

197

you or die in the attempt. Where are you going?"

"Home. To my boardin'-house," she said, a little mockingly.

"Well, I'll pack your load for you," returned Jim. He dropped one of them, and in securing it let several others slip, and had quite a time recovering them all. As he rose he thought he detected Molly averting dusky hungry eyes. Just on the moment Sue Henderson passed. She gave them a bright smile and said: "Hello, you-all! Everybody Christmasing. See you tonight."

Jim answered with a cheerful, "Howdy!" but Molly's response was unintelligible. Then she said: "If you must make it wuss for me—"

"Darling, don't say wuss. Say worse. . . . Come—which way?"

That epithet had the desired effect. Jim had discovered its potency and had used it sparingly. Just now it caused Molly's blaze to dim and pale. She started off. Jim caught up with her at the corner, which she turned into the side street. They walked in silence. The bleak wind swept straight down this street from the mountains and it was like icy blades. Molly did not look warmly clad. Her coat was wholly inadequate for such weather. Jim longed to speak of the fur coat he had bought for her, but this was not the moment.

"You played me a low-down trick," she said, presently, coldly.

"Me? I sure did not. How so?"

"You set thet Diamond outfit onto me."

"Molly! I swear I didn't. Honest. You know I wouldn't lie," replied Jim, most earnestly.

"You shore would. You'd do anythin'."

"But I protest my innocence."

"Innocence?—You!" She gave him her eyes for a second. Jim felt shot through with black and gold arrows.

"Sure I'm innocent. I thought how good it'd be to send the gang in on you—if for nothing else than to remind you of my existence. But I didn't. Not only that, Molly, but yesterday I actually kept Slinger from hunting you up."

"Wal, you shore didn't this heah day. . . . Oh, it was—turrible!" Her voice broke, close to a sob.

"Molly!—I'm sorry. What'd Slinger do?"

"I wouldn't tell you. I—I wouldn't give you the satisfaction. But I'll never forgive him—or you either."

"Gee! he must have given you 'most as much as you deserve," said Jim, laconically.

Molly's recollection, coupled with Jim's good-natured sarcasm, proved too much for her reticence. "He disgraced me," she burst out, almost weeping. "Right there in the store—before two of the clerks, an' thet gabby old Mrs. Owens—who'll tell it all over."

"What'd Slinger say, honey?"

"Stop callin' me them sweet names," flashed

Molly, in desperation. "I cain't stand it. I'll run away from heah or do somethin' turrible."

"You have already done something 'turrible,' only you don't know it," responded Jim. "I'll try to remember not to be sentimental. . . . Tell me what Slinger said."

"Nothin' 'cept 'come heah, you moon-eyed calf!' . . . I was paralyzed when I seen him come in. I couldn't run. Slinger's eyes are shore turrible. He reached over the counter an' said—what I told you. Then he grabbed me by my blouse—it's a way he has—only this time he pulled me half over the counter—face down—an'—an' smacked me so hard you could have heahed it out in the street. . . . I won't be able to—to set down at dinner! . . . An' then he said he'd see me later."

Jim kept a straight face, gazing ahead on the wintry street. How he wanted to shout!

"Turrible," he agreed. "For a grown girl. . . . And what did the cowboys do?"

"Drove me mad. One by one, in two an' threes—the whole outfit," said Molly, woefully. "Not one single word about you, Jim Traft, but all the same it was all for you. The sweet things they said to me aboot the dance tonight—aboot the party Unc—Mr. Traft was goin' to give me—Christmas presents—"

"Uncle *is* going to give the party for you," interposed Jim.

"They were darned nice," went on Molly,

ignoring his statement. "You know durin' the holidays Mr. Babbitt gives us clerks ten per cent on all sales. Curly Prentiss heahed aboot thet. An' Jim, the sons-of-guns cleaned me out. Bought every last thing in my department. Mr. Babbitt was thunderstruck an' tickled to death. He complimented me, as if *I* had anythin' to do with the idiots squanderin' their money. They spent all the cash they had, an' went in debt for hundreds of dollars. They'll never get the money to pay up. An' thet Bud Chalfack! . . . I cain't tell you aboot him."

"Sure you can Molly. Go on. It's very thrilling. And maybe telling me will make it easier for you," persuaded Jim.

"I've only Curly's word for it," returned Molly. "But he swore Bud bought the finest set of fur-niture—a bedroom set—Babbitt's had on hand. For me. For a Christmas present—an'—an' weddin' present together. Bud said he'd shore be daid broke when thet weddin' comes off. . . . An' I'm afraid he'll be daid."

"The extravagant sons-of-guns!" ejaculated Jim, amazed and chagrined. "They had to go overdo it. Buyin' you some presents—or even buyin' out the store—was all right. But I reckon the—the rest was tactless, to say the least. Molly, you'll have to excuse it. They can't take you seriously, any more than can I."

Molly stopped before a modest little brown

cottage, almost at the end of the street. Jim made a note of the single large pine tree in the yard, for future emergency, when he wished to find Molly after dark.

"This is where I board," she said, simply.

"Are you comfortable here?" asked Jim, anxiously.

"I'm used to cold. But there's a stove in the parlor. Come in."

Jim was elated that she should trust him so far as to ask him inside. The modest little parlor was warm and comfortable indeed, compared with the blustery outdoors. Jim deposited Molly's bundles in a chair, and turning discovered that she had removed her hat and coat and was warming her hands over the stove. She looked healthy and pretty, yet somehow forlorn. What was to prevent him taking her in his arms then and there? He longed to. That had been his intention, should opportunity offer. Nevertheless, something inhibited him. Probably it was a divination that Molly, during the few minutes' walk with him, had unconsciously been drawn to him again. She betrayed it now. That was what he had prayed for, but he could not act upon it.

"Thanks for asking me in, Molly," he said. "I suppose you expect me to get my trouble off my chest—then let you alone. . . . Well, I won't do it now. When that time comes we'll have a grand row. And I just won't spoil your Christmas. . . .

But I ask you—will you send word to Darnell that you will not go to the dance with him tonight?"

"Thet'd be a low-down trick," replied Molly, quickly.

"It does appear so. There are good reasons, however, why it would be wise for you to do so—unless you want to lose your good name in Flag."

"Glory said thet. I don't believe either of you. An' it's not square of you to—"

"You needn't argue the point. Answer me. Will you go with me instead?"

She hung her head, she clenched her little trembling hands, she shook all over. What a trial that must have been! Jim sought to add to it.

"With me and Glory, of course. She wants you. And she thinks *this* is the time for you to come back. Before you've made me the laughing-stock of Flag."

"But it cain't do thet," she cried.

"Yes it can. And it will. Not that I care a hang for what people think or say. We want you to avoid—well, Molly, being misunderstood, not to say worse."

"You hit it on the haid, Jim," she replied with spirit. "Thet's what I'm not goin' to avoid."

Jim regarded her speculatively. If he had had a vehicle of some kind out in the street he would have picked her up right there as she was, and packed her out, and carried her off home. But this drastic action could scarcely be undertaken now, though his finger tips burned to snatch her.

"I am not angry with you now, but I shall be presently," he said.

"Who cares?" she rejoined, flippantly, and he realized he had brought her reply on himself.

"Oh, I see. . . . Do you then care—something for this gambler and embezzler, Ed Darnell?"

"How dare you?" retorted Molly, but she was shocked. Jim realized that Gloriana had not told her a great deal, after all.

"I'm a darin' cowpuncher," said Jim.

"I'll tell Mr. Darnell. Then mebbe you won't be so darin'."

Jim, despite self-control, grew a little hot under the collar. There was not anything soothing in Molly's championship of a cheap adventurer.

"By all means tell him. . . . You're a queer kid, Molly. Just to hurt me you'll flirt with this stranger, forgetting or pretending to forget that Slinger Dunn, your brother, perhaps the hardest nut in Arizona next to Croak Malloy, is my partner."

"Jim Traft, I'm no flirt—an' Slinger isn't a hard nut," she retorted, pugnaciously.

"Well then, you're going to do it?"

"Do what?"

"Make me an object of scorn. These Flag girls never cottoned to me. The young fellows, except cowboys, have no use for me. The old women don't like me. When they all see—actually see you've jilted me—"

"They won't. I'll make it the other way round," she interrupted, passionately.

Jim saw this tack was useless. The only thing that would move Molly at this particular moment, and perhaps at any other time, was physical force. Slinger knew how to handle her. Jim essayed another argument.

"You saw one of my Christmas presents—for you. What you think of it?"

"Gave me nightmare."

"Have you any curiosity about the other?"

"Nope. I may be a poor little country girl, but you cain't buy me—you Mizzouri villain."

"You used to call me Mizzouri, with a kiss. Do you remember when we went wild-turkey hunting?"

"I'm tryin' to forget. Oh, Jim, you've been so good—I—I—I—" She bit her tongue. "An' I will forget, if I have to go to the bad."

"You've made a fair start, Molly Dunn," replied Jim, curtly. "Say, has this Darnell so much as laid a hand on you?"

"No! You insult me," she cried, with flaming face.

"But, Molly, be reasonable. You hinted that you'd encourage such things," protested Jim, justly nettled.

"I will—if you drive me."

Then there was a deadlock. Molly and Jim glared at each other across the stove, above which extended hands almost met. Jim found it hard to tear himself away, especially in view of her anger. He pondered a moment. Finally he said, gently: "Darling, do you have *any* idea to what extremes you may drive me?"

She shook her head dubiously.

"Don't you know I worship you?"

Her glossy head drooped.

"Don't you realize you'll ruin me if you persist in this madness? I can't believe it. But you might convince me, eventually."

Then she covered her face with her hands and the tears trickled through her fingers.

Jim grasped at the right moment to make his escape.

"I won't distress you any more," he said. "Don't cry and make your eyes red. I'll see you tonight. Please save a dance for me."

Then he rushed out to find the cold wind soothing to a heated brow. He trudged home, his mind in a whirl. It was nearly dark when he arrived. Gloriana was not in the living-room. Wherefore Jim threw himself into the armchair and reclined there until he had reestablished the Western character he had recently adopted.

Before supper he went out to the bunk-house, to find the place a bedlam of jolly cowpunchers and a storeful of the men's furnishings, goods which they had bought so indiscriminately. All of the boys were sober—a remarkable circumstance on the eve of Christmas. When he entered—and he had stood in the open door a moment—they whooped and began to throw packages at him.

"Merry Christmas!" yelled Bud.

"Son-of-a-gun from Mizzouri!" yelled Curly.

"Whoopee, you diamond-buyer!" yelled Cherry.

"You lovesick, dyin' duck!" yelled some one Jim did not pick out, for the reason that he had to dodge. And so it went until they had exhausted their vocabularies and their missiles.

"Am I to understand that this fusillade is kindly meant?" he asked, with mock solemnity.

"Means we shore went broke on you an' Molly Dunn," replied Bud.

"Boys, that was a cowboy stunt—your buying out Babbitt's," said Jim. "I'm broke, too, but I'll share the debt."

Some one observed that he would, like the old lady who kept tavern out West, and as Jim had learned that that was a very disreputable thing, he made no further comment.

"Slinger, I hope you didn't tell these wild men what *you* did in Babbitt's," he returned.

"I shore did, an' the outfit's with me, Mister Traft," answered Dunn.

"Boss, Slinger had an inspurashun," observed Bud, sagely. "Soon as a feller learns to treat bull-haided sisters an' fickle sweethearts thetaway he'll get some obedience."

"I'm afraid it won't work on high-spirited girls like Molly and my sister."

"It shore would. Wimmen is all the same. What you say, pard Curly?"

"But, on this heah Christmas Eve my heart is shore sad," rejoined Curly. "Peace on earth an' good will toward men is a lot of guff. There's battle an' murder in the air. Some of us won't even see another Christmas."

"Then we oughta get turrible drunk," said Bud.

Approval of this statement was not wanting.

"Curly, what's eating you?" asked Jim, grasping that his favorite cowboy had something besides the festivities of the season on his mind.

"Ask Bud," replied Curly, gloomily.

"Wal, Boss, it ain't nuthin' much, leastways oughtn't fuss us till after Christmas," replied Bud. "Curly an' I made a round of the gamblin'-places this afternoon. I didn't know what was in Curly's mind. Anyway, the doorkeeper at Snell's tried to bar Curly out. Shore it's a swell place, but we reckoned it wasn't none too good fer the Diamond. After I got in I seen why Curly pushed his gun against the doorkeeper's bread-basket. A bartender friend of Curly's had tipped him off thet there was a big game goin' on at Snell's. Wal, there was. Bambridge, Blodgett, another rancher we didn't know, an' Blake, a hotel man from Winslow, an' last this hyar Darnell hombre was sittin' in. You should of seen the coin of the realm on thet table. Wal, we watched the game. I seen Bambridge was bettin' high an' losin'. Looked like he'd whoop up the pots, an' Darnell would rake them in. Blake is no slouch of a gambler, an' he was shore sore at the game, either from losin' or somethin'. All I seen about Darnell was thet he was mighty slick with the cards. They jest flew out of his hands. Curly, you know, is a card sharp hisself, an' he swore Darnell stacked the deck on every deal he had. An' Blodgett an' the strange rancher, anyhow, was gettin' a hell of a fleecin'."

"Ahuh. So that's it," returned Jim, seriously. "Curly, I don't see anything in that to make you sad on Christmas Eve."

"Boss, there's shore two things," drawled Curly. "I've got to raise enough money to set in that game at Snell's. An' I'm wonderin' if Darnell is as slick with a gun as he is with the cairds."

"Life is orful hard fer a cowpuncher when he's in love," observed Bud. "Sky so blue an' grass so green, flowers an' birds, dance an' holdin' hands, an' kisses sweeter'n ambergris—an' jest round the corner bloody death lurkin'."

"What's the idea, Curly?" asked Jim, quickly interested.

"Boss, it's a fine chance to get rid of Mister Darnell without involvin' any of our lady friends, you know. Flag is such a hell of a place for gossip. An' I reckon there's shore enough right now."

"Get rid of Darnell!" ejaculated Jim, curiously.

"Shore. I can set in thet game if I've a good-sized roll. Shore I'd flash it an' let on I was a little drunk. Savvy? Wal, I can nail Darnell at his cheatin' at cairds. If he pulls a gun—well an' good. If not he'll shore find Flag too hot a town in winter."

"Curly, it's a grand idea, except the possibility of Darnell's throwin' a gun. I hardly believe he'd have the nerve. He's an Easterner."

"We don't know for shore," said Curly. "He might even be from Texas."

"Aw, guff an' nonsense!" burst out Bud. "Thet handsome white-mugged sharper won't go fer a gun. But whatinhell's the difference if he does? Save us the trouble of stringin' him up to a cotton-wood. . . . An', Boss, an' Curly, an' all you galoots, thet's what Darnell is slated fer. I seen it—I felt it. . . . Now I ask you, knowin' how few my hunches are—do you recollect any of them far wrong? What's more, Bambridge ain't genuine Western. He's too cock-sure. He reckons us all easy marks."

"Curly, I'll dig up the money and go with you to Snell's," said Jim.

The Diamond immediately voted upon a united presence at that occasion. Curly made no objection, provided they dropped in unobtrusively.

"I heahed this poker game has been goin' on most in the afternoons," he said. "An' course it's kind of private—Snell's is—an' you may not get in. But don't start a fight. Aboot four o'clock would be a good hour, Jim."

"How much money will you require?" queried Jim.

"Wal, I ought to have a roll of greenbacks big enough to choke a cow, with a century as a wrapper. Shore I'll have to flash this roll or they'd never let me set in. But you can gamble I won't lose much of it."

"That makes it easier," said Jim. "I can manage somehow. . . . Now, fellows, about this dance tonight. It's at the hotel and the big bugs in town are back of it. No knock-down and dragout cowboy dance. Savvy? . . . I—I tried to coax Molly not to go with this Darnell, but she's stubborn. She's going. And we can't help it. I'm curious to see what comes off. Also a little worried about you boys. Anything up your sleeves?"

"Nope. We're layin' low, Boss, honest Injun," averred Bud.

"Jim, I met Sue Henderson this afternoon," spoke up Curly, "an' she asked me if it was true that Molly wasn't goin' with *you*. Sue's the biggest gossip in Flag, except her ma, so I tried to use my haid. I said yes it was true—that Molly an' Jim had a tiff an' she got mad an' dished Jim fer this dance. Sue looked darned queer an' asked me if that also applied to your engagement. I said Lord, no. But I didn't convince Sue. I reckon it's goin' to look bad fer Molly."

"Serve her darn right," said Slinger.

"You see, Jim, Molly's picked the quickest way to queer herself with Flag folks," went on Curly. "But the crazy kid—she's not smart enough to see that Darnell won't queer himself with these Flag girls fer her. Shore as shootin' Molly Dunn of the Cibeque will be a wallflower at the dance."

"But you boys—" began Jim, haltingly.

"Shore we'll cut her daid," interrupted Curly, and his drawling voice had a steel ring. "Molly's a darlin', but she cain't play didoes with the Diamond."

When Jim related this bit of conversation to Gloriana, after supper, he was amazed to note she did not show any surprise. He had been shocked at Curly's ultimatum. Those loyal cowboys whom Molly could wind round her little finger! But this was only another proof to Jim how little he knew the cowboys and the West. Gloriana, with her feminine perspicacity, saw much more clearly than he.

"It'll be a good lesson, Jim," said Glory. "If only Ed Darnell runs true to form!"

"And what's that?"

"Molly is only pretty game for him. He'll play with her, but he won't champion her. He's keen after Sue Henderson. All these Flag girls have regular beaus who take them to dances. Darnell couldn't get any one except Molly. And you can bet he won't dance exclusive attendance on her."

"I don't like it, Glory," returned Jim, moodily.

"No wonder. It'll be a beastly Christmas Eve for you, Jim. Small return for your affection and generosity. But life is like that. I'm sure, though, this dance will settle Molly's hash, to be slangy, and work to your interest. . . . I think you'd better vamoose now, so I can dress."

"What are you going to wear, Glory?" asked Jim, with interest.

"Well, it's an occasion not to overlook. I want your town of Flag to see you have a sister you can be proud of, anyway."

"Good! Knock 'em dead, Glory. And that goes for the cowboys, too."

"I shall avail myself of the opportunity, to my utmost . . . Jim, how are we to go? In that breezy buckboard?"

"Yes; we have to. The snow's 'most gone. But we might use the sleigh in a pinch."

"I'd like that, with the buffalo robe. And, Jim, don't forget a couple of hot stones in a burlap sack. It'll save me from pneumonia."

Jim ran into the living-room to have a word with his uncle before dressing.

"Son, I'm goin' to pass on this dance," said the rancher, with a chuckle. "I reckon it wouldn't be any fun for me. I'll wait for Molly's party hyar next Wednesday. An' you see to it she's back home by then."

"Uncle, I'll do it or die."

"Fetch Glory in before you leave. I can stand havin' my eye knocked out once more."

While Jim dressed his mind was active. If his cowboys and acquaintances snubbed Molly that night it might give him an opening for the wild plot he meant to carry out. And if Darnell played up to it as Gloriana had declared he would play— then the hour would be ripe for Jim's coup. He had to choke down his shame, his resentment that he must resort to such means to recover his sweetheart. Whatever he was going to do must be done quickly, for Molly's sake more than his.

Molly's room at the ranch-house had been kept precisely as she had left it. Jim went to the kitchen and gave the housekeeper instructions to light Molly's lamps about midnight, to start a fire in the grate, and to be careful about the screen. Lastly Jim took from his closet the fur coat he had bought for Molly, and with this on his arm, and his own overcoat he made the stone-floored corridor ring with his footsteps. Gloriana's room was dark, except for the flicker of wood fire behind the screen. Whereupon Jim hurried to the living-room.

Glory stood in the bright flare of lamps and fire, her furs on the floor, and she was pivoting for the benefit of her uncle.

Jim was not prepared for this vision of loveliness. Glory, in white gown with flounces of exquisite lace, and a hint of blue, her beautiful arms and neck bare, with a smile of pure joy on her face, and that dancing purple lightning in her eyes, was an apparition and a reality that sent the blood thrilling from Jim's heart.

"Glory, you look a little like your mother," Uncle Jim was saying. "But I reckon, only a little. . . . Lass, I—I hope we Western folks are not too rough an' plain to—to make you happy. It shore makes *me* happy, an' almost young again, to look at you."

"Thank you, Uncle; that *is* a sweet compliment," said Glory and she stepped out of her furs to kiss him. "Don't you worry about me and all my finery. It'll wear out—and by that time I hope I'll deserve to be happy in your great West."

It was late according to Western custom when Jim and Gloriana arrived at the hotel, and the lobby was crowded. Red and green decorations, upon which shone bright lights, lent the interior of the hotel the felicitous color of the season. Entrance to the dining-hall, from which emanated strains of Spanish music and the murmur of gay voices, was blocked by a crowd of lookers-on, some of whom surely had the lithe build of cowboys.

Jim saw Gloriana to the wide stairway which led to the ladies' dressing-room, and then went in search of his own. Curly and Bud were there, immaculate in dark suits and white shirts, which rendered them almost unrecognizable to Jim. Curly, particularly, looked handsome and clean-cut, and he did not appear unomfortable, as did Bud. Slinger also showed up on Jim's entrance, sleek and dark and impassive, as striking in his black suit as when he wore the deerskin of the forest.

"Where's the gang?" asked Jim.

"Wal, they're shore out there hoofin' it. Up an' Lonestar an' Cherry an' Jack all dug up gurls somewhere. Hump says he's too crippled yet an' will only look on."

"Boss, you oughta see the lady who came in on the arm of Jackson Way," observed Bud. "Out-of-town gurl an' she'll run Molly close fer looks. Jack never seen us atall. Son-of-a-gun! We gotta get a dance with her."

"Sure. I'll fit it, boys," Jim assured them.

"Jim, I see you've disobeyed Ring Locke's orders," drawled Curly, disapprovingly.

"Curly, darn it, I couldn't pack a gun with this rig," complained Jim, designating the trim suit of black. "Where'd I wear that cannon you insist on my carrying?"

"Wal, if you went slappin' around me you'd shore hurt your hand. An' if you watch me you'll notice I don't turn my back to nothin'."

Jim sighed. Almost he had forgotten the menace of the time and place.

"I'll risk it. And if Croak Malloy shows up I'll dive somehow."

"Wherever you are you want to see Croak first," returned Curly. "He's not liable to show up heah, but he might. An' to look fer him is the idea."

"Slinger, you're going to dance?" asked Jim.

"I shore ain't hankerin' to make a sliding fool of myself. But I promised this mawnin', an' I reckon I cain't back out."

Curly looked rather fierce, and chewed at his cigarette, something unusual for the cool Texan.

"Well, come on, you Diamond," said Jim, at length. "Let's go get Glory."

She was waiting for Jim on the stairway, queenly and beautiful, her great eyes brilliant with excitement and interest.

"My Gawd! Curly, lemme hold on to you," whispered Bud.

Curly let out a little gasp which was not lost on Jim, but Slinger showed no sign of being transfixed by Gloriana's loveliness. She came down to meet them, with just a hint of eager gaiety, and apparently unconscious of the gaping crowd. After a moment of greeting Curly elbowed an entrance for the others in the colorful hall.

"Pretty nifty, I'll say," observed Bud. "What do you think of the style Flag's puttin' on, since you come Miss Glory?"

"Very different from Jim's letter descriptions of

217

Western dance-halls," laughed Gloriana. "I like this."

"Jim, hurry an' dance with your sister so we can get a chance," added Bud, very business-like.

"Say, don't you gazabos fight over Glory or dance her off her feet," replied Jim. "That happened last time. Glory came West to get well, and not to be buried. . . . Come on, Glory, see if boots and chaps have made me clumsy."

When he swung his sister out into the eddying throng of dancers she said: "Jim, I saw Molly in the dressing-room. Sue Henderson and her mother cut her dead. Mrs. Henderson, you know, is the leading social light of Flag. Molly looked wonderfully sweet and pretty in her new dress. But scared, and dazed in spite of her nerve. Jim, she won't be able to carry it through. Darnell will fail her. Then your chance will come."

"Poor crazy kid!" choked Jim. "This'll be a rotten night for her—and sure a tough one for me. . . . Glory, if it wasn't for that, I'd be the proudest escort you ever had at any dance. Even as it is I just want to bust with pride. I'll bet you Curly squeezed my arm black and blue, when he saw you on the stairs. And Bud whispered: 'My Gawd! Curly, lemme hold on to you!' "

"They are dears," replied Gloriana, dreamily. "Only—just too much in earnest. . . . Slinger scares me."

"Well, enjoy yourself. These affairs are few and

far between. . . . It ought to be a great night for you. All eyes are on you, Glory. . . . How terribly pretty you are!—Gosh! pretty isn't the word. . . . And you dance like—like a dream. . . . Glory, dear, haven't you wasted a good deal of your life doing this?"

"Yes, I have, Jim," she replied, regretfully.

At the expiration of that waltz they were at the far end of the large room, and had to make their way through a whispering, staring crowd of dancers. Jim espied Jackson Way with a very pretty brunette girl. Jack tried to escape in the press, but Jim nailed him gaily, "Where you going, cowboy?" And so the blushing Jack and his fair damsel were captured and led across to Curly and Bud and Slinger.

"Glory I'll leave you to the tender mercies of the Diamond," said Jim, after there had been a pleasant interchange of introductions and some gay repartee. "But I'll keep an eye on you. . . ."

"Jim, there are Ed Darnell and Molly," interrupted Gloriana, suddenly. Her voice had an icy edge.

Before Jim glanced up he felt a jerk of his whole frame, as released blood swelled along his hot veins. He saw Molly first, and knew her, yet seemed not to know. As he met her dusky eyes, unnaturally large and bright, with almost a wild expression, his passion subsided. He smiled and bowed to her as if nothing untoward had hap-

pened. And it pleased him that Gloriana did likewise. The others of Jim's company, however,
pointedly snubbed Molly. Then Jim's glance
switched to Darnell. In this good-looking and ele-
gant gentleman Jim scarcely recognized the man
he had seen with Bambridge in the station at
Winslow. At least that was a first impression,
which had not the test of proximity or consistence;
and he concluded it would be wiser to be deaf to
his jealousy and await developments.

That moment, however, was the beginning of a
most miserable experience. Jim left Gloriana with
the gathering group of young people, and strolled
away on his vigil. His purpose was fixed and unal-
terable; his embarrassment and humiliation now
actual pain; and not all of these states of mind
could render him oblivious to his position there. He
had only to make the rounds of the dance-hall, the
corridors and lobby, to realize his status. His cowboys, and his other friends, and Flagerstown folk
who were close to old Jim Traft, had shown and
were still showing their contempt for Molly Dunn.
These people represented the rather small élite of
the Arizona town. A majority of those present,
however, were made up of cowboys, and young
men about town, all accompanied by the girls of
their choice; and it was plain gossip had run rife
among them, and they did not conceal their
curiosity and satisfaction. Little Molly Dunn of the
Cibeque, sister of the gun-thrower, and a plain girl

of Arizona backwoods, had jilted the young Easterner, the favorite nephew of rich old Jim Traft. It was all as plain as print, and it grew so much plainer, as time progressed, that Jim might have been reading it through a microscope. There was only one good thing about the miserable situation, and that was that Molly Dunn could not fail to see the humiliation she had brought upon her lover.

Jim danced with Sue Henderson, and two others of the Flagerstown girls who had been friendly to Gloriana, and it was an ordeal, for they were both sympathetic and vindictive. Common little hussy—Molly Dunn! And Jim had to resent that, and try to make excuses for Molly.

Darnell did precisely what Gloriana had predicted. He neglected Molly for the girls of higher social standing, and it seemed to Jim that when Darnell grasped the significance of the situation he showed his true colors. He left Molly to the cowboys and the clerks. She danced and flirted wildly. She was too gay, too indifferent, and before long she broke and went to the other extreme. Jim watched her sit out three dances alone, trying to hide in a corner. But Molly Dunn could not hide at that dance.

Jim thought it was time to do something, and approaching Gloriana, who sat with Curly, he said, "Come on, you." And he dragged them up.

"You're going to dance with Molly," replied Gloriana, gladly. "It is high time."

"Yes, if she will. But, anyway, we can show this crowd where we stand."

As they approached Molly she appeared to shrink, all except her big dark eyes. Gloriana sat down beside her and said something nice about Molly's new dress and how sweet she looked.

"Molly, won't you dance the next with me?" asked Jim.

Curly gazed down upon her, his fair handsome face clouded, and his flashing blue eyes full of sorrow.

"Molly Dunn, you've shore played hell heah tonight," he said.

Molly surely was ready to burst into tears when the music started again. Dancers from all sides rushed upon the floor, and Curly, with a gay call to Jim, drew Gloriana into the thick of the whirling throng. Jim did not wait for Molly's consent; he took her hand, and pulled her to her feet and led her out into the maze. Then when he had her close and tight in his arms, he felt that he had surely understood himself.

"Oh—Jim," she whispered, "it's been awful! . . . An' the worst was when Glory came to me jest now—before them all—an' spoke so sweet—as if nothin' had happened. . . . Oh, I wanted the ground to open an' swallow me."

Jim thought that a strange speech, full of contrition and shame as it was. What about him! But

222

Gloriana had been the great factor in Molly's downfall.

"Glory is true blue, Molly," Jim whispered back. "That ought to prove it. You've doubted her."

Jim felt a gradual relaxing of Molly's stiff little hand and then a sinking of her form against him.

"I'm ashamed," she replied, huskily. "I'll go drown myself in the Cibeque."

"Yes, you will!" In the press of the throng it seemed to Jim that he had her alone and hidden safe from the inquisitive eyes. He could hug her without restraint and he did. Molly hid her dusky head on his shoulder and danced as one in a trance.

Chapter Twelve

ALL too soon that dance ended, and Jim got Molly into an out-of-the-way corner, where a few other couples, evidently lovers, were too concerned with themselves to look at anyone else.

Jim believed the tide had turned in his favor, though tragic little Molly was unconscious of it. She gazed up at him as if fascinated, with almost a terrible yearning and hopelessness. "Don't do it," whispered Jim, "or I'll kiss you right here."

"Do—do what?"

"Look at me like that. . . . Molly, you've sure made a mess of Christmas Eve, but it's not too late."

223

"Oh yes, Jim dear, it *is* too late," she sighed, mournfully.

"They all gave me—the cold shoulder. Except Glory, bless her! I—I cain't realize she didn't take me at my word."

"Not Glory. And what do you care for the others? You won't have to live with them. . . . Molly, you were mistaken in this Darnell. He's no good. He very nearly ruined Gloriana. What she told you was true. Look how he has treated you."

"Jim, I don't need to be told now," she interrupted, bitterly. "He's made a fool out of me. . . . But only tonight did I learn he's no good. Before we got here. He—he insulted me, Jim."

"Did he?—Well, that's not surprising. Just how?" returned Jim, in cool, hard query. "I hope he didn't lay a hand on you."

"He laid two hands on me," she said, frankly. "An' he was 'most as bad as Hack Jocelyn, if you remember. Jim. . . . I was aboot ready to bite when some one came into the hall."

"Ahuh!—Why did you come with him, then?" queried Jim, serenely.

"I had to come to this dance or die. Besides, I reckon I was some to blame. I told Darnell I wasn't good enough for the Trafts an' their crowd."

"Molly, you're generous, but you can't save him now."

"You leave him alone," flashed Molly. "He carries a gun. He might hurt you—an' thet'd shore kill me. . . . I'll tell Slinger. Honest, I will. But Slinger has never even looked at me tonight. He must despise me."

"No. Slinger is just angry with you. . . . Now, Molly, you must not let Darnell take you home. Promise you won't—or I'll go right out now—"

"I promise, Jim. Please ask Slinger to take me away. I'm sick of this dance. I want to go home."

"Out to the ranch?" he asked, hopefully.

"Home to the Cibeque, where I belong."

"All right, I'll find Slinger," rejoined Jim, thinking fast and furiously. "But let's dance again. There goes the music."

Jim did not break the sweet tumultuousness of that dance by a single word. When it was over he asked Molly to wait near the door, and left her back somewhat out of the throng. Then he instituted a wild search for Gloriana, whom he found presently with Curly.

"Gee! you two must be having the time of your lives!" he exclaimed, surprised at Gloriana's radiance and something indescribable about Curly.

"Jim, I am enjoying myself," admitted Gloriana, with a blush.

"Boss, this heah is aboot as near heaven as I ever hope to get," drawled Curly.

"Fine. Then you see Glory home. I'm going to be—engaged. . . . Glory, don't stay late." And Jim rushed away to find Slinger. In this he was also fortunate, as he found him in the smoking-room, alone and watchful. His dark face wore rather a sad expression. He was out of his element at a dance.

"Slinger, I want you. What're you doing? Dancing any?"

"I had one with Glory. Thet'll be aboot all fer me. If I wasn't worried about the kid I'd chase myself back to the ranch. I've been hangin' around heah listenin' to this fellar Darnell." Slinger spoke low and indicated a noisy group of young men. They had a flask and were exchanging it. Darnell had here the same ingratiating manner, the same air of good fellowship, which Jim had noted in the dance-hall. He appeared to be a man nearing thirty, well set up, handsome in a full-faced, sensual way, and unmistakably egotistical. He would go far with young people.

"What of him?" whispered Jim.

"Wal, I shore ain't crazy aboot him. Strikes me sort of tincanny. . . . Jim, he's packin' a gun. Can you see thet?"

"No, Slinger, I'll be hanged if I can."

"Wal, he is, an' thet's kind of funny. If I could find a reason, I'd mess up this heah place with him. But it'd look all the wuss fer Molly—"

"Yes, it would. Let Darnell alone. And, Slinger, listen. Molly has had enough of this. She sent me to ask you to take her home. But I've got an idea.

You run over to the stable and send a boy with a sleigh. Pronto. I'll let Molly think you're going to take her. But I'll take her myself, and out to the ranch. Savvy, pard?"

"I shore do. An' damn if you ain't a good fellar," declared Slinger. "Molly had better sit tight this time. . . . Jim, this heah deal eases my mind."

"Rustle, then, you Indian."

Jim saw Slinger glide out with his inimitable step, and then he went to get his overcoat and hat. For the moment he had forgotten the fur coat, which he had folded inside his. But there it was. With these he hurried back to the hall, eager and thrilling, afraid, too, that Molly might have bolted or that Darnell might have come out. To his relief, however, he found her waiting, strained of face, her eyes like burnt holes in a blanket. They leaped at sight of him.

"Slinger has gone for a sleigh," said Jim, as he reached her, and he tried to be natural. "Here, slip into this. You won't need to go upstairs. I'll get your coat tomorrow. And no one will see you as you go out."

"Whose coat is this? . . . Oh, what lovely fur!— Glory's?"

"Hurry!" he replied, holding it for her.

"Slinger can fetch it right back."

Jim turned up the high collar of the coat, and against the dark fox fur Molly's eyes shone beautifully. What a difference fine feathers made!

"Come," he said, taking Molly's arm. He led her out, relieved that but few dancers paid attention to their departure. In the lobby entrance they ran square into Darnell, gay, heated of face.

"Hello, kid—Where the deuce are you going?" he shot out, and his gaiety suddenly fled. Two men behind him came up, evidently his companions, and curious. Jim did not recognize either.

"Home," replied Molly, and she flashed by.

Darnell took a step forward to confront Jim.

"We've met before?" he said, and both voice and look were uncertain.

"Yes. I happen to be Jim Traft—Miss Dunn's *fiancé*. And if you don't step aside this meeting will be somewhat like the one you spoke of."

It was certain that long before Jim completed this deliberate speech Darnell had recognized him. One of the strangers drew him aside, so Jim could pass. And as Jim went out he heard Darnell curse. Molly was already out in the corridor. As Jim joined her Slinger came up the steps.

"Any ruction heah?" he queried, sharply. "I seen Darnell stop you."

"No. I got out of it all right, Slinger. Come on," replied Jim, grimly, and he laughed inwardly at the thought of what this Ed Darnell had happened upon. His luck, at least, was out.

A two-seated sleigh, with a Mexican driver, stood at the curb. Jim bundled Molly into the back seat, and stepping in he tucked the heavy robe round her and himself. Molly uttered an exclamation which was surely amazed protest.

"Slinger, I'll see Molly—home," said Jim, and for the life of him he could not keep the elation out of his voice.

"Shore, Jim, you see her home," drawled Slinger, meaningly. And he leaned over the side of the sleigh. "Sister, you've messed up things considerable. But somehow Jim still loves you, an' I reckon I do, too. We jest cain't help it. All the same, don't go triflin' with strange fellars no more. I'll see you in the mawnin'."

"Slinger, you lay off Darnell," insisted Jim, forcefully.

"All right, Boss. But I'll jest watch him a little. Shore is an interestin' cuss. I seen him gettin' gay with one of them rich gurls."

Jim laughed and told the Mexican boy to drive straight out the main street.

"It's closer, turnin' heah," spoke up Molly, a little alarmed. As yet, however, she had no inkling of the plot.

"More snow out this way. This bare ground is hard on the runners," replied Jim, and indeed the rasping sound of iron on gravel was irritating to nerves as well. Jim felt for Molly's hand under the robe, and found it, an ungloved cold little member. She started and tried to draw it away. In vain! Jim held on as a man gripping some treasure he meant to keep. Soon they were on the snow, and then the sleigh glided smoothly with the merry bells ringing. Soft heavy flakes were falling, wet and cool to the face.

"Heah—turn down heah," called Molly, as they reached the last side street.

"Boy, drive straight out to the Traft ranch," ordered Jim.

Molly stood up, and would have leaped out of the sleigh had not Jim grasped her with no uncertain hands, and hauled her down, almost into his arms. She twisted round to look up at him. The darkness was thick, but he could see a pale little face, with great staring eyes.

"You—you want to get somethin' before takin' me home?" she asked.

"Why, of course, Molly. This is Christmas, you know," he returned, cheerfully.

"I—I didn't know you could be like this." And Jim imagined he had more cause to be happy.

No more was said. Jim endeavored to secure Molly's hand again, but she had hidden it somewhere. Thwarted thus, Jim put an arm round her. When they reached the big pine trees, black against the snow, Jim knew they were nearing the ranch. He nerved himself for the crisis. There was no use of persuasion or argument or subterfuge. Then the ranch-house loomed dark, with only one light showing. The bells ceased jangling in a crash.

"Molly, come in for—a minute," said Jim, easily, as he stepped out.

"No, thanks, Jim," she replied, with pathos. "I'll stay heah. Hurry, an' remember—I—I cain't accept no Christmas presents."

Jim leaned over, as if to rearrange the robe, but he snatched her bodily out of the sleigh.

"All right, boy, drive back," he ordered, and as the bells clashed again he turned with the kicking Molly in his arms. He heard her voice, muffled in the furs, as he pressed her tight, and he feared she used some rather strong language. Up the steps, across the wide veranda and into the dark ranch-house he packed her, fighting all the while, and on into the dim-lighted living-room, where he deposited her in his uncle's big armchair. Then he flew to lock the door. It was done. He felt no remorse—only a keen, throbbing, thick rapture. He turned up the lamp, and then lighted the other one with the red shade. Next he removed the screen from before the smoldering fire, to replenish it with chips of cedar and pine cones.

"Jim Traft—what've you done?" cried Molly, huskily.

Jim turned then, to see her in the chair, precisely as he had bundled her.

"Fetched you home, Molly," he said, with emotion.

"It was a trick."

"Reckon so."

"You didn't mean to take me to my boardin'-house?"

"I'm afraid I never thought of that."

231

"An' thet damn Slinger! He was in the deal with you?"

"Yes. Slinger was implicated—to the extent of getting the sleigh."

"Wal, now you got me heah—what you think you're goin' to do?" she demanded.

"Oh, wish you a merry Christmas and a happy New Year."

"Jim—honest I wish—you the same," she responded, faltering a little.

"Thanks. But it's not Christmas yet," rejoined Jim, consulting his watch. "Only eleven o'clock. At midnight I'll give you the other Christmas present."

"Other?—Jim Traft, are you loony? Or am I dreamin'? You didn't give me nothin'. You tantilized me with thet—thet ring, which was shore low-down. But thet's all."

"Molly, you have one of your presents. You've got it on. . . . That fur coat."

Uttering a cry of surprise and consternation, she bounced out of the chair to slip out of the rich, dark, fragrant coat. She handled it with awe, almost reverence, stroked it, and then with resignation laid it over the table.

"Pretty nice, don't you think?" queried Jim, pleasantly. "Becomes you, too."

"I'm findin' out you're as much of—of a brute as any cowboy," she asserted, tearfully. "How'm I to get back to my boardin'-house? When Glory comes? You'll send me then, Jim?"

"Molly, you're not going back to your boarding-house—tonight—or ever again," he replied, confronting her and reaching for her, so that Molly backed into the armchair and fell into it.

"I am—too," she retorted, but she was vastly alarmed.

"No, this is home, till you've grown out of your schoolgirl days."

"Kidnappers—you an' Slinger!"

"I reckon we are, Molly."

"You're wuss than Hack Jocelyn," she cried, wildly. "Are you goin' to hawg-tie me heah?"

"No. I don't believe you'll want to leave, after tomorrow when you see Uncle Jim and Glory."

"Jim—I cain't see them. It'd hurt too bad. Please let me go."

"Nope. . . . You hurt me, didn't you?"

"All fer your good, Jim. . . . Cain't you see thet?"

"Indeed I can't. You just almost broke my heart, Molly Dunn. If it hadn't been for Uncle and Glory—Well, never mind. I don't want to heap coals of fire upon your head."

"What did Uncle Jim an' Glory do?" she asked, poignantly.

"They both have faith in you. Faith!"

"I cain't stand thet, Jim. I cain't," she wailed.

He slipped into the big chair and gathered her in his arms. What a tight, quivering little bundle!

"Molly, both Uncle and Glory love you."

"No—no. Thet's not so," she cried, half smothered. "Let me go, Jim."

"Ha, ha! I see myself. . . . Hold up your head, Molly."

"If you dare kiss me—Jim Traft—I—I. . . . Oh—"

"Don't you dare me, Molly Dunn," added Jim, quite beside himself now. Molly's lips were sweet fire, and she could not control them. But she was strong, and as slippery as an eel. Jim had to confine his muscular efforts to holding her merely.

"Molly, you are mussing a perfectly beautiful little dress," he said, mildly, "besides, darling, you're making a very indecorous, not to say immodest, display of anatomy."

"I don't care," panted Molly, red of face, blazing of eye. But she did care. She was weakening.

"Darling." Jim divined this word had considerable power; at least enough to make Molly hide her face.

"Sweetheart," he went on.

And this appeared to end her struggling.

"Don't you love me, Molly?"

"Thet has been—all the trouble. . . . Too much—to disgrace you," she replied, haltingly, and she looked up with wet eyes and trembling lips. Jim was quick to kiss them and when he desisted this time, she lay back upon his arm, her eyes closed, heavy-lidded, her face pale and rapt.

"Don't you *want* to stay, Molly," he went on, tenderly.

"No—no. . . . But I'm a liar," she replied, brokenly, without stirring.

"To be my wife?"

She was mute and therefore won. Jim found the little box in his pocket and extracting the diamond ring from it he slipped it upon her finger, where it fitted tight and blazed triumphantly.

"There!"

Moreover, it had potency to make her eyes pop open. She stared. Slowly a transformation set in. She became ecstatic and ashamed, filled with sudden wild misery and joy, all at once.

"Oh, I—I've been jest what Slinger called me," she cried.

"What was that?"

"It's too turrible to tell. . . . How can you be so good—to make me love you more? . . . Jim, honest I thought I was thinkin' only of you. If I was fit for you I wanted to—an' sometimes deep down in me I reckoned I was, because love ought to count—I wanted to make myself unfit. . . . Yet when thet mouthin' pawin' Darnell laid hold of me—when I had my chance to disgrace you an' degrade myself—I couldn't. My very soul went sick. An' then I only wanted to get free of him at any cost. I did. An' afterward he begged so hard, an' I longed so to go to the dance, thet I went."

"Well, I'm glad you did since we had to have this ruction. But don't mention Darnell to me again, at least tonight."

"After all, people won't know how bad it was," she said, with a passion of hope and regret.

"They'll think it was only a lovers' quarrel," replied Jim, happily, and he was glad to believe that himself.

"If only Glory will forgive me!"

"Glory! Why, she has already."

"You don't know thet lovely sister of yours, Jim. . . . The more she persuaded me I was doin' wrong, the kinder an' sweeter she talked, the proud way she looked—the more I wanted to do somethin' awful. I wanted to hide thet I loved her, too. . . . Oh, she seemed so wonderful—so far above me. But if she'll forgive I'll never do wrong again, so help me Gawd!"

"Molly, that's a vow. I'll hold you to it. . . . And now, honey, make up to me for all I suffered—for every miserable moment."

"I cain't, Jim," she replied, mournfully. "What's done is done. Oh, if only I could."

"Well, then for every wretched moment you spent with *him*. Could you count how many?"

"I reckon I could," she said, thoughtfully. "What's a moment? Same as a minute."

"More like a second. Some are utterly precious, like this one. Others are horrible."

"Wal, with sixty seconds to the minute and sixty minutes to the hour—an' I reckon aboot five hours, all told—thet would be how much?—A lot to make up for!"

"Will you try? That will be your repentance."

"Yes," she promised, shyly, yet fearfully, as if remembering.

"Put your arms around my neck. . . . There!— Now start kissing me once for every one of those heart-broken minutes."

Molly was not very far on this tremendous penance, considering sighs and lulls, and spasms of quick tender passion to make amends, when a knock on the living-room door startled her violently.

"Well, if that isn't tough!" ejaculated Jim, and putting Molly down he rose to go to the door. "Must be Gloriana May."

And she it was who entered, radiant and beautiful, with swift hopeful flash of purple eyes that moved from Jim to Molly, and back again. Curly stepped in behind her.

"Jim, dear, I hope we didn't intrude," she said, sweetly, with mischief and gaiety underlying her speech. "Were you aware that this is Christmas?"

"Jim, many happy returns of this heah evenin'— I mean the last of it," drawled Curly, as he came forward, so cool and easy, and already within possession of the facts. "Molly, I've been shore daid sore at you. But I'm an understandin' cuss. . . . Suppose I kiss you my Christmas greetin's."

And he did kiss her, gallantly, though withal like a brother, while Molly stood stiff, blushing and paling by turns.

"Curly Prentiss, do you kiss *every* girl on Christmas?" she had spirit to retort.

"Nope. Thet privilege I reserve fer particular gurls," he drawled, and turned to Jim with extended hand. "Boss, I'm shore glad. This is the second time the Diamond's near been busted. Never no more! . . . Good night, all. I'll see you in the mawnin'."

When Jim had closed the door upon him there was an eloquent silence in which Gloriana and Molly gazed into each other's eyes. Certain it was that Jim trembled. Yet his hopes ran high. Molly approached Gloriana and stood bravely, without trace of the shame Jim knew she felt.

"Glory, I'm heah again—to stay," she said, simply. "Jim kidnapped me—an' I reckon saved me when he did it. . . . I'm shore powerful sorry I've been such a dumbhaid. But you cain't doubt my love for him, at least. . . . Will you forgive me?"

Gloriana took Molly into her arms, and bending over her spoke with emotion. "I do indeed, Molly, as I hope to be forgiven. . . . Come with me to my room. . . . Good night, brother Jim; it's late. We'll see you in the morning."

Chapter Thirteen

SNELL'S gambling-hall was crowded on the afternoon of Christmas Day, when Jim Traft and Curly Prentiss arrived rather late. Evidently no open sesame was required on this occasion, and no doortender. Curly said this was because the business men of Flagerstown, who liked to buck the tiger, would be conspicuous for their absense on this holiday. But there would be a big game going, and Darnell would be in it.

Curly appeared to be under the influence of liquor, which Jim knew he was most decidedly not. But Curly excited no interest whatever, for the good reason that he differed very little in garb and manner from other cowboys present. Some, in fact, were hilariously drunk.

They strolled around to watch the faro game, the roulette wheel, and other games of chance, more or less busy with customers, until they approached a ring of lookers-on which surrounded the heavy poker game Curly wanted to sit in, provided Darnell was one of the players.

By looking over the heads of spectators they ascertained that Darnell was indeed there, and also Bambridge. Then Curly whispered to Jim that the other three gamblers were precisely the same he and Bud had watched yesterday afternoon.

"All set," concluded Curly, his blue eyes flashing like a northern sunlit sky. "Big game an' all daid sore. Darnell is ridin' them high an' handsome."

Then he turned to the circle of watchers and lurched into it. "Heah, lemme in, you geezers," he called out, in a loud and good-natured drawl. "I'm a-rarin' to set in this heah game."

But Curly's action was more forceful. Without waiting for the men to open up he swept them aside. Jim followed until he secured a place just back of the front row, where he could see and yet keep out of sight.

"Gennelmen, I wanta set in," said Curly. "There's only five of you heah. Thet shore ain't no good game. You oughta have six. An' heah I am."

Darnell looked up and gave Curly a hard glance. But if it were one of recognition he certainly did not connect Curly with the little meeting in Winslow some time previous.

"This is poker for men of means and not casino for two-bit cowpunchers," he said.

"Hell you shay," replied Curly, without offense, as he wiped a hand across his face, after the fashion of the inebriated. "Reckon you don't savvy I ain't no two-bit cowpuncher."

"Get out or I'll have you thrown out," snarled Darnell. His concentration on the game was such that an interruption jarred him Yet even in anger there was no heat in the sharp dark eyes. His

240

cheek and the line of his chin were tight. Here Jim saw the man as a handsome cold-faced gambler.

"My Gawd! man, you must be a stranger heah-aboots," drawled Curly, and he clumsily pulled out the one vacant chair left and fell into it, knocking against the table. With one hand he dropped his sombrero beside the chair and with the other he slammed down a huge roll of greenbacks, the outside one of which bore the number one hundred.

"My money ain't counterfeit, an' I reckon it's as good as anybody's," said Curly, lolling over the table in the careless laxity of a drunken man. His curly hair, wet and dishevelled, hid his eyes. He gave his mouth and chin the weakness character-izing the overindulgence in drink.

At sight of the roll of greenbacks Darnell's eyes leaped, but before he could speak, which it was evident he intended to do, Bambridge came out with: "Sure your money's as good as anybody's, cowboy. Sit in an' welcome."

"Much obliged, Mister," replied Curly, grate-fully, as he snapped the rubber band off his roll. "What's the game, friends?"

"You make your own game. No limit," replied the dealer, who happened to be the man from Winslow. "Your ante."

"Make it five call ten," drawled Curly, but he labored long over the roll of greenbacks trying to find one of small numeration. "Doggone!—This heah legacy of mine is shore dwindlin' of change."

The game proceeded then with Curly apparently a lamb among wolves. Still, though betting with reckless abandon, he did not risk much. "Dog-gone-it! Wait till I get some cairds," he complained, "an' I'll show you fellars how a cowboy bets."

Altogether he carried out his pretense of a drinking range-rider come into possession of much money that was destined to make rich pickings for one of the gamblers presently. Once or twice the Winslow man kindly cautioned Curly about betting, which act incurred the displeasure of Bambridge.

"I'm two thousand out," he growled. "This cowpuncher insisted on joining us. Now let him play his own game."

"Bambridge, I'm out more than that," replied the Winslow rancher, sarcastically. "But I reckon it's lowdown to rob this boy."

"Rob!—Are you casting any reflections?" spoke up Darnell, sharply.

"Not yet," answered the rancher, steadily, his eyes veiled.

"See heah, Boss," began Curly, to the Winslow man. "I'm shore appreciatin' your advice. But since it 'pears to rile this gamblin' couple, you let me play my own game. I ain't so dumb. But at thet I only started in fer fun."

Jim was all eyes when the deal passed to Darnell. He had long slim white hands, flexible, and manipulated the cards marvelously. Yet when he dealt them out he was very slow and deliberate, as if to show his antagonists that his deal was open and fair. There was some stiff betting on that hand, which Curly passed and which Bambridge won. The game seesawed on. Finally Curly won his first hand, and he was jubilant. After that he staked his winnings recklessly. He had injected something of humor in the game, from a spectator's point of view, judging from the comments round the circle. Jim heard a cowboy whisper: "Thet's Curly Prentiss, an' you wanta look out."

Upon Darnell's next deal the play was a jack-pot, with the dealer's privilege of making the ante.

"Throw in one of your hundreds, cowboy," he said, as he chipped in one hundred dollars.

"Wal, century plants ain't nothin' in my young life," drawled Curly. "There you air, my Mississippi River gazabo."

Darnell gave a slight start, and eyed the cowboy intently. Curly's head was bent rather low, as usual, with his eyes hidden under that wave of bright hair any girl might have envied. He was smiling, easy, and happy in the game. Perhaps his remark was merely a chance one and meant nothing. But Jim's reflection was that Darnell certainly did not know cowboys of the Arizona-range stripe.

The Winslow man opened the jack-pot, the two players between him and Curly stayed, and then

Bambridge raised before the draw. Presently they were all in, in a jack-pot carrying more than six hundred dollars. The watchers of the game looked on with intense interest. Each player called for what cards he wanted. Darnell said casually: "Three for myself—to this little pair." And he slid the three cards upon the table and laid the deck aside.

Suddenly like a panther Curly leaped. His left hand shot out to crack down upon Darnell's and crushed it flat on the table. Then his right followed, clutching a big blue gun, which he banged on the table, making the players jump, then freeze in their seats. Curly sank back and threw up his head to show blazing eyes as clear as crystal. His frank young face set cold. How vastly a single moment had transformed him!

Darnell turned a greenish livid hue. He had been trapped. Malignance and fear betrayed him.

"You—low-down — — — —— of a caird sharp!" drawled Curly, in a voice with a terrible edge. "You reckoned I was drunk, eh?"

The circle of men back of Darnell split and spread, with shuffling feet and hoarse whispers, in two wings, leaving the space there clear. That act was as significantly Western as Curly's. Jim had seen it before.

"Don't anybody move a hair," ordered Curly, and the pivoting of his gun indicated the other players. Bambridge gasped. Only the Winslow man remained cool. Perhaps he knew or guessed the nerve behind the gun-hammer, which plainly rose a trifle, sank back, to rise again, almost to full cock.

"Gentlemen, look heah," went on Curly, bitingly, and he turned Darnell's crushed hand over. Bent and doubled in his palm were three cards that dropped out. Aces!

"Pretty raw, I must say," spoke up the Winslow man. "At that, I had a hunch."

"Darnell, we Westerners don't often hang caird sharps, like we do cattle thieves. But on second offense we throw a gun," said Curly, and the menace of him seemed singularly striking. Then in the same cool, careless voice he called Darnell all the profane epithets, vile and otherwise, known to the range. "You get out of Flag. Savvy? . . . An' anytime anywhere after this—if you run into me—you pull a gun!"

Darnell whirled on his chair, knocking it to the floor, and he rushed through the opening in the crowd to disappear.

Curly moved the gun, by accident or intent—no one could tell—until it had aligned itself with Bambridge.

"Mister Bambridge, you've laid yourself open to suspicion round heah—long before this poker game," said Curly, as cutting as before. "I told your daughter thet, an' naturally it riled her. I reckon she's a fine girl who doesn't savvy her Dad."

"Who the hell is this hyar lyin' cowpuncher?" demanded Bambridge, yellow of face, as he appealed to the other players.

Curly's arm moved like a snake. "Don't you call me a liar twice! . . . I'm Curly Prentiss, an' I belong to the Diamond. *We* are on to you, Bambridge, if no other outfit round heah is. *We* know you're a damn sight crookeder cattle thief than Jed Stone himself. . . . Now listen closer. What I said aboot gun play, to your gamblin' new hand, Darnell, goes for you, too. Savvy? . . . Right now an' heah, or anywhere after."

"You—you drunken puncher—you'll pay for this holdup of an innocent—and unarmed man," panted Bambridge, as he got up, his face ghastly, sweating, and his eyes bulging with a fury of passions. He swept the edge of the crowd aside and thumped away.

"Gentlemen, I apologize for breaking up your game," said Curly, sheathing his gun. "But I reckon I saved you money. Suppose we divide what's on the table an' call it quits."

"Agreed," replied the Winslow man, gruffly. "Prentiss, we sure owe you a vote of thanks."

It was Jim, and not Curly, who told the rest of the Diamond what had happened at Snell's late on Christmas Day.

Bud and Cherry, who had already been surreptitiously looking upon red liquor, promptly went on the rampage, eventually getting Lonestar and Up Frost with them. Jackson Way, owing to his new girl, manfully refused to drink more than one glass with his comrades.

"No, siree," avowed Jack, seriously. "Sometime in a man's life he parts with bad whisky—an' company."

"You disgrash to Diamond," roared Bud.

Jim, learning of this from Ring Locke, rode back to town, perturbed in mind, but the cowboys could not be located, at least in a hasty search. So he went home to supper. Later Curly came in, serene and drawling. "They're shore a bad bunch of punchers. They've busted out. In the mawnin' we better go find them an' hawg-tie them an' pack them in, or they'll never be fit fer Molly's party."

It seemed incredible to Jim that the quiet evening at home was real. How strange to glance at Curly now and recall the tremendous force he had exhibited at Snell's only a few hours before! He was so easy-going, so droll and tranquil, as he unmercifully teased Molly, subtly including Gloriana in his philosophy.

"You cain't never tell aboot girls, Jim," he said, sorrowfully. "I've shore had a deal of experience with all kinds. Red-headed girls, I reckon, are best to gamble on. Blondes are no good. Brunettes are dangerous. They're like mules, an' fer a spell will be powerful good, just to get a chance to kick you. Christmas an' birthdays, though, a fellar's girl can be relied upon to stand without a halter. But these girls between blondes an' brunettes, the kind with hair like the ripple of amber moss, an' eyes like violets under water—they're scarce, thank the Lord. . . . I've heahed of a few, only never saw but one."

Uncle Jim roared, Molly threw something at Curly, while Gloriana was convulsed with laughter. Curly evidently was a perpetual source of surprise, delight, and mystery to Gloriana. There dawned in Jim a hope that she would grow to find more.

They had a pleasant hour in the bright living-room, then the rancher left the young folk to themselves. Curly stayed awhile longer.

"Wal," he said, presently, "I'll say good night, Miss Glory."

"What's your hurry?" queried Gloriana, in surprise. "Don't be so outlandishly thoughtful of my brother. He and Molly don't know we exist. . . . Oh, maybe you want to go to town."

"Wal, I had thought aboot it," drawled Curly.

"And maybe join in the general painting the Diamond is giving Flag?" went on Gloriana.

"Wal, they shore cain't do much paintin' or anythin' without me," he admitted, his keen blue eyes studying Gloriana.

Despite Gloriana's conviction of Jim's utter absorption, he still had eyes and ears for his sister and his best friend. Molly saw nothing except the ruddy coals of the fire, until Jim gave her a nudge.

"Very well, Mister Prentiss, good night," said Gloriana, icily, as she rose.

"Say, do you care a whoop aboot whether I get drunk or not?" demanded Curly, his face flaming. Gloriana was the one person who could stir him out of his nonchalance or coolness.

"Certainly not," replied Gloriana, in amaze. "Why should I? . . . But you are my brother's right-hand man. And I had hoped you would develop some character, for his sake."

"Cain't a man take a drink an' still have some character?" asked Curly, stoutly.

"Some men can," replied Gloriana, with emphasis that excluded Curly from her generalization.

"Wal, I reckon I'll go get awful drunk. Good night, Miss Traft."

"Good-by! . . . Mister Prentiss."

Curly departed hastily. His heavy steps sounded faster and faster, until they died away.

"Jim, this Curly cowboy irritates me," remarked Gloriana, coming to the fire.

"What?—Oh, I'm sorry, Glory. I thought you liked him," replied Jim, innocently.

"I do. He's a fine upstanding chap, so kind, easy-going, and big-hearted. He worships you, Jim. And of course that goes a long way with me. But it's the *other* side of him I can't—savvy, isn't it? It's that plagued cowboy side. . . . For instance, just a moment ago he saw you holding Molly's hand. So he possessed himself of mine. And I give you my word I could hardly get it away from him."

How sweet to hear Molly's laugh trill out! And the perplexity of Glory's expressive face, with its suggestion of color, likewise pleased Jim.

"Glory, the way to get along with Curly—and amuse yourself—is to let him hold your hand," said Jim.

"Don't be silly. I—I did that very thing, at the dance, until I got scared. In fact, I scarcely knew I *was* letting him."

"Glory, I told you Curly was the finest fellow I ever knew, for a man's friend, or a pard, as they call it out West. If you could stop his drinking he'd be that for a woman, too."

"I want to stop his drinking," admitted Gloriana, now gravely, "but I—I am not prepared to—to—"

"Sure you're not," interposed Jim, apologetically. "Don't misunderstand me, Glory. On the other hand, don't be cold to Curly just because you wasted some admiration—and sentiment— perhaps some kisses and caresses that would have raised poor Curly to the seventh heaven—on that Ed Darnell. . . . By the way, Glory, Curly threw a gun on Darnell today. Cussed him!—Whew! I never heard such language. He cast our cook, Jeff Davis, in the shade. And he drove Darnell out of Flag!"

"My—heavens! . . . Jim!" cried Gloriana, and Jim could find no suggestion of indifference now.

"Yes, by heavens—and any other place," nodded Jim, emphatically. He had the satisfaction of seeing Molly come out of her trance.

"Not on my account?" queried Gloriana, breathlessly.—"Oh, I hope not. I had all the slander and gossip I could stand—back home."

"Your name will never be heard of in connection with Darnell," said Jim. "And fortunately he chased half a dozen girls more than Molly. He—"

"The big liar!" interrupted Molly, disgustedly. "He swore *I* was the only one. . . . Aren't men lowdown, Glory?"

"Some of them are assuredly," agreed Gloriana. "But tell us, Jim. What happened? How did Curly do it?"

Whereupon Jim, warning the girls not to tell Uncle Jim just yet, related the experience of the afternoon, punctuating the story with mention of his own thrills and fears. He wanted to do justice to Curly's nerve—to that side of his character which seemed so incomprehensible to Gloriana. She was as horrified and fascinated as she was relieved.

"This was no trick for Curly Prentiss," went on Jim. "He had Darnell sized up. Knew he was a bluff, as well as a cheat. That there was not the slightest chance of a fight. And never will be so far as Darnell risking an even break."

"What's that?" asked Gloriana, her eyes still large and full of wondering awe.

"An even break is where two men go out, with intention to fight, and each has his chance to draw."

"Draw!—Draw what?" queried Gloriana, bewildered.

"Gosh! how dumb you are, Glory. Do you think I mean to draw pictures on the side of a barn?—The draw means to pull, throw, jerk a gun."

"Oh, I see. . . . I guess I am very stupid. . . . Then you don't think Curly will have one of those draws—even breaks with Darnell?"

"Not a chance in the world. Curly says Darnell will come to the end of his rope pretty pronto—and that will be swinging from a cottonwood tree."

"Hanged!"

"I reckon that was what Curly was driving at.—Glory, it shocks you terribly, I see. But please realize that Darnell has come to Arizona, first hounding a girl who happens to be my sister. Then he affiliates himself with a crooked cattleman—Bambridge. In Arizona, mind you! . . . Try to steel yourself to facts. The West is still raw, hard, sudden, bloody. It sickened me for months and even now I get a jar occasionally. But it's grand with all its stings. You'll find that out."

"I'm afraid I'm finding out a good deal already," murmured Gloriana, still with that fixed look in her beautiful eyes. "And some of it is—maybe I'm

252

not big enough for this West. . . . Well, I'll go to bed and leave you to yourselves. . . . Good night, Molly, little Western sister. This Christmas Day has been a happy one, after all. *'Quién sabe?'* as Curly says. Forget all the rest, Molly. . . . Good night, brother Jim. After all, you're smiled upon by the gods."

After Gloriana had gone Molly whispered, dreamily: "She called me sister! . . . Oh, I adore her! . . . Jim, shore as beans she fallin' in love with Curly. Only she doesn't even dream of it. An' Curly is ravin' crazy aboot her. He'll get drunk, Jim. Jest you wait an' see. I know these heah cow-boys. . . . An' Bud—he's as bad. An' poor Slinger!—Lordy! what's to become of us?"

"Love is indeed a very destructive agent, my dear," replied Jim dreamily.

"It darn near destroyed me, Mizzouri," she said, plaintively. "Oh, Jim, it'll shore do it yet—if you make me love you more an' more."

"Well, sweetheart, if you want to know, I'm quite satisfied and happy now. And I'd rather not risk another of your demonstrations—if it were to take the form of another Ed Darnell."

"You're makin' fun of me now," returned Molly, reproachfully, and then she slipped back into his arms. "I'm heah—for good."

Next morning the bunk-house was incredibly quiet when Jim knocked and stamped in. Jeff was cooking a lonely breakfast. "Outfit's stampeded, Boss. I seen it comin'."

"Dog-gone their hides!" complained Jim. "Now I'm afraid to go downtown."

Before he started, however, he consulted his uncle and advised a postponement of Molly's party until New Year's Eve.

"Fine idee," agreed the rancher. "But don't be hard on the boys, Jim. Remember that Diamond was the toughest outfit in Arizona. Lovable punchers, if I ever knew any, but sure blue hell on holidays. Better go downtown an' drag them out. Reckon thet four-flush Sheriff Bray had his chance at us last night. Don't tell the girls."

Jim had no intention of that, though so far as Molly was concerned she would know. He had a talk with Ring Locke and told him about the affair at Snell's. The foreman seemed both vastly concerned and pleased. "Son-of-a-gun, thet Prentiss boy. . . . Jim, thet'll settle Bambridge. He'll have to shoot or git out. An' he ain't the shootin' kind. All the same, I wish the Diamond was out of town."

Some of the cowboys might as well have been out of town, for all Jim could find of them. Jackson Way, of course, had gone to Winslow with his girl. Hump, Cherry, and Uphill had disappeared, after a bloodless and funny fight with some rival cowboys over a pool game. Lonestar Holliday was discovered lurching out of a cheap

Mexican lodging-house, almost speechless, and certainly lost to a sense of direction. Jim bundled him into the buckboard. "Sit on him, Charley," ordered Jim, "and take him home. Then hurry back."

Bud was in jail, and all Jim could find out, in the nature of offense, was a charge of disorderly conduct, including unusual profanity. Bray, the sheriff, was not to be found on the moment, and probably that was a good thing for all concerned. Bud was locked up with a tramp, two Mexicans, and a Navajo, and a madder cowboy Jim never had seen. "Boss, I'm gonna shoot thet — — — coyote of a sheriff!" he asserted. Jim paid his fine and got him out, greatly relieved that it had been no worse.

"Where's Curly?" demanded Jim.

"Shore haven't the slightest idee. I reckoned *he'd* stay home on Christmas—considerin'."

"When'd you see him last?"

"Yestiddy sometime, I think it was, but I ain't shore. The last time I seen him was when he was helpin' Miss Glory in the sleigh, after the dance. My Gawd! you'd took him fer the Prince of Wales."

"Then you went an' got drunk?"

"Must have, Boss, or suthin' like. My haid feels sorta queer."

"Fine lot of cowboys!" ejaculated Jim, meaning the expression literally. He had lived long enough in the West to learn that such derelictions of the Diamond were now the exception instead of the rule, which had been the case before his uncle put the outfit in his charge. Bud, however, took the assertion as a calumny and proceeded to burst forth. "Boss, celebratin' Christmas an' Fourth of July are religus duties every cowpuncher holds sacred. An' this hyar is the fust time the Diamond, all together, has busted out since last Fourth. You don't appreciate us. We oughta get pulverized every Saturday night."

"I'd fire every last man jack of you," averred Jim, stoutly.

"Dog-gone-it! When you was a tenderfoot you had some human feelin's. But now thet you're a moss-backed Westerner—an' turrible in love— you're wuss'n a sky pilot. If I fell in love I'd do somethin' won-n-derful."

"If *you* fell in love!—Why, you moon-eyed, dying-duck, tenor-singing lovesick calf—everybody knows what ails you," declared Jim, dryly.

"Hellyousay?" replied Bud, good-naturedly. "News to me. I'd like to know who she is. An' say, Boss, I'm not tellin' you what I'd do to anyone else for such disrespectful talk."

"Shut up, and think, if you're capable of it. I'm worried. I want to find Curly."

But that was impossible. Jim went back to the ranch considerably concerned over Curly's disappearance. Lonestar and Bud were back, and late that night Uphill came, so Ring Locke informed Jim. The next day and the next passed. On the third Hump and Cherry rolled in, more or less dilapidated. But no Curly! Jim discovered that he was not the only one who missed the drawling-voiced cowboy. Gloriana passed from coldness to disdain and then to pique, and from that to a curiosity which involved her own state of mind as well as interest in Curly's whereabouts.

"Curly is a proud fellow," observed Jim, for Gloriana's benefit, though he directed the remark to his uncle. "Belongs to a fine old Southern family. Rich before the war. He has taken offense at something or other. Or else he's just gone to the bad. I don't know what the Diamond will do without him."

Later, Gloriana, with one of those rare flashes of her eyes, said to Jim: "Brother mine, your remarks were directed at me. Very well. The point is, not what the Diamond will do without Curly, but what *I* will."

"Glory!—What are you saying?" expostulated Jim, both thrilled and shocked. "It's just pique. You don't care a rap for Curly. But because he bucked against your imperious will your vanity is hurt."

"Some of your deductions are amazingly correct," retorted Gloriana, satirically. "But you're off on this one. And I'm afraid your prediction about my bucking up the Diamond must be reversed. If you were not blind you'd see that."

"Glory, hang on to this strange new sweet loving character you've developed, won't you?"

"I'll hang on for dear life," laughed Gloriana, finally won over.

The last day of the old year dawned—the day of Molly's party. The cowboys, excepting Bud, had given up ever expecting to see Curly Prentiss again, who, they claimed, had eloped. Bud, however, was mysterious. "You cain't ever tell aboot thet son-of-a-gun. He'll bob up, mebbe."

Jim was not sanguine, and felt deeply regretful. Had he unduly lectured Curly? But he could not see that he had, and he resigned himself to one of those inexplicable circumstances regarding cowboys which he had come to regard as inevitable.

Jim's small family were all in the living-room early that morning, planning games for the party, when there came a familiar slow step outside, and a knock on the door. Jim opened it.

There stood Curly, rosy-cheeked as any girl, smiling and cool as ever.

"Mawnin', Boss," he drawled.

"How do, Curly! . . . Come in," replied Jim, soberly. It was too sudden for him to be delighted.

Curly sauntered in. He wore a new colored blouse, new blue jeans, and new high top boots, adorned with new spurs. He did not have on a coat or vest, the absence of which brought his worn gun-belt and gun into startling prominence.

"Mawnin', folks. I dropped in to wish you-all a happy New Year," he drawled.

Uncle Jim, Molly, and Gloriana all replied in unison. The old rancher's face wreathed itself into smiles; Molly looked delighted;. and Gloriana tranquil, aloof, with darkening eyes.

"Where you been—old-timer?" queried Jim, coolly. Curly's presence always steadied him, whether in amaze, anger, or indecision.

"Wal, I took a little holiday trip to Albuquerque—to see a sweetheart of mine," replied Curly. "Shore had fun. I wanted particular to brush up on dancin'. An' my girl Nancy shore is a high stepper. I got some new steps now that'll make Bud green."

"Albuquerque!" exclaimed Jim, beginning to realize this was Curly Prentiss.

"Curly, I never heahed of no Albuquerque girl before," said Molly, bluntly.

"Molly, this was one I forgot to tell you aboot."

"Did you fetch her down for my party?"

"No. I couldn't very well. Nancy's married an' her husband's a jealous old geezer. But I shore would have loved to fetch her."

It was the expression in Molly's big dark eyes that gave Jim his clue. The cowboy did not live who could deceive Molly Dunn. Curly's story was a monstrous fabrication to conceal his drunken spree. Yet how impossible to believe this clear-faced, clear-eyed cowboy had ever been drunk!

Not the slightest trace of dissipation showed in Curly's handsome fair face. He looked so innocent that it was an insult to suspect such a degrading thing. Suddenly Molly shrieked with mirth, which had the effect of almost startling the others.

"Say, anythin' funny aboot me?" queried Curly,

"Oh, Curly Prentiss!—You're so funny I—I could kiss you."

"Wal, come on. I've shore been in a particular kissable spell lately."

Gloriana was the quiet, wondering one of the group. She had been gullible enough to believe Curly's story, and had no inkling from Molly's mirth. Moreover, the growing light in her beautiful eyes gave the lie to coil indifference to Curly's presence. She was too cool. Gloriana could never wholly hide her true feelings. That was part of the price she had to pay for those magnificent orbs of violet.

"Molly," put in Jim, "if you have an urge to kiss anybody, you can come to me. I won't have you wasting kisses on this handsome, heartless cowboy. . . . Well, let's get back to our plans for the party. . . . Curly, we'd be glad to have you sit in with us on this discussion—that is, of course, if you're coming to the party."

"Wal, you shore flattered me, postponin' Molly's party once on my account," he drawled, with a blue flash of eyes upon Gloriana. "An' I wouldn't want you to do thet again. I gave up the society of a wonderful damsel to come to this heah party."

"You dog-gone lovable fraud!" burst out Molly, unable longer to conceal her feelings.

Chapter Fourteen

IF EVER a cowboy outfit need to get out of town and back to hard food and hard work the Diamond was surely it— so said Ring Locke. By New Year's they were a spoiled bunch. Bud went round looking for somebody to fight; Jackson Way got married on the sly and broke the outfit in more ways than one; Lonestar grew lonesome and sad, and swore he was pining for Texas; Uphill and Hump developed acute hysteria over some trick or joke which only they seemed to share; Cherry scoured the town for a girl; and Curly, according to united verdict, became a star-gazing idiot. Nevertheless, they had daily uproars in the bunk-house, drove Jim and Molly nearly crazy with their pranks, and Gloriana to her wit's end; and at the last, as if to make amends, they made Molly's party a huge success.

The day after New Year's they rode forty miles ahead of the chuck-wagon, down out of the snow and cold, to the sunny cedared and piñoned forest. Back to saddle and chaps, to sour-dough biscuits and flapjacks, to chopping wood and smoky campfires—in a word—back to the range! And as if by magic they were all in a day the same old Diamond. Jim felt that he could burst with pride and affection. Where was there to be found another group like this? Yet that was only his personal opinion, for Uncle Jim and Locke had laughed at his conceit and told him of other noted Arizona outfits. "You get an outfit that sticks together for a spell—anywhere in Arizona—an' you have the makin's of another Diamond," declared Locke.

But Jim had his doubts. He took the Cibeque for example, and he shuddered in his boots. They, however, had been a rustling outfit. Jim gazed at the lean, quiet, youthful faces around the camp-fire, and he just gloried in the fact that he was one of them. Perhaps the dual characters of these boys were the secret of their fascination for him.

Next camp they were in the pines, and once more Jim lay awake at night, listening to that mighty roar of the wind in the tree tops. It was a storm wind from the north, from the mountains, and it swelled and lulled, moaned and sighed its requiem. Sometimes it sounded like an army approaching on horses.

And the fourth day they rode along their blazed trail, down into wild and beautiful Yellow Jacket. All the long way down that zigzag trail Jim whistled or stopped his horse at the turns to gaze down. Once he heard Bud remark, laconically: "My Gawd! it must be great to be in love like the boss. Jest soarin'. He'll come down with a hell of a thump pronto."

Jim laughed at Bud, but a couple of hours later, when he gazed at a huge blackened, charred mass, all that remained of the wonderful peeled pine logs which had been cut to build his ranch-house, he did come down with a sickening thump.

"Haw! Haw!—Reckon the Hash Knife has had a party, too," yelled Bud, shrilly.

"Croak Malloy's compliments, Boss. See the latest cut in the aspen there," added Curly, grimly, pointing to the largest of the beautiful white-barked quaking-asps near at hand.

Curly had sharp eyes. Jim dismounted and walked over to the tree. The crude, yet well-fashioned outline of a hash knife had been cut in the bark, and inside the blade was the letter M. Jim had seen enough of these hash-knife symbols to be familiar with it, but not before had he noticed the single letter. That was significant. It seemed to eliminate Jed Stone. In a sudden violent burst of temper Jim wheeled to his men and cursed as never before in his life.

"Wal, Boss, thet's shore fine," drawled Curly.

"Dog-gone! The boss is actooly riled," observed Up, in delight.

"Pard Jim, you aboot hit plum center, thet time," cut in Slinger Dunn's inimitable voice, something to make the nerves tingle.

"Jim Traft, so help me Gawd, I've got an inspirashum," chimed in Bud. "I'll cut down thet aspen, split out thet section an' dress it up fer Croak Malloy's grave."

"*Yippy—yip—yippee!*" yelled some of the cowboys, in unison.

Jim caught the infection of their grim and merry mood, but gave no further indication.

"Boys, throw the packs. And three of you go back to the wagon for another load. The rest of us will pitch camp."

According to Slinger the tracks around the cabin site and pile of charred logs were old, and probably had been made the day after the Diamond rode home to Flagerstown before Christmas.

"Which means the Hash Knife had a scout watching us," asserted Jim, quickly.

"Boss, you shore hit it on the haid," remarked Curly, admiringly.

"Dog-gone if he ain't gettin' bright," agreed Bud.

"Speaks kinda bad fer me, but I shore do think jest thet," went on Slinger.

"Slinger, all you could hope to do heah is to watch the trails down in the canyon," said Curly. "Thet greaser of Jed Stone's, the sheep-herder Sonora, has been keepin' tab on us from the rim."

"Shore. I was afeered of jest thet. Wal, I hate to kill a man when he ain't out in the open. But he's spyin' on my pardner."

"Slinger, don't be so sorrowful an' apologetic

aboot it," replied Curly. "He's a greaser. He's a low-down skunk, a murderer. Next trick he'll shoot one of us in the back. Don't forget he's Croak Malloy's pard, an' not Jed Stone's."

"Smoke him up, Slinger," added Bud, with a sting in his flippant speech. "We've had all our parties an' dances an' spoonin' bees—leastways *I* have, an' thet's no joke. This hyar Sonora better keep out of my sight, fer I'll take him fer a deer or a turkey or a bob-cat."

Jim drew a deep hard breath that actually hurt his lungs. "God, it *is* hell—to wake up to this! . . . Boys, my softy days are past. We'll start this long job slow, and watch as much as we work. Slinger, your job is the same as before, only it's more. Bud, you hunt meat for camp, and I don't need to tell you what else."

"Now you're shore talkin', Boss," drawled Curly, with fire in his eyes. "We'll fall down on this job if we don't forget home an' mother an' sweetheart."

"Say wife an' baby, too," added Bud, indicating the sober-faced Jackson Way. "Jack's so damn sudden an' mysterious I reckon—"

"Shet your loud trap," yelled Jackson, not seeing any humor in Bud's talk, "or I'll beat your head into a puddin'."

"Aw, Jack, I was only tryin' to be funny, to cheer up the boss," explained Bud, contritely,

Thus began the Yellow Jacket task of the

Diamond. They set grimly to it, like pioneers with Indians lurking in the woods, wary and watchful. Here Jim sensed the tremendous pride of the members of the Diamond. Even Curly's carelessness now vanished, he glided at a task with the steps of a hunter and always his matchless eyes had the roving, searching look of a hawk. Rifles took precedence of axes, or any other working tools. When one of the cowboys went forth to pack in some firewood or a bucket of water, he did not leave his rifle behind. They changed the open camp to a wide dry cavern in the side of the yellow cliff, the only ingress to which was by a pine tree dropped across the brook.

Nevertheless, the new pile of peeled pine logs slowly grew as the days passed.

Slinger spied upon the Hash Knife camp, reporting several of their number absent. They were inactive, waiting for spring. "I couldn't get no closer than top of a rock wall," said Slinger. "But I seen Stone, walkin' to an' fro, his haid bent, as if he had a load on his back. Couldn't make out Malloy, an' reckon he's away. Same aboot the greaser."

"Take my field-glasses next time," said Jim, tersely. "We want to know who's there and what they're doing."

When more days, that lengthened into weeks. passed without any sign on the part of Stone's gang that they were even aware of the return o the Diamond to Yellow Jacket, Jim felt the easing of a strain.

"Wal, we'll heah from them when Malloy comes back," said Curly, meditatively. "He'll come. I cain't conceive of thet hombre bein' daid or quittin' this range. Can you, Slinger?"

"Not till he raises some more hell," returned the backwoodsman. "Malloy an' thet Texan an' the greaser must be down-country, hatchin' up somethin', or huntin' up cattle to rustle in the spring."

"Wal, spring will be heah some fine mawnin'," replied Curly. "An', dog-gone-it, Jim, your uncle will be shovin' all thet stock down in heah. He's in too darn big a hurry."

"Anyway, Uncle can't be stopped," rejoined Jim. "This rustler nest has long been a sore spot with him. And really, he doesn't see any more than a scrap or two for us, like we had with the Cibeque. The Hash Knife outfit simply doesn't faze Uncle Jim."

"He's shore a tough old cattleman an' he's been through the mill. But I cain't quite agree with him aboot only a little scrap or two. Shore there may be aboot only *one*."

In spite of these convictions and misgivings, the weeks went on without any untoward happening at Yellow Jacket. And while vigilance did not relax there was a further lulling of apprehension. It was not wholly improbable for the Hash Knife outfit to be through. Other Arizona gangs had come to an end. In the past the Hash Knife itself had rounded out both meritorious and vicious cycles.

March brought spring down into the brakes under the giant rim of the Mogollans; violets and bluebells and primroses, as well as trout rising to flies, and the bears coming out of their hibernation, to leave muddy tracks on all the trails. The brown pine needles floated down to make room for fresh green, the sycamores showed budding leaves, long behind the cottonwoods. Smoky blue water ran in the hollows, and that was proof of snow melted off the uplands. And lastly the turkey gobblers began to gobble; early and late they kept up their chug-a-lug, chug-a-lug-chug-a-lug chug.

March also brought the vanguard of Mexican laborers to blast out and grade the road down into Yellow Jacket. Already the road was cut and leveled through the forest to the rim. And at the nearest ranch lumber and framework, cement and pipe, bricks and hardware, had begun to arrive.

Coincident with this arrived also more food supplies, and mail and news, all of which were avidly devoured by the cowboys. Curly had received a letter which rendered him oblivious to his surroundings, even to Bud's sly intrusions into his dream. Jim's uncle had taken Gloriana to California, while Molly went to stay with Mrs. Locke and diligently pursued her studies.

"Jim, lemme see thet letter from Miss Glory,"

asked Bud, casually. "I jest want to admire thet lovely handwritin'."

And the innocent Jim handed over the letter.

"I knowed it," declared Bud, after a quick glance, but on the moment he did not explain what it was he knew. Jim guessed readily enough that Bud had seen the handwriting on Curly's letter, and now he was in possession of the secret of Curly's trancelike abstraction.

News from Uncle Jim and Ring Locke, from friends of the cowboys, from the weekly newspaper recently started in Flagerstown, furnished debate, not to mention endless conversation, for many a camp fire.

Bambridge had sent his family away from Flagerstown, no one knew where, and had moved to Winslow to conduct his cattle business. Darnell had not been seen in town since Christmas, when he boarded a late east-bound train, after buying a ticket for Denver. But a cowboy friend of Uphill's had seen Darnell in Holbrook right after New Year's, and hinted that he kept pretty well hidden there. Croak Malloy had shot a man in Mariposa, according to range rumor. Blodgett, who operated a ranch south of the brakes, complained of spring rustling.

"Uncle Jim says to expect our five thousand head of cows and calves, with a sprinkling of steers, just as soon as the road dries up. . . . Darn his stubborn hide!"

"Then he's back from California?" asked Curly, with a naïve hopefulness.

"Sure; long ago. Says he's rarin' to come down. I'll bet he comes, too. And Glory—she raved about California. Let me read you gazabos some of her letter." And Jim sorted over the closely written pages, and finding one, he read aloud a beautiful tribute to the sunny golden state. Then he went on: "And Jim, dear, something will have to be done or I'll sure go back on Arizona for California. I didn't meet any boys out there that can compare with our cowboys. But I can't be loyal forever, without any reward. Tell the outfit that, will you, Jim? And tell them Molly and I are coming down there just as soon as ever Uncle Jim will let us. We're making life almost unendurable for him now. . . . Tell Bud he must take me hunting—(no, Molly is going to teach me to call wild turkeys)—but fishing for trout and gathering flowers. Tell Lonestar, who's the best rider in the outfit, that *he* is to teach me the flying mount, not to say how to get on a horse any old way at first. Tell Jackson—but I forgot, Jack is married, and of course, having become friends with his wife, who's a dear girl, I can't ask him to take me on long lonely walks, and climb up cliffs, where it would be necessary to support me—at least. . . . Come to think of it, I don't know that there is any other of the outfit I'd ask to fill such capacity. . . . Oh yes, Bud must show me how to carve my name on aspen trees. . . . I have favors to ask of Cherry and Up and Hump. And lastly, *somebody* must show me a real live desperado."

Not a word about Curly or Slinger! It was an omission which the impassive faces of these two individuals did not betray. Nevertheless, no violence was needed on the part of Curly and Slinger to raise pandemonium in camp. The other cowboys had incentive enough. After they had finished their remarkable demonstration Jim calmly remarked: "Certainly I would never allow Glory and Molly to visit this wild camp, even if Uncle Jim would, which I greatly doubt."

"Haw! Haw! Haw!" roared Bud, derisively, to the four winds.

"Boss, shore it'll be safe when summer comes," said Curly eagerly, without the drawl.

"How'll it be safe?" asked Jim, bluntly.

"'Cause, dog-gone-it, Slinger an' I will make it safe—if we have to kill off the whole darned Hash Knife outfit."

"I wasn't thinking of danger to my sister and my sweetheart—from that source," remarked Jim, subtly—and he felt deeply gleeful at the glaring glances of the suspicious cowboys.

"Jim, the outfit has aboot given up whisky and fighting, not to say the society of questionable women—all for you. Don't rub it in," rejoined Curly, in cool, curt drawl, and he stalked away rather too stiff and erect to look his usual graceful self.

It was a rebuke Jim acknowledged he deserved, but he did not take occasion then to explain he had been exercising the cowboys' privilege of being cryptically funny.

The road came on down into Yellow Jacket, and all too soon the horde of bawling cattle followed, to spread over the great wild canyon and to go on down into the brakes below, and on their heels rolled the wagons with materials for Jim's ranch-house. It took days to transport the lot. And meanwhile the two builders Jim's uncle had sent down drove the cowboys to desperation with log-lifting. Jim labored mightily with them, and had the joy of the primitive pioneer, in seeing his habitation go up in the wilderness. Bud ran a pipe-line from Yellow Jacket spring, and had water on the place before the house was up. The canyon had never resounded to such unfamiliar noise. Its tranquillity had been disrupted. And this kept on while the log house grew, one log above the other, and the high-peaked, split pine-shingle roof went on, with its wide eaves sloping out over wide porches. Then while the carpenters were busy with the doors and windows and inside finish, the big barn was started, and long slim poles cut and hauled for corrals.

It was well on in May when the expert workmen

left to go back to Flagerstown, leaving Jim possessed of a spacious new pine house that flashed yellow in the sunlight. But much labor there was still, and Jim realized it would take months before that habitation coincided with the picture in his mind.

"Jim, heah you have a log-cabin palace aboot ready," drawled Curly, and did not add whether he meant ready for furniture or a bride or for another bonfire for the rustlers.

After the workmen left, the old vigilance was observed. Spring was at its height, and up and down the wild canyon, and far down in the brakes, cows and steers and unbranded calves roamed at will, an irresistible temptation to range men of Croak Malloy's type. Then came the spring round-up—the first ever ridden at Yellow Jacket—and for days the yells of cowboys, the bawl of calves, and the acrid smell of burning hair filled the canyon. The Diamond brand went on hundreds of calves and yearlings. Whether he liked it or not, Jim had begun his ranching, and the cowboys had settled down once more to life in the saddle.

"Wal, the longer thet Hash Knife waits the wuss they'll ride over us," summed up the pessimistic Bud.

"Boss, it's shore the range twenty miles an' more down in the brakes that'll take our cattle," added Curly. "You can pen up a few hundred haid heah in the canyon. But your range is below. An' thet damned country is big, an' lookin' for a lost cow will be huntin' fer a needle in a haystack. It's yours, though, an' worth fightin' fer. You can double your stock in two years. Grass an' water mean a fortune to a rancher. To find 'em an' hang on to 'em—thet's the ticket."

"Aw, you gotta hang on to the *cattle,*" rejoined Bud. "I've known many a rancher who'd made his pile—if he could only have hanged on."

"Wal, it's lucky fer Jim thet the Hash Knife is peterin' out."

"Shore. . . . Say, did you fellars heah a rifle-shot?" Curly threw up his head like a listening deer.

"By gum, I heerd somethin'," replied Bud.

"What's strange about it—if you did?" queried Jim, uneasily.

"Get back under the porch," ordered Curly, sharply. "We made one mistake aboot buildin' this cabin. A good rifle could reach you from thet cliff."

"Wal, it's a safe bet Hump heerd somethin'. Look at him."

The cowboy designated by Bud's speech and finger appeared hurrying under the pines toward the cabin.

"Shot came from high up," observed Curly, warily. "Back a ways from the rim. I wonder would Slinger be up there?"

"Slinger'd be anywhere where he ought to be," said Lonestar.

They waited for Hump.

"Fellars," he said, sharply, running up on the porch. "I heerd a forty-four crack up on the rocks!"

"We heahed a rifle-shot, Hump. But I couldn't swear to it's bein' a forty-four. . . . Thet would be Slinger."

"Mebbe shot a deer on the way to camp."

"An' pack it around an' down? Not much. Somethin' wrong. You could hear it in thet shot."

The Diamond waited, with only one member absent; and every moment increased speculation. When Slinger appeared down the trail there was only one exclamation, which was Curly's "Ahuh!"

They watched the backwoodsman glide along. He had the stride of the deer-stalker. But there seemed to be force and menace, something sinister, in his approach.

"Packin' two rifles," spoke up the hawk-eyed Curly. "An' what's thet swingin' low?"

"Pard, it's a gun-belt," declared Bud.

"By Gawd! so it is!" ejaculated Curly, and then, as they watched Slinger come on, he sat down to light a cigarette. "Boss," he said, presently, now with his lazy drawl, "I reckon you have one less of the Hash Knife to contend with."

"Wal, it's been some time comin'," added Bud, as if excusing a flagrant omission.

Slinger soon reached the porch. His dark face betrayed nothing, but his glittering eyes were something to avoid. He laid a shiny, worn carbine on the ground, muzzle pointing outward. It was the kind of rifle range-riders liked to carry in a saddle sheath.

"Wal, Slinger, what'd you fetch it heah thet way fer?" demanded Curly, sharply.

"Dog-gone if it ain't cocked!" exclaimed Bud. Jim, too, had just made this discovery.

"Jest the way he left it," replied Slinger. "I wanted to show you-all how near somethin' come off."

He bent over to touch the trigger, which action discharged the rifle with a spiteful crack.

"Funny it didn't go off up there," observed Slinger. "Hair trigger, all right." Then he laid a gun-belt full of shells, and also burdened with a heavy bone-handled gun, at Jim's feet on the edge of the porch. But Jim did not have any voice just then. He sensed the disclosure to come.

"Slinger, whose hardware are you packin' in?" demanded Curly.

"Belonged to thet Hash Knife greaser, Sonora," replied Slinger, who now removed his cap and wiped his wet face. "I struck his fresh track this mawnin' down the trail, an' I followed him. But never seen him till a little while ago, up heah on the rim. He was lyin' flat on his belly, an' he shore had a bead on Jim. Pretty long shot for a greaser, but I reckon it was aboot time I got there."

Jim stood stricken, as he gazed from the porch

276

steps where he had been sitting up to the craggy rim. Surely not a long shot! He could have killed a deer, or a man, at that distance. He suddenly felt sick. Again a miraculous accident, or what seemed so to him, had intervened to save his life. Would it always happen? Then he became conscious of Curly's cold voice.

"You — — —!" cursed that worthy, red in the face, and with a violence that presupposed a strong emotion. "Heah I've been tellin' you to keep under cover! Is it goin' to take a million years of Arizona to teach you things? . . . My Gawd! boy—thet greaser shore would have plugged you!"

Chapter Fifteen

JED STONE regarded his Texas confederate with a long unsmiling stare of comprehension.

"Shore, Jed," repeated Pecos, "you're goin' to draw on Croak one of these days. You can't help yourself. . . . I'd done it myself if I hadn't been afeered of him."

"Pecos, you tell me thet?" queried Stone, harshly. "You know then? He's got you beat on the draw? You're not hankerin' to *see?*"

"Not a damn hanker, Jed," drawled Pecos. "I'd shore like to see him *daid*—the crooked little rattlesnake—but I still love life."

"Ahuh. . . . An' thet's why you're leavin' the Hash Knife?"

"Not by a long shot, Jed. I'd gone with Anderson, but for you. An' I'd gone when Malloy killed thet cowboy Reed, who throwed in with us. But I stuck on, hopin' Malloy had spit out his poison. I'm goin' because I reckon the Hash Knife is done. Don't you know thet, too, Jed?"

"Hell!—If we are done, what an' who has done us?"

"Reckon you needn't ask. You know. Malloy was the one who took up Bambridge. Arizona will never stand a cattle thief like Bambridge. She shore hates him most as bad as Texas. It's Bambridge's pretense of bein' honest while makin' his big cattle deals thet riles Jim Traft, an' other ranchers who are the real thing. Mark my words, Bambridge won't see out this summer."

"Huh! If he doesn't fork over the ten thousand he owes me he shore won't, you can gamble on thet," returned Stone.

"Wal, all those deals thet have brought us up lately were instigated by Bambridge. Runnin' off the Diamond brand up at Yellow Jacket an' shippin' the stock from Winslow—of all the damn-fool deals, that was the worst. We could have gone on for years heah, appropriatin' a few steers now an' then, an' livin' easy. No, Malloy has done us. These last tricks of his—they make me sick an' sore."

"You mean thet cattle-drive in April, without me knowin'?"

"Not thet particular. I mean buildin' this heah cabin, fer one thing. Shore it's a fort. An' only twenty miles from Yellow Jacket!"

"Ha! Ha!—Croak runs up this cabin, he said, because he liked the view down over the brakes, an' the wall of the Mogollans standin' away there so beautiful."

"Wal, I ain't gainsayin' the view. But to take Malloy serious, except regardin' life an' death, is sheer nonsense. He aims to hang on heah whether you like it or not."

"Mebbe he will hang—an' from a rope," muttered the outlaw.

"Not Croak Malloy! He'll die with his boots on, sober an' shootin'. Don't have vain hopes, Jed. . . . Malloy will run the Hash Knife—an' run it to hell. Take, for instance, these two hombres he's lately rung in on us. Just a couple of town rowdies, drinkin' up what they steal. No stuff for the Hash Knife!"

"I had the same hunch when I seen them," said Stone, pacing to and fro.

"Wal, heah's Lang an' Madden, both scared of Croak, an' they'd double-cross you any day. An' Sonora, he's Croak's man, as you know. Right now, Jed, the Hash Knife, outside of you an' me, is done."

"I reckon so. It's been keepin' me awake nights."

"Wal, then, shake the onery outfit an' come away with me?"

"Where you goin', Pecos?"

"Reckon I'll lay low fer a spell."

"Shore. But where? I want to know."

"Jed, I'll ride straight for the haid of the Little Colorado. I told you I had word last fall from an old Texas pard who's layin' low up there."

"Uh-huh. Pecos, have you got any money?"

"Shore. Malloy hasn't won all I had."

Stone turned with a jerk of decision. "All right, Pecos, if I don't join you up there before the snow flies, you can reckon Malloy's done fer *me,* as he has fer the Hash Knife."

"Jed, shore there's no call fer you to risk an even break with Croak," said the Texan, gravely. "He's no square gunman. He'd have murdered young Traft over there at Yellow Jacket thet day."

"Yes, I remember. An' my kickin' his gun up made him hate me. . . . Honest to Gawd, Pecos, the only reason I'd ever risk an even break with Croak—if I did—would be just to see if he could beat me to a gun."

"I savvy. I had the same itch. It's the one weakness of a gunman. It's plain vanity, Jed. Don't be a damn fool. Come away with me now."

Stone thought for a long moment. "No, not yet. I'm broke. I want thet money from Bambridge. An' I want to—" His pause and the checking of his thought suggested an ominous uncertainty of himself rather than meaning not to confide in the Texan. "But, Pecos, I'll promise you, barrin' ordinary accidents, thet I'll meet you at the haid of the Little Colorado sometime before the summer's over."

"Thet shore sounds good," replied Pecos, rising to his lofty stature. "Shake on thet."

Stone gripped his lieutenant's hand, and their eyes locked as well. It was one of the moments that counted with men of the open. Then Pecos strode out to his horse, and while he mounted Stone untied the halter of the pack-mule.

"Reckon you'd better work out through the woods," he said casually. "If Croak happened to meet you on the trail he'd be curious. He took Anderson's desertion as a slap in the face. . . . Good luck, Pecos."

"Same to you, Jed. I'll shore be countin' the days."

Pecos rode out from under the shadow of the great cliff, keeping to the grass, and soon headed into the fringe of timber below. Stone watched him go with mingled regret and relief. Pecos was the last of the old Hash Knife, except himself. Malloy represented a development of a later type of Arizona rustler. There was such a thing as straight rustling, about which the ranchers had never made any great hullabaloo. But these new fellows, who had corrupted some of the old, stealing cattle barefaced and wholesale, were marked for a bullet or a rope. Of course Malloy would get a bullet.

And that thought focused Stone's plodding mind on the hint he had given Pecos. The Texan had admitted as much. That was a strange coincidence, and it shamed Stone a little. Pecos, no doubt, was as good a man with a gun as Malloy. But he rode away and now he would never be certain. The outlaw leader acknowledged to himself that he was not built that way. He hated Malloy, the same as every square shooter in the Tonto. Likewise he shared their fear of the notorious gunman.

Stone sat down on the rude seat which had been fashioned by Malloy, and where he sat so often, to smoke and watch the sunset over the Mazatzals. What a grand wild view it was out and down over the black brakes to the purple ranges! But did the crooked-faced little murderer really care anything about the beauty and grandeur of that scene? Stone, inquiring into the intricacies of his own habits, was constrained to admit that most probably Croak Malloy loved Arizona and particularly this wild and lonely and colorful corner of the Tonto. It was an amazing conviction to dawn upon Stone.

Malloy had certainly selected this site for a cabin with more than its superb view in mind. It stood high up, above a long fan-shaped bare slope of grass, and had been built in a notch of the great wall of rock. It could only be approached from the front, facing downhill. The spruce logs, of which it had been constructed, had been cut right on the spot. They were heavy, too green to burn for a long time, and significant indeed were the narrow chinks left open between the logs, some close to the floor, others breast high, and not a few in the loft. A spring of clear cold water ran from under the cliff, and the cabin had been erected right over it. The wall above bulged far out, so far that neither avalanche nor bullets from any point above could reach the cabin. With store of meat and provisions a few vigilant and hardened outlaws could hold that cabin-fort indefinitely. No Arizona posse of sheriff's sworn-in deputies, or any reasonable outfit of cowboys, were going to rush that retreat, if it sheltered the Hash Knife. Stone conceded Malloy's sagacity. But it was a futile move, simply because he and his new accomplices would spend very little time there. They had made three cattle-drives already this spring, one of which was as bold and as preposterous as the raiding of the last of the Diamond stock on Yellow Jacket. Bambridge, with his new man, Darnell, was back of these. Stone had not needed to meet Darnell more than once to get his status. Darnell would hardly bother the Hash Knife long. He was too sharp a gambler. Presently, if he won too much from Croak Malloy, very suddenly he would turn up his toes.

But it was Malloy who stuck in Jed Stone's craw. Jed had never before admitted even to himself that he meant to kill the gun-thrower. When, however, he had intimated so much to Pecos, he realized the grim thing that gripped him. He did mean to kill Malloy. It had been in his dreams, in that part of his mind which worked when he was asleep, and now it possessed him. How and when to do the deed were matters of conjecture; the important thing was the decision, and Stone imagined he had arrived at it. Nevertheless, conscience awakened a still small voice. Bad as Malloy was, he trusted Stone, had fought for him, would do so again at the drop of a card, and that meant, of course, he stood ready to die for him. Stone faced the issue uneasily.

"An' the little cuss likes to set here fer the view," soliloquized the outlaw.

Stone did not blame him. Where in Arizona was there a more wonderful scene for a fugitive from justice? The black expanse of tangled rock and timber sloped many miles down, and on each side the high unscalable walls stood up with bold protection. Four days' hard riding from Winslow or Flagerstown, and more from points south, Malloy's cabin retreat seemed safe from intrusion. Moreover, it would have to be found, which task would be no slight one. Slinger Dunn probably knew of it already, and perhaps more of the backwoodsmen and hunters of the Cibeque. Stone took satisfaction in convincing himself that the Hash Knife had no more need of concern about the Diamond. Still, an afterthought was that he no longer controlled the Hash Knife. Suppose that doughty old cattleman, Jim Traft, did throw a few thousand head of steers down into Yellow Jacket! He was fool enough, and bull-headed enough, to do it. And if he did, nothing but death could ever prevent Croak Malloy from stealing them. Wherefore the ghastly idea of death for Malloy again held sway over Jed Stone.

It was a beautiful morning in May, and the brakes were abloom with fresh foliage and spring flowers. All the way down the slope bright blossoms stood up out of the grass. And the voices of birds were rich and sweet on the morning air. Pecos had ridden away, and Stone was left alone to fare for himself, as had so often been the case of late. Somebody had to stay there, and it might better be he. Any day now Malloy would return with his new men; and Madden, who had taken a message to Winslow for Stone, ought to be back. Sonora rode to and fro over the trails of the brakes, in accordance with Malloy's orders, which for once coincided with Stone's judgment.

This section of Arizona, so long a refuge, would be hard to leave. Stone did not know the headwaters of the Little Colorado, except that it was a very thickly forested country, inhabited only by Apaches and a few straggling outlaws and trappers.

But Jed Stone loved the rock walls, the colored cliffs, the canyons, the byways of the rims of the Mogollans. There was no other country like that—none so full of hiding-places—none with the labyrinth of gorge and thicket and cavern, where the wild game was tame, and where men of his kind could sleep of nights. That was the shibboleth Stone hugged to his breast. But was it all?

He confessed, as he gazed away down the sea of treetops, so green and tufted and bright, at the gray crags standing up as if on sentinel duty, at the wandering lines of the insulating walls, that there might be more to his obsession than just a sense of security.

"Never will be no different," he muttered. "They can't fence these brakes, or cut the timber or live down here. It belongs to us—and the Indians. Fire could never run wild down here. Too green and rocky! Too many streams! . . . All they can do is throw cattle in, and even then a thousand head would be lost. Nope, this corner of the Tonto never will be no different. . . . Reckon thet's another reason why I hate to leave."

Jed Stone had been twenty years a fugitive—a criminal in sight of the law. But he knew in his heart that the crime which had outlawed him and not been his. He held no bitterness, no resentment. Never in all those hard years would he have changed that sacrifice. Nevertheless, it was natural for him to resent the encroachment of civilization, as if he had an actual right. He had arrived at a time in his life when he balked at things as they were, at things he must do.

Stone's quick eye, ever roving from habit, detected movement of gray down in the foliage. He thought it was a deer until he saw brown and heard a distant thud of hoofs. Horses! Probably Malloy was returning. But Stone took no chances with suppositions, and his hand went to the rifle leaning against the bench.

When three horses emerged from the green below he recognized the first of the riders to be Madden, but they were halfway up the hill before he made out that the second was Bambridge. The outlaw's thought changed, and conjecture that was not friendly to this visit took the place of hard vigilance. Bambridge riding down into the Black Brakes must certainly have something to do with Malloy. It was unwise, especially for this pseudo rancher. Stone arose and walked to the high step.

The dusty horses limped wearily up the hill, to be halted before the cabin. The men were travel-stained and tired. Bambridge's big face appeared haggard, and it did not express any pleasure.

"Hullo, Boss! I fetched a visitor," called out Madden, busy with saddle packs.

"So I see. . . . Howdy, Mr. Bambridge!" replied Stone, coolly.

"Mornin', Stone. I expect you're surprised to see me," said Bambridge, bluntly.

"Shore am. Glad, though, for more'n one reason," answered the rustler.

Bambridge unstrapped a coat from his saddle, and mounted to the porch, heavy of step and dark of eye. He flopped down on the bench, dropping his coat and sombrero. Evidently he had not slept much, and it was plain his sweaty and begrimed apparel had not been changed for days. He packed a gun, which Stone had taken note of first.

"Malloy failed to show up," he said, sourly.

"Ahuh. It's a way Croak has. But he'll show up when you least expect him an' don't want him. Where'd you go to meet him?"

"Tanner's out of Winslow," returned Bambridge, shortly, his dull gray eyes studying the outlaw, as if he was weighing that remark about Malloy.

"Tanner's. So Malloy meets you there, eh?— Wal, I reckon he might as well go into Winslow or Flag," said Stone, dryly.

Bambridge seemed uncertain of his ground here, but was indifferent to it. Stone grasped the fact that the cattle dealer did not take him for the dominant factor in the Hash Knife.

"You can bet I'd rather he had. Eighty miles ride, without a bed, an' practically nothin' to eat, is enough to make a man bite nails."

"What's the reason you undertook it?"

"It concerns me an' Malloy," said the other.

Whatever sense of fair play Jed Stone felt

toward this man—and he confessed to himself that it was little—departed here.

"Any deals you make with Malloy concern me. I'm boss of this Hash Knife outfit."

"Not so any one would notice it," rejoined Bambridge, with scant civility.

The man was on dangerous ground and had no intimation of it. Steeped in his absorption of his greedy sordid plans, if he had the wit to understand Jed Stone he did not exercise it. Stone paced the narrow porch, gazing out over the brakes. For the moment he would waive any expression of resentment. Bambridge was in possession of facts and plans that Stone desired to know.

"Wal, mebbe you're right aboot Croak bossin' the outfit pretty generally," he said, at length. "But only in late deals that I had little to do with. What I don't advise I shore don't do. Thet deal of Diamond cattle last winter—thet was an exception. I've kicked myself often enough. . . . By the way, you can fork over thet ten thousand you've owed me on thet deal. I sent Madden in to get it."

"Man alive! I gave the money to Darnell, with instructions to hand it to Malloy for you," ejaculated Bambridge, in genuine surprise.

"You did? When?"

"Weeks ago. Let's see. It was the ninth of April that I drew that ten thousand. Next day Darnell was to ride out to Tanner's. He met Malloy there and delivered your money."

"Not to me," declared Stone.

"Why!—the man is reliable," replied Bambridge, in exasperation. "Are you quite—honest, about it? . . . Have you seen Malloy since?"

"Wal, Bambridge, I've seen Malloy several times since then. He never mentioned no money—for me. Appeared to be pretty flush himself, though. . . . An' much obliged for the hint about my honesty."

Bambridge let the caustic rejoinder go by without apology.

"Honesty is not your trade, Stone. I'll say, though, you've kept your word to me, which is more than Malloy has. . . . You suspect this new man of mine, Darnell?"

"No, I don't suspect him. I *know* him to be a Mississippi River gambler, run out of St. Louis—accordin' to his own statement. I've seen a few of his kind hit the raw West. They didn't savvy us Westerners an' they didn't last. Darnell has double-crossed you. He'll try it on Croak Malloy, which will be bad for his health."

"No wonder Darnell can't savvy you Westerners. Who the hell can, I'd like to know?"

"Wal, not you, thet's shore."

"Give me proof Darnell has done me dirt," demanded the other, impatiently.

"Wal, I saw him right here after the tenth of April—along aboot the twentieth, I reckon, for it was after Malloy made a raid on Blodgett's range. . . . Darnell did not give me any money. He had a big roll, for I saw him flash it when he was gamblin' with the men. . . . Thet was the day Croak shot young Reed."

"Aw, I'd want more proof than that," returned Bambridge. "You might have been drunk when Darnell gave it to you."

"Shore. I might have been anythin'. Us outlaws are pretty low-down, I reckon. But I, for one, am not as low-down as some who call themselves cattlemen. . . . Bambridge, am I to hold you or Darnell responsible fer thet ten thousand?"

"Not me, you can bet. Or Darnell, either. Malloy is your man. He seems to be runnin' your outfit now, an' no doubt appropriated your money."

"Nope. Croak is square aboot money," said the outlaw, meditatively.

"Bah!—What you givin' me?" retorted Bambridge, harshly. "Stone, you talk queer for a rustler. Here you are hidden down in this God-forsaken wilderness—afraid to go near any town—with a price on your life, yet you talk of honesty in yourself an' men. Thet's a joke about honor among thieves."

"Wal we needn't argue aboot it," replied Stone. A Westerner would have gauged something from the cool quality of his voice and the averting of his eyes. "I've served your turn. An' now thet Malloy is doin' it, why, you've no call to get nasty. What

I'd like to know is—how'd you come to ride out here? Shore is a long ride fer anyone."

"I want action. That's why I came," almost yelled Bambridge, red in the face. "Malloy has failed me twice, both times because I didn't pay first. Here I have a chance to sell ten thousand head of cattle—to the government buyer in Kansas City—an' I haven't the cattle."

"Chance to sell quick an' get out of Arizona, huh?"

"You've hit it, Stone. An' that's why I'm here. I want cattle. Old Traft lately drove a big herd down into Yellow Jacket. I'm after it. Malloy agreed to drive it. I've built a corral along the railroad, halfway between Winslow an' Holbrook. Short-cut idea, see? An' I can load there. He also agreed to make away with this damned young smart Alec, Jim Traft. Took the money quick enough, by damn."

"Took what money?" queried Stone, with no apparent interest.

"What I offered for the job," fumed the cattleman. "Then afterward he said it was the kind of job Croak Malloy couldn't do. But he'd put his man Sonora on it. A Mexican."

"Job to do away with young Jim Traft," mused Stone, drumming the bench with his fingers. "Wal, I reckon thet's a fine idee—fer *you*. I'll tell you somethin', though. Sonora will never do it."

"More double-crossin', eh?"

"No. The greaser is straight. Funny fer a greaser,

ain't it? But he simply won't, because Slinger Dunn will kill him. I wouldn't go prowlin' around Yellow Jacket for anythin', an' you can gamble Malloy wouldn't, either."

"So that's why he's slow about drivin' the Diamond cattle. Damn his crooked mug! . . . Stone, did you know Malloy was in with that Tanner outfit an' has been workin' on Blodgett's stock?"

"No. Thet's news to me. Who told you?"

"Darnell. In fact, he made the deal. This was against my orders, I'm bound to admit. I'm pretty sore at him an' I'm through with him. But Malloy has got to square himself with me."

"Your man is playin' both ends against the middle," observed the outlaw, thoughtfully. "He's smart enough to try to use Malloy—same as you—an' get a big raid off. Then he, too, can jump Arizona. Wal, my advice is to be jumpin' quick. We decent rustlers don't work thet way. We never rob any cattleman of enough stock to ruin him. Thet's why Hash Knife has lasted twenty years."

"My daughter married a cowboy in Flag last winter," said Bambridge. "An' I'm ready to get out quick, without any advice from you. Can you jack up Malloy on this job?"

"Shore I can, if I like," replied the outlaw, easily. "I can handle Croak on any deal, providin' I give him the big share. I'm not keen, though, to egg him along—for nothin'."

Bambridge was no match for Stone in subtlety.

He had been led on to tell his business with Malloy; now all the outlaw leader wanted to know was whether or not he had brought the money.

"Malloy wanted twenty thousand dollars," said Bambridge. "That was out of all reason. He can't deliver cattle enough. So we jawed about it. He came down to fifteen—an' I've got ten thousand with me. Suppose you persuade Malloy to make the drive—with as few men as can possibly be needed. An' the day you land the cattle at my corral I'll fork over another five thousand."

"How many cattle?" asked Stone, tremendously interested, but not in any case in the query he made.

"I don't stipulate any number. Only as many as can be rounded up quick an' driven out quick."

"Ahuh. . . . Suppose you let me see the color of thet ten thousand," suggested the rustler, as if he needed a little more material persuasion.

Bambridge unbuttoned his bulging vest, and from an inside pocket drew forth a packet of clean new greenbacks, with the bank wrapper still round them. He flipped it upon the bench. Money was only so much paper to him! His large features worked.

"You've as much right to doubt me as I have you," he said, blandly. "There you are!—Nice fresh green color!"

"Wal, it ain't so much money, after all, considerin'," reflected Stone.

The cattleman's face fell. He had calculated upon this last card.

"I've got about five hundred more in gold. I'll throw that in. Will you pull off the deal?" And he jingled the heavy coins, which evidently were what had made his vest bulge.

Stone's veins leaped as the released blood gushed hot and bursting along them. All his talk had been pretense, except wherein he had wanted to find out if Bambridge really carried the money with him.

"Let me see thet, too. . . . The gold! The good old yellow stuff with the music—an' hell hid in it."

Bambridge reacted slowly to that suggestion. Something wedged into his eager one-ideaed mind. Instead of complying with Stone's request he ceased jangling the gold and snatched up the packet of bills, which he returned to his pocket. Then he buttoned up his vest.

"Fork it all over!" suddenly called the outlaw, and in a single second such a remarkable transformation occurred in him that Bambridge's eyes popped wide.

"Wha-at?" he stammered.

"Hand me thet money."

"I will not. No pay in advance. Malloy—"

"Pay hell! I wouldn't drive a steer fer you. But I want the ten thousand. You owe it to me."

"See you in hell first," burst out Bambridge,

furiously. He stood up, and stepped out as if to go off the porch.

Stone gave him a sudden hard shove, which staggered him backward. "You —— fool! You will brace me on my own ground? Fork over thet money or—"

"You're a low-down thief! No wonder Malloy's quit standin' for you. . . . An' if you want to know it—there's talk of collectin' the reward on your head."

Bambridge's ignorance of such men as Jed Stone could not have been better expressed. And if he had known how to inflame this outlaw it was doubtful if he could have done so more subtly. For years that price on Stone's head had been a thorn in his flesh. There was still a mother and a father living, not to forget a sacrificed sweetheart; and the thought of them hearing of this reward was torture.

Stone drew his gun and struck Bambridge over the forehead. Not a violent blow, though it brought blood! The cattleman fell over the bench, against the wall.

"Get that through your thick skull?" demanded Stone, as he menacingly straddled the bench. "*Hyar!* Don't pull—"

But Bambridge, like a madman, his face ablaze, reached back toward his hip.

"Take it then!" hissed the outlaw. His shot broke Bambridge's draw. The gun slipped out on the floor and spun round. Bambridge uttered a horrible groan, sagged back, his huge face going out, like an extinguished light.

Stone stood an instant. Then with swift movement he picked up the gun from the floor, fired it into the wall, and dropped it again. Then, bending over the dead man, he ripped open his vest and extracted the money, which he transferred to his own pocket. That done, he stepped to the porch. The gun in his hand still smoked. Sheathing it, he glanced along the wall of the cliff to see Madden coming on a run. His next move was to light a cigarette, and his fingers were as steady as a rock. He had shot Bambridge as he would have a hydrophobia skunk, than which there is no more despised beast of the wilderness.

Chapter Sixteen

MADDEN thumped up to the cabin, breathless and alarmed. "Boss, I heerd—shootin'," he panted.

"Reckon you did," replied Stone, removing his cigarette to puff a cloud of smoke.

The right-hand man of Croak Malloy took his cue from that—no need for concern!

"What come—off?"

"Wal, you can see fer yourself."

Madden stamped up the high porch steps, his beady eyes working as if on points, until suddenly they fixed on the dead man, the little stream of red blood running out toward the gun lying on the floor. It seemed to be an accusing finger.

"——! Throwed on you?" ejaculated Madden, in amaze.

Stone nodded.

"What's thet cut on his haid?" asked the other, curiously.

"Wal, he fell all over the place," replied Stone, casually. "I reckon he hit the bench. . . . Better search him, Madden."

The outlaw picked up the gun, took a look at the chamber, and laid it on the bench. Then he extracted watch, papers, and a handful of gold coins from the pockets, which he placed beside the gun. His next move was to look for a money-belt.

"Wasn't well heeled," he remarked, in disgust. "I recollect he an' Croak had a hell of a row at Tanner's. There was a game on. An' Bambridge lost. Swore he'd never fetch any more money where there was a lot of robbers. Haw! Haw!"

"You're welcome to thet, Madden. I shore don't want it."

"Thanks, Boss. An' what about all these papers?"

"Wal, I reckon you can keep them for Croak," said Stone, with humor. "By the way, Madden, when do you expect him?"

"Today, sure. Thet's why I near rode Bambridge

off his laigs gettin' hyar. . . . What'd you an' Bambridge fight aboot?"

"Wait till Croak comes," replied the rustler leader. "I don't want to tell it all over again."

"Shall we drag Bambridge an' bury him, or wait fer thet, too?"

"Reckon we'd better wait. Put the gun back on the floor where you found it. An' cover him over."

"Haw! Haw! Pertickler on Croak seein' the evidence huh? . . . Don't blame you. Croak will be a-rarin'. But at thet he wasn't so fond of Bambridge, an' don't you overlook it."

Stone sat down on the porch steps and smoked a cigarette, while Madden fetched a tarpaulin from the canyon corral where the horses were fenced in. The tight cold tension within Stone slowly relaxed its grip, but did not disappear. He felt that he might as well make a day of it, if opportunity afforded. Malloy would undoubtedly be rancorous at the killing of Bambridge. Stone did not concern himself even to think out an explanation. What did he care what the little rattlesnake thought? The hard fierce creed of outlaws had not been transgressed—that Stone knew in his heart. It might be, presently, but that was another matter. He would wait to see how Malloy took the situation.

"Firewood runnin' low," said Madden. "I'll pack up some. Funny how we all have to lug wood up the hill."

Stone watched the short, sturdy figure in its

dust-crusted garb go down the hill to the edge of the timber, and come staggering up again, under a load of faggots. He wondered how soon Croak Malloy would come, and still felt sure of himself. There was no time like the first moments of the inception of a resolve. Who would be with Malloy? Perhaps a new man or so, and surely that hulking specimen of town-dive riffraff Blacky Reeves, as Malloy called him. Stone reflected that he might as well have a shot at him, too, while he was at it, and the thought was pleasing.

But the afternoon wore on, and the croaking Nemesis of the Hash Knife did not appear. Stone sat for hours on Malloy's seat on the porch, waiting and watching.

The long shadows crept over the breaks, the purple veils drooped into the canyons, the high rims caught the gold of sunset and shone in winding zigzag lines. Then dusk intervened, the air chilled, the night-hawks began their piercing-noted quest. Gloom settled down over the wilderness, and silence, and soon night. Malloy would not come up that rough trail in the dark.

Call to supper at last brought the outlaw leader inside the cabin, where bright fire and smoking pans and pots attested to Madden's practical application to duties surely neglected by others of the Hash Knife.

"No sign of Croak?" he asked.

"Nary. An' mebbe it's jest as well," replied Stone.

"Shore. Tomorrer you'll feel less testy. . . . Wal,
Croak's been in a fight, you can lay to thet. Else
he'd been hyar. I seen him at Tanner's about a
week ago—yep, jest seven days, an' we set the
day for me to get hyar with Bambridge. . . . Thet
feller Darnell has messed things up again, I
reckon."

"Madden, I appreciate your cookin', if not your
company," said Stone.

"Shore kind of you, Boss," replied the other, sarcastically. "But when the final row between you
an' Croak comes don't take any of it out on me. I
was Croak's pard before we come to the Hash
Knife. An' if I do see some queer deals I hardly
approve of, I can't do nothin'."

"I'll remember thet, Madden," rejoined Stone,
in a surprise he did not show. "Thet's straight talk.
I didn't think it was in you."

They finished the meal, after which Stone
smoked in front of the fire, where Madden
presently joined him.

"Forgot aboot thet dead hombre out there," he
said. "We ought to have planted him."

"Maddy, you've slept before where there was a
dead man lyin' around."

"Shore. But I ain't crazy aboot it."

After a while, which was mostly silence, they
sought their blankets. Stone's bed happened to be
in the corner just inside where Bambridge lay, and
he could smell the blood. Sleep did not come

readily, so presently he got up, and carrying his blankets to another unoccupied bough-couch in the cabin, he spread them in that. It was a quiet night, with no sound except a low moan of wind in the caverns of the great overhanging cliff. And some hours elapsed before Stone fell into slumber.

Next morning he was up with the sun, and something, as black and uncanny as the vanished night, had left him. Stone walked along the wall, as far as the intersecting canyon which the rustlers used as a corral for the horses. He reminded himself that he did this quite often. There seemed no sense in deceiving himself—he would soon be riding away from the rendezvous and the brakes. Which presupposed that he did not mean to give Malloy a chance to kill him!

On his return he heard a halloa, and quickening his steps soon turned a corner of wall to see riders coming up the slope. Three—with pack-animals!

Madden hailed him from the door. "Croak comin' with Blacky an' some fellar I cain't make out yet."

Stone, in action of which he was unaware, hitched his heavy belt, as if about to mount a horse or undertake something physical. As he went up the porch steps his quick eye took in the tarpaulin that hid Bambridge. The body looked like some covered packs.

"Maddy, no hurry aboot tellin' Croak," said Stone, indicating the dead man.

"All right, Boss. I'd jest as lief see Croak cheerful as long as possible."

Then they both went into the cabin, Madden to bustle around the fire, and Stone to watch through one of the chinks between the logs. The three rustlers came very slowly up the slope, to halt before the cabin. A lean dark rider, the stranger, sagged in his saddle. A bloody bandage showed from under his sombrero. He was the last to dismount, but they were all ridden out. Without speaking they threw saddles and packs, and left the weary horses standing.

"Wal, if thar's anybody home they shore ain't powerful glad to see us," said Malloy, gruffly.

Madden ran out, his hands white with flour. "Howdy, men! We seen you comin', but didn't think it no call fer a brass band."

"Haw!—I should smile not. . . . Anybody hyar?" returned Malloy.

"Only the boss."

Whereupon Stone stalked out, and a singular incomprehensible fact was that he was glad to see the gunman. Croak radiated the raw hard force of the range. He was, at best, an ally to depend upon in times that tried men. On the other hand, Stone certainly had a wavering thought—this was the moment! Nevertheless, he did not take advantage of it.

"Mornin', Croak. How's tricks?" he said, cheerfully.

"Hullo there, you old son-of-a-gun!" replied Malloy. "Got news fer you—an' somethin' else."

Malloy limped. Something beside sweat and dust had caked on his worn yellow chaps—something dark and sinister. Stone's sharp eye caught a bullet-hole in the leather. Malloy carried a rifle, saddle-bag, and an extra gun-belt, minus shells. His leather jacket looked as if he had slept in wet clay that had hardened. His crooked face somehow appeared wonderful to look at, or else Stone's mind at the moment was steeped in strong feeling. Malloy might have been wearing a death mask, yet his eyes were alight, and it seemed that in them was a smile. His boots dragged across the floor, his spurs jangled, as he went into the cabin, to deposit wearily what he carried.

"Howdy, you cook!" he called. "Then thet four-flush cattle thief didn't come out?"

"Croak, I've shore got bad news," returned Madden. "But s'pose you rest a little—an' eat somethin'—before I spring it on you."

"Good idee. I'm mad as a tarantula-wasp anyhow. . . . I reckoned Bambridge wouldn't come. . . . An' mebbe I like it jest as well as if he did. No more deals fer me with thet — — —!"

"Sounds good to me, Croak," returned Stone, with satisfaction. "Reckon I can give you a reason why you can't take up any more deals with Bambridge. But it's bad news. An' suppose you have a shot of my bottle first."

Malloy took a long drink of fiery liquor that made him cough huskily and brought color to his ashen cheeks.

"Ugh!—If I'd hed thet two days ago—mebbe I'd never got hyar," he said, enigmatically.

"Where's Lang?"

"Ha!—Feedin' the buzzards."

"You don't say," returned the outlaw leader, coolly, though the statement had struck fire from him. Another of the original Hash Knife gone! Lang was not loyal, but he belonged to the old school, and once he had been respectable.

Slow footfalls thudded up the steps outside, across the porch. The bar of light from the door darkened. Reeves entered with the lean-jawed stranger.

"Hed to shoot thet bay. She was bad crippled," announced Reeves.

"Should have been done before," replied Malloy. "Boss, shake hands with Sam Tanner. . . . Cousin of Joe's from up Little Colorado way."

"Howdy, Tanner," said Stone, civilly, though he did not move toward Malloy's new man. Perhaps this omission was not noticed, as table and packs and also Malloy stood between. Tanner merely bowed his bandaged head, which, with sombrero removed, showed matted hair, and dark stains extending down over the left temple and ear.

"Must have jagged your haid on a snag or somethin'," went on Stone.

"Nary snag. I got sideways to a lead slug," returned Tanner. He had a low voice, and a straight, level look from his black eyes. Stone gauged men of the range with speed and precision. This fellow, since he was kin to Joe Tanner, and in the company of Croak Malloy, could be only another of their ilk, but he seemed a man to consider thoughtfully.

"Croak, I reckon you'll be tellin' me you've had a little brush with somebody," said Stone, dryly.

"Brush?—Haw! Haw!" rejoined the gunman, and his flaring glance, his crisp query, and his deadly little croak of a laugh made Stone's flesh creep. He guessed there were some dead men somewhere who would never tell the tale of what had happened.

"Wal, take your time tellin' me," drawled the leader.

"Come an' get it," yelled Madden.

They sat at the rude table, upon which the cook thumped steaming utensils. The keen-eyed Stone remarked that all three men were ravenously hungry, yet only Malloy could eat. That to Stone was most significant. So far as Malloy was concerned, however, it would take a great deal to sicken him.

"A good stiff drink with some hot grub—an' a fellar's able to go on," he said, as he rose. "But I'll shore sleep most like our pard Lang hangin' down there on thet cottonwood."

Stone did not reveal his curiosity; he knew he would soon be enlightened, and if his intuition was not at fault most weighty things had happened. But when Malloy drew a heavy roll of soiled greenbacks from his pocket and tossed it over, Stone could not hide a start.

"Bambridge sent thet money he owed you," said Malloy. "Like the muddlehaid he is he trusted it to Darnell. . . . An' I'm tellin' you, pard, if it hadn't been fer me you'd never seen it."

"I reckon. Thanks—Croak," replied the outlaw chief, halting. This was one of the surprising attributes of the little gunman. Vicious and crooked as he was, he yet had the quality which forced respect, if not more, from Stone's reluctant mind.

Malloy laboriously took off his chaps and flapped them into his corner of the cabin. Then a bloody wet spot showed on the leg of his jeans. "Some hot water, Maddy, an' a clean rag. I've a crease on my laig."

"What's the fellar got who gave you thet cut, Croak?" queried Stone.

"He got nothin', wuss luck. I was shore damn near my everlastin', Jed, an' don't you overlook it . . . Sam, you better have Madden wash thet bullet hole of yours. He's pretty handy."

Stone curiously watched the deft Madden dress the wounds of the injured rustlers.

"Ouch!—What'd you put in it, you idjet? Feels like salt," shouted Malloy.

"Croak, you're wuss'n a baby aboot little hurts. What'd you do if you got shot bad?"

"Haw! Haw! Thet's a good one. I can show more bullet scars than any damn rider in these brakes. An' I know who made each one. Some of the men are livin' yet, which speaks pore fer me. I never lived up to my reputation."

In due time the ministering was ended, after which Malloy asked for another drink. "Reckon I'd better get some of my news off my chest. Then after I hear yours I'll have a nap of about sixteen hours. . . . Boss, would you mind comin' out on the porch where I can set down an' talk?"

They went outside, and Stone experienced a qualm when Malloy hobbled to his favorite seat. The foot of his injured leg rested upon what he must have thought was a pack, but it happened to be Bambridge's head under the tarpaulin.

"Jed, you know thet trapper's cabin down hyar a ways—reckon aboot three hours stiff ridin'?— Thet old one under the wall, where a spring runs out by a big white sycamore?"

"Shore. I know it. Slept there often enough. Full of mice an' bugs."

"Wal, it ain't no more," said Malloy, with a grim chuckle. "It's a heap of ashes."

"Burnt, eh? What you fellars doin'—burnin' all the cabins around?"

"Hellno. We didn't do it. That tarnel Slinger Dunn!"

"Ah, I see. . . . Wal, Slinger is a bad hombre. Too much like an Apache! . . . Hope you didn't brush with the Diamond."

"Jed, your hopes air only born to be dashed. Me an' you left of the Hash Knife, 'cept Maddy hyar—an' you can lay it to thet damned slick tracker Dunn an' the outfit he's throwed in with. You oughta have killed him long ago."

"Not so easy to do as to say," replied Stone, sarcastically.

"Ha—you're talkin'. Wal, I had a chanct to kill Slinger, but it'd have meant me gettin' it too."

"You're learnin' sense late—mebbe too late, Croak. . . . I hope to God, though, you didn't raid this new stock of Jim Traft's."

"No, Jed, we didn't," replied Malloy, frankly. "I was sore at you fer talkin' ag'in it, but after I got away an' seen what a mess Bambridge an' his card sharper got me into I changed my mind. Not that I wouldn't of druv the cattle later! But this hyar wasn't the time. An' if Bambridge had come to meet me hyar, as he promised, with a new deal on fer this Diamond stock, I'd shore have taken the money, but I wouldn't have made a single move. Not now."

"Wal, you puzzle me. Suppose you quit ridin' round in a circle," declared Stone, impatiently.

"Fust aboot the money Bambridge sent you by Darnell," began Malloy. "I seen he was flush at Tanner's, an' he was losin' fer a change. Joe is pretty keen himself with the cairds. I set in till I was broke. We hung round Joe's ranch fer a week, waitin', an' finally I got wind of this backhand game Darnell was playin'. He was the mouthpiece between me an' Bambridge. But all the time he was hatchin' a deal on his own hook. An' this one was to make a raid on Blodgett's range without lettin' Bambridge in on it. Joe Tanner never was no smart fellar, an' shore he was always greedy. So he double-crossed us, too. Wal, it was Sam hyar who put me wise. An after figgerin' some an' snoopin' around I seen the deal. Funny I didn't shoot Darnell. But I jest held him up. Then he swore the big roll he had was fer you from Bambridge. I reckoned thet was the truth. . . . Wal, a day or so after they druv the lower end of the brakes an' got some odd thousand head of Diamond stock up on the open range below Tanner's. I was hoppin' mad when I found out, but neither Darnell or Joe came back to Tanner's. Sam's sweet on the sawmill man's daughter, an' thet's how he come to be out of what followed. He told me, an' also thet Darnell, Joe, Lang, an' some riders he didn't know were comin' up to get another whack at the Diamond cattle. Then I was a-rarin' to get at them. I seen it all too late. Bambridge, by playin' on my hopes, had got me in on his deals. He was aimin' fer a big stake—then to duck out of Arizona. Now Darnell carried his messages to an' fro, an' he seein' a chanct himself, double-crossed Bambridge an', as I said, persuaded Joe Tanner to throw in with him."

Malloy refilled his pipe and called for Madden to fetch him a light. After puffing thoughtfully, his cramped, wrinkled brow expressive of much, he went on:

"I took their trail with Sam. Night before last, jest before sundown we come damn near gettin' run down by a stampede of cattle. We rustled to thet trapper's cabin, an', by Gawd! we hadn't hardly hid our horses an' slipped in there when hyar come Joe, Lang, Darnell, an' his seedy-lookin' outfit. Some of them had sense enough to ride on. But both Darnell an' Tanner had been shot an' found ridin' hard. I never seen a madder man than Tanner, nor a scareder one than Darnell. We'd jest started to have hell there—with me readin' it to them, when we found out who an' what was chasin' them. . . . No less than the Diamond outfit, Jed, led by Slinger Dunn an' thet Prentiss cowpuncher.—Dog-gone, I'd always wanted to run ag'in' him! . . . Wal, there they had us, an' you can bet we didn't sleep much thet night. When daylight come I took a look out, an' was surprised when the bullets begun to fly. Them darned punchers all had rifles!—An' there we was, with only our guns, no shells to spare, little grub, an' no water atall. We was stuck, an' you bet I told them. Thet glade is open in front of the cabin, as you can recollect, an' there them dare-

311

devil cowboys dodged along the edge of the timber, like a bunch of Apaches, an' kept shootin'. We couldn't do nothin'. Say, wasn't I hot under the collar? Worried, too, Jed, an' don't you overlook thet. . . . Wal, they was cute enough to guess it, an' this Prentiss hombre yelled for us to throw out all guns an' belts, an' to come after, hands up, an' line up ag'in' the cabin wall. . . . Haw! Haw!"

Malloy laughed in grim recollection of the images or ideas his words called up. Stone could not divine any humor in them. Probably Malloy laughed at the suggestion for him to put up his hands.

"I yelled back," resumed Malloy, " 'Hey, Prentiss, what'll you do to us—in case we surrender?'

" 'Wal, we'll shore hang you an' thet caird sharp, anyways,' called back the cowboy. Orful cheerful he was, an' sort of cocky. . . . Gawd! but I wanted to get out there to throw a gun on him. Then I yelled back, 'Reckon you'll have to come take us.'

"It wasn't long after thet when I smelled smoke," resumed Malloy, after a pause. "Thet damned redskin Dunn had set fire to the cabin roof. It was an old roof of shacks an' brush, an' shore dry. Burn? You should have heerd it! We didn't have a hell of a lot of time. Fire began to drop on us. Lookin' out, I seen thet the cowboys had bunched over at the edge of the woods, jest out of gunshot. I seen also thet the smoke from the cabin was blowin' low an' gettin' thicker. 'Men,' I says, 'we've got one chanct an' a slim one. Take it or leave it. I'm gonna run out under cover of thet smoke, an' make a break fer cover. Anyway, it's better to be shot than burn up or hang. Take your choice. But whoever's comin' with me start when I yell.' "

Malloy took another long pull at his pipe, and his wonderful eyes, flaring with lightning, swept down over the wild brakes and along the wandering gray wall of rock.

"I waited till a thick lot of smoke rolled off the roof," went on Malloy, "an' then I yelled, 'Let 'er rip!' An' I run fer it, a gun in each hand. To do 'em credit, every last man in the cabin charged with me. But what'n hell could they do? . . . Wal, I got a bullet in the laig fust thing, an' I went down. But I got up an' run as best I could. You'd thought an army had busted loose—there was so much shootin'. An' bullets—say, they was like bees! But we had the smoke with us, or not one man jack of us would have escaped. Shore I was shootin', but bein' crippled an' on the run, I was shootin' pore. I nailed one of them punchers, though, an' I seen another one fall. Thet one was daid before he hit the ground. But some one else allowed fer him. . . . I got to the timber an' fell in the brush, where you bet I laid low. I reckoned my laig was broke. But I wasn't even bad shot, an' when I got it tied up I felt better. The shootin' an' yellin' soon ended. I peeped through the brush . . . an' what do you reckon I seen?"

"Some rustler swingin'," returned Stone, hazarding a guess.

"Nope. It was thet caird sharp, Darnell. But when I seen him fust they hadn't swung him up. I could hear him beggin'. But thet Diamond bunch was shore silent an' swift. They jerked him clear, till he kicked above their haids. I seen his tongue stick out . . . then his face go black. . . . An' next went up Lang an' Joe Tanner. They had their little kick. . . . I watched, but seen no more rustlers swing. But shore Prentiss an' Dunn would have nailed some of them on the run. I crawled away farther an' hid under a spruce thet had branches low on the ground. I lay there all day, till I was shore the cowpunchers had rid away. Then I went into the spruces where me an' Blacky had hid our horses. His was gone, but mine was there. I sneaked him off into the woods, an' worked round to the trail. All night! This mawnin' I run into Blacky, who'd got away without a scratch. An' Sam, who hadn't been in the cabin, seen us from his hidin'-place, an' whistled. . . . An' wal, hyar we air."

"Croak, you might have reckoned on some such mess as thet," said Stone, gravely.

"Shore I might, but I didn't. Jed, I've had too damn much money lately. Thet gambler het up my blood. I'm sorriest most thet I didn't plug him.

314

But it was a hell of a lot of satisfaction to see him kick."

"No wonder. I'd like to have been there. . . . So the Hash Knife is done!—Croak, what do you aim at now?"

"Lay low an' wait," replied the gunman. "We shore can find men to build up the outfit again."

"Never—if young Traft got killed in thet fight," retorted Stone, vehemently. "Old Jim would rake the Tonto with guns an' ropes."

"Course I don't know who got shot, outside of the two cowboys I see drop. The one I shot wasn't young Traft, an' neither was the other. An' they wasn't Slinger Dunn or Prentiss, either. . . . Boss, have you seen Sonora?"

"No. He hasn't been in fer days," replied Stone.

Malloy held his pipe far away from him and sniffed the air.

"Damnit, am I loony, or do I smell blood?"

"I reckon you smell blood all right, Croak, old boy," returned Stone, jocularly.

"How so? I'm shore washed clean." Suddenly, with his gaze on Stone, narrowing and shrewd with conjecture, he felt with his foot the pack upon which it had rested. "What the hell?"

Then with a singularly violent action he swept away the tarpaulin, to disclose Bambridge, a ghastly sight for even calloused men; and the pool of blood, only partly dried up; and the gun lying near on the floor.

"Bambridge!" he exclaimed, in cold and ringing speculation. "Boss, you done fer him?"

"I reckon. He throwed a gun on me, Croak," replied Stone, rising to go to the wall, where he poked a finger in a bullet hole in one of the yellow logs. "Look here."

"Ahuh. . . . Wal, you saved me the trouble, mebbe. . . . Shot yestiddy, I reckon. What'd he have on him?"

"Ask Madden. He searched him."

"Hyar, Maddy, come out pronto," he yelled, and when the cook ran out breathless and anxious, he went on. "This was your bad news, eh?"

"Nope, I didn't reckon thet bad. But he had only aboot five hundred on him, an' some papers."

"Huh. Five hundred what?" demanded Malloy.

"Dollars—in gold double-eagles."

"An' this two-bit cattle thief reckoned he'd bribe me with thet!" he ejaculated, in disgust. "Wal, Maddy, give me one of them gold birds fer luck, an' keep the rest. . . . An' say, somebody'll have to plant this stiff. . . . Blacky, you an' Madden gotta dig a grave fer our departed guest. Dig it right out hyar alongside the porch, an' put up a stone or somethin', so when I see it I'll be reminded of what a foolish galoot I am."

"Reckon you'd better search him again, Madden," added Stone. "Bambridge was the kind of hombre who'd sew bills up inside his clothes."

The two outlaws, enthusiastic in obedience, lost

no time complying. Stone turned away from the gruesome sight. But Malloy watched with a sardonic grin.

"Jed, I don't notice thet you've gone back any on the draw," he remarked. "You shore hit him plumb center. . . . An', wal, I guess I gotta take it as friendly act on your part, though I seen red fust off."

Malloy had his strong fascination for all men who came in contact with him, and never had Jed Stone felt it more certainly than now. Over all men he exerted a fascination of fear, but this was hardly what influenced the rustler leader here. He still bore the hatred for Malloy, because the gunman had broken up the Hash Knife; nevertheless, his deadly intent began to lose the keenness of its edge. A deep resolve, however, was something so fixed in Stone that to change it, let alone eradicate it, was a slow, painful process. It had its inception at this hour, however, and began its gradual disintegration.

Malloy went to bed and to sleep. His slumber, however, was as strange a thing as any other connected with him. He slept, yet seemed to be awake. The slightest sound would make him wide awake in a second. This was not conscience or fear, for the man possessed neither, it was the defensive instinct of the gunman most highly developed.

That day and the night passed. Stone grew more thoughtful. It did not surprise him to see Sam Tanner saddle a horse and ride away while Malloy lay asleep. These two men would never have gotten along.

Stone walked under the wall, and found his way into the hidden recesses of a wide fissure which opened out into a canyon, choked with green thicket and splintered sections of cliff, where silence and peace reigned. He could not stay longer at the cabin. Any hour that wild Diamond outfit might ride up there. Stone realized that Malloy expected it and certainly would not remain. Tanner had taken no chances. But Stone was reluctant to relinquish his revenge.

He lay on the pine-needle mat of brown, and fought the thing out. Malloy, so far as was possible for one of his character, had certain virtues worthy of respect, if not regard. He had not approved of the leadership of the Hash Knife and had openly opposed it. On the other hand he was not an enemy of Stone's. He trusted him. He would not have cheated him. And so Stone beat down the insistent voice that called to him to murder Malloy in cold blood. He would be truer to the old creed of the Hash Knife. Let Malloy go his way, build up another rustler outfit, and meet his inevitable end. That must come soon. These young Arizonians like Dunn and Prentiss were not to be stopped, or if they were, others as resouceful and deadly would arise. Arizona was slow but sure. Jed Stone would disappear and never be heard of again. That idea had its strong attraction. The range rumor would go abroad—the Hash Knife leader gone.

Stone felt an amazing relief at the joint renunciation of his desperate resolve and the sense of his vanishing from the Tonto. As he lay under its spell the pain at giving up these wild lonely canyons and tangled brakes he loved so, seemed to mitigate. There were other places where wilderness survived—where the forest was sweet and insulating.

And from that strange hope it took only a single leap of consciousness to land him on the verge of abandoning forever the crooked trail of the rustler, the outlaw. Almost before he realized it the transformation happened—not to character, for he was too old to change, but to its objective—to the necessity of stealing to live, and of fighting to survive. He had in his possession now more money than he had ever had at one time, enough to start ranching as he had dreamed of it twenty years before. Something had clarified his intelligence. Where were the clamoring fears attendant on the fugitive from justice? Vanished. It was a joke that he might be apprehended for that old crime of which he bore the stigma. And outside of Arizona who would know him or want to pry into his past? Many a successful cattleman or sheepman had gotten his start by questionable means. Stone knew this because he knew such men.

No—there was nothing to prevent him—nothing to fear. When he gave up his intention to kill his most notorious partner he had freed himself from intricate and subtle fetters. That was the secret of his surprise, his relief, his elation. Because when he abandoned that bloody revenge on Malloy he was in reality abandoning his position as a leader of outlaws.

Pecos would be waiting for him up at the headwaters of the Little Colorado. Stone decided that the sooner he started the better for him. There was a shadow over the yellow cabin built by Malloy, and more than that cast by the bulk of the looming wall. Besides he hardly trusted himself, so long as he remained in propinquity to the remnant of the Hash Knife.

Upon Stone's return to the cabin, at sunset, he found it deserted. Malloy and his two comrades had departed in a hurry, leaving the interior of the cabin in a state of confusion. He felt no surprise. It had happened before. Still, there might have been good reason for such a departure. Sonora might have returned or anything could have happened. Hastily packing some food supplies and a blanket, Stone made his way under cover of the wall to the corral. His horse was among the several horses left. In a few moments Stone rode down the slope into the darkening forest.

Chapter Seventeen

THREE mornings later, in the first rosy flush of sunrise, when the black squirrels were chattering and the blue jays screeching, Jed Stone struck into a blazed trail new to him and which led to a newly graded road. This he concluded was the road recently cut down into Yellow Jacket.

He would have suffered a pang for this desecration of the wilderness but for the satisfaction and even melancholy happiness which had increased during his slow and wary working up towards Clear Creek and Cottonwood Canyon, from which junction he could find his way to the Little Colorado. He had meat and salt, hard biscuits and coffee, enough to last him for the journey.

Up out of the canyon country now, on the level of the slowly rising plateau, where forest of pine began to be sprinkled with open patches of desert of cedar and piñon and sage, he relaxed something of vigilance and made much faster time. Because of this he discovered, presently, that he had ridden some distance over fresh horse tracks before he had observed them.

"That's queer," he soliloquized, halting. "They shore weren't in the road back there a ways."

Riders had come along here that very morning, and they had certainly cut off into the woods somewhere between this point and back where Stone had noticed the clean untracked road.

The fact was disturbing, but after he had reflected a moment he made sure that he would have heard and seen them long before they could have discovered him. For he had been alone, and though relaxed somewhat from strain he still exercised keen eyes and ears. They had turned off not to avoid him, but for reasons of their own.

Stone spurred on and rode at a brisk canter for a while, anxious to get to the Cottonwood country, where again he could take to the deep forest. But when he came to the junction of the new road with the old one he was halted by plain evidences of a hold-up. A vehicle of some sort had come along here headed south and had gone no farther, along either road. Stone found a canvas bag, open and rifled of its contents, and thrown aside. The ground about had been so cut up with hoofs that he could read but little from the tracks. But soon he ascertained that the wheel tracks turned back the way they had come.

"Wal, now, jest what come off heah?" he muttered. He was accustomed to read the signs of the open. These might have meant little, and again they might have meant a great deal. Stone sensed the latter, and he searched the roadside until he found along the wheel tracks a bloody glove that had fallen into the weeds.

"Ahuh. I smelled it—as Croak would say,"

declared Stone. "I'm jest curious now to catch up with whatever had these wheels."

Whereupon he put his horse to a gallop, walk and trot, and lope, according to the stretches of road open far ahead or turning through the cedars. And in an hour or less he sighted a buckboard with one occupant driving slowly north. Stone kept on. He would have a look at that driver and his vehicle. A strong instinct prompted this, not all curiosity. He did not need to come to close quarters with the driver. This individual wore no hat; he had gray hair; he sagged in his seat, now with his head hunched between square shoulders and again with it lifted doggedly. Stone, after the manner of riders of his kind, like hounds on scent, caught the color of blood on stones along the roadside. Then he spurred his horse into a run.

Before he caught up with the buckboard it stopped, and the man turned, evidently having heard the thudding hoofs behind. As Stone flashed up, to haul his horse to a sliding halt, he caught sight of the dark face of a Mexican lying on the floor behind the back seat. Stone had seen too many dead men not to know this one.

"Hey, old-timer—" Then he experienced a violent heart-stabbing start. He was staring into the hard convulsed visage of a man he had not seen for twenty years, yet whom he instantly recognized. A wrench tore Stone. "Dog-gone-me if it ain't Jim Traft!"

"Howdy, Jed!" replied the rancher, grimly. "An' what do *you* want?"

"Me!—Hell, nothin', except to ask what's happened? I run across your tracks a ways back. Looked like a hold-up to me. An' I knew it when I found this glove."

Stone pulled out the stained glove, which he had tucked under the pommel of his saddle.

"Belonged to my driver, Pedro, lyin' there," said Traft, nodding at the dead man. "But, shore, you know what come off."

"I don't. I know nothin'. I've been three days ridin' out of the brakes. I jest run across you."

"Jed Stone, can you expect me to believe thet?" queried Traft, incredulously.

"Reckon I expect it, Jim, 'cause I swear it's true," replied Stone, and gazed straight into the steel-blue eyes bent so piercingly and accusingly, and yet so strangely, upon him. That look bridged the long cruel years back to the dim cowboy days.

"You don't know I've been held up an' robbed by Croak Malloy?" demanded Traft, derisively.

"By God! . . . You have? . . . No, Jim, I didn't know."

"Nor thet he killed my driver?"

"I didn't know, Jim," repeated Stone, now with terrible earnestness to be believed by this old rancher.

"Jed, I reckon I don't see any reason for you lyin' to me. Many years ago you lied to me—an' that lie ruined you an' saved me. But don't lie now."

"Jim, I'm not lyin'. I swear to God! . . . I'd quit the Hash Knife. I left our hole down in the brakes three days ago. My outfit's done. Malloy broke it up. I'm leavin' Arizona forever—an' this life I've led."

After a protracted study of Stone's face the rancher burst out: "My Gawd! Jed, I'm glad. An' it's shore a queer meetin' for me an' you. . . . But listen. I was goin' down to Yellow Jacket to surprise my nephew Jim. I had his sweetheart, Molly Dunn, with me, an' his sister, Gloriana. We slept last night at Miller's sheep-ranch, I reckon some fifteen miles up the road. An' at the turn-off down there we got held up by three men. I didn't know Malloy till one of his pardners called him Croak. . . . Wal, when Pedro drove on, at my order, Malloy rode up an' shot him. An' you bet he'd have done fer me but fer an idee he got. Anyway, they robbed me an' yanked the girls out of the buckboard. They had to hawg-tie Molly. She shore fought. Malloy says, 'Traft, I'll give you three days to come to Tobe's Well with ten thousand dollars. Put the money in the loft of the cabin, next the chimney. We'll see you come, or whoever you send. An' these girls will be set free. Mebbe a little wuss fer love-makin'!' . . . The little ruffian said jest thet, an' grinned aboot it. I agreed. An' he let me go."

"Jim, if I know Malloy he let you off easy," declared Stone, sharply, and he reined his horse over close to the buckboard. "I struck their tracks down by the new road. An' I know aboot where they cut off into the woods. . . . Jim, I'll trail Malloy, an' go round an' haid him off, or come up on him at Tobe's Well. Mebbe I better make a short cut an' beat him there. . . . But I'll come up on him before dark. An' I'll get the girls."

"Jed Stone, are you aimin' fer thet ten thousand?" demanded Traft.

"I don't want a dollar. I'll do this because, wal, because I liked young Jim an' because I'd starve before I'd do you another dirty deal. At thet Malloy an' Bambridge rung me into the only one. An' I killed Bambridge fer doin' it."

"You killed Bambridge?" ejaculated the rancher.

"I shore did. An' Croak told me he'd seen thet gambler Darnell kickin' at the end of a rope. But, Jim, you'll hear all thet pronto. I'll have to rustle. . . . One thing more. Malloy may kill me. I reckon I can outfigger him, but to be on the safe side you'd better send a trusty rider with thet money, an' after you do, make a bee line for Yellow Jacket. I'll fetch the girls there."

"Jed Stone, by—heaven! . . . wait!" faltered the old cattleman.

But Stone had spurred away, to call over his shoulder, "So long, Jim—old pard!"

Like the wind Stone raced back down the road,

and as soon as he was sure of direction he cut across the cedared desert and into the woods, where gallop and trot soon brought him upon Malloy's tracks. He followed them, and marveled in mind at the inscrutability of chance, at the inevitableness of life—at this meeting with Jim. After all, he was not to ride away from the brakes without the blood of Cloak Malloy on his hands. How his heart leaped at the just cause! For as surely as his keen eyes were finding the tracks over moss and pine needles, he realized he would kill Malloy. Very likely all three of the rustlers! He must come up to them before night, otherwise the young women would be subjected to abuse and worse. Malloy had always made much of his few opportunities to degrade women. Probably owing to his misshapen body and repulsive face all women, even the slatterns of the towns, had wanted none of his acquaintance, which had made the little gunman a woman-hater.

The hours of the day were as moments. Forest and ravine, pine and spruce, rock and log, all looked alike to Stone. Yet he recognized familiar country when he rode into it. By mid-afternoon he had approached the vicinity of Tobe's Well, a wonderful natural hollow in the high escarpment overlooking the Cibeque. Stone left the trail he was hounding, and going around came up on the rim from the south. Horses rolling below in the sandy patches! Smoke curling from the stone chimney of the log cabin! Saddles and packs under the great silver spruce!

Jed Stone led his horse around the rim and down a dim seldom-trodden trail to the opening into the circular gorge. And never in all his twenty years of hard wild life had he been more Jed Stone.

No one hailed him as he strode along the mossy bank of the brook, under the stately pines, and on toward the cabin. The lonely isolation of the place invited carelessness. But Stone muttered: "They must be powerful keen on what's inside. Reckon I didn't get here too soon."

Dropping the bridle reins, he strode on to the open door. It was a big bright cabin, open on the lee side. And as he glanced in he heard a girl's low cry, deep, broken with emotion. He saw a dark little girl with gold-brown hair, all tossed and tangled, lying bound half upright against a pile of packs. That was Molly Dunn. He did not need to look twice. His eyes swept on.

Madden was on his knees, his hand white with flour, but on the moment he appeared riveted. Reeves stood back, his face set toward Malloy, who manifestly had just torn the blouse off a white-faced, white-shouldered girl, shrinking before him.

The moment had been made for Jed Stone. He recognized it, and saw, as if by magic, how far in the past it had its incipiency and now had reached fulfillment. He gloried in it. What debts he would pay here!

He stepped inside to call out, harshly, "What the hell's goin' on?"

It was the first occasion on which he had ever seen Malloy surprised, but perhaps the thousandth when he had seen him angry. Stone felt his sudden presence had been decidedly inopportune for his erstwhile partner and his accomplices.

"Aw, it's the boss!" gasped Madden, in explosion of breath that suggested relief.

"Who's been chasin' *you?*" burst out Malloy, and with gesture of impatience he flung down the torn blouse.

"Jed Stone!" screamed Molly Dunn, and if ever a voice thrilled Stone this one did then. She had recognized him. Even on the moment he remembered the times he had patted Molly's curly head when she was a mere tot, had bought her candy at the store in West Fork, had often lifted her upon his horse, and in later years, when she was grown into a pretty girl, he had talked with her on occasions when he rode to and fro from the Cibeque to the Tonto.

"Wal, I reckon ten thousand devils might be chasin' me, fer all you'd care, Croak," replied Stone. "I jest happened in on you here."

"Damn queer, an' I call it tough. You're wuss'n an old woman," complained Malloy.

"Who're these girls an' what're you doin' with them?"

"Jed, we got into another brush down in the

brakes," replied Malloy. "Damn if it wasn't full of cowpunchers. But we give them the slip. An' comin' out we run plumb into old Jim Traft an' these gurls. It gave me a great idee. An' hyar air the guns while old Jim is raisin' the dust back to Flag."

"My Gawd!—Not old Jim Traft—the rancher?" burst out Stone, loudly, in pretended consternation.

"Shore. I said old Jim didn't I?"

"An' these girls are friends or kin of his?"

"Shore. I reckon you'd know Molly Dunn if you'd look. She knowed you all right. The other is young Jim Traft's sister."

"An' you aim to make money out of them?"

"I shore do."

"An' make game of them while the money's comin'?" demanded Stone, harshly.

"Wal, thet's none of your bizness, Jed," rejoined Malloy, testily. Habit was strong upon him. This interruption had upset him and he had scarcely adapted himself to it.

But Stone, acting his part, intense and strung, saw already that Malloy's mind had not grasped the situation.

"Man, are you crazy?" shouted Stone. "Jim Traft will have a hundred cowboys ridin' on your trail. You couldn't hit it—with nine horses. They'll catch you—they'll hang you."

"Hang nothin'. Jed, you're the one who's crazy.

What's got into you lately?" replied Malloy, in plaintive amaze and disgust. "You're gettin' old or you've lost your nerve."

"Croak, you've done fer the Hash Knife, an' now this deal will set the whole country ablaze."

Malloy stared his amaze. Stone, seizing the instant, strode to and fro in apparent despair, and wringing his hands, he wheeled away. But when he turned, swift as light, he held a gun spouting red. The little gunman died on his feet, without a movement, even of that terribly sensitive right hand. But he fell face down, showing where the bullet had blown off the back of his head.

Madden, with a bawling curse, swept one of his flour-covered hands for his gun. Too late, for Stone's second shot knocked him over as if it had been a club.

Reeves leaped for the door, just escaping the bullet Stone fired after him. And he was visible running madly in the direction of the horses. Stone let him go. Then he surveyed the cabin. A glance sufficed for Madden and Malloy, but it was a dark and terrible one, of reckoning, of retribution.

The girl Malloy had half stripped had slipped to the floor in a faint, her white arms spread. Then on the instant Molly Dunn's eyes opened, black and dilated with terror.

"How do, Molly!" said Stone, as he bent over her to slash the thongs of buckskin round her boots. He had to roll her over to free her hands. "I reckon I got here none too soon, but not too late, either."

"Oh, Jed—you've come—to save us?" cried Molly.

"Shore. An' as I said I hope not—too late."

"We're all right, Jed. But, oh, I was scared. Thet croakin' devil! . . . Is he daid?"

"Malloy has croaked his last, Molly," went on Stone. "I happened to run across old Jim out on the road. Thet's how I got on your trail. Brace up, now, Molly. Why, this little affair shouldn't faze Molly Dunn of the Cibeque."

"I knowed—knew you at first sight, Jed. An' oh, my heart leaped! . . . Jed, thank God you came in time. I was aboot ready to die. I'd fought Malloy till he hawg-tied me. . . . Oh, how can I ever thank you enough? How will Jim ever do it?"

Her passion of gratitude, her wet eloquent eyes, her trembling little hands, so prodigal of their pressure on his, warmed all the ghastly deadliness out of Jed Stone's veins. Happy moments had vanished forever, for him, he had imagined. But this one was reward for all the lonely starved past.

"Wall, you needn't try to thank me, Molly," he replied. "Now let's see. . . . It's 'most dark already. We'd better camp here tonight. An' tomorrow we'll start for Yellow Jacket. . . . Reckon I'd better pull these disagreeable-lookin' hombres outside."

Madden was of heavy build and took considerable strength to drag out, but Malloy was slight and light.

"With your boots on, Croak, old man!" ejaculated Stone, as he let the limp body flop down. Then Stone possessed himself of the bone-handled gun and the belt with its shiny shells. As an afterthought he rifled the dead man's pockets, to extract considerable money, watch and knife, and one golden double-eagle Malloy had taken from. Madden for luck.

Inside the cabin Stone saw Molly had somehow gotten the torn blouse on the unconscious girl, and was now trying to bring her to.

"Let nature take its course, Molly," he advised. "She'll come to presently of her own accord, an' mebbe the shock to her will be less. . . . Lord! what a pretty girl! I never seen her like. . . . An' she's young Jim's sister?"

"Yes. An' isn't she just lovely?"

"Here, we'll lift her up on this bed of spruce. Somebody cut it nice an' fresh. You can both sleep there tonight."

"Jed, fetch me some cold water. I'm near daid of thirst. Thet wretch tried to make us drink whisky. Ughh!"

Stone found a pail and went to fill it at the spring. His mind seemed full of happy yet vague thoughts. He felt sort of boyish, and warm deep down within. Going back inside, Stone filled a cup with water and watched Molly drink. What a glossy head she had! Two such pretty girls at once quite took his breath. One Western and the other

Eastern! Stone regarded them with interest, with a growing sense of the importance he had played in their lives, with an assurance of the food for memory that there would be in the future.

"Glory—you called her?"

"Shore. But her name's Gloriana."

"An' she's a city girl from the East?"

"Yes. An', Jed, she's come to live out West always."

"Fine, if you can keep her. Proud-lookin' lass! Won't this little adventure sicken her on the West?"

"It'll be the best thing that ever happened to her," avowed Molly, with bright eyes. "Jed, she shore was aboot the proudest girl I ever met. An' Jim's sister. His family, really! Gosh! it was hard on me. I made a mess of things. Jed, I went back on Jim because I thought I wasn't good enough for him—for his aristocratic family. But he kidnapped me—thank the good Lord. I reckon I was jealous, too."

"Small wonder, Molly. It was tough on you—to stack up against these Trafts, you just fresh from the Cibeque. But you're good enough fer anybody, Molly Dunn. I shore hope it'll come out all right."

"Oh, it will, Jed," replied Molly, hopefully. "Glory has a heart of gold. I love her—an' indeed I believe she's comin' to love me. But she can't savvy me. Heah I've had only two years' schoolin', an' lived all my life in a log cabin no better'n this, almost. Never had any clothes or nothin'. An' she has had everythin'. Uncle Jim says the West will win her an' thet she an' I will get along an' be sisters soon as Glory is broke in. He says she must get up against the real old West—you know, an' thet will strike the balance. I don't savvy jest what Uncle Jim means, but I believe him."

"Molly, I reckon I savvy what Uncle Jim is drivin' at," replied Stone, smiling thoughtfully at the earnest girl. "The real old West means hard knocks, like this one she's gettin', cowboys an' cattle, work when you want to drop, an' no sleep when you're dyin' fer it. Cold an' wet an' dust an' wind! To be starved! To be scared stiff! . . . A hundred things thet are nothin' at all to *you,* Molly Dunn, are what this city girl needs."

"Jed, thet's exactly what Uncle says. . . . I'm to marry Jim soon," she went on, with a blush. "They all wanted it this spring, but I coaxed off till fall."

"Ahuh. I reckon you love him heaps, Molly?"

"Oh!—I'm not really Molly Dunn any more. I've lost myself. I'm happy, though, Jed. I'm goin' to school. An' if only Glory could see me as I see her!"

"Wal, I'll help her see you true, Molly," returned Stone, patting her hand. "Now, I'd better go outside while you fetch her to. Sight of the desperado who came a-rarin' in here, swearin' an' shootin', mightn't be good."

"Jed, she was simply crazy aboot desperadoes," said Molly. "An' I honestly believe she was tickled when Malloy carried us off. Leastways, she was till he got to pawin' her."

"Dog-gone! Thet's good. . . . Now, Molly, don't you say one word aboot me till I think it over. I'll go outside an' see to my horse. An' when she's all right, you come out to tell me. Mebbe by then I'll have a plan."

"Jed Stone, never in my life—an' I've always known you—did I ever think of you as a rustler, a killer, a bad man. An' now I *know* you're not really."

"Thanks, Molly; thet'll be sweet to remember," he replied. "Fetch her to, now, an' say nothin'."

Stone went outside, unsaddled his horse and turned him loose, then walked to and fro, in his characteristic way when deep in thought. Presently Molly came running to him. What pleasure that afforded the outlaw whose life had been lived apart from the influence of women!

"She's come to, Jed. An' she's not so knocked out as I reckoned she'd be," said the girl, happily. "I darn near exploded keepin' our secret—thet we're safe with you an' will start in the mawnin' fer Yellow Jacket."

"Wal now, Molly Dunn, you stick to me," rejoined Stone, eagerly. "We'll let on I'm wuss than Croak—thet I jest killed them fellars an' drove the third off so I could have you girls to myself. It's a good three-day ride to Yellow Jacket, fer you, anyhow. Thet gives us time to cure Miss Gloriana of all her bringin'-up. I'll be a real shore-enough desperado—up to a certain point. Savvy, Molly?"

"Oh, Jed, if I only dared do it!" exclaimed Molly, pale with excitement. How her dark eyes glowed! "But she'll suffer. An'—an' I love her so!"

"Shore. All the same, if she's got the real stuff in her thet's the way to fetch it out. It's the only way, Molly, to strike thet balance between you an' her which your Uncle Jim meant. If you've got the nerve, girl, an' do your part, you'll never regret it."

"Jed, you don't mean never to tell Glory you're good instead of bad. I couldn't agree to thet."

"Wal, of course, she's bound to find out sometime thet I'm not so bad, after all. But I'd advise you to put Uncle Jim wise an' keep the secret for a while. Molly, I'll be disappointed in you if you fall down on this chance. I'll bet you young Jim would jump at it."

"He would—he would," panted Molly. "Jed, Heaven forgive me—I'll do it. I'll trust you an' do my part."

"Thet's like a girl of the Cibeque," replied Jed, heartily. "Go back now, an' tell her you both have fallen out of the fryin'-pan into the fire."

Chapter Eighteen

LIFE played even an outlaw queer pranks, thought Jed Stone, as he stalked toward the cabin, conscious of a strange elevation of spirit. When a young man he had shouldered the sin of his friend, for the sake of the girl they both loved—and the noble deed had earned him twenty years of loneliness, misery, and infamy. Just now he had actually committed a crime—he had murdered his confederate, who, vile as he was, had yet the elements of loyalty, the virtue of trust; and out of this circumstance, again in the interest of woman, he divined that he would climb out of the depths. It was an enigma.

Stone entered the cabin, as once he had seen the villian in a melodrama. The Traft girl was sitting up, with Molly fluttering around her. He sustained a shock—like wind rushing back through his veins to his heart. It was as if he had not before seen this girl. In all his life such eyes had never before met his. They were large, dark violet, strained with an expression which might have been horror or terror, or fascination. How wondrously lovely! Stone doubted that he could play his part before their gaze.

"Wal, what'd this Dunn kid tell you?" he demanded, with a fierce glare.

"Oh—sir—she said you—you were Jed Stone,

the desperado," faltered the girl, in haste. "That we'd fallen out of the frying-pan into the fire—that you killed those men so you could have us all—to yourself."

"Correct. An' now what do you think?" queried Stone, studying the girl. She was frightened, and still under the influence of shock, but she was no fool.

"Think? About—what?"

"Why, your new owner, of course. Reckon I always was jealous of Croak Malloy—of his gun-play an' his way with wimmen."

"Mister Stone, when you came in this cabin—when that little beast was tearing my clothes off—I *knew* you were going to save me from him."

"Wal, you're the smart girl," he replied, and almost wavered before those searching, imploring eyes. "Shore I was." Then he reached down with a slow hand and clutched the front of her blouse and jerked her to her feet. Holding her to the light, he bent his face closer to her. "You're a beautiful thing, but are you good?"

"Good? . . . I think so—I hope so."

"Wal, you gotta know—if *I* ask you. Are you a *good* girl?"

"Yes, sir, if I understand you."

"Wal, thet's fine. I've shore been hungry fer one of your kind. Molly Dunn there, she's a Western kid, an' a little wildcat thet's not afraid of desper-adoes. She comes of the raw West, same as me.

339

She'll furnish game fer me. But you're different. You belong to the class that made me an outlaw. An' I'm gonna take twenty years of shame an' sufferin' out on you. . . . Make you slave for me! . . . Make you love me! Beat you! Drag you down."

She sagged under his grasp, without which she would have fallen. Her face could not have been any whiter. "I—I am at your mercy. . . . But, for God's sake—if you had the manhood to kill those brutes—can't you have enough to spare us?"

Stone let her sink down upon the couch. Tenderfoot as she was, she had instinctively recognized or at least felt the truth of him. He would need to be slow, careful, and probably brutal to convince her.

"If you're gonna flop an' faint every time I grab you or speak to you this'll be a picnic fer me," he said, disgustedly. "Where's your Traft nerve. Thet brother of yours, young Jim, has shore got nerve. He braced me an' my whole outfit. Come right to us, an' without a gun. I shore liked him. Thet was the day he knocked the stuffin's out of Croak Malloy. . . . No, Gloriana, you ain't no real Traft."

That stung red into her marble cheeks and a blaze to her wonderful eyes.

"I haven't had half a chance," she flashed, as much to herself as to him.

"You'd never make a go of the West, even if you hadn't had the bad luck to run into Jed Stone," he went on. "You're too stuck up. You think you're too good fer plain Western folks, like Molly there, an' her brother, an' me, an' Curly Prentiss. An' you really ain't good enough. Because here it's what you can *do* thet counts. Wal, I'll bet you cain't do much. An' I'm shore gonna see. Come hyar!"

He dragged her across the floor to the fireplace, where Madden had opened packs and spread utensils and supplies.

"Get down on your knees, you white-faced Easterner," he ordered, forcing her down. "Bake biscuits fer me. If they ain't good I'll beat you. An' fry meat an' boil coffee. Savvy?"

With trembling hands she rolled up her sleeves and began to knead the flour Madden had left in the pan. Stone observed that she was not so helpless and useless as he had supposed. Then he turned to Molly.

"Wal, my dusky lass, you can amoose me while Gloriana does the housework."

"I shore won't. Stay away from me!" shouted Molly, bristling like a porcupine. When Stone attempted to lay hold of her person she eluded him, and catching up a pan she flung it with unerring aim. Stone dodged, but it took him on the back of the head with a great clang, and then banged to the floor.

"You'll pay fer thet, you darned little hussy," he roared, and made at her.

Then followed a wild chase around the cabin,

that to an observer who was not obsessed with fear, as was Gloriana, would have been screamingly funny. As an actor Jed was genuine, but he was heavy on his feet as an ox, and he had to face the brunt of missiles Molly threw, that never failed to connect with some part of his anatomy. When she hit him on the knee with a heavy fruit-can he let out a bawl of honest protest. Molly finally ran behind the half-partition which projected out from the wall, and here allowed Jed to catch her. The partition was constructed of brush. He tore out a long bough and cracked the wall with it.

"Take thet—you darned—little Apache squaw," he panted, and he whacked away with his switch. Then he bent over Molly, who was convulsed on the pine-needle floor, and whispered in her ear, "Yell—scream!"

Whereupon Molly obeyed: "Ah! . . . *Oh!* . . . Ouu!"

Stone paused for effectiveness, while he peeped through the screen. Gloriana knelt erect, her breast heaving, her eyes wildly magnificent. They were searching round for a weapon, Jed concluded.

"Now—Molly Dunn—mebbe thet'll learn you not to monkey with Jed Stone. . . . Come hyar, an' kiss me."

He had to shake her to keep her remembering her part. Stone made smacking sounds with his lips, capital imitations of lusty kisses.

"Oh—you crazy—desperado!" burst out Molly, choking. "Jim Traft—will kill you—for this!"

"Haw! Haw! Thet's funny. . . . Now, you be good fer a minnit." Whereupon he picked her up and carried her, along with the wicked whip, out to the couch, where he dropped her like a sack of potatoes. Molly's face was a spectacle. It was wet and working. She hid it on the green spruce boughs and then she kicked like a furious colt. Her smothered imprecations sounded like: "Brute! Beast! Coyote! Skunk!"

Stone had made a discovery. His keen sight caught Gloriana concealing the butcher knife, clutched in her hand and half hidden in the folds of her dress. She, too, was a spectacle to behold, but beautiful and marvelous to him—her spirit so much greater than her strength.

"Say, what're you goin' to do with thet knife?" demanded Stone.

"You're no desperado! You're a dog," she cried. "If you lay a hand on Molly again I—I'll kill you."

Here indeed was a quick answer to the primitive instincts which Stone and Molly had wished to rouse in the Eastern girl. Indeed, Stone thought she might develop too fast and spoil the game. Most assuredly she had to be intimidated. "You'd murder me—you white-faced panther?" he shouted, ferociously. "Drop thet knife!" And whipping out his gun he fired, apparently point-blank at her; but he knew the bullet would hit the bucket of water. The crash in the encompassing cabin walls was loud. Gloriana not only dropped the knife—she dropped herself. However, she did not quite faint. Stone lifted her up, with feeling vastly different from what he pretended, then he made a show of collecting everything around which she might have used as a weapon.

"Get back to work," he ordered.

Just then Gloriana was a pitiful sight, verging on collapse. It quite wrung Molly's heart, as Jed saw. But he was adamant. He had divined the thing had gone beyond them both. It was serious, earnest business; and if they kept on, simply making situations for Gloriana to react to, the benefit to her would be incalculable. She had a suprising lot of courage for a tenderfoot placed, as she believed she was, in a terrible, irremediable situation. She weakly brushed back her amber hair, leaving a white blot of flour on it and her forehead, and then went at the biscuit dough again.

"Say, darlin', did you wash them slim little hands of yourn?" asked Stone, suddenly.

"No. I—I never thought to," she faltered.

"Wal, you wash them. There's the washpan. . . . What're you tryin' to do—poison me with dirty hands? I'll have you know, Gloriana Traft, thet I'm a clean desperado an' any woman who cooks fer me has gotta be spick an' span."

Suddenly Molly, with an almost inarticulate cry,

leaped off the bed and bolted out the door. Stone did not understand her move, but yelling, he thudded after her. But she was not trying to escape. Manifestly she had to get outside, away from Gloriana. She waited behind the young spruces for Stone.

"What's the matter, lass?" he asked, anxiously. "It's shore goin' fine. You're a grand aktress. You beat thet Siddons woman all holler."

Molly had a hand pressed into her heaving bosom. Her eyes were distended.

"Oh, Jed—I—I cain't bear it!" she wailed. "I'm afraid it'll do her some harm. . . . Please, Jed, let me tell her you're not the—the devil you seem?"

"An' spoil it all!—No, Molly, I jest won't," he replied, stubbornly. "Cain't you see the good it'll do? Look at the spunk she showed. She'd knifed me, too!—Molly, fer Heaven's sake, stick it out. We'll make a man out of her."

"But—but you'll overdo it," cried Molly.

"You dog-gone little simpleton," he retorted. "I cain't overdo it with thet girl. She'll lick us both yet, if we don't watch out."

"Wasn't she jest—wonderful? When I seen her with thet knife I aboot went stiff. . . . Jed, what we're doin' is turrible wrong. Heah you've killed two men. Right before her eyes! There's blood all over the floor yet. . . . You've pretended to beat me—an' *kiss me*—which I didn't reckon was in the play. An' you've shot at her! . . . Jed, people can die of fright. You scare me into thinkin' you're not actin'—you *mean* it all. . . . An' oh, I'm sick—sick."

"Molly, I swear to Gawd I wouldn't harm one hair of thet girl's haid," he avowed, earnestly. "But I had a hunch. I seen what *she* needs—an', by thunder, if you don't show yellar, she'll get it! . . . Molly, I've knowed you since you was a baby, an' I used to call you 'Little wood-mouse.' Slinger got thet name from me. Shore you can trust me. It's hard to do—an' the hardest of all is to come fer her. But, honest, Molly. I reckon this deal's a Godsend to her, an' to you, an' to *me*."

"You!—How come, Jed?" she queried, sharply.

"Dog-gone-it, Molly, I cain't tell all in a minnit. But I feel it's somethin' big an' wonderful fer me—to remember all my life after as the thing which helped change me."

"Jed!—You're goin' to give up rustlin'?" she asked, breathlessly.

"I shore am, Molly Dunn."

"Gawd! I'm glad! 'Most as glad as when my brother quit. I reckon it's gettin' through my thick haid. . . . Go on, Jed, with our play. I'll stick, but fer my sake don't—don't hurt her."

"You're shore real Arizona," returned Stone, feelingly. "Run back in, now. I've some diggin' to do before dark."

"But you'd better drag me back," objected Molly.

Wherefore Stone presently heaved a kicking rebellious young woman into the cabin, with a fiercely appropriate command. And he followed that with an order to put some pine cones on the fire. Then Stone searched among the packs to find a short-handled shovel, with which he proposed to dig Croak Malloy's grave. The thing was monstrously impelling. Jed Stone digging Croak Malloy's grave! Arizona would learn some day, and the range-riders would marvel as they talked about the campfires, adding bit by bit to the story of the doom of the Hash Knife.

Stone had sense enough of the dramatic to choose the most striking spot at Tobe's Well and that was under the monarch of a silver spruce which dominated the place, and where the cowboys, hunters, trappers, as well as outlaws, always camped in pleasant weather. Stone found the ground soft. He dug a deep grave, and dragging Madden over he tumbled him into it, with scant ceremony. While performing a like office for Malloy he got blood on his hands. It seemed to burn, and before filling up the grave he went to the brook to wash it off.

"Wal, Croak, you shore didn't end as you always swore you would," mused the outlaw, as he plied the shovel. "You shore wasn't back against the wall—your guns shootin' red. . . . You an' Madden were pretty close these late years. Now you can rot together an' go to hell together."

The job done, he placed a huge rock at the foot of the grave, with the prophetic remark: "Shore some wag of a cowpuncher will plant a haidpiece."

Whereupon Jed's active mind reverted to the issue in the cabin, and on the way back he picked up a good-sized stone which he concealed under his coat. The light of blazing pine cones revealed two girls working frantically to get supper for him. He caught the tail end of Molly's conversation: "—an' no use lyin', Glory—I'm as scared as you."

"O Heaven! how false men are!" sighed Glory. "When this desperado came in I had a wild thought he was a hero."

"Hey, don't talk aboot me," put in Stone. "I'm a sensitive man."

Silence ensued then. The girls did not look up. And Stone, profiting by this, threw some sacks over the blood pools on the hard-packed clay floor. Also he surreptitiously laid the stone on the box seat where he intended to sit at the rickety old rough-hewn table. This he cleared by piling Malloy's trappings on the ground, and covering it with the cleanest piece of canvas he could find. Then he sat down to watch and wait. He realized he had fallen upon the most delicious situation of his life—if he had ever had one before—and he wanted to live every second of it to the full. Finally the girls put the supper on the table.

"Thet's right, wait on me, Gloriana," he said. "An' you, Molly, set down an' eat. . . . Gimme one of them turrible-lookin' biscuits. . . . Ou! Hot!"

He contrived to drop the biscuit and at the same instant push the heavy rock off the box seat. It fell with a solid thump. Gloriana actually jumped. Her eyes opened wide.

"Golly! Did you heah thet biscuit hit?" ejaculated Stone, as if dumbfounded.

"I heahed somethin' heavy," corroborated Molly, serious-faced, but her sweet red lips slightly twitched.

"Say, gurl, air you aimin' to poison me?" demanded Stone, suspiciously. "What'n hell did you put in thet biscuit?"

Gloriana stammered something, and then walking round the table, she espied the rock, which, unfortunately, had fallen upon the biscuit.

"It was a rock," she said, slowly.

"Wal, dog-gone! So it was. Must have been on the box. I shore didn't see it. . . . I offer my humble apologies, Miss Traft."

No doubt Gloriana's mind was so steeped in fright that it could not function normally, yet she gazed with dubious tragic eyes at the desperado.

Stone then devoted himself to the meal, which he soon discovered was the best he had sat at for many a weary moon. Days on end he had prepared frugal meals for himself, and the last few he had lived on dried meat, hard biscuits, and coffee. This was a repast—a feast, to which he did ample justice.

"Wal," he drawled, when he could eat no more, as he transfixed Gloriana with eyes he tried to make devouring, "if you can love as well as cook, I'm shore a lucky desperado. . . . Get out now and I'll wash up. No sweethearts of mine ever had to do the dirty work round my camp."

While he was noisily banging pans, cups, and other utensils around his trained ear caught Gloriana's whisper. "Now—let's run!"

"An' get lost in the woods—for the bears to eat!" whispered Molly.

Stone dried the camp utensils and placed them on the shelf, after which he washed his hands in hot water.

"Put some wood on the fire," he said, filling his black pipe. "Pass me a red coal on a chip. . . . Thet's it, darlin'; you're shore learnin' fast."

The interior of the cabin brightened with blazing cones and sticks. Molly sat as in a trance. Gloriana stood awaiting another command, nervous, with great blank eyes. She might have been a bird fascinated by a snake.

"Spread some blankets on the bed there," he said, pointing to the pack he had opened. While this order was being complied with he puffed his pipe, and opened his big hands to the fire with an air of content. Molly's reproachful glance might have been lost upon him. Jed reasoned it out that the little Cibeque girl had lived too long among Western men to trust him wholly. That gave Stone more thrills. He would fool Molly, too. At length he got up to view the bed.

"Kinda narrow fer three to sleep comfortable," he said, laconically. "I always wear my boots an' spurs to bed—in case I have to hurry to a hoss— an' I kick when I have nightmare. But I reckon there's room fer two. Now, Molly, you an' Gloriana draw lots to see who'll sleep fust night with me."

"Jed Stone, I'll see you in hell before I'd do it," cried Molly, passionately. "You'll have to tie me, hand an' foot."

"Wal, you needn't take my head off. I kinda lean to Glory, anyhow."

Gloriana gazed at him with eyes full of a sickening horror and desperate defiance.

"You'll have to kill me—you monster!" she said, hoarsely.

"Wal, both buckin' on me, huh," replied Stone, as if resigned to the nature of women. "All right, I don't want no tied gurl sleepin' with me, an' shore no daid one. So I'll pass. You can sleep together an' I'll be a gentleman an' go outdoors. But you gotta entertain me before. Molly, you sing, 'Bury me not on the Lone Prairie.' "

"I cain't sing a note an' I wouldn't if I could," avowed Molly.

"Gloriana, my duckie, can you sing?"

"I used to sing hymns, in Sunday school. But they would scarcely be to your taste, Mister Stone," was the partly satiric reply.

"Say, where'd you think I was brought up?" queried Stone, as if deeply insulted. "I used to go to church. I had a gurl once who took me to prayer-meetin'."

"You did? Impossible to believe! I wish she were hear now to pray for us."

"Ahuh. So do I. . . . But she's daid—these many years," replied Stone, and was lost in reverie for a moment. He saw that girl, and the little church, and the gate where he bade her good night. "I bet you can dance," he went on, looking up. "You've shore got dancin' feet an' ankles. I never seen such boo-tiful laigs, if you'll excoose me bein' familiar."

"Yes, I can dance, and I'll try," replied the girl, as if relieved to get off so easily. Whereupon she began a swaying of her graceful body, a sliding of her little feet. But she appeared unsteady.

"Hold on. You need a bracer," said Stone, and going to his pack he took out a black bottle, from which he emptied some liquor into a cup. This he diluted with water and offered with the curt word, "Drink."

"No!"

"Say, it's fine old stuff. It'll do you good. An' when you get to be a grandma you can tell your grandchildren you once drank out of Jed Stone's flask."

"The honor does not appeal to me."

"Glory, he's gettin' mad," spoke up Molly, in alarm. "An' it shore won't hurt you."

"I—I won't," replied Gloriana, backing away weakly.

"Gurl, I'll pour it down your lily throat," said Stone, in a terrible tone, while he reached for her. But Gloriana eluded him. Then Stone whipped out his gun and aimed at her feet. "You drink an' you dance—or I'll shoot at your feet."

At this dire threat Gloriana took the cup with trembling hands and drank the contents.

"Ag-hhh," she choked, and then stood with distended eyes, with hand on her breast, as if feeling fire within. "Oh, Molly—such stuff! . . . Is there no way out of this nightmare?"

"Dance!" thundered Stone.

And then he was to see the girl waltz fantastically over the open space of the clay floor, with the firelight shining fitfully on her wan face, until she gave out and collapsed upon the bed.

"Thanks, Glory," he said, huskily. "You're shore a fairy on your feet. . . . Now, I reckon, I'll let you go to bed. You gotta sleep, for we have a long tough ride tomorrow."

Stone picked up one of the bed rolls, and carrying it out back through the open side of the cabin he unrolled it in the gloom of the cliff and stretched himself as if he never meant to move again. He could see the flicker of the firelight on one wall of the cabin, but the girls were out of his sight. He heard their low voices for what seemed a long time.

Sleep did not come readily. He doubted if it would that night, and welcomed wakefulness. When had he lain down in such strange sweet sense of security? Was it peace? What had happened to him? And he rested there trying to understand the vast change. It was not the little service he had rendered these young woman, or the strenuous and agonizing experience he meant to give Gloriana Traft, out of which would come the wholesome good. No—it was that he was free. The Hash Knife outfit was dead—every one dead, since he, too, Jed Stone, was dead to all that strife. He had no enemy in the world, it seemed, except every honest rancher and cowboy. But they were no longer enemies. He had squared himself. He could lie down without fear, without one eye kept open, without distrust of comrades, of the morrow, of the future. Without certainty of the inevitable death at the crack of a gun or the end of a rope! For years Malloy had been the dark shadow over him—the step on his trail. And Malloy would never awaken again—never ruin another rancher—never spread fear and hate about him— never exercise that fatal draw—never by reason of his personality cause better men to lose poise and serenity in their desire to kill him.

The flicker of the fire died out, as did also the

low voices. They slept—those two pretty girls, destined to make two lucky cowboys happy and Arizona the better for their worth. Arizona! The name lingered in Stone's consciousness. He had been born and bred in this country of arid zones, of canyon and forest, of the clear streams with the gray salt margins along the sand. But who—what Arizonian had ever loved a country more than had he?

The night wind arose, mournful as always, cold off the heights. Yet it seemed a different music, as if it blew from far-off forests, as yet unknown to the fame of Jed Stone.

Chapter Nineteen

JED STONE awoke with the first pink streak of dawn flushing the sky. The old somber distrust of the new day had departed. He seemed young again.

Going to the door of the cabin, he called: "Hey, babes in the woods! Roll out an' rustle."

He heard a gasp, and then a low moan, but he did not look in. He went out to fetch the horses. There had been nine in the canyon the night before; now he could see but six, including his own. One was a pretty pinto mare which he selected for Gloriana, with a chuckle at the thought of how all her life she would remember this ride. He drove four horses in, haltered them, and chose the best saddles for the girls, the stirrups of which he shortened to fit them. It tickled him to see blue smoke curling up from the cabin, and a little later his keen nostrils took note of the fragrance of coffee. When he got a pack-saddle strapped on the fourth horse he was ready to go in, but he tarried a moment. How sweet, rich, melodious, and rose-green the sunrise-flushed canyon! Henceforth Tobe's Well would be famous as the last resting-place of the great Croak Malloy.

Presently he repaired to the cabin.

"Mawnin', gurls," he bawled, stalking in.

Gloriana had been listlessly brushing her lustrous hair, while Molly attended to the breakfast chores.

"Ha, makin' yourself look pretty," remarked Stone. "Wal, you can't bamboozle the boss of the Hash Knife. An' you ought to be ashamed—lettin' Molly do all the work."

"I started the fire and made the biscuits," she retorted. Stone had grasped before that she seemed peculiarly susceptible to criticism, and decided he would work on her sensitiveness to the limit.

"Wal, we can't pack much of this outfit," observed Stone. "You gurls pick out what belongs to you."

Molly designated two duffle-bags and one small grip. Stone carried them outside. Then returning, he rolled some blankets. He remembered that he had some hard bread and dried meat in his saddlebags, which supply he would add to without letting the girls know. His plan precluded an insufficiency of food on this three-day ride down to Yellow Jacket. When he had packed the horses Molly called from the cabin, "Come an' get it!"

"You come hyar yourself an' get somethin'," he replied.

Molly came running, anxious and big-eyed. "What—Jed?"

"Pitch in now, an' show this Eastern gurl what a Western lass is made of. Savvy?"

"I reckon."

"I'm givin' you the chance, Molly. Don't fall down. Take everythin' as a matter of course. Help her, shore, but give her a little dig now an' then."

"Jed, you're a devil," returned Molly, slowly, and turned away.

Stone stamped into the cabin, upon her heels: "Feed me, now, ladylove. An' then we gotta rustle. I'm a hunted desperado, you know. Soon as your Uncle Jim gets back to Flag the woods will be full of cowboys, sheriffs, deputies, an' a lot of gallants who'd like to win the hearts of my captives. Haw! Haw!"

The breakfast was even more tasteful than had been the supper the night before. Stone ate with the appetite of an Indian, and the wisdom of a range-rider who had to go far.

"You ain't eatin' much," he observed, addressing Gloriana.

"I'm not hungry," she replied.

"Wal, you eat. Heah me? Or I'll be givin' you another drink."

This threat had the desired result.

"Gurls, I've gotta hurry, so can't pack much grub," said Stone, rising to gather up a few utensils, some coffee and meat, and what biscuits had been left. These he tied up securely, and took them out to put upon the pack-animal. The rest of the outfit he would leave until his return that way. His last service to Croak Malloy was pounding and smoothing the grave.

Presently the girls appeared. Molly had taken the precaution to don a riding-skirt and boots, but Gloriana wore the thin dress which Malloy had torn considerably.

"Where's your hat?" asked Stone.

"It blew off, yesterday. . . . I—I forgot to look in my bag—and change. If you'll give me time—"

"Nope. Sorry, Gloriana. Didn't I tell you I was a hunted man? You'll have to ride as you are. Strikes me the Lord made you wonderful to look at, but left out any brains. You'll do fine in Arizona. . . . Here, wear Croak's sombrero. . . . Haw! Haw! If your ma could see you now!"

She had to be helped upon the pinto, which promptly bucked her off upon the soft sward. What injury she suffered was to her vanity. She threw off the old sombrero, but Stone jammed it back on her head.

"Can't you ride?" inquired Stone, gazing down upon her.

"Do you think I was born in a stable?" she asked, bitterly.

"Wal, it'd be a darn sight better if you was. An' far as thet is concerned the Lord was born in a stall, so I've heerd. So it ain't no disgrace. . . . I'm curious to know why you ever come to Arizona?"

"I was a fool."

"Wal, get up an' try again. This little mare isn't bad. She was jest playin'. But don't let her see you're afraid. An' don't kick her in the ribs, like you did when you got up fust."

"I—I can't ride this way," she said, scarlet of face.

"Wal, you are a holy show, by golly!" observed Stone. "I never seen so much of a pretty gurl. You shore wouldn't win no rodeo prizes fer modesty."

"Molly, I can't go on," cried Gloriana, almost weeping. "My skirt's up round my neck!"

"Glory. I don't see what else you can do. You'll *have* to ride," replied Molly.

"Thet's talkin'. Glory, you'll get some idee of the difference between a no-good tenderfoot from the East an' a healthy Western cowgurl. . . . Now, you follow me, an' you keep up, or there'll be hell to pay."

The ease with which Molly mounted her horse,

a wicked black animal, was not lost upon Gloriana, nor the way she controlled him.

"Molly, you better lead this pack-hoss. I'll have to keep my eye on our cultured lady-friend hyar," drawled Stone, and he started off. At the gateway of the canyon, where a rough trail headed up toward the rim he turned to caution Gloriana. "Hang on to her mane."

When they reached the top he had satisfation in the expression of that young woman's face. Stone then struck out along the rim, and he did not need to pick out a rough way. The trail was one seldom used, and then only by riders who preferred to keep to the wilder going. It led through thickets of scrub oak, manzanita, and dwarf pine, with a generous sprinkling of cactus. To drag Gloriana Traft through them was nothing short of cruelty. Stone kept an eye on her, though he appeared never to turn his head, never to hear her gasps and cries. Molly, who came last, often extricated her from some tangle.

Stone, from long habit, was a silent and swift traveler, and did not vary his custom now. But he had to to stop more often to let the girls catch up. The condition of Gloriana's dress—what was left of it—seemed satisfactory to the outlaw. She had lost one of the sleeves that Malloy had almost torn from her blouse, and her beautiful white arm showed the red and black of contact with brush. What a ludicrous and pathetic figure she made, hunched over her saddle, with the gunman's battered and bullet-marked sombrero on her head! She had pulled it down now, to protect eyes and face, thankful for it. Where was her disgust and horror? Nothing could have better exemplified the leveling power of the wilderness. Before Gloriana Traft got through this ride she would give all her possessions for a pair of blue jeans.

About the middle of the morning Jed came out on the high point of the Diamond Mesa. And he halted. The girls came up, to gaze out and down.

"Oh-h!" cried Miss Traft, her voice broked, yet deep and rich with feeling. She did not disappoint Stone here.

"The Tonto!" screamed Molly, suddenly beside herself. "Jed, why didn't you *tell* me you were comin' heah? . . . Oh, Glory, look—look! It's my home."

"Home!" echoed Gloriana, incredulously.

"Yes. *Home!* . . . An', oh, how I love it! See thet thin line, with the white? Thet's the Cibeque windin' away down through the valley. See the big turn. Now look, Glory. There's a bare spot in the green. An' a gray dot in the middle. Thet's my home. Thet's my cabin. Where I was born."

"I see. But I can hardly believe," replied Gloriana. "That tiny pin-point in all the endless green?"

"Shore is, Glory. You're standin' on the high rim of the Diamond, a mile above the valley. But it looks close. You should see from down there. All my life I've looked up at this point. It was the Rim. But I was never heah before. . . . Oh, look, look, Glory, so you will never forget!"

The Eastern girl gazed silently, with eyes that seemed to reflect something of the grandeur of the scene. Stone turned away from her, glad in his heart that somehow she had satisfied him. Then he had a moment for himself—to gaze once more and the last time over the Tonto.

The Basin was at its best at sunrise or sunset, or in storm. Tranquil and austere now, it withheld something which the outlaw knew so well. The dotted green slopes from the Rim merged in the green-black forest floor, so deceivingly level, but which in reality was a vast region of ridges and gorges. Molly called it home, and so it was for backwoodsmen, deer, bear, and wild turkeys, and outlaws such as he. He liked best the long sections of yellow craggy Rim stepping down into the Basin toward the west. They showed the ragged nature of the Tonto. Away beyond them rose the purple range, spiked as a cactus plant, and to the south, dim on the horizon, stood up the four peaks that marked the gateway of the Cibeque, out into the desert. But nowhere was the desert visible. Doubtful Canyon called to Stone. He had killed a man there once, in an argument over spoil, and he had never been sure of the justice of it. Doubtful had been well named. It was deep and black and long, a forest and cliff-choked rent in the vast slope of the mountain.

"Molly, don't forget to show Gloriana some other places," said Stone, with a laugh. "There's West Fork, the village I used to ride through an' see you at Summer's store. An' buy you a stick of candy. . . . Not for years now. . . . An' never again. . . . There's Bear Flat an' Green Valley, an' Haverly's Ranch, an' Gordon Canyon. An' see, far to the east, thet bare yellow patch. Thet's Pleasant Valley, where they had the sheep an' cattle war which ruined your dad, though he was only a sympathizer, Molly. I reckon you never knew. Wal, it's true. . . . Miss Traft, you're shore the furst Eastern gurl ever to see the Tonto."

Though they wanted to linger, Stone ordered them on. Momentarily he had forgotten his role of slave-driver. But Gloriana had been too engrossed in her own sensations to notice his lapse.

Straight back from the Rim he headed, through trailless forest of stunted pines and wilderness of rock and cactus, toward the far side of the mesa, which sloped to the east, and gradually varied its rough aspect with grassy levels and healthier growth of pine. When Stone crossed the drift fence, which along here had been cut by the Hash Knife, he halted to show the girls.

"Traft's drift fence. Gloriana, this is what the old man saddled on your brother Jim. There's nine miles of fence down, which Jim an' his uncle can

363

thank Croak Malloy fer. But I will say the buildin' of this fence was a big thing. Old Jim has vision. Shore I'm a cattle thief, an' the fence didn't make no difference to me. I reckon it was a help to rustlers. But Malloy hated fences. . . . Wal, it'll be a comfort to Traft an' all honest ranchers to learn he's dead."

"Jed Stone, you—you seem to be two men!" exclaimed Gloriana.

"Shore. I'm more'n thet. An' I reckon one of them is some kin to human. But don't gamble on him, my lovely tenderfoot. He's got no say in my make-up."

Molly Dunn lagged behind, most intensely interested in that drift fence, the building of which had made her lover, young Traft, a marked man on the range, and which had already caused a good deal of blood-spilling. Stone had to halloa to her, and wait.

"What's ailin' you, gurl?" he queried, derisively. "Thet fence make you lovesick fer Jim? Wal, I reckon you won't see him again very soon, if ever. . . . Get off an' straighten thet pack."

While Molly heaved and pulled to get the pack level on the pack-saddle again, Stone rolled a cigarette and watched Gloriana. Her amaze at Molly Dunn amused him.

"Wal, Glory, she used to pack grub an' grain from West Fork on a burro, when both of them wasn't any bigger'n jack-rabbits."

"There's a lot I don't know," observed Gloriana, thoughtfully, as for the hundredth time she tried to pull her torn skirt down to hide her bare legs.

"Shore," agreed the outlaw. "An' when a fellar finds thet out there's hope fer him."

He led on, calling for his followers to keep up, as they were losing time and the way was rough and long. As a matter of fact, Stone could have led down into Yellow Jacket that very day, but this was not his plan. He intended to ride these girls around, through the forest, up and down canyons, across streams, and among the rocks until one of them, at least, could no longer sit in the saddle. He was enjoying himself hugely, and when he saw how Gloriana had begun really to suffer he assuaged his conscience in the same way that a surgeon excused his cruel bright blade. Stone believed now that the Eastern girl would come off in the end with flying colors, even if she went down flat on her back. She had something, he began to divine, and it would come out when physically she was beaten.

The rest of that day he rode through a maze of wild country, at sunset ending up on a weathered slope where he had to get off and walk.

"Hey, there!" he called back. "Fall off an' walk. If your hoss slides, get out of his way. An' step lively so you won't go down in one of these avalanches."

All of which would have given a cowboy something to do. Molly had to stop often to rescue her friend, and more than once a scream rent the air. But at length they got across and down this long slant of loose shale, and entered a grassy wooded flat where water ran. Here Stone halted to make camp.

Gloriana came staggering up, sombrero in hand, leading her horse, and her appearance would have delighted even the most hardened Westerner who was inimical to tenderfeet. Her face was wan where it was not dirty, her hair hanging dishevelled and tangled with twigs, her bare arms all black and red, and her dress torn into tatters. One stocking hung down over her shoe, exposing a bloody leg, and the other showed sundry scratches.

"Wat-er!" choked Gloriana, huskily, as she sank down on the sward.

"Aha! Spittin' cotton, my proud beauty?" ejaculated the outlaw.

"Reckon you'd better have a drink out of my bottle." But she waved the suggestion aside with a gesture of abhorrence. And when Molly came carrying a dipper of water, Gloriana's great tragic eyes lit up. She drank the entire contents of the rather large vessel.

"Wal, Glory, you have to go through a good deal before you find the real value of things," remarked Stone, thoughtfully. "You see, most folks have life too easy. Take the matter of this drink of cold pure spring water. Sweet, wasn't it? You never knowed before how turrible sweet water could be, did you? It's the difference between life an' death."

"Thanks, Molly," said Gloriana, gratefully. "Aren't you—thirsty?"

"Not very. You see, out heah we train ourselves to do without water an' food. Like Indians, you know, Glory," replied Molly.

Plain indeed was it that Gloriana did not know; and that she was divided in emotion between her pangs and the surprise of this adventure.

"Hey, Molly, stop gabbin' an' get to work," ordered Stone, dryly. "Our St. Louis darlin' here will croak on us, if we ain't careful."

He slipped the ax out from under a rope on the pack, and proceeded to a near-by spruce, from which he cut armloads of the thick fragrant boughs. These he spread under an oak tree, and went back for more, watching the girls out of the tail of his eye. Once he caught Gloriana's voice, in furious protest—"The lazy brute! Look at the size of him—and he makes you lift those packs!" And Molly's reply: "Aw, this heah's easy, Glory. An' I'm tellin' you again—don't make this desperado mad."

Then Stone slipped behind the spruce and peered through the branches. Molly did lift off those heavy packs, and unsaddled the animal. Next she turned to remove the saddle from her horse. At this Gloriana arose with difficulty, and limping to the horse she had ridden she tugged at the cinches, and labored until she got them loose. Then she slid the big saddle off. It was a man's saddle and heavy, which of course she had not calculated upon, and down she went with it, buried almost out of sight. Molly ran to lift it off. Stone saw the Eastern girl wring her helpless hands. "Dog-gone tough on her," he soliloquized, and proceeded to get another load of spruce boughs, which he carried over to the oak tree.

"Hey, Gloriana, fetch over thet bed roll," he called.

She paid no attention to him. Then he bellowed the order in the voice of a bull. He heard Molly advise her to rustle. Whereupon Gloriana lifted the roll in both arms and came wagging across the grass.

"Untie the rope," he said, not looking at her, and went on spreading the boughs evenly. Presently, as she was so slow, he looked up. She was wearily toiling at the knot.

"I—I can't untie it," she said.

"Wal, you shore are a helpless ninny," he returned, in disgust. "What in Gawd's name *can* you do, Miss Traft? Play the concertina, huh? An' fix your hair pretty, huh? It's shore thunderin' good luck for some fine cowboy thet I happened along an' saved him from marryin' you."

The marvel of that speech lay in its effect upon Gloriana, whose piteous mute appeal to Molly showed she had been driven to believe it was true.

"See heah, Jed Stone," demanded Molly, loyally, "how could Glory help the way she was brought up? Everybody cain't be born in Arizona."

"Misfortune, I call thet. . . . But see heah, yourself, Molly Dunn. The more you stick up fer this wishy-washy tenderfoot the wuss I'll be. Savvy?"

"You bet I savvy," rejoined Molly, resignedly.

"Wal then, rustle supper. I'm tired after thet ride. My neck's stiff from turnin' round to watch Miss Traft. It was a circus, though. . . . Gather some wood, start a fire, put on the water to boil, mix biscuits, an' so forth."

No one could ever have guessed that Molly Dunn had packed a horse and led him, and had ridden over thirty miles of rough wilderness during the hours of daylight. She was quick, deft, thorough in all camp tasks; and it gave the outlaw pleasure to watch her, outside of his diabolical plot to subjugate the Eastern girl.

"Say, if this heah's all the grub you fetched we'll eat it tonight," said Molly.

"Go light on grub, I tell you. Mebbe I didn't pack enough. But I was a-rarin' to get away from Tobe's Well."

"Molly, I'll help you—or die trying," offered Gloriana. "But if that queer pain comes to my side again—farewell."

"What pain, honey?"

"Reckon she's got appendixitis," drawled Stone, who allowed no word to get by him unheard.

"It was in my left side—and, oh, it was awful!"

"Thet comes from ridin' a hoss when you're not used to it. But it'll not kill you."

"Yes, it will, if I live long enough to mount that wild mustang again," avowed Gloriana. Then in a lower tone she added. "Molly, I thought Ed Darnell was a villain. But, my, oh!—he's a saint compared with this desperado."

"Oh no, Glory. Jed Stone is an honest-to-Gawd desperado," expostulated Molly.

"What's she sayin' aboot thet fellar Darnell an' me?" demanded Stone, going to the fire.

"Jed, she knew Darnell back in Missouri," explained Molly.

"You don't say. Wal, thet's interestin'. Hope she didn't compare me to him. Two-bit caird-sharp before he hit the West. An' then, like a puff of smoke, he lit into crooked cattle-dealin'. . . . An' did he last longer than any of them dude Easterners who reckon they can learn us Westerners tricks? He did not."

"What do you mean, Jed?" queried Molly, who divined when he was lying and when he was not.

"Croak Malloy was in thet outfit Traft's cow-boys rounded up in a cabin down below Yellow Jacket. They'd been rustlin' the new Diamond stock an' had to ride fer their lives. Wal, they didn't ride fer, not with your redskin brother an'

Curly Prentiss an' thet rodeo-ridin' bunch after them. Croak said they set fire to the cabin, an' burned them out, an' he got shot in the laig. But he escaped, an' it was when he was hidin' in the brush thet he seen the cowboys string up Darnell along with two rustlers. Croak said he never seen a man kick like thet white-cuff caird-slicker, Darnell."

Gloriana's eyes were great black gulfs.

"Mr. Stone, among other things you're a liar," she said, deliberately.

"Wal, I'll be dog-goned!" ejaculated the outlaw, genuinely surprised and not a little hurt. "I am, am I? Wal, you'll see, Miss Traft."

"You're trying to—to frighten me," she faltered, weakening. "Have you no heart—no mercy? . . . I was once engaged to—to marry Darnell, or thought I was. He followed me out here."

"Ahuh. What'd he foller you out heah fer?"

"He swindled my father out of money, and I suppose he thought he could do the same with Uncle Jim."

"Not old Jim Traft. Nix come the weasel! Old Jim cain't be swindled. . . . Wal, Miss Gloriana, I must say you was lucky to have Darnell stack up against Curly Prentiss. I remember now thet Madden was in Snell's gamblin'-den when Curly ketched Darnell cheatin' an' drove him out of Flag. Funny he didn't bore thet caird-sharp. Reckon he savvied how soon Darnell would come to the end of his rope. He did come soon—an' it was a lasso."

"I don't believe you," replied Gloriana, steadily.

"Sweet on him yet, huh?"

"No, I despise him. Any punishment, even hanging, would be too good for him," retorted Gloriana, with passion.

"See there, Molly. She's comin' round," drawled Stone. "We'll make a Westerner of her yet."

"Jed, was there a—a fight down below Yellow Jacket?" asked Molly, with agitation.

"Shore was. Malloy said he seen two cowboys shot, one of which he accounted fer himself But he didn't know either. An' so they couldn't have been Jim or Slinger or Prentiss."

"Oh—how'll we find out?" cried Molly, in honest agony. And the tone of her voice, the look of her, about finished Gloriana, who fell in a heap.

"Wal, what difference does it make," queried Stone, "to one of you, anyhow? One of you gurls is shore goin' with me, an' cowboys won't never be no more in your young life. Haw! Haw!"

"I could stick this in you, Jed Stone," cried Molly, brandishing the wicked butcher knife.

The outlaw reached down and lifted Gloriana upright. Gloriana's head rolled. "Brace up," he said, and shook her. She found strength left to resist. Then he clasped her in his arms and hugged her tight. And while he did this he winked and grinned at Molly, who stood there aghast. "You need a regular desperado hug to stiffen your spine. . . . There! Now you stand up an' do your work."

She did keep her feet, too, when he released her, and such eyes Jed Stone had never seen. If he had been the real desperado he pretended, he would have flinched and quailed under their magnificent fury.

"Call me when supper's ready," he ordered Molly. "I smelled a skunk out there, an' I afeerd it's one of them hydrophobia varmints. They shore stink wuss."

As he strode off he heard Gloriana ask in Heaven's name what he would think of next, and what was a hydrophobia skunk anyway. Luckily Stone had smelled a skunk, and any kind of one would serve his purpose, so presently he fired his gun twice, and then went back to camp.

"Missed him, by gosh!" he said, greatly annoyed. "An' it shore was a hydrophobia, all right. Molly, you gurls will have to sleep with me tonight. 'Cause thet skunk will come round camp, an' it'd be shore to bite Glory's nose. Hydrophobia skunks always pick out a fellar with a big nose. An' I'll have to be there to choke it off."

"I'd be eaten up by skunks with hydrophobia and lions with yellow fever before I'd obey you," declared Gloriana.

"Haw! Haw! Yes, you would. Wait till it gets dark an' you smell thet varmint."

While they sat at the meager supper, Stone bedeviled Gloriana in every way conceivable, yet to his satisfaction it did not prevent her from eating her share. That was the answer. Let even the effete Easterner face the facts of primal life and the balance was struck.

Darkness soon settled down, and twice Gloriana fell asleep beside the fire. "Let's sit up—all night," she begged of Molly.

"I'd be willin', if he'd let us. But, Glory, dear, you jest couldn't. You'd fall over. An' by mawnin' you'd be froze. We'll *have* to sleep with Stone. He's put all the blankets on thet bed. An' I'll sleep in the middle—so he cain't touch you."

"You'll do nothing of the sort," retorted Gloriana. And when they reached the wide bed under the oak tree she crawled in the middle and stretched out, as if she did not care what happened.

"Wal, now, thet's somethin' like," declared the outlaw, as he saw the pale faces against the background of blankets. He sat down on the far side of the bed and in the gloom contrived to remove his boots and spurs. "Gurls, I'm liable to have nightmare. Often do when I'm scared or excited. An' I'm powerful dangerous then. Shot a bedfellow once, when I had nightmare. So you wanta kick me awake in case I get to dreamin'. . . . An', Molly, don't forget if thet skunk gets its teeth fastened in Glory's nose you must choke it off."

It was not remarkable to Stone that almost before he had ceased talking Gloriana was asleep. He knew what worn-out nature would do. Nevertheless, as soon as Molly had dropped off he made such a commotion that he would almost have awakened the dead. Then he began to snore outrageously, and between snores he broke out into the thick weird utterance of a man in a nightmare.

"Molly—Molly!" cried Gloriana, in a shrill whisper, as she clutched her friend madly. "He's got it!"

"Sssh! Don't wake him. He won't be dangerous unless he wakes," replied Molly.

Jed made the mental reservation that his little ally was all right, and began to rack his brain for appropriate exclamations: "AGGH! I'll—carve—your—gizzard!" And he sprang up to thump back. Then he gave capital imitations of Malloy's croaking laugh. Then he shouted: "You can't have the gurl! She's mine, Croak, she's mine! . . . I'll have your heart's blood!" After which he snored some more, while listening intently. He did not hear anything, but he thought he felt the bed trembling. Next he rolled over, having thrown the blankets, to bump hard into Gloriana. But that apparently did not awaken him. He laid a heavy arm across both the girls and went on snoring blissfully.

"Molly," whispered Gloriana, in very low and

bloodcurdling voice. *"Lets—kill him—in his sleep!"*

"Oh, I wish we could, but we're not strong enough," replied Molly, horrified. "Don't you dare move!"

Stone could scarcely contain himself, and wanted to roar his mirth and elation. So his acting had been so good, so convincing that it had driven this lovely tenderfoot to consider murder! He could not have asked more. She was responding nobly to the unplumbed primitive instincts which, happily for her and those who loved her, she shared in common with the less sophisticated characters of the West.

Lastly Jed thought he would try the love-making of a man suffering from delusions in a nightmare. This rather taxed his capacity. His actual experience had never gone so far. But he bawled out endearments of every kind, and he hugged both girls until they appeared to be squeezed into one. Suddenly there came a terrific tug at his hair. He bawled in earnest. A tight little fist was fast in his hair and pulling fiercely. It was Molly's, and he had trouble in tearing it loose. After that rebuke Jed rolled back against the tree, and pulling his blanket free he composed himself to slumber.

In the gray of dawn he got up, pulled on his big boots, and went at the camp-fire tasks, careful not to make noise. His two babes in the woods were locked in sleep, also in each other's arms. Stone cooked the last of the meat and boiled the last of the coffee. A few biscuits were left, hard as rocks. Then he went to awaken the girls. Their heads were close together, one dark, the other amber, and their sweet pale faces took the first flush of the sunrise. It was a picture the outlaw would carry in his memory always, and he found himself thanking God that he had come upon Croak Malloy before they had suffered harm.

"Gurls, roll out," he called.

Molly awakened first and was bright and quick in an instant. She smiled, and Jed thought he would treasure that smile. Then Gloriana's eyes popped open. Dim gulfs of sleep! Stone turned away from them with a conscious-stricken pang.

"Rustle an' eat. I gotta hunt the hosses," he said.

Upon his return they had finished eating. Molly said: "Glory's bag is missin'. With all her outdoor clothes!"

"Shore. I hid it. I don't want her dressin' up. She looks so cute in thet outfit," he replied. "Saddle your hoss, you starin' idgit," he said to Gloriana. "An', Molly, rustle with the bed an' packs while I eat."

Molly proved as capable as any cowboy, but poor Gloriana could not get the saddle up, and when the pinto bit and kicked at her, which was no wonder, she gave up coaxing and struck it smartly with a branch.

"Hyar! Don't beat thet pony," expostulated

377

Stone. "Who'd ever think you'd show cruelty to a dumb beast?"

"Dumb! He sure is," replied Gloriana, "and he's not the only be—thing around that ought to be beaten."

"Molly, you cain't never tell aboot people till you get them in the woods," said Stone, reflectively. "Their real natoor comes out. I reckon Glory, hyar, would have murdered Croak Malloy in cold blood if he'd got away with her. It's turrible to contemplate."

Soon they were mounted and riding in single file, as on the day before. Stone led them out of this gorge, miles and miles through the forest, out into the sunny desert, and back again, and finally, without a halt to the rim of the Black Brakes. He followed along that until mid-afternoon, when he came to a trail he knew, which was seldom used even by rustlers, unless pressed. Here they had to walk down and it was no fun. "Don't let your hoss fall on you," was all Stone said. At a particularly bad descent Gloriana and her pinto both fell, and she miraculously escaped being rolled on. "Whew!" ejaculated Stone. "I reckoned you was a goner then. The Lord shore watches over you."

"I don't—care," panted the girl. "I'd sooner die—that way—than some other way." Her spirit was hard to break. She seemed to recover her courage after each successive trial. But her strength was almost spent. Once down in the brakes Stone eased up on rough going, and wended a leisurely course through the labyrinthine glades and aisles, groves and fields of broken cliff. The gold slants from the westering sun fell across their path, and the wilderness appeared more than usually beautiful. Stone calculated their position at that hour was less then a dozen miles below Yellow Jacket. And his intention was, if Gloriana could stand it, to climb out of the brakes, and ride to the head of Yellow Jacket, where he could show the girls their way and then take leave of them. There was a risk of being held up along the trail by one or more of the Diamond outfit, but since he had the girls to credit him with their rescue he had little to worry about. Still he did not want that to happen. He had planned a climax to his plot.

The sun set behind the western wall of the brakes; a mellow roar of running water filled the forest with dreaming music. Stone thought it about time to choose a place to camp, and he desired it to be remote from the trail, which he believed ran somewhat to his left along the stream. With this end in view he wormed his way through the woods toward the wall they had long since descended.

It loomed above him, gray and lofty, always silent and protective. And suddenly he emerged into an open space, where tall spruces and wide-spreading sycamores dominated the green. The glade appeared familiar, and as Gloriana and Molly rode out of the forest he reined his horse.

"Oh my God—look!" cried Molly, in accents of horror.

Simultaneously then Stone's senses accounted for a smell of burned wood, the pile of charred logs that was once the trapper's cabin, and three grotesque and hideously swaying figures of men, hanging limply by their necks from a prominent branch of a sycamore.

Stone's shock had its stimulus in Gloriana's shriek. She swayed and slid out of the saddle. He caught her and lifted her in front of him, a dead weight.

"Jed—this heah is too much," expostulated Molly, hoarsely. She looked as if she, too, would faint.

Cursing under his breath, he turned to the girl. "I swear it was accident," he avowed, earnestly. "We were east of the trail, an' if I thought aboot it at all, I reckoned we were far from thet old cabin. By Gawd! I'm sorry, Molly. It *is* too much."

"Jed, I'll be—keelin' over, too," gasped Molly. "Thet's a hard sight for *me,* let alone Glory. . . . If I recognized Darnell, *she* recognized him, you bet."

"Shore she did. I never seen him but once, an' I knew him. An' there's my old Sheriff Lang, his star still a-shinin' on his vest. An' Joe Tanner. . . . Wal, thet's shore a cowboy job, slick an' clean. Thet's the way of the West!"

Darnell's distorted and discolored features had been stamped by an appalling surprise and terror, something wholly wanting from the visages of the other two dead men. They swayed as the evening breeze moved the sycamore branch. Darnell's watch fob dangled from his vest.

"Jed, come on—fetch her," implored Molly. "I'll hate you forever—if she doesn't get over this."

"Molly, it's shore sickenin', but mebbe jest as well she seen it."

"I—I wasn't above bein' took in myself—by thet handsome gambler," admitted Molly, with intense humility. "What an end! . . . An' Jim an' Slinger were responsible. I'll never get—"

"Don't you believe it," interrupted Stone. "Thet's the work of Arizona range-riders. Prentiss an' his pards are back of thet. . . . An' see there. Graves! But wait, Molly."

The outlaw's sharp eyes, in further survey of the glade, had fallen upon freshly made graves.

"Wal, there are no cowboys buried here, thet's shore. . . . Ride on, Molly."

Stone halted in the first likely spot for camp, and slipping out of his saddle with Gloriana in his arms, he laid her down on a soft pine-needle mat. She was conscious.

"Tend to her, Molly," said Stone, briefly, and he turned to look after the horses. Then he cut ample spruce boughs for two beds, and made them, one of which, for the girls, he laid in a protected niche of the cliff. Having finished these tasks, he approached his prisoners.

"There's nothin' to eat."

"Small matter, Jed. Our appetites are shore not a-rarin'," replied Molly.

Gloriana transfixed him with solemn tragic eyes.

"I take back—calling you a liar," she said, simply.

"Thanks. I accept your apology."

"Who—who did that?" she asked, with a gesture to indicate the tragedy down the valley.

"What? Who did what?"

"Hanged those men?"

"I reckon thet was Curly Prentiss an' his pards. Shore young Jim had a hand in it, onless, of course, Curly an' Jim got killed by the rustlers. Some of the Diamond were done for, thet's shore."

"But—you—said—" she faltered, piteously.

"Shore. I said I reckoned it wasn't Jim or Curly. I forgot thet. Must have been one or more of them daredevils. Bud or Lonestar—an' mebbe Slinger. I seen where blood had dripped on the leaves, about saddle-high, along the trail. Some cowboys packed out, shore."

That surely finished Gloriana and all but did the same for Molly. She just had strength left to help Stone carry Gloriana to bed. The outlaw then sought his own rest, and the meditations inspired by the latest developments. This adventure had not lost its sting, despite the knocking at the gate of his conscience. Tomorrow would see the end of it and he must not fail in the task he had set himself.

Morning disclosed Molly to be herself again, and Gloriana able to get up, though she could not stand erect. She could do nothing but watch the others saddle and pack. Still, her perceptions were all the keener, and she paid Molly mute and eloquent tribute of appreciation.

"I'm made of straw and water," she said, humbly.

"Wal, Gloriana, darlin', a thing of beauty is a joy forever," rejoined Stone, with gallant cheerfulness.

Once more they were mounted and off. Stone led up out of the brakes through the narrow hidden crack in the east wall, a secret exit known only to outlaws. It was a long gloomy ascent which took an hour of labored climbing on foot. From the outlet Stone made his way along the rim, north, and in the direction of Yellow Jacket. He led the pack-horse, while Molly supported Gloriana in her saddle. Stone kept close to them, fearing Molly might weaken and betray him. But she did not. And the outlaw recalled what she had confessed about her brother giving up rustling. Slinger had once belonged to the Cibeque outfit, and the years were not many since Stone had tried to get him into the Hash Knife. Molly could be generous and strong.

Before they reached the head of Yellow Jacket, which Stone was approaching, he had fears the Eastern girl would not make it. Yet a little rest enabled her to go on, without complaint, without appeal for mercy.

At last Stone espied the new road, where it turned to go down into the canyon. He halted before the girls noticed it and dismounted near the rim.

"Wal, we've reached the partin' of the trails," he said. "There's a ranch down heah where one of you can go an' send word to the cowboys. 'Cause I cain't take you both with me any farther. I'm a hunted desperado, you know. An' I've gotta hole up till all this blows over. One of you goes with me."

"Take us both—Jed," implored Molly, and that plainly was her last word in this trick perpetrated upon an innocent tenderfoot.

"No, Molly, *I* will go," interposed Gloriana. "You love Jim. He worships you. . . . There's no one cares for me or—or whom I care for. . . . And I'm not strong, as you've seen from my miserable frailty on this ride. I won't live long, so it'll not matter much."

Molly, with eyes suddenly full of tears, averted her gaze. Stone regarded the Eastern girl with poignant emotion he gladly hid.

"Ahuh. So you'll go willin'?"

"Yes, since you compel me. But on one condition."

"An' what's thet?"

"You must—marry me honestly. I have religious principles."

"Wal, I reckon I could fetch a padre down into the brakes—where we'll be hidin'," replied Stone. "An' so—Miss Gloriana Traft—you'd marry me—Jed Stone of the Hash Knife—thief, killer, outlaw, desperado—to save your friend?"

"Yes, I'll do even that for Jim and Molly."

Suddenly Jed Stone turned away, gripped by a whirlwind of passion. It had waylaid him, at this pathway of middle life, like a tiger in ambush. All the hard bitter years of outlawry rose like a hydra-headed monster to burn his soul with the poison of hate, revenge, lust, and the longing to kill. To wreak his vengeance upon civilization by despoiling the innocence and crushing the life of this young girl! The thing roared in his brain, a hell-storm of fury. He had never realized the depths into which he had been thrust until this madness wrapped him in a whirling flame.

But the instant he understood that this was actual temptation—that it had tripped him with surprise and feeling he never dreamed he pos- sessed—he rejected it with the hard stern courage of the outlaw who had survived baseness. That kind of crime was for Croak Malloy—never for Jed Stone.

He stepped through the brush to the rim and gazed down into Yellow Jacket. The canyon seemed to lift to meet his eye, with all the gold and green beauty, the noble gray cliffs, the singing amber stream, and with some indefinable peacefulness of solitude that he grasped then and there, forever to be a possession of his lonely soul.

Then he returned in thought to the issue at hand. Far beyond his hope had he succeeded in forcing latent good into being. This Eastern girl had really defeated him. What could be greater than sacrificing virtue and life itself for her friend? Stone bowed under that. Gloriana Traft had love—which was greater than all the fighting instincts he had meant to rouse. It would have been an error of nature to have created such a beautiful being as this girl and not have endowed her with unquenchable spirit. She was as noble, in her extremity, as she was beautiful. Her eyes and lips, the turn of her face, were no falsehoods. And so Jed Stone divined how he was to profit by the courage of a girl he had driven to such desperate straits. The lesson, the good would rebound upon him.

"Ride over hyar a step," he said to the girls, and he pointed down into the canyon. "This is Yellow Jacket, an' thet new house you see way down there in the green is Jim Traft's."

While they stared he went back to mount his own horse and turn to them again.

"The road is right hyar," he went on, as coolly

and casually as if that fact was nothing momentous. "Shore you can make it thet fer."

Then he patted Molly's dusky tousled head: "Good-by, little wood-mouse. Be good—"

"Oh, Jed," cried Molly, wildly, with tears streaming down her cheeks. "Remember aboot never—rustlin' no more!"

Stone turned to the Eastern girl. "Big-eyes!" he called her, for that was the most felicitous of all names for her then. "So long!—Marry Curly or Bud, an' have some real Western kids. . . . But don't never forget your desperado!"

As he spurred away he heard her poignant call: "Oh wait—wait!" But Jed Stone rode as never had he from sheriffs and posse, from vengeful cowboys who pursued with gun and rope.

Chapter Twenty

"— — — LUCK!" shouted Jim Traft, slamming down his pencil, and crumpling the white sheet of paper to fling it into the fire.

"Why, James!" exclaimed Curly, looking in grave surprise from his game of checkers, which he was playing with the crippled Bud, on his bed.

"Boss, thet shore's amazin' fine example fer us—on a Sunday night, too," added Bud, plaintively.

"Shore the way Jim can cuss now is somethin'

frazzlin' on the nerves," put in Jackson Way, who, as usual during any leisure, was writing to his young wife.

"Aw, you weren't listening," returned Jim, exasperated. "I said, 'Dod blast the dog-gone luck.'"

"Yes, you did. Haw! Haw!"

"Jim, you're shore demoralizin' what's left of the Diamond."

"Next an' last it'll be red-eye, an' then good-by."

It was Sunday evening at the ranch-house down in Yellow Jacket. The big living-room shone bright and new with lamp and blazing fire. Jim had been endeavoring to write a letter to his uncle, reporting loss of two thousand head of Diamond-brand stock, and the fight at the cabin down in the brakes, which had entailed a more serious loss. But the letter for many reasons was difficult to write. For one thing, Molly and Gloriana would surely see it, and as Gloriana took care of her uncle's mail she would be very likely to read it first. And it had to be bad news. Jim could not gloss over the deaths of Uphill Frost and Hump Stevens, nor the serious condition of Slinger Dunn and Bud Chalfack. Moreover, he found it impossible to confess his part in that fight. On the moment Curly was trying to keep the fretful and feverish Bud from reopening wounds. Lonestar Holliday read quietly by the lamplight across the table from Jim, but he could not sit still, and as he moved his bandaged foot from one resting-place to another he betrayed the pain he was suffering. Jack Way wore the beatific smile which character-ized his visage while writing to the absent bride.

"Jump, dog-gone you," said Curly, mildly, to his opponent. "Cain't you see a jump when you have one?"

Bud reluctantly made the required move, when Curly promptly jumped three men, practically winning the game. Bud gave the home-made checker-board a shove, sending the checkers flying.

"Skunked again! Thet's three games, without me gettin' a king," complained Bud, fiercely. "Of all the lucky gazabos I ever seen, you're the dingest. . . . Lucky in fights—lucky in good looks—lucky at games—lucky at shenanagin out of work—an' lucky with wimmen! It do beat hell!"

"Bud, what's eatin' you? I've got brains, which shore was left out of your make-up. I think aboot things. I don't yell an' run into a lot of bullets, like you do. I take care of my face, hair, teeth, an' so on. When I play cairds or checkers I use my haid an' figger out what the other fellar is aimin' at. An' it's a damn lie aboot me gettin' out of work. As fer the ladies—wal, I cain't help it if they like me."

"Go out an' drown yourself," shouted Bud, who plainly was angry for no reason at all, unless because he was all shot up.

"Wal, pard, you can gamble on this heah," drawled his handsome friend. "If I turn out as unlucky as you with a certain lovely person, I shore will drown myself in drink."

"Aw, I said wimmen. The way you talk, anyone would reckon there was no plural number of wimmen atall. Jest one woman in the world!"

"Which is correct."

Jim broke into the argument. "Shut up, you gamecocks. Listen. I can't write to Uncle Jim. If he doesn't show up here in a few days I'll have to ride to Flag."

"An' take Jack with you?" queried Bud, in a terrible voice.

"Yes. Jack has a wife, you know."

"An' leave the rest of us hyar fer Croak Malloy to wipe out, huh?"

Jim paced the floor. The matter was not easy to decide, and more than once he had convinced himself that the longing to see Molly had a good deal to do with the need to go to Flagerstown.

"Of course, if you boys think there's a chance of Malloy coming back—"

"Wal, Jim," interposed Curly, coolly. "As I see it you'd better wait. We've managed to get along without a doctor, an' I reckon we can do the same without reportin' to old Jim. He'll roar, shore, but let him roar. This last few weeks hasn't been any fun fer us. Somebody will get wind of thet fight an' Flag will heah aboot it."

"All right, I'll give up the idea about going, as well as writing. It'll be a relief," replied Jim, and indeed the outspoken renunciation helped him. "You know one reason I wanted to go was to block Uncle Jim's fetching Molly and Glory down here."

"Aw!" breathed Bud, reproachfully. "An' me dyin' hyar by inches."

"Let Uncle Jim fetch the girls," rejoined Curly, stoutly.

"Curly, you're a cold-blooded Arizonian," declared Jim, with both irritation and admiration. "Here's the deal. We had to take Slinger home to West Fork, shot to pieces. Bud's on his back, full of bullets and bad temper. Lonestar hobbles about making you grind your teeth. And out there under the pines lie two of the Diamond—in their graves!"

"Wal, it's shore sad," replied Curly, "but the fact is we got off lucky. An' we cain't dodge what's comin' because of what's past. I reckon thet fight aboot broke the Hash Knife fer keeps. I'm pretty shore I crippled Malloy. I was shootin' through smoke, but I seen him fall. An' then I couldn't see him any more. He got away, an' thet leaves him, Madden, an' Jed Stone of the Hash Knife. Stone won't stand fer the kind of rustlers Malloy has been ringin' in of late. Thet Joe Tanner outfit, let alone such hombres as Bambridge an' Darnell. So heah we are, not so bad off. An' I reckon we could take care of your uncle an' the girls."

Cherry Winters came in at that juncture, carrying a rifle and a haunch of venison. The cool fragrance of the night and the woods accompanied him.

"Howdy, all!" he said, cheerfully.

"What kept you late, Cherry?" asked Curly.

"Nothin'. I jest ambled along. Reckon I was pretty fur up the crick. Got to watchin' the beaver."

"Jeff has kept supper on for you," added Jim. "You know how sore he gets when we're late? Rustle now."

Jim went out on the porch. Night down in Yellow Jacket was always dark, by reason of the looming walls, which appeared so much closer and higher and blacker than by day. No air was stirring, consequently no sound in the pine and spruce tops, and the warm fragrant atmosphere of the sunny hours lingered in the canyon. The stream murmured as always, mellow and low; and the crickets were chirping. White blinking stars watched pitilessly out of the blue above.

The trouble with Jim was that he had not been weaned of his tenderfoot infancy; he had swallowed too big a dose of Arizona and he was sick. Beginning with Sonora's ambush—which only Slinger's timely shot had rendered futile—a series of happenings had tested Jim out to the limit. He had been found wanting, so far as stomach was concerned, and he knew it. Asleep and awake, that fight before the burning cabin had haunted him. No use to balk at the truth! He had taken cool bead with rifle at an oncoming and shooting, yelling rustler, and well he knew who had tumbled him over, like a bagged turkey. Afterward Jim had looked for a bullet-hole where he had aimed, and had found it. That was harsh enough. But the fact that he had, in common with his cowboys, turned deaf ear alike to the cursings and pleadings of the gambler Darnell, and had himself laid strong hands on that avenging rope, had like a boomerang rebounded upon him. All the arguments about rustlers, raids, self-preservation, had not been sufficient to cure him. Reality was something incalculably different from conjecture and possibility. In the Cibeque fight, rising out of the drift fence, he had been unable to take an active part; and so the killing of Jocelyn and the Haverlys by Slinger Dunn had rested rather easily upon his conscience. But now he was an Arizonian with blood on his hands. He still needed a violent and constant cue for passion.

Curly came outside presently: "Fine night, Boss. An' it's good to feel we can peek out an' not be scared of bullets. I reckon, though, thet feelin' oughtn't be trusted fer long. We'll heah from Croak Malloy before the summer is over."

"Yes, it's a fine night, I suppose," sighed Jim. "But almost—I wish I was back in Missouri."

"Never havin' seen Arizona an' Molly?" drawled the cowboy, with his cool, kindly tone.

"Even that."

"But more special—never havin' killed a man?"

"Curly!"

"Shore you cain't fool me, Jim, old boy. I was aboot when it come off. I seen you bore thet rustler. Fact is I had a bead on him myself."

"I—I didn't dream anybody knew," replied Jim, hoarsely. "Please don't tell, Curly."

"Wal, I cain't promise fer the rest of the outfit. Bud seen it, from where he fell. An' what's more, he seen thet rustler shoot Hump daid."

"He did!" cried Jim, a dark hot wave as of blood with consciousness surging to his head. A subtle change marked his exclamation.

"Shore. An' Lonestar reckoned he seen the same. Wal, thet rustler was Ham Beard. We searched him, before we buried him. Used to be a Winslow bartender till he murdered some one. Then he took to cattle-stealin'. Sort of a lone wolf an' shore a daid shot. If it hadn't been fer thet smoke he an' Croak might have done fer all of us. Though I reckon in thet case, if they'd charged us without the cover of smoke, we'd have stopped them with our rifles. . . . It was a mess, Jim, an' you ought to pat yourself on the back instead of mopin' around."

Jim realized this clearly, and in the light of

Curly's cool illuminating talk he felt the relaxing of a gloomy shade.

"If Glory an' Molly never hear of it—I guess I'll stand it," he said.

"Wal, you can bet your last pair of wool socks in zero weather thet our beloved Bud will spring it on the girls."

"No!"

"Shore. An' not because of his itch to talk. It'll be pride, Jim, unholy pride in your addition to the toll of the Diamond."

"I'll beg him not to, and if that's not enough I'll beat him."

"Wal, Mizzouri, it cain't be did," drawled Curly.

The cowboys had given the brakes a wide berth for days, notwithstanding the pertinent and baffling fact that most of the Diamond stock had been driven or had stampeded as far south as Yellow Jacket. Jim was strong to ride down, at least as far as the burned cabin, and to bury the rustlers they had left hanging to the sycamore. But Curly took as strong exception to leaving crippled cowboys unprotected at the ranch-house; and as for the hanging rustlers, he said, "Let 'em sun dry an' blow away!"

Curly was not as easy in mind as might have appeared to a superficial observer. He was restless; he walked up and down the canyon trail. Jim noted that Curly's blue flashing eyes were ever on the alert. And when Jim finally commented about this, Curly surprised him with a whisper: "Nix on thet, Mizzouri. I don't want Bud or Lonestar to worry. They make fuss enough. But I'll tell you somethin'. This very day, when you were eatin' dinner, I seen a rider's black sombrero bobbin' above the rim wall there. On the east rim, mind you!"

"Curly! . . . A black sombrero? You might have been mistaken," replied Jim.

"Shore. It might have been a black hawk or a raven. But my eyes are pretty sharp, Jim."

Hours of uneasiness on Jim's part followed, and apparently casual strolling the porch on Curly's. Nothing happened, and at length Jim forgot about the circumstance. He went back to his accountbooks, presently to be disturbed by the nervous Bud.

"Boss, I thought I heerd a call a little while ago, but I didn't want to bother you. But now I shore heerd hosses."

"You did?" Jim listened with strained ears while he gazed around the living-room. Lonestar was asleep, and so was Cherry, while Jack, writing as usual, could not have heard the crack of doom. But Jim distinctly caught a soft thud, thud, thud of hoofs.

"Curly!" he called sharply. That jerked the sleepers wide awake, but it did not fetch Curly.

"Boys, something up. We hear horses. And Curly doesn't answer. Grab your rifles."

"Listen, Boss!" ejaculated Bud.

Then Jim caught a call from outside: "Jim—oh, Jim!"

"Molly!" he shouted wildly, and rushed out, to be followed by the three uninjured cowboys. No sign of horses down the trail. But under the pines in the other direction moved brown fingers, now close at hand, emerging from the grove. Molly led, on a big raw-boned bay horse. Hatless, her dusky hair flying, she called again: "Jim—oh, Jim!"

Roused out of stupefaction, Jim rushed to meet her. "Molly! for Heaven's sake, how'd you get here?" he cried as she reined in the bay. She dropped a halter of a pack-horse she was leading. Then Jim saw that she was brush-covered and travel-stained. Her hair was full of pine needles, and her eyes shone unnaturally large and bright. Jim's rapture suffered a check. He looked beyond her, to see Curly supporting Gloriana in the saddle of a third horse. Her head drooped, her hair hung in a tawny mass.

"My God! what's happened?" he exclaimed, in sudden terror.

"Shore a lot. Don't look so scared, Jim. We're all right. . . . . Help me down."

She slid into his arms, most unresisting, Jim imagined, and for once his kisses brought blushes without protest. If she did not actually squeze him, then he was dreaming. He set her down upon her feet, still keeping an arm around her.

"What—what's all this?" he stammered, looking back to see Gloriana fall into Curly's arms. As Curly carried her up the porch steps Jim caught a glimpse of Gloriana's face. Then he dragged Molly with him into the house.

"Curly, let me down," Gloriana was saying.

But Curly did not hear, or at least obey. "For Gawd's sake, darlin', tell me you—you're not hurt or—or anythin'."

No longer was Gloriana's face white. "Let me down, I say," she cried, imperiously. Whereupon Curly became aware of his behavior, and he set her down in the big armchair, to gaze at her as at a long-lost treasure found.

"Glory!—What crazy trick—have you sprung on us?" gasped Jim, striding close, still hanging to Molly. He stared incredulously at his sister. Her flimsy dress had once been light-colored. It seemed no longer a dress, scarcely a covering, and it was torn to shreds and black from contact with burned brush. But that appeared only little cause for the effect she produced upon Jim and his comrades. One arm was wholly bare, scratched and dirty and bloody: her legs were likewise. To glance over these only forced the gaze back to Gloriana's face. The havoc of terrible mental and physical strain showed in its haggard outlines. But her eyes seemed a purple radiant blaze of rapture, or thanksgiving. They would have reassured a cynic that all was well with heart and soul—that life was good.

"Oh—Jim," she whispered, lifting a weak hand to him, and as he clasped it, to sink on one knee beside her chair, she lay back and closed her eyes. "I'm here—I'm safe—oh, thank Heaven!"

"Glory, dear, what in the world happened?" begged Jim.

On the other side of the chair Curly lifted her hand, which clung to a battered old sombrero, full of bullet holes.

"Jim, this heah's what I seen bobbin' above the rim," he said, in amazing conjecture. "Whose hat is this? Reckon it looks some familiar."

He could not remove it from the girl's tight clutch.

"Thet sombrero belonged to Croak Malloy," interposed Molly, who stood back of Jim, smoothing the pine needles out of her tangled hair.

"Holy Mackeli!" burst out Curly. "I knew it. I recognized thet hat. . . . Jim, as shore as Gawd made little apples thet croakin' gun-thrower is daid."

"Daid? I should say he is," corroborated Molly, laconically. "Daid as a door nail."

The tremendousness of that truth, which no one doubted, commanded profound silence. Even Curly Prentiss had no tongue.

"Jed Stone killed Malloy, an' Madden, too," went on Molly, bright-eyed, enjoying to the full the sensation she was creating.

Jim echoed the name of the Hash Knife leader,

but Curly, to whom that name had so much more deadly significance, still could not speak.

"Molly Dunn, I'm a hurted cow-puncher," called Bud from his bed. "An' if you don't tell pronto what's come off, I'll be wuss."

Gloriana opened her eyes, and let them dwell lovingly upon her brother, and then Molly, after which they wandered to the standing wide-eyed cowboys, and lastly to the stricken Curly, whose adoration was embarrassingly manifest.

"Tell them, Molly," she whispered. "I—can't talk."

"We planned to surprise you, Jim," began Molly. "It took some persuadin' to get Uncle Jim in on our job. But we did. An' let's see—five days ago—early mawnin' we left Flag in the buckboard, Pedro drivin'. That night we slept at Miller's ranch. Next mawnin' at the fork of the road we got held up by Croak Malloy, an' two of his pards, Madden an' Reeves. They'd jest happened to run into us. Uncle Jim didn't know Malloy until he shot Pedro. Malloy robbed Uncle, took our bags, an' threw us on horses. An' he told Uncle to go back to Flag, dig up ten thousand dollars, an' send it by rider to Tobe's Well, where it was to be put up in the loft by the chimney. Malloy drove us off then, into the woods, an' along in the afternoon we reached Tobe's Well. We'd jest been dragged in, an' they'd hawg-tied me, an' Malloy was tearin' Glory's clothes off, when in comes Jed Stone. He shore filled thet cabin. . . . Wal, Croak was sore at bein' interrupted, an' Jed raved aboot what Uncle Jim would do. Queer what stress he put on Uncle Jim! Called him Jim! . . . Croak got sorer at all the fuss Jed was makin' over nothin'. But when quick as a cat he turned one of them held a boomin' gun. I shut my eyes. Jed shot two more times. I heahed one of the rustlers run out, an' when I looked again Malloy an' Madden were daid, an' Reeves had escaped."

"Wal, of all deals I ever seen in my born days!" ejaculated Curly Prentiss as Molly paused, gradually yielding to excitement engendered by her narrative. Her big eyes glowed like coals.

"Wal, it turned out we'd fallen out of the fryin' pan into the fire," went on Molly, presently. "Jed had run into Uncle Jim, an' learnin' aboot the holdup, he'd trailed us, an' he killed them men jest to have us girls all to himself. It began then. . . . Whew, what a desperado Jed Stone was! He had to beat me with a switch. An' when he was fightin' an' kissin' me Glory grabbed up the butcher knife to kill him. She'd been put to makin' biscuits while Jed made love to me. He had to shoot at her, an' she fainted again. . . . Wal, Glory cooked his supper, an' afterward he made her drink whisky, an' then dance fer him. Thet played poor Glory out. He let us alone then. Next mawnin' we rustled off quick, without hardly any grub, an' he rode us all over the Diamond. He got lost, he said. We had two more days of ridin', up an' down, through the brush, over rocks. Oh, it was bad even for me. All the time Jed made me do the work an' near drove Glory crazy. One night he forced us to sleep in the same bed with him, an' gave us choice of who was to lie in the middle. Glory wouldn't let me. He had a nightmare, an' raved aboot hydrophobia skunks an' how we'd have to choke one off Glory's nose. . . . Yesterday, late afternoon, we slid an' rolled down into the canyon, an' soon we rode plumb into thet place where you hanged Darnell an' the two rustlers. . . . The sight near keeled me over. An' poor Glory—But enough said aboot thet. We camped above there, an' this mawnin' climbed out again. Glory was all in, starved, an' so sick after seein' those daid men, hangin' like sacks by their necks, thet she couldn't sit up in her saddle. I had to hold her. We went along the rim till we came to the road. An' there Jed said he'd located himself again, an' we'd have to seperate, as he could only take one of us with him, the other goin' to a ranch he said was down heah. I begged him not to separate us . . . an' then Glory told Jed she would go with him, *to save me!* . . . Thet flabbergasted Jed, as you could see. He hadn't savvied Glory. He'd been daid set to make her squeal an' show yellow—which she shore didn't. . . . An' then what do you reckon he said?"

Only questioning eyes made any return to that.

"He patted me on the haid, called me Wood-mouse, an' then to Glory, 'Big-eyes, go marry Curly or Bud, an' have some real Western kids, an' never forget your desperado.' . . . Then he rode off like mad. An' after Glory had braced up we found the road. An' heah we are!"

"Of all the strange things!" exclaimed Jim.

The cowboys were mystified. Curly ran his lean brown hand through his tawny locks, in action of great perplexity.

"Molly, was Jed drunk?"

"No. He had a bottle, an' he made Glory drink some of the stuff. But he didn't drink any."

"Bud, you heah Molly's story?" went on the nonplussed Curly.

"Yes, an' if she ain't lyin', Jed Stone was locoed. Thet happened, mebbe, when he seen Glory, an' it ain't no wonder."

"Bud Chalfack, don't you dare hint I'm not tellin' the truth," declared Molly, approaching his bed, and then seeing how white and drawn his face was, how prone his sunk frame, she fell on her knees, with a cry of pity.

"Wal, ain't you only a kid, an' turrible in love?" he growled. "You couldn't see straight, let alone tell anythin' straight. . . . I'm a dyin' cowpuncher, Molly. I reckon you'd better kiss me."

"Oh, Bud, I'm so sorry. Are you in pain?" she asked.

"I shore am, but you an' Glory might ease it some."

Whereupon she kissed his cheek and smoothed the damp hair back from his wrinkled brow. That fetched a smile to Bud's face, until it almost bore semblance to the cherubic visage he possessed when in good health and spirits.

"Glory, ain't you comin' over to kiss me, like Molly done?" he asked plaintively.

"I am, surely, Bud, as soon—as I'm able," she replied, smiling wanly. "I hope and pray you're not serious—about dying."

"Aw, I am, Glory. But I might be saved," he said, significantly. "If only I jest didn't want to croak."

"Hush, you sick boy. Molly and I will nurse you."

At that Curly arose with a disgusted look, muttering under his breath: "If it takes thet, I reckon I can get shot up some."

Jim came out of his trance. "Boys, in our surprise and joy we're forgetting the girls. . . . Curly, fetch hot water, and tell Jeff to fix something fit for starved people. Cherry, bring in the bags. . . . Now, Glory, I'll carry you upstairs. . . . Come, Molly."

"Oh, such a wonderful, sweet-smelling house!" murmured Gloriana as he carried her along a wide hall, into the end room, sunny and open. It was bare except for a built-in bed of sycamore branches, upon which lay a thick spread of spruce foliage. He gently deposited Gloriana there, only to find her arms round his neck.

"Jim, brother—my old world came to an end today," she murmured, dreamily.

"Yes. But you can tell me all when you're rested again," he replied, and kissing her cheek he disengaged himself and turned to meet Molly, who had followed. "Molly, you two use this room. Make her comfortable. Put her to bed. Feed her sparingly. And have a care for yourself. . . . What a kid you are! To go through all that ride and come out like this!—Damn Jed Stone. Yet I bless him! I can't make it out."

Curly and the cowboys came up, packing things, and Curly lingered, unmindful of Jim or Molly.

"Glory, I beg pardon for callin' you darlin', in front of the outfit," he said, humbly. "I was shore out of my haid. But they all know aboot me."

She transfixed him with eyes of awe and reproach, almost horror.

"Curly, I—I ought to shudder at sight of you," she said, very low. "But I—I don't."

"There! That'll be about all for you," interrupted Jim, and he shoved the shy and stricken cowboy out of the room, to follow at his heels.

"What'd she mean, Jim?" Curly asked, huskily.

"I don't know, but I imagine it's a lot—from Gloriana Traft."

Curly stalked downstairs and out into the open,

like a man who did not see where he stepped. He remained absent until sunset. At supper, which was a silent meal, in deference to the sleeping girls up stairs, he ate but little, and that with a pre-occupied air. Later he sought out Jim.

"Boss, I been thinkin' a heap aboot Molly's yarn," he said, ponderingly. "An' it's shore a queer one. The idee of Jed Stone bein' lost! . . . Heah's what I make of it—if you swear on your knees you'll never squeal on me."

"I promise, pard," returned Jim, feelingly.

"Wal, you remember how crazy Glory was to heah aboot desperadoes. Now she took Jed fer one, an' I'll bet he was cute enough not to disap-point her. Jed must have hatched up some deal with Molly, to fool Glory, to scare her, to find out if she had any real stuff in her. Thet an' thet only can account fer Jed's queer doin's an' Molly's queer story."

"But, Curly, was that motive enough?" asked Jim, incredulously.

"No, I reckon it wasn't," admitted the cowboy. "They had to have a deeper one. Now, Jed knew Molly when she was a baby, always was fond of her. Molly is shore Arizona, Jim. So is Jed. But you cain't savvy thet because you're an Easterner. An' to boil it down I reckon Jed scared Glory an' starved her an' drove her jest fer Molly's sake. An' in the end Glory took the brim off their cup by meanin' to give herself up to save Molly's honor.

Glory was plumb fooled, an' clean honest an' as big as life. It was great, Jim. An' if I hadn't been in love with her before, I shore would be now."

"If that's true, Molly is an awful little liar," said Jim, dubiously.

"Wal, yes an' no. It depends on how you see it. Molly worships Glory, an' she couldn't have meant anythin' but good. An' good it shore was an' is. Thet gurl is changed."

"Ahuh. I begin to savvy, maybe. I believe I did notice some little difference, which I put down to her joy at being safe again with us."

"Shore it was thet. But more. If I don't miss my guess, Gloriana will never see through Jed an' Molly. An' thet's jest as well. I hope the lesson wasn't too raw. But thet sister of yours has guts. . . . When she gets rested she'll appreciate things as they *are* out heah."

Next day Molly showed up downstairs, in changed garb, merry and shy by turns; and she surely was beleagured by the cowboys. Eventually Jim contrived to get her away from Bud, and to walk out to look over Yellow Jacket. She was enraptured.

"Molly, the end of the Hash Knife makes a vast difference," Jim was saying as he halted with her on the log bridge across the amber stream. "We can actually live down here, eventually. But not till next year, and then you must have frequent visits to Flag. . . . You haven't forgotten your promise to marry me this fall, have you?"

"Oh, did I promise, Jim?" she asked, in shy pretense of surprise.

"You sure did."

"Wal, then, say late November."

"But that's winter!"

"November? Oh no, thet's the last of fall."

"Gosh! how long to wait! . . . But I love you so and you're such a wonderful girl—I guess I can wait."

"Maybe—the middle of November," she whispered, whereupon Jim, with a glad shout, snatched her into his arms, to the imminent peril of their falling off the log that bridged the brook.

Next morning late a lovely and languid Gloriana trailed shakily down the winding stairs into the living-room. Dark shadows enhanced the depth and hue of her eyes. She wore white, and to Bud and Curly, at least, she might have been an angel. But to Jim she appeared spent and shaken, completely warped out of her old orbit. She was made much of by the cowboys, except Curly, who worshiped and glowered by turns, from afar. Bud took advantage of Gloriana's pledge of the day before and held her to it, after which he held her hand. At length Curly lunged out of the room, as if he meant to destroy himself, and then almost immediately he lunged back again. Jim understood his pangs, and when Curly gravitated to him, as always happened when he was cast down, Jim whispered:

"Pard, it doesn't mean anything!"

"Wal, I'll shore find out pronto," replied Curly, in heroic mood. "Never do to let her get hold of herself again."

Presently the other cowboys went out on the porch, to take up tasks, or to amuse Lonestar, who had a chair outside. This left Jim and Molly at the table. Gloriana sat on the edge of Bud's bed, which consisted of blankets over spruce boughs, laid on the floor. Curly, who had before wandered around like a lost dog, now watched his friend and his sweetheart with flashing blue eyes. They apparently were oblivious of the others.

"Glory, you're the beautifulest gurl," Bud was saying.

"Silly, you've seen prettier ones," she replied, but she was pleased, and she stroked his hair with her free hand.

"Nope. They don't walk on Gawd's green earth," returned her champion.

"Bud, I'm to be here all summer," she said, with a smile of enchantment. "Oh, it's so heavenly here. I didn't know. . . . Will you be all right soon—so you can ride with me—teach me how to handle a horse? I'm so stupid—so weak. Why, that pinto bucked me off!"

"She did? Son-of-a-gun! I'll beat her good fer thet."

"No you won't. I love her."

"Love a pinto! . . . Is thet all?"

"Bud, I love every horse—everything—everybody in Arizona."

"Aw, thet's wuss."

Jim, entranced at this byplay, suddenly felt a tug. "Look at Curly," whispered Molly.

Curly seemed to have become transformed back to the old cool, easy cowboy, an unknown quantity, potent with some secret of imperturbable assurance. Yet Jim divined his was the grandeur of despair.

"Glory," drawled Curly, as he sat down on the bed, opposite her, and possessed himself of Bud's other restless hand, "we've been like brothers for six years. . . . Bud an' I. . . . An' I reckon this last fight I evened up an old debt. When Bud went down, thet rustler would have killed him but fer me."

"Pard, what's ailin' you—thet you never told me before?" demanded Bud, his voice deep and rich.

"No call fer it, Bud."

Gloriana looked from one to the other, fascinated, and vaguely troubled. Her intuition distrusted the moment.

"Dog-gone! I had a hunch you did. Shore as hell thet's why you missed the chance at Croak Malloy."

"I reckon." Then Curly looked up at the girl. "I

jest wanted you both to know, in case I don't stay on heah."

"Stay on—heah?" faltered Gloriana, in her surprise actually imitating him. Then her eyes dilated with divining thoughts.

"Now what I want to know—seein' Bud an' I are the same as brothers—which of us is to call you sister?"

"Curly!" she entreated.

"Aw, pard!" burst out Bud.

"This son-of-a-gun ain't bad hurt," went on Curly. "I've seen him with more and worse gunshot wounds. He's only workin' on your sympathy. Wal, thet's all right. But it makes me declare myself right heah an' now."

"Please, Curly—oh, don't."

"You know I love you, Glory," he continued, coolly and slowly. "Only it's more since I told you first. An' I asked you to marry me an' let me be the one to help you tackle this tough Arizona. . . . Wal, thet was Christmas-time, aboot. You promised to write your answer. But you never did. An' I reckon now I'm wantin' to heah it."

"But, Curly—how unreasonable! Wait, I beg of you. I—I'm upset by this adventure. I don't know myself."

"Wal, you know whether you love me or not. So answer pronto, lady."

She drooped her lustrous head a moment, then raised it, fearlessly, as one driven to the wall.

"Curly, you're not greatly different from Jed Stone," she said.

"I reckon thet a compliment."

"I'm not sure yet how or what I feel toward you, Curly, except that I know I'm not worthy. But since you insist—I—I say yes." And with wistful smile she held out her free hand to him. Curly clasped it in both his and carried it to his breast, his face pale, his eyes intense.

"Whoopee!" yelled Bud, in stentorian tones. "I knowed I could fetch him. All the time I knowed it—the handsome jealous geezer!"

Next day Uncle Jim Traft drove down into Yellow Jacket.

No suggestion of the hard old cattleman! He was merry and keen, full of energy to see and hear, and somehow mysteriously buoyant. At Jim's hurried report of the lost cattle he replied: "Pooh-pooh! Only an incident in a rancher's life!" But he gazed sorrowfully down at the graves of those cowboys who had died for the Diamond. They had not been the first, and perhaps they would not be the last.

Curly related the story of the fight at the trapper's cabin. Molly led him aside to tell her version of their adventure with Croak Malloy and Jed Stone. And Bud with rare pride exhibited the headpiece of carved aspen which he vowed he would place on Croak Malloy's grave.

"Wal, wal, we have our ups an' downs," replied

412

the old rancher, when all was said. "An' I say you got off easy. . . . My news is good news. Blodgett's riders rounded up your stampeded stock. All the range knows Malloy is dead an' the Hash Knife no more. Spread like wildfire. Yellow Jacket will prosper now, an', my! what a gorgeous place! An', Jim you won't be lonesome, either, when you settle down with the little wife. Allen Blodgett is takin' charge of his father's range, an' he'll live there. Jack Way's wife's father will start him ranchin'. Miller is goin' to move down. An' in no time this valley will be hummin'. An' I near forgot. The doctor come back from West Fork, reportin' Slinger Dunn out of danger."

That, of all news, was the best for Jim, who found his joy and gratitude in Molly's brimming eyes.

"Rustlin' will go on," continued Uncle Jim, "but no more at the old Hash Knife rate. It'll be two-bit stealin' an' thet we don't mind."

After supper, when the old rancher had Jim, Gloriana, Molly, and Curly alone, he pulled a soiled paper from his pocket. His air was strikingly momentous.

"I'm askin' you never to tell what I read you now. Promise?"

Surprised at his earnestness, at his fine softened face, strangely pale, they solemnly pledged themselves, whereupon Uncle Jim adjusted his eyeglasses and began to read slowly:

413

DEAR JIM:

I changed my mind about the money your rider fetched down. I appropriated it an' am leavin' this letter instead. You owe me thet, to make a new start in life.

Thet niece of yours, Gloriana, offered to make a sacrifice. Same as I did twenty years ago, to save my pard. For the sweetheart we both loved an' which he never got, after all. It sort of faced me back on the old forgotten trail. Jim, it's never too late.

Tell her, if she ever has a boy, to call him

JED.

Center Point Publishing
600 Brooks Road ● PO Box 1
Thorndike ME 04986-0001 USA

(207) 568-3717

US & Canada:
1 800 929-9108
www.centerpointlargeprint.com